THE
COLLECTED TALES OF
NIKOLAI GOGOL

THE
COLLECTED TALES OF
NIKOLAI GOGOL

TRANSLATED AND ANNOTATED BY
RICHARD PEVEAR AND LARISSA VOLOKHONSKY

PANTHEON BOOKS

NEW YORK

Library of Congress Cataloging-in-Publication Data

Gogol', Nikolaĭ Vasil'evich, 1809–1852.
[Short stories. English. Selections]
The Collected Tales of Nikolai Gogol / Nikolaĭ Gogol ; translated and
annotated by Richard Pevear and Larissa Volokhonsky.
p. cm.
Contents: St. John's Eve—The night before Christmas—The terrible
vengeance—Ivan Fyodorovich Shponka and his aunt—Old world
landowners—Viy—The story of how Ivan Ivanovich quarreled with Ivan
Nikiforovich—Nevsky Prospect—The diary of a madman—The nose—The
carriage—The portrait—The overcoat.
ISBN 0-679-43023-7
1. Gogol', Nikolaĭ Vasil'evich, 1809–1852—Translations into English.
I. Pevear, Richard, 1943– . II. Volokhonsky, Larissa.   III. Title.
PG3333.A6   1998
891.73'3—dc21   97-37228
CIP

Random House Web Address: http://www.randomhouse.com

Book design by Julie Duquet

Printed in the United States of America
First Edition

2   4   6   8   9   7   5   3   1

CONTENTS

PREFACE

Art has the provinces in its blood. Art is provincial in principle, preserving for itself a naive, external, astonished and envious outlook.

— Andrei Sinyavsky,
In Gogol's Shadow

Nikolai Vassilyevich Gogol was born on April 1, 1809, in
the village of Sorochintsy, Mirgorod district, Poltava province, in
the Ukraine, also known as Little Russia. His childhood was spent
on Vassilyevka, a modest estate belonging to his mother. Nearby
was the town of Dikanka, once the property of Kochubey, the
most famous hetman of the independent Ukraine. In the church
of Dikanka there was an icon of St. Nicholas the Wonderworker,
for whom Gogol was named.

In 1821 Gogol was sent to boarding school in Nezhin, near
Kiev. He graduated seven years later, and in December 1828, at the
age of nineteen, left his native province to try his fortunes in the
Russian capital. There he fled from posts as a clerk in two government ministries, failed a tryout for the imperial theater (he had not
been a brilliant student at school, but had shown unusual talent as a
mimic and actor, and his late father had been an amateur play-

wright), printed at his own expense a long and very bad romantic poem, then bought back all the copies and burned them, and in 1830 published his first tale, "St. John's Eve," in the March issue of the magazine *Fatherland Notes*. There followed, in September 1831 and March 1832, the two volumes of *Evenings on a Farm near Dikanka*, each containing four tales on Ukrainian themes with a prologue by their supposed collector, the beekeeper Rusty Panko. They were an immediate success and made the young provincial a famous writer.

Baron Delvig, friend and former schoolmate of the poet Alexander Pushkin and editor of the almanac *Northern Flowers*, had introduced Gogol to Pushkin's circle even before that, and in 1831 he had made the acquaintance of the poet himself. Writing to Pushkin on August 21 of that year, Gogol told him how his publisher had gone to the shop where the first volume of *Evenings* was being printed and found the typesetters all laughing merrily as they set the book. Shortly afterwards, Pushkin mentioned the incident in one of the first published notices of Gogol's work, a letter to the editor of a literary supplement, which began: "I have just read *Evenings on a Farm near Dikanka*. It amazed me. Here is real gaiety—honest, unconstrained, without mincing, without primness. And in places what poetry! What sensitivity! All this is so unusual in our present-day literature that I still haven't recovered." At twenty-two Gogol was well launched both in literature and in society.

In 1835 came *Mirgorod*, another two-volume collection of Ukrainian tales, and *Arabesques*, a group of articles and tales reflecting the life of Petersburg, including "Nevsky Prospect," "The Diary of a Madman," and the first version of "The Portrait." By then Gogol had also begun work on the novel-poem *Dead Souls*. When Pushkin began to publish his magazine *The Contemporary* in 1836, he included tales by Gogol in the early issues—"The Carriage" in the first and "The Nose" in the third. April of that same year saw the triumph of his comedy *The Inspector General*.

In June 1836, at the height of his fame, Gogol left Russia for Switzerland, Paris, and Rome. Of the remaining sixteen years of his life, he would spend nearly twelve abroad. He returned in the fall of 1841 to see to the publication of the first volume of *Dead Souls*. When the book finally appeared in May 1842, its author again left the country, this time for a stretch of six years. Later in 1842, a four-volume edition of Gogol's collected writings (minus *Dead Souls*) was brought out in Petersburg. Among the previously unpublished works in the third volume was his last and most famous tale, "The Overcoat." By then, though he was to live another decade, his creative life was virtually over. It had lasted some twelve years. And in terms of his tales alone, it had been even briefer, condensed almost entirely into the period between his arrival in Petersburg and his first trip abroad in 1836.

The road that brought Gogol from the depths of Little Russia intersected with Nevsky Prospect, "all-powerful Nevsky Prospect," in the heart of the capital. His art was born at that crossroads. It had the provinces in its blood, as Andrei Sinyavsky puts it, in two senses: because Little Russia supplied the setting and material for more than half of his tales, and, more profoundly, because even in Petersburg, Gogol preserved a provincial's "naive, external, astonished and envious outlook." He did not write from within Ukrainian popular tradition, he wrote looking back at it. Yet he also never entered into the life of the capital, the life he saw flashing by on Nevsky Prospect, where "the devil himself lights the lamps only so as to show everything not as it really looks"—this enforced, official reality of ministries and ranks remained impenetrable to him. Being on the outside of both worlds, Gogol seems to have been destined to become a "pure writer" in a peculiarly modern sense.

And indeed Gogol's art, despite its romantic ghosts and folkloric trappings, is strikingly modern in two ways: first, his works are free verbal creations, based on their own premises rather than on the conventions of nineteenth-century fiction; and, second, they are highly theatrical in presentation, concentrated on figures and gestures, constructed in a way that, while admitting any amount of digression, precludes the social and psychological analysis of classical realism. His images remain ambiguous and uninterpreted, which is what makes them loom so large before us. These expressive qualities of Gogol's art influenced Dostoevsky decisively, turning him from a social romantic into a "fantastic realist," and they made Gogol the father of Russian modernism. His leap from the province to the capital also carried him forward in time, so that, at the beginning of the twentieth century, the symbolist Andrei Bely could say: "We still do not know what Gogol is."

A vogue for Little Russia already existed when Gogol arrived in the capital. The novelist Vassily Narezhny (1780–1825) had recently published two comic novels portraying Ukrainian life and customs—*The Seminarian* (1824) and *The Two Ivans, or The Passion for Lawsuits* (1825). In 1826 a leading romantic of Ukrainian origin, Orest Somov (1793–1833), had begun to publish a series of tales based on the folklore of the region. And Anton Pogorelsky (1787–1836), superintendent of the Kharkov school district, had used a Ukrainian setting for a volume of fantastic tales entitled *The Double, or My Evenings in Little Russia* (1829). The province offered an ideal combination of the native and the exotic, the real and the fantastic, peasant earthiness and pastoral grace. The landscape of Little Russia is open steppe, not the forests of the north; the climate is sunny, warm, southern, conducive to laziness and merry-making; the earth is abundant; the cottages, built not of logs but of cob or whitewashed brick, are sunk in flourishing orchards; the men wear drooping mustaches, grow long topknots on their shaved heads, and go around in bright-colored balloon trousers. Here was a whole culture, with its heroic past of successful struggle against the Turks on one side and the Poles on the other, that could be taken as an embodiment of the Russian national spirit. And so it was taken in the Petersburg of the 1820s.

Gogol, however, seems to have paid little attention to the details of Ukrainian life while he lived there. He was bent on putting the place behind him, on winning glory in the capital, on performing some lofty deed for the good of all Russia, on becoming a great poet in the German romantic style (the title of his burnt poem was *Hans Küchelgarten*). It was only in Petersburg that he discovered the new fashion for the Ukraine and sensed, in Sinyavsky's words, "a 'social commission' from that side, a certain breath of air in the literary lull of the capital, already sated with the

Caucasus and mountaineers and expecting something brisk, fresh, popular from semi-literate Cossackland." Four months after his arrival, on April 30, 1829, he wrote to his mother:

> You know the customs and ways of our Little Russians very well, and so I'm sure you will not refuse to communicate them to me in our correspondence. That is very, very necessary for me. I expect from you in your next letter a complete description of the costume of a village deacon, from his underclothes to his boots, with the names used by the most rooted, ancient, undeveloped Little Russians; also the names, down to the last ribbon, for the various pieces of clothing worn by our village maidens, as well as by married women, and by muzhiks . . . the exact names for clothing worn in the time of the hetmans . . . a minute description of a wedding, not omitting the smallest detail . . . a few words about carol singing, about St. John's Eve, about water sprites. There are lots of superstitions, horror stories, traditions, various anecdotes, and so on, current among the people: all of that will be of great interest to me. . . .

So it was with the help of his mother's memory, plus a few books of local history and old Ukrainian epic songs, that Gogol set about creating the Little Russia of *Evenings on a Farm near Dikanka* and *Mirgorod*.

It is a world of proud, boastful Cossacks, of black-browed beauties, of witches, devils, magic spells and enchantments, of drowsy farms and muddy little towns—that is, a stage-set Ukraine, more operatic than real. Holidays and feasting are always close by—in "St. John's Eve" and "The Night Before Christmas" obviously, but also in the wedding that begins "The Terrible Vengeance," in the banqueting that runs through the *Mirgorod* tales and appears again in "The Carriage," a perfect little anecdote that belongs to this same world. Festive occasions grant special privileges; on festive nights fates are revealed or decided, lovers are separated, enemies are brought together; the natural and the supernatural mingle for good or ill, for comic or horrific effect. The expanded possibilities of festive reality justified the freedom with which Gogol constructed his narratives. But of the real peasant, of conditions under serfdom, of Ukrainian society and its conflicts at the time, there is no more trace in Gogol's tales, even those of the most realistic cast, than there was in his father's comedies. His characters, as Michel Aucouturier notes in the preface to his French translation of *Evenings*, "are not typical representatives of the Little Russian peasantry, but the young lovers and old greybeards of the theater, Ukrainian descendants of the Cléantes and Elises, the Orgons and Gérontes of Molière."

The more surprising is the reputation Gogol acquired early, among both conservatives and liberals, as a painter of reality, the founder of the "natural school." Gogol's appearance in Russian literature was so enigmatic that it seems his first critics (Pushkin excepted), while they liked what they read, could not account for their liking of it and invented reasons that were simply beside the point. The real reason was no doubt the unusual texture of Gogol's writing. His prose is a self-conscious artistic medium that mimics the popular manner but in fact represents something other, something quite alien to the old art of storytelling.

In his essay "The Storyteller" (1936), Walter Benjamin wrote: "Experience passed on from mouth to mouth is the source from which all storytellers have drawn." And he noted further that "every real story . . . contains, openly or covertly, something useful. The usefulness may, in one case, consist in a moral; in another, in some practical advice; in a third, in a proverb or maxim. In every case the storyteller is a man who has counsel for his readers. . . . Counsel woven into the fabric of real life is wisdom." If we turn to Gogol's tales with such words as "experience," "practical advice," "counsel," and "wisdom" in mind, we will see that they are total strangers to the "real story" as Benjamin defines it. Memory is the medium of storytelling, both in the experience that is passed on from mouth to mouth and in the storyteller's act of telling, which is always a retelling. Though he may vary the tale each time he tells it, he will insist that he is faithfully repeating what he heard from earlier storytellers; otherwise it would be something made up, a fiction, a lie. Memory is the storyteller's

authority, the Muse-derived element of his art. He has the whole
tale, the plot, the sequence of events, even the embellishments, in
mind before he tells it. Gogol, we might say, has nothing in mind.
Memory plays no part in his work. He does not know where the
act of writing will lead him. In other words, he belongs not to
the order of tradition but to the order of invention. And his best
inventions come to him in the writing; he happens upon them—
Ivan Fyodorovich Shponka's dream, for instance, which is so unexpected and so transcends the rest of the story that he simply breaks
off after it. Hence his way of proceeding by digressions, which
often turn out to be the main point of the tale; hence his scorn for
the accepted rules of art—unity of action, logical development,
formal coherence—and his avoidance of "meaning" and motiva-
tion. The discovery of the unaccountable, of the absence of an
experience to be passed on, left him permanently surprised. His
work was the invention of forms to express it.

If we take what might seem the most traditional of Gogol's
tales—"The Terrible Vengeance," for example, or "Viy" (which
Gogol calls a "folk legend" and claims to retell almost as simply as
he heard it)—we will see that their procedure is precisely antitra-
ditional. "The Terrible Vengeance," far from being a naive epic tale
of Cossack life, is a studied imitation of the epic manner, a con-
scious experiment in rhythmic prose, with inevitable elements of
parody and a quite unconvincing pathos. No folktale or epic song
would end with what amounts to its own prologue, explaining the
action after the fact. The structure is highly artificial and peculiarly
Gogolian (it occurs again in "The Portrait" and in the first part of
Dead Souls), showing his concern with the act of composition and
his unconcern with meaning. So, too, in folktales about Ivan the
Fool, the hero traditionally undergoes three tests and wins the
beautiful daughter in the end. Gogol's "Viy" belongs to the same
general type, but the daughter is hardly a prize, and the hero,
Khoma Brut, comes to a sorry and quite untraditional end. What
makes these stories are countless unpredictable incidents, details,
and turns of phrase scattered along the way, and such bravura passages as the famous description of the Dnieper River in "The Terrible Vengeance," the erotic rendering of Khoma Brut's flight with

the witch, and the tremendous finale of the tale with the appearance out of nowhere of the monster Viy (who, incidentally, has no source in folklore; he is Gogol's creature and appears literally out of nowhere).

Of this untraditional procedure Sinyavsky writes:

> . . . the accent shifts from the object of speech to speech as a process of objectless intent, interesting in itself and exhausted by itself. Information that is a priori contentless shifts our attention from the material to the means of its verbal organization. Speech about useless objects enters consciousness as a thing, as a ponderable mass, as a fact of language valuable in itself. That is why we perceive Gogol's prose so distinctly as prose, and not as a habitual manner and generally accepted form of putting thoughts into words, nor as an appendix to the content and subject of the story. It has its content and even, if you wish, its subject in itself—this prose which steps forth in the free image of speech about facts not worth mentioning, speech in a pure sense *about nothing.*

If there is still a mimicry of traditional storytelling in a number of the earlier Ukrainian tales, in others we see much more clearly this shift to "a process of objectless intent," to "speech . . . *about nothing*"—particularly in "Ivan Fyodorovich Shponka and His Aunt," the last written of the *Evenings*, and in "Old World Landowners" and "The Story of How Ivan Ivanovich Quarreled with Ivan Nikiforovich" from *Mirgorod*. The element of the supernatural that triggers events in the other Ukrainian tales is almost entirely absent from "Shponka" and "Landowners." Almost, but not quite: Shponka's dream of the multiplying wife, and the she-cat that precipitates the end of the otherwise endless banality of the landowners' existence, are decisive incursions of the supernatural, or the other-natural, into the idyllic placidity of Little Russian farm life. In the story of the two Ivans, however, nothing of the sort happens, and the quarrel of the two friends proves unresolvable. The narrator ends with a dispirited exclamation: "It's dull in this world, gentlemen!" Beneath the unbroken surface of this banal local anecdote (there was in fact such an inseparable, litigious pair living in the town of Mirgorod) some extraordinary transformation should be about to happen, some new reality should be about to appear. For Gogol, the non-occurrence of this transformation became the most "supernatural" subject of all. He developed it in *Dead Souls*.

In the Petersburg tales the unaccountable sits squarely in the midst of things, like Major Kovalev's nose in the barber's loaf of bread. "Petersburg has no character," Gogol wrote to his mother in 1829, "the foreigners fattening themselves here no longer resemble foreigners, and the Russians in turn have become some sort of foreigners here and are no longer either the one or the other." Where identity is so fluid, memory finds nothing to grasp, no experience is durable enough to be passed on. The phantasmal Petersburg of later Russian literature—of Dostoevsky, Alexander Blok, Andrei Bely—made its first appearance in "Nevsky Prospect," the idea for which came to Gogol as early as 1831, when he wrote down some sketches of the Petersburg landscape. It is a landscape of mists, pale colors, dim light, the opposite of his native province, and peopled mainly by government officials of various ranks, among whom Gogol singled out a certain type of petty clerk, the "eternal titular councillor"—Mr. Poprishchin of "The Diary of a Madman," Akaky Akakievich of "The Overcoat"—a type that became as perennial in Russian literature as the phantasmal city that somehow exudes him but will not house him.

Nothing stands still on Nevsky Prospect. People of various ranks appear, disappear, reappear in other guises, changing constantly with the light. "The deceptive nature of reality," as Sinyavsky notes, "is nowhere so openly and declaredly expressed by Gogol as in 'Nevsky Prospect.' It is not by chance that 'Nevsky Prospect' sets the tone for the other Petersburg tales." The unusual structure of the tale underscores the theme, framing two opposite cases of deception with a more general evocation of the city's atmosphere. Interestingly, in a note published in *The Contemporary*, Pushkin (who did not live to read "The Overcoat") called "Nevsky Prospect" the fullest, the most complete of Gogol's tales.

The order of ranks is also revealed in these tales as a deception, a pure fiction. Major Kovalev, hero of "The Nose," is a "collegiate assessor made in the Caucasus," meaning made rather quickly. He was "made" rather recently, as well, and is still quite proud of his advancement. One day his nose disappears and then turns up "by himself" in the street wearing the uniform of a state councillor, a civil-service rank roughly equivalent to the military rank of general. Major Kovalev is not even sure of the proper way to address him. The fiction of ranks is also at the center of "The Diary of a Madman." Here, for instance, the awarding of a decoration is described from the family dog's point of view. The dog notices that her usually taciturn master has begun talking to himself, saying, "Will I get it or won't I?" over and over again. A week later he comes home very happy:

> All morning gentlemen in uniforms kept coming to him, congratulating him for something. At the table he was merrier than I'd ever seen him before, told jokes, and after dinner he held me up to his neck and said: "Look, Medji, what's this?" I saw some little ribbon. I sniffed it but found decidedly no aroma; finally I licked it on the sly: it was a bit salty.

The keeper of the "Diary," Mr. Poprishchin, also broods on the question of rank, because he is unhappily in love with his chief's daughter, who is in love with a handsome kammerjunker:

> Several times already I've tried to figure out where all these differences come from. What makes me a titular councillor and why on earth am I a titular councillor? Maybe I'm some sort of count or general and only seem to be a titular councillor? Maybe I myself don't know who I am . . . can't I be promoted this minute to governor general, or intendant, or something else like that? I'd like to know, what makes me a titular councillor? Why precisely a titular councillor?

In the end he decides he is the king of Spain, an act of perfect fictionizing for which he is taken off to the madhouse.

"The Diary of a Madman" is Gogol's only first-person story,

and Mr. Poprishchin is perhaps the most human of his characters. For brief moments a piercing note comes into his voice, as when he asks, "Why precisely a titular councillor?" or when he calls out his last words to his mother: "Dear mother, save your poor son! shed a tear on his sick head! see how they torment him! press the poor orphan to your breast! there's no place for him in the world!" We hear the same note, more briefly still, in the voice of that other titular councillor, Akaky Akakievich, when his fellow clerks torment him unbearably and he finally says: "Let me be. Why do you offend me?" There is something so strange, so pitiable in his voice that one young clerk never forgets it:

> And long afterwards, in moments of the greatest merriment, there would rise before him the figure of the little clerk with the balding brow, uttering his penetrating words: "Let me be. Why do you offend me?"—and in these penetrating words rang other words: "I am your brother." And the poor young man would bury his face in his hands. . . .

These moments of pathos led certain radical critics of Gogol's time, the influential Vissarion Belinsky first among them, to see Gogol as a champion of the little man and an enemy of the existing social order. The same view later became obligatory for Soviet critics. But whatever semblance of social criticism or satire there may be in the Petersburg tales is secondary and incidental. The pathos is momentary, and Gogol packs his clerks off to the madhouse or out of this world with a remarkably cool hand.

The young Dostoevsky, in his first novel, *Poor Folk,* challenged Gogol's unfeeling treatment of his petty clerk. Dostoevsky's hero, Makar Devushkin, is also a titular councillor and clearly modeled on Akaky Akakievich. He lives by the same endless copying work and suffers the same humiliating treatment from his fellow clerks. But instead of being an automaton whose highest ideals are embodied in a new overcoat, Makar Devushkin is endowed with inner life, personal dignity, and the ability to love. He is also a writer of sorts, concerned with developing his own style. And he is a literary critic. Makar Devushkin reads Gogol's "The Overcoat"

and is offended: "And why write such things? And why is it necessary? . . . Well, it's a nasty little book . . . It's simply unheard of,
because it's not even possible that there could be such a civil
servant. No, I will make a complaint . . . I will make a formal
complaint." Makar Devushkin shows the influence of sentimental
French social novels on Russian literature of the 1840s. Nothing
could be further from the spirit of such writing than Gogol's
strange humor. The "laughter through tears of sorrow" that Pushkin noted elsewhere in his work is precisely *laughter*. The images it
produces are too deeply ambiguous to bear any social message.
He saw the fiction of ranks not as an evil to be exposed but as an
instance of the groundlessness of reality itself and of the incanta-
tory power of words.

Gogol labored more over "The Portrait" than over any of his
other tales. The expanded second version was published seven
years after the first, in the *Collected Works* of 1842. Belinsky considered it a total failure and thought he knew how it should have been
written. He would have purified Gogol's "realism" of what he
considered its alien admixture of the fantastic, "a childish fantas-
magoria that could fascinate or frighten people only in the igno-
rant Middle Ages, but for us is neither amusing nor frightening,
but simply ridiculous and boring." He goes on to explain:

> No, *such* a realization of the story would do no particular
> credit to the most insignificant talent. But the thought of
> the story would be excellent if the poet had understood it
> in a *contemporary* spirit: in Chartkov he wanted to portray a
> gifted artist who ruined his talent, and consequently himself,
> through greed for money and the fascination of petty fame.
> And the realization of this thought should have been sim-
> ple, without fantastic whimsies, grounded in everyday reality:
> then Gogol, given his talent, would have created something
> great.

Belinsky's suggestion amounts to the negation of the artist Gogol
and his replacement by a "critical realist" of the dullest sort, a useful chicken instead of a bird of paradise. The contemporary spirit

that Belinsky called for was of no interest at all to the author of "The Portrait." (A century later, in his little book on Gogol, Vladimir Nabokov, though no disciple of Belinsky, offered a similarly rationalizing reduction of Gogol's work, rejecting all the fantastic tales as juvenilia and allowing as the real Gogol only "The Overcoat," *The Inspector General,* and the first part of *Dead Souls.* His criterion was not social utility, however, but artistic idiosyncrasy, an appeal to "that secret depth of the human soul where the shadows of other worlds pass like the shadows of nameless and soundless ships.") Gogol had a different understanding of the artist's task and of his temptation. The fantastic and the diabolical were always essential dimensions of his world, never more so than in "The Portrait."

He toiled over "The Portrait" because it involved a judgment of his own work and its central question tormented him personally. It was not a question of the harmful influence of money or fame, but something more primitive and essential: the ambiguous power of the artistic image itself. And the more lifelike the image, the more perplexing the question. The ambition to achieve a perfect likeness might go beyond the artist's control and bring into the world something he never intended. Thus the portrait in Gogol's tale looks back at its viewers, looks back with the eyes of the Antichrist whose life it has magically prolonged. The corrupting power of the gold it bestows on its new purchaser, the painter Chartkov, is only a secondary effect, an extension of the evil present in the painted image itself. The question the tale explores is whether art is sacramental or sacrilegious, godlike or diabolical, and at what point it may change from one to the other. Some years later, in 1847, Gogol wrote a letter to his father confessor in which he declared himself "guilty and cursed" not only for having portrayed the devil, which he had done with the intention of mocking him, and not only for having painted nothing but grotesque images, being unable to describe a positive character properly, but first of all for having attemped to re-create each thing "as alive as a painter from life." In "The Portrait," the terms of this self-condemnation were already embodied dramatically.

Nature is always doubled by the supernatural in Gogol's tales, and the ordinary is always open to the assaults of the extraordinary. The reality of the capital is a closed fiction, an unrelieved banality, but filled with gigantic, unexpected forces, like the huge fist "the size of a clerk's head" that suddenly comes at Akaky Akakievich out of the darkness. If Akaky Akakievich transgressed the order of things by desiring a new overcoat (by desiring anything at all), and is punished most terribly for it in the phantasmal world of Petersburg, he also returns as a phantom himself and has his revenge. He momentarily becomes one of those unexpected forces, robs the *important person* of his overcoat, frightens a policeman away with "such a fist . . . as is not to be found even among the living," and, having grown much taller, vanishes completely into the darkness of night.

Gogol was made uneasy by his works. They detached themselves from him and lived on their own, producing effects he had not foreseen and that sometimes dismayed him. He would write commentaries after the fact, trying to reduce them to more commonplace and acceptable dimensions. But their initial freedom stayed with them. It was inherent in his method of composition, and in his astonishing artistic gift—astonishing first of all to himself.

RICHARD PEVEAR

TRANSLATORS' NOTE

THIS TRANSLATION HAS been made from the Russian text of the six-volume Khudozhestvennaya Literatura edition (Moscow, 1952–53).

We have arranged the tales in the order of their composition. They include four of the eight tales from *Evenings on a Farm near Dikanka* (1831–32): "St. John's Eve" from the first volume, and "The Night Before Christmas," "The Terrible Vengeance," and "Ivan Fyodorovich Shponka and His Aunt" from the second. We have eliminated the forewords of the beekeeper Rusty Panko, but kept his footnotes, as well as the author's, for individual stories. We include three of the four tales from the two volumes of *Mirgorod* (1835), omitting only "Taras Bulba." Of the Petersburg tales (1835–42; the collective title is not Gogol's but has become traditional), we include all except "Rome." "The Carriage" is a slight anomaly in this group but belongs to the same period. We give the expanded 1842 version of "The Portrait."

The question of rank is of central importance to the Petersburg tales. The following is the table of the civil service ranks as established by the emperor Peter the Great in 1722, with their military equivalents:

Chancellor	Commander in Chief
Actual Privy Councillor	General
Privy Councillor	Lieutenant General
Actual State Councillor	Major General
State Councillor	———
Collegiate Councillor	Colonel
Court Councillor	Lieutenant Colonel
Collegiate Assessor	Major (or Captain)
Titular Councillor	Staff Captain
Collegiate Secretary	Lieutenant
Secretary of Naval Constructions	———
Government Secretary	Second Lieutenant
Provincial Secretary	———
Collegiate Registrar	———

The rank of titular councillor conferred personal nobility; the rank of actual state councillor made it hereditary.

UKRAINIAN
TALES

St. John's Eve

A True Story Told by the Beadle of the ——— Church

FOMA GRIGORIEVICH WAS known to have this special sort of quirk: he mortally disliked telling the same thing over again. It sometimes happened, if you talked him into telling something a second time, that you'd look and he'd throw in some new thing or change it so it was unrecognizable. Once one of those gentlemen—it's hard for us simple folk to fit a name to them: writers, no, not writers, but the same as the dealers at our fairs: they snatch, they cajole, they steal all sorts of stuff, and then bring out booklets no thicker than a primer every month or week—one of those gentlemen coaxed this same story out of Foma Grigorievich, who then forgot all about it. Only there comes this same young sir from Poltava in a pea-green caftan, whom I've already mentioned and one of whose stories I think you've already read, toting a little book with him, and opening it in the middle, he shows it to us. Foma Grigorievich was just about to saddle his nose with his spectacles, but remembering that he'd forgotten to bind them with thread and stick it down with wax, he handed the book to me. Having a smattering of letters and not needing spectacles, I began to read. Before I had time to turn two pages, he suddenly grabbed my arm and stopped me.

"Wait! first tell me, what's that you're reading?"

3

I confess, I was a bit taken aback by such a question.

"What's this I'm reading, Foma Grigorievich? Why, your true story, your very own words."

"Who told you those are my words?"

"What better proof, it's printed here: *told by the beadle So-and-so.*"

"Spit on the head of the one who printed it! He's lying, the dad-blasted Muscovite! Did I say that? The devil it's the same! He's got a screw loose! Listen, I'll tell it to you now."

We moved closer to the table and he began.

MY GRANDFATHER (God rest his soul! and may he eat nothing in that world but white rolls and poppyseed cakes with honey!) was a wonderful storyteller. Once he began to talk, you wouldn't budge from your place the whole day for listening. No comparison with some present-day babbler, who starts spouting off, and in such language as if he hadn't had anything to eat for three days— you just grab your hat and run. I remember like now—the old woman, my late mother, was still alive—how on a long winter's evening, when there was a biting frost outside that walled us up solidly behind the narrow window of our cottage, she used to sit by the comb, pulling the long thread out with her hand, rocking the cradle with her foot, and humming a song that I can hear as if it was now. An oil lamp, trembling and flickering as if frightened of something, lighted our cottage. The spindle whirred; and all of us children, clustered together, listened to our grandfather, who was so old he hadn't left the stove[1] in five years. But his wondrous talk about olden times, about Cossack raids, about the Polacks, about the mighty deeds of Podkova, Poltora Kozhukha, and Sagai-dachny,[2] never interested us as much as his stories about some strange marvel of old, which sent shivers all through us and made our hair stand on end. Now and then fear would take such hold of you that everything in the evening appeared like God knows what monster. If you happened to step out of the cottage at night for something, you'd think a visitor from the other world had gone to lie down in your bed. And may I never tell this story another time if I didn't often mistake my own blouse, from a distance, for a curled-up devil at the head of the bed. But the main thing in my grandfather's stories was that he never in his life told a lie, and whatever he used to say, that was precisely what had happened. I'll tell one of his wonderful stories for you now. I know there are lots of those smart alecks who do some scribbling in the courts and even read civic writings, and who, if they were handed a simple prayer book, wouldn't be able to make out a jot of it—but display their teeth shamefully, that they can do. For them, whatever you say is funny. Such disbelief has spread through the world! What's more—may God and the most pure Virgin not love me!—maybe even you won't believe me: once I made mention of witches, and what do you think? some daredevil turned up who didn't believe in witches! Yes, thank God, I've lived so long in the world, I've seen such infidels as find *giving a priest a ride in a sieve*[3] easier than taking snuff is for the likes of us; and they, too, go in fear of witches. But if they were to dream . . . only I don't want to say what, there's no point talking about them.

Way, way back, more than a hundred years ago—my late grand-father used to say—no one would even have recognized our vil-lage: a farmstead, the poorest of farmsteads! Some dozen huts, cobless, roofless, stuck up here and there in the middle of a field. Not a fence, not a decent barn to put cattle or a cart in. It was the rich ones that lived like that; and if you looked at our sort, the poor ones—a hole in the ground, there's your house! Only by the smoke could you tell that a creature of God lived there. You may ask, why did they live like that? It wasn't really poverty, because almost everybody then went Cossacking and got no small amount of goods in other lands; but more because there was no need to have a decent cottage. What folk weren't hanging about then: Crimeans, Polacks, Litvaks![4] It also happened that bunches of our own would come and rob their own. Everything happened.

In this farmstead a man often appeared, or, better, a devil in human form. Where he came from and why he came, nobody knew. He'd carouse, drink, then suddenly vanish into thin air, without a trace. Then, lo and behold, again he'd as if fall from the sky, prowl the streets of the hamlet, of which there's no trace left now and which was maybe no more than a hundred paces from

Dikanka. He'd pick up passing Cossacks: laughter, songs, money flowed, vodka poured like water . . . He used to accost pretty girls: gave them ribbons, earrings, necklaces—more than they knew what to do with! True, the pretty girls would hesitate a bit as they took the presents: God knows, maybe they really had passed through unclean hands. My grandfather's own aunt, who kept a tavern at the time on what is now Oposhnyanskaya Road, where Basavriuk—so this demonic man was known—used to carouse, she it was who said she wouldn't agree to take presents from him, not for all the blessings in the world. But, again, how not take: anybody would have been filled with fear when he knitted his bristling eyebrows and sent such a scowling look at you that you'd gladly let your legs carry you God knows where; and once you did take it—the very next night some friendly visitor from the swamp, with horns on his head, drags himself to you and starts strangling you, if you've got a necklace on your neck, or biting your finger, if you're wearing a ring, or pulling your braid, if you've braided a ribbon into it. God be with them, these presents! But the trouble is that you can't get rid of them: throw the devilish ring or necklace into the water, and it comes floating right back to your hands.

There was a church in the hamlet, of St. Panteleimon if I remember rightly. A priest lived by it then, Father Afanasy, of blessed memory. Noticing that Basavriuk did not come to church even on Easter Sunday, he decided to reprimand him and put him under a church penance. Penance, hah! He barely escaped. "Listen, my good sir!" the man thundered in reply, "you'd better mind your own business and not go meddling in other people's, unless you'd like to have that goat's gullet of yours plugged with hot kutya!"[5] What could be done with the cursed fellow? Father Afanasy merely announced that anyone who kept company with Basavriuk would be regarded as a Catholic,[6] an enemy of Christ's Church and of the whole human race.

In that hamlet one Cossack called Korzh had a man working for him who was known as Pyotr Kinless—maybe because nobody remembered either his father or his mother. The church warden, it's true, said they'd died of the plague the next year; but my grandfather's aunt wouldn't hear of it and tried the best she could to endow him with kin, though poor Pyotr needed that as much as we need last year's snow. She said his father was still in the Zaporozhye,[7] had been in captivity to the Turks, had suffered God knows what tortures, and by some miracle, after disguising himself as a eunuch, had given them the slip. The dark-browed girls and young women cared little about his kin. They merely said that if he was dressed in a new coat tied with a red belt, had a black astrakhan hat with a smart blue top put on his head, had a Turkish saber hung at his side, was given a horsewhip for one hand and a finely chased pipe for the other, not a lad in the world could hold a candle to him. But the trouble was that poor Petrus had only one gray blouse, with more holes in it than there are gold coins in a Jew's pocket. And that still wasn't so great a trouble, the real trouble was that old Korzh had a daughter, a beauty such as I think you've hardly chanced to see. My late grandfather's aunt used to say—and you know it's easier for a woman to kiss the devil, meaning no offense, than to call another woman a beauty—that the Cossack girl's plump cheeks were as fresh and bright as the first pink poppy when, having washed itself in God's dew, it glows, spreads its petals, and preens itself before the just-risen sun; that her eyebrows were like the black cords our girls now buy to hang crosses and ducats on from the Muscovites who go peddling with their boxes in our villages, arched evenly as if looking into her bright eyes; that her little mouth, at the sight of which the young men back then licked their lips, seemed to have been created for chanting nightingale songs; that her hair, black as the raven's wing and soft as young flax (at that time our girls did not yet wear braids with bright-colored ribbons twined in them), fell in curly locks on her gold-embroidered jacket. Ah, may God never grant me to sing "Alleluia" in the choir again if I wouldn't be kissing her here and now, even though the gray is creeping into the old forest that covers my head, and my old woman's by my side like a wart on a nose. Well, if a lad and a girl live near each other . . . you know yourself what comes of it. It used to be that at the break of dawn, the traces of iron-shod red boots could be seen at the spot where Pidorka had stood gabbling with her Petrus. But even so, nothing bad would ever have entered Korzh's mind, if Petrus hadn't decided one time—well, it's obvious none but the evil one prompted him—without taking a good look around the front hall, to plant a hearty kiss, as they say, on the Cossack girl's rosy lips, and the same evil one—may the son-of-a-bitch dream of the Holy Cross!— foolishly put the old coot up to opening the door. Korzh turned to wood, gaping and clinging to the doorpost. The cursed kiss seemed to stun him completely. It sounded louder to him than the blow of a pestle against the wall, something our peasants usually do to drive the clootie away, for lack of a gun and powder.

Having recovered, he took his grandfather's horsewhip from the wall and was about to sprinkle poor Pyotr's back with it, when Pidorka's brother, the six-year-old Ivas, came running from nowhere, grabbed his legs with his little arms in fear, and shouted, "Daddy, daddy! don't beat Petrus!" What could he do? A father's heart isn't made of stone: he put the horsewhip back on the wall and led him quietly out of the cottage: "If you ever show up in my cottage again, or even just under the windows, then listen, Pyotr: by God, that'll be the end of your black moustache, and your top-knot[8] as well; here it is going twice around your ear, but it'll bid farewell to your head or I'm not Terenty Korzh!" Having said that, he gave him a slight cuff, so that Petrus, not seeing the ground under him, went flying headlong. There's kisses for you! Our two doves were grief-stricken; and then a rumor spread through the village that some Polack had taken to calling on Korzh, all trimmed in gold, with a moustache, with a saber, with spurs, with pockets that jingled like the little bell on the bag our sacristan Taras goes around the church with every day. Well, we know why someone comes calling on a father who has a dark-browed daughter. So one day Pidorka, streaming with tears, picked up her Ivas in her arms: "Ivas my dear, Ivas my love! run to Petrus, my golden child, quick as an arrow shot from a bow; tell him everything: I would love his brown eyes, I would kiss his white face, but my lot forbids me. More than one napkin is wet with my bitter tears. It's hard on me. I'm sick at heart. And my own father is my enemy: he's forcing me to marry the unloved Polack. Tell him the wedding is being prepared, only there won't be any music at our wedding: deacons will sing instead of pipes and mandolins. I won't step out to dance with my bridegroom: they will bear me away. Dark, dark will be my house: of maple wood it will be, and instead of a chimney there will be a cross on its roof!"

As if turned to stone, not moving from the spot, Petro listened while the innocent child babbled Pidorka's words to him. "And I thought, luckless me, that I'd go to the Crimea and Turkey to war myself up some gold, and then come to you with wealth, my beauty. That's not to be. An evil eye has looked on us. There'll be a wedding for me, too, my dear little fish: only there won't be any deacons at that wedding; a black raven will crow over me instead of a priest; a smooth field will be my home and a gray cloud my roof; an eagle will peck my brown eyes out; the rains will wash the Cossack's bones, and the wind will dry them. But what am I doing? of whom, to whom shall I complain? God must will it so—if I perish, I perish!" and he plodded straight to the tavern.

My late grandfather's aunt was slightly surprised to see Petrus in the tavern, and that at an hour when good people go to church, and she goggled her eyes at him, as if just waking up, when he ordered a jug of vodka as big as half a bucket. Only it was in vain that the poor fellow thought to drown his grief. The vodka pricked his tongue like nettles and tasted bitterer to him than wormwood. He pushed the jug off onto the ground. "Enough of this grieving, Cossack!" something rumbled in a bass voice behind him. He turned around: Basavriuk! Ohh, what an ugly mug! Bristly hair, eyes like an ox! "I know what you lack: it's this!" Here, grinning devilishly, he clanked the leather purse that hung from his belt. Petro gave a start. "How it glows! heh, heh, heh!" he bellowed, pouring gold coins into his hand. "How it rings! heh, heh, heh! And I'll ask just one thing for a whole heap of such baubles." "The devil!" shouted Petro. "Let's have it! I'm ready for anything." And they shook hands. "Watch out, Petro, you came just in time: tomorrow is John the Baptist.[9] It's only on this one night in the year that the fern flowers. Don't miss it. I'll be waiting for you at midnight in Bear's Gully."

I don't suppose chickens wait so impatiently for the housewife who brings them grain as Petrus waited for that evening. He kept looking to see if the tree's shadow was getting longer, if the setting sun was getting redder—and the more impatiently as it went on. So drawn out! God's day must have lost its end somewhere. Now there's no more sun. The sky is red only on one side. That, too, is fading. It's getting colder in the fields. Dusk thickens, thickens, and—it's dark! At last! His heart nearly jumping out of his breast, he set off on his way and descended cautiously through the dense forest into the deep ravine known as Bear's Gully. Basavriuk was already waiting there. It was blind dark. Hand in hand they made their way over the boggy marsh, getting caught in thickly growing thorns at almost every step. Here was a level place. Petro looked around: he had never chanced to come there. Basavriuk also stopped.

"Do you see the three knolls standing before you? There will be many different flowers on them; but may the otherworldly powers keep you from picking so much as one. Only as soon as the fern begins to flower, grab it and don't turn around, whatever you fancy is behind you."

Petro was about to ask . . . behold—he was no longer there. He approached the three knolls: Where are the flowers? Nothing could be seen. Wild weeds stood blackly around, stifling everything with their thickness. But now lightning flashed in the sky and a whole bank of flowers appeared before him, all wondrous, all never seen before; there were also simple ferns. Doubt came over Petro, and he stood before them pondering, arms akimbo.

"What's so extraordinary about it? Ten times a day you may happen to see such stuff; where's the marvel? Is that devilish mug making fun of me?"

But, lo—a small flower bud showed red, moving as if it were alive. A wonder indeed! Moving and growing bigger and bigger, and reddening like a hot coal. A little star lit up, something crackled softly, and the flower unfolded before his eyes, shining like a flame on others around it.

"Now's the time!" thought Petro, and he reached out. He saw hundreds of hairy hands stretching toward the same flower from behind him, and something behind him was running to and fro. Closing his eyes, he pulled at the stem, and the flower stayed in his hand. All became hushed. Basavriuk appeared, sitting on a stump, all blue like a dead man. Not moving a finger. Eyes fixed motionlessly on something visible only to himself; mouth half open and unresponding. Around him nothing stirs. Ugh, horrible! . . . But now a whistling was heard, at which everything went cold inside Pyotr, and he fancied that the grass rustled, the flowers began talking to each other in voices thin as little silver bells; the trees rumbled, pouring out abuse . . . Basavriuk's face suddenly came to life; his eyes flashed. "At last you've come back, yaga!"[10] he growled through his teeth. "Look, Petro, presently a beauty will stand before you: do whatever she tells you, or you'll be destroyed forever!" Here he parted the blackthorn bush with his stick, and before them appeared a hut, as they say, on chicken's legs. Basavriuk pounded on it with his fist and the wall shook. A big black dog came running to them and, with a squeal, turned into a cat and hurled itself at their eyes. "Don't rage, don't rage, old witch!" Basavriuk said, spicing it with such a word as would make a good man stop his ears. Behold, where the cat had been there stood an old hag, all bent double, with a face as shriveled as a baked apple; her nose and chin were like the jaws of a nutcracker. "A fine beauty!" thought Petro, and gooseflesh crept over him. The witch snatched the flower from his hand, bent down, and whispered something over it for a long time, sprinkling it with some water. Sparks poured from her mouth; foam came to her lips. "Throw it!" she said, handing the flower back to him. Petro threw it up and— oh, wonder!—the flower did not fall straight back but for a long time looked like a fiery little ball amidst the darkness, floating like a boat in the air; at last it slowly began to descend and fell so far away that the little star was barely visible, no bigger than a poppyseed. "There!" the old hag croaked hollowly; and Basavriuk, handing him a spade, said: "Dig there, Petro. You'll see more gold there than either you or Korzh ever dreamed of." Petro, spitting on his hands, grabbed the spade, drove it in with his foot, turned up the earth, again, a third time, yet again . . . something hard! . . . The spade clangs and won't go any further. Here his eyes begin to make out clearly a small ironbound chest. He was about to take hold of it, but the chest started sinking into the ground, deeper, deeper; and behind him came a laugh that more closely resembled the hiss of a snake. "No, you won't see any gold until you get some human blood!" said the witch, and she brought him a child of about six, covered with a white sheet, making a sign that he should cut its head off. Petro was dumbfounded. A small thing, to cut off a person's head for no reason at all, and an innocent child's at that! Angrily he pulled off the sheet that covered its head, and what then? Before him stood Ivas. The poor child folded his little arms crosswise and hung his head . . . Like a madman, Petro jumped at the witch with his knife, and was already raising his hand . . .

"And what did you promise for the girl? . . ." thundered Basavriuk, and it was as if he put a bullet through his back. The witch stamped her foot: blue flame burst from the ground; its whole inside lit up and looked as if it were molded from crystal; and everything under the ground became visible as in the palm of your hand. Gold coins, precious stones, in chests, in cauldrons, were heaped up right under the place where they stood. His eyes glowed . . . his mind darkened . . . As if insane, he seized the knife and innocent blood spurted into his eyes . . . A devilish guffawing thundered on all sides. Hideous monsters leaped before him in throngs. The witch, clutching the beheaded corpse, drank its blood like a wolf . . . Everything whirled in his head! Summoning all his strength, he broke into a run. Everything before him was covered with red. The trees, bathed in blood, seemed to burn and groan. The sky, red hot, was trembling . . . Fiery spots, like lightning, came to his eyes. Exhausted, he ran inside his hut and collapsed as if he had been mowed down. A dead sleep came over him.

For two days and nights Petro slept without waking. On the third day, having come to, he looked around at all the corners of his house for a long time; but his efforts to recollect were all in vain: his memory was like an old miser's pocket, not even a penny could be coaxed out of it. He stretched a little and heard a clank at his feet. He looked: two sacks of gold. Only then, as if through sleep, did he remember looking for some treasure, being afraid in the forest alone . . . But what the price had been, how he had obtained it—that he simply could not understand.

Korzh saw the sacks and—went all soft: "Petrus is this and that and the other! And haven't I always loved him? hasn't he been like my own son to me?" And the old coot went off into such fancies that the fellow was moved to tears. Pidorka began telling him how Ivas had been stolen by some passing Gypsies. But Petro couldn't even remember his face: so addled he was by that cursed devilry! There was no point in delaying. The Pole got a fig under his nose, and the wedding was cooked up: they baked a lot of cakes, sewed a lot of napkins and kerchiefs, rolled out a barrel of vodka; the young couple was seated on the table; the round loaf was cut; they struck up the bandore, cymbals, pipes and mandolins—and the fun began . . .

Weddings in the old days were no comparison with ours. My grandfather's aunt used to tell us—oh, ho, ho! How girls in festive headdresses of yellow, blue, and pink stripes trimmed with gold braid, in fine shirts stitched with red silk and embroidered with little silver flowers, in Morocco boots with high, iron-shod heels, capered about the room as smoothly as peahens and swishing like the wind; how young women in tall headdresses, the upper part made all of gold brocade, with a small cutout behind and a golden kerchief peeking from it, with two little peaks of the finest black astrakhan, one pointing backward and the other forward, in blue jackets of the best silk with red flaps, stepped out imposingly one by one, arms akimbo, and rhythmically stamped away at the gopak.[11] How young lads in tall Cossack hats and fine flannel blouses with silver-embroidered belts, pipes in their teeth, bobbed and pranced before them, cutting all sorts of capers. Korzh himself couldn't hold back, looking at the young ones and remembering bygone times. With a bandore in his hands, puffing on his pipe and humming at the same time, the old fellow put a glass on his head and, to the loud shouts of the revelers, broke into a squatting dance. What people won't think up when they're tipsy! They used to dress in disguises—my God, they no longer looked like human beings! No comparison with the costumes at our weddings nowadays. How is it now? They just copy the Gypsies or the Muscovites. No, it used to be one would dress up as a Jew and another as a devil, and first they'd kiss each other and then grab each other's topknots . . . God help us! you had to hold your sides from laughter. They'd get dressed up in Turkish or Tartar costumes: everything on them blazes like fire . . . And when they start fooling and pulling tricks . . . well, saints alive! A funny thing happened with my grandfather's aunt, who was at this wedding: she was dressed then in a loose Tartar dress and went around offering glasses to the guests. The devil put one of them up to splashing some vodka on her from behind. Another—no flies on him either—struck a fire straight away . . . the flame blazed up, the poor aunt got frightened and started pulling her dress off in front of everybody . . . Noise, laughter, turmoil arose, like at a street fair. In short, the old people remember no merrier wedding ever.

Pidorka and Petrus started living like lord and lady. Everything in abundance, everything shining . . . However, good people shook their heads slightly, looking at their life. "No good can come from the devil," everybody murmured with one voice. "Where did he get his wealth, if not from the seducer of Orthodox people? Where could such a heap of gold come from? Why, suddenly, on the very day he got rich, did Basavriuk vanish into thin air?" Now, just tell me people were making it up! Because, in fact, before a month was out, nobody could recognize Petrus. What happened to him and why, God knows. He sits in one place and won't say a word to anyone. He keeps thinking and thinking, as if he wants to remember something. When Pidorka manages to make him talk about something, he seems to forget it all and starts to speak, and even almost cheers up; then he glances inadvertently at the sacks and cries out: "Wait, wait, I forgot!" and falls to thinking again, and again strains to remember something. Once in a while, after sitting in the same place for a long time, he fancies it's all just about to come back to him . . . and then it all goes again. He fancies he's sitting in the tavern; they bring him vodka; the vodka burns him; the vodka's disgusting to him. Somebody comes up, slaps him on the shoulder . . . but then it's as if everything gets misty before him. Sweat streams down his face, and he sits back down, exhausted.

What didn't Pidorka do: she consulted wizards, she poured out

a flurry and boiled a bellyache*—nothing helped. So the summer
went by. Many Cossacks had reaped their hay and harvested their
crops; many Cossacks, the more riotous sort, had set out on campaign. Flocks of ducks still crowded our marshes, but the bitterns
were long gone. The steppes were turning red. Shocks of wheat
stood here and there like bright Cossack hats strewn over the
fields. On the road you would meet carts piled with kindling and
firewood. The ground turned harder and in places was gripped by
frost. Snow had already begun to spatter from the sky, and the
branches of the trees were decked with hoarfrost as if with hare's
fur. On a clear, frosty day, the red-breasted bullfinch, like a foppish
Polish gentleman, was already strolling over the snowdrifts pecking
at seeds, and children with enormous sticks were sending wooden
whirligigs over the ice, while their fathers calmly stayed stretched
on the stove, stepping out every once in a while, a lighted pipe in
their teeth, to say a word or two about the good Orthodox frost,
or to get some fresh air and thresh some grain that had long been
sitting in the front hall. At last the snow began to melt, and *the pike
broke the ice with its tail*, and Petro was still the same, and the further
it went, the grimmer he became. As though chained down, he sat
in the middle of the room with the sacks of gold at his feet. He
grew wild, shaggy, frightening; his mind was fixed on one thing,
he kept straining to remember something; and he was angry and
vexed that he could not remember it. Often he would get up
wildly from where he sat, move his arms, fix his eyes on something
as if wishing to catch it; his lips move as if they want to utter some
long-forgotten word—and stop motionless . . . Fury comes over
him; like a demented man, he gnaws and bites his hands and tears
out tufts of his hair in vexation, until he grows calm, drops down
as if oblivious, and then again tries to remember, and again fury,

---

*A flurry is poured out in cases when we want to find out the cause of a fear; melted tin or
wax is dropped into water, and whatever shape it takes is what has frightened the sick person;
after that the fear goes away. We boil a bellyache for nausea and stomachache. A piece of hemp
is set alight and thrown into a mug, which is then turned upside down in a bowl of water and
placed on the sick person's stomach; then, after some whispered spell, he's given a spoonful of
the same water to drink. (Author's note.)

and again torment ... What a plague from God! Life was no longer life for Pidorka. At first she dreaded staying alone in the house with him, but later the poor thing grew accustomed to her misfortune. But the former Pidorka was no longer recognizable. No color, no smile: worn, wasted, she cried her bright eyes out. Once someone evidently took pity on her and advised her to go to the sorceress who lived in Bear's Gully, who, as rumor had it, could heal any illness in the world. She decided to try this last remedy; one word led to another, and she talked the old hag into coming home with her. This was in the evening, just on the Baptist's eve. Petro lay oblivious on the bench and did not notice the new visitor at all. And then gradually he began to raise himself and stare. Suddenly he trembled all over, as if on the scaffold; his hair rose in a shock ... and he laughed such a laugh that fear cut into Pidorka's heart. "I remember, I remember!" he cried with horrible merriment and, swinging an ax, flung it with all his might at the hag. The ax sank three inches into the oak door. The hag vanished and a child of about seven, in a white shirt, with covered head, stood in the middle of the room ... The sheet flew off. "Ivas!" Pidorka cried and rushed to him; but the phantom became all bloody from head to foot and lit up the whole room with a red glow ... Frightened, she ran out to the front hall; then, recovering a little, she wanted to go back and help him—in vain! The door slammed shut so tightly behind her that it was impossible to open it. People came running; they began to knock; they forced the door: not a soul. The whole room was filled with smoke, and in the middle only, where Petrus had been standing, was a heap of ashes from which smoke was still rising in places. They rushed to the sacks: instead of gold coins there was nothing but broken shards. Eyes popping, mouths gaping, not daring even to move their mustaches, the Cossacks stood as if rooted to the spot. Such fright came over them on account of this marvel.

What happened after that, I don't remember. Pidorka made a vow to go on a pilgrimage; she collected the property left by her father and a few days later was indeed no longer in the village. Where she went, no one could say. Obliging old women had already sent her to the same place Petro had taken himself to; but a

Cossack come from Kiev told that he had seen a nun in the convent, all dried up like a skeleton and ceaselessly praying, in whom the villagers by all tokens recognized Pidorka; that supposedly no one had yet heard even one word from her; that she had come on foot and brought the casing for an icon of the Mother of God studded with such bright stones that everyone shut their eyes when they looked at it.

Sorry, but that was not the end yet. The same day that the evil one laid hands on Petrus, Basavriuk appeared again; only everybody ran away from him. They knew now what kind of bird he was; none other than Satan, who had taken human form in order to dig up treasures—and since treasures can't be taken with unclean hands, he lured young fellows away. That same year everybody abandoned their dugout homes and moved to the village; but there was no peace from the accursed Basavriuk there either. My late grandfather's aunt used to say that he was vexed with her the most, precisely for having abandoned the former tavern on Oposhnyanskaya Road, and he tried with all his might to vent his anger on her. Once the village elders gathered in the tavern and were having, as they say, a proper conversation at table, in the middle of which stood a roast lamb of a size it would be sinful to call small. They chatted about this and that, about all sorts of marvels and wonders. And they fancied—it would be nothing if one of them did, but it was precisely all of them—that the lamb raised its head, its mischievous black eyes came to life and lit up, and that instant a black, bristling mustache appeared, twitching meaningfully at those present. Everybody recognized the lamb's head at once as Basavriuk's mug; my grandfather's aunt even thought he was about to ask for some vodka . . . The honorable elders grabbed their hats and hastily went their ways. Another time the church warden himself, who liked now and then to have a private little chat with an old-time glass, before he even reached the bottom, saw the glass bow to the ground before him. Devil take it! he began crossing himself! . . . And then another wonder with his better half: she had just started mixing dough in a huge tub when the tub suddenly jumped away. "Stop, stop!"—but nothing doing: arms akimbo, with an imposing air, it broke into a squatting dance all around the room . . . Go on and laugh; but our grandfathers were in no mood for laughter. And even though Father Afanasy walked around the whole village with holy water and chased the devil down all the streets with the sprinkler, all the same, my late grandfather's aunt complained that as soon as evening came, somebody started knocking on the roof and scratching at the wall.

Not only that! Now, for instance, on this same spot where our village stands, everything seems quiet; but not so long ago, my late father and I still remembered that a good man couldn't pass by the ruins of the tavern, which the unclean tribe[12] kept fixing up at their own expense for a long time afterwards. Smoke poured from the sooty chimney in a column and, rising so high that your hat would fall off if you looked at it, poured hot coals all over the steppes, and the devil—no need to mention that son-of-a-dog—sobbed so pitifully in his hovel that the frightened jackdaws rose in flocks from the nearby oak grove and with wild cries dashed about the sky.

The Night Before Christmas

The last day before Christmas had passed. A wintry, clear night came. The stars peeped out. The crescent moon rose majestically in the sky to give light to good people and all the world, so that everyone could merrily go caroling and glorify Christ.* The frost had increased since morning; but it was so still that the frosty creaking under your boots could be heard for half a mile. Not one group of young lads had shown up under the windows of the houses yet; only the moon peeked stealthily into them, as if inviting the girls sprucing themselves up to hurry and run out to the creaking snow. Here smoke curled from the chimney of one cottage and went in a cloud across the sky, and along with the smoke rose a witch riding on a broom.

If the Sorochintsy assessor had been passing by just then, driving

---

*Among us, to go caroling [*koliadovat*] means to sing songs called *koliadki* under the windows on Christmas Eve. The master or mistress of the house, or anyone staying at home, always drops into the carolers' sack some sausage or bread or a copper coin, whatever bounty they have. They say there used to be an idol named Koliada who was thought to be a god, and that is where the koliadki came from. Who knows? It's not for us simple people to discuss it. Last year Father Osip forbade going caroling around the farmsteads, saying folk were pleasing Satan by it. However, to tell the truth, there's not a word in the koliadki about Koliada. They often sing of the nativity of Christ; and in the end they wish health to the master, the mistress, the children, and the whole household. (The Beekeeper's note.)

a troika of hired horses, in a hat with a lamb's wool band after the uhlan fashion, in a dark blue coat lined with astrakhan, with the devilishly woven whip he used to urge his coachman on, he would surely have noticed her, for no witch in the world could elude the Sorochintsy assessor. He could count off how many piglets each woman's sow had farrowed, and how much linen lay in every chest, and precisely which of his clothes and chattels a good man had pawned in the tavern of a Sunday. But the Sorochintsy assessor was not passing by, and what business did he have with other people, since he had his own territory. And the witch, meanwhile, rose so high that she was only a black spot flitting overhead. But wherever the spot appeared, the stars disappeared from the sky one after another. Soon the witch had a sleeve full of them. Three or four still shone. Suddenly, from the opposite direction, another little spot appeared, grew bigger, began to spread, and was no longer a little spot. A nearsighted man, even if he put the wheels of the commissar's britzka on his nose for spectacles, still wouldn't have been able to make out what it was. From the front, a perfect German:* the narrow little muzzle, constantly twitching and sniffing at whatever came along, ended in a round snout, as with our pigs; the legs were so thin that if the headman of Yareskov had had such legs, he'd have broken them in the first Cossack dance. To make up for that, from behind he was a real provincial attorney in uniform, because he had a tail hanging there, sharp and long as uniform coattails nowadays; and only by the goat's beard under his muzzle, the little horns sticking up on his head, and the fact that he was no whiter than a chimney sweep, could you tell that he was not a German or a provincial attorney, but simply a devil who had one last night to wander about the wide world and teach good people to sin. Tomorrow, as the first bells rang for matins, he would run for his den, tail between his legs, without looking back.

Meanwhile the devil was quietly sneaking toward the moon and had already reached out his hand to snatch it, but suddenly pulled

---

*Among us, anyone from a foreign land is called a German, whether he's a Frenchman, a Swiss, or a Swede—they're all Germans. (The Beekeeper's note.)

it back as if burnt, sucked his fingers, shook his leg, and ran around to the other side, but again jumped away and pulled his hand back. However, despite all his failures, the sly devil did not give up his pranks. Running up to it, he suddenly seized the moon with both hands, wincing and blowing, tossing it from one hand to the other, like a muzhik who takes a coal for his pipe in his bare hands; at last he hastily hid it in his pocket and ran on as if nothing had happened.

In Dikanka nobody realized that the devil had stolen the moon. True, the local scrivener, leaving the tavern on all fours, saw the moon dancing about in the sky for no reason and swore to it by God before the whole village; but people shook their heads and even made fun of him. But what led the devil to decide on such a lawless business? Here's what: he knew that the wealthy Cossack Choub had been invited for kutya[1] by the deacon, and that there would also be the headman, a relative of the deacon's in a blue frock coat who sang in the bishop's choir and could hit the lowest bass notes, the Cossack Sverbyguz, and others; that besides kutya there would be spiced vodka, saffron vodka, and lots of other things to eat. And meanwhile his daughter, the beauty of the village, would stay at home, and this daughter would certainly be visited by the blacksmith, a stalwart and fine fellow, whom the devil found more disgusting than Father Kondrat's sermons. The blacksmith devoted his leisure time to painting and was reputed to be the best artist in the whole neighborhood. The then still-living chief L——ko himself had summoned him specially to Poltava to paint the wooden fence around his house. All the bowls from which the Dikanka Cossacks supped their borscht had been decorated by the blacksmith. The blacksmith was a God-fearing man and often painted icons of the saints: even now you can find his evangelist Luke in the T—— church. But the triumph of his art was one picture painted on the church wall in the right-hand vestibule, in which he portrayed Saint Peter on the day of the Last Judgment, with the keys in his hand, driving the evil spirit out of hell; the frightened devil is rushing in all directions, sensing his doom, and the formerly confined sinners are beating him and driving him about with whips, sticks, and whatever else they can find. All the while the artist was working on this picture, painting it on a big wooden board, the devil tried as hard as he could to hinder him: shoved his arm invisibly, raised up ashes from the forge in the smithy and poured them over the picture; but the work got done despite all, the board was brought to church and set into the wall in the vestibule, and ever since then the devil had sworn vengeance on the blacksmith.

One night only was left him to wander about the wide world, but on this night, too, he sought some way to vent his anger on the blacksmith. And for that he decided to steal the moon, in hopes that old Choub was lazy and not easy to budge, and the deacon's place was not all that close to his: the road went beyond the village, past the mills, past the cemetery, and around the gully. If it had been a moonlit night, the spiced vodka and saffron vodka might have tempted Choub, but in such darkness you would hardly succeed in dragging him down from the stove[2] and getting him out of the cottage. And the blacksmith, who had long been on bad terms with him, would never dare visit his daughter with him there, for all his strength.

So it was that, as soon as the devil hid the moon in his pocket, it suddenly became so dark all over the world that no one could find the way to the tavern, to say nothing of the deacon's. The witch, seeing herself suddenly in the dark, cried out. Here the devil, sidling up to her, took her under the arm and started whispering in her ear what is usually whispered to the whole of womankind. Wondrous is the working of the world! All who live in it try to mimic and mock one another. Before, it used to be that in Mirgorod only the judge and the mayor went about during the winter in cloth-covered sheepskin coats, and all of petty clerkdom wore plain uncovered ones; but now both the assessor and the surveyor have got themselves up in new coats of Reshetilovo astrakhan covered with broadcloth. Two years ago the clerk and the local scrivener bought themselves some blue Chinese cotton for sixty kopecks a yard. The sacristan had baggy summer trousers of nankeen and a waistcoat of striped worsted made for himself. In short, everything tries to get ahead! When will these people cease their vanity! I'll bet many would be surprised to see the devil getting up to it as well. What's most vexing is that he must fancy he's a handsome fellow, whereas—it's shameful to look him in the face. A mug, as Foma Grigorievich says, that's the vilest of the vile, and yet he, too, goes philandering! But it got so dark in the sky, and under the sky, that it was no longer possible to see what went on further between them.

"So, CHUM, YOU haven't been to the deacon's new house yet?" the Cossack Choub was saying as he came out the door of his cottage to a tall, lean muzhik in a short sheepskin jacket with a stubbly chin that showed it hadn't been touched in over two weeks by the broken piece of scythe a muzhik usually shaves with for lack of a razor. "There'll be good drinking there tonight!" Choub continued, with a grin on his face. "We'd better not be late."

With that, Choub straightened the belt that tightly girded his coat, pulled his hat down hard, clutched his knout—a terror and threat to bothersome dogs—but, looking up, he stopped . . .

"What the devil! Look, look, Panas! . . ."

"What?" said his chum, and also threw his head back.

"How, what? There's no moon!"

"What the deuce! It's a fact, there's no moon."

"None at all," said Choub, somewhat vexed at the chum's unfailing indifference. "Not that you care, I suppose."

"But what can I do?"

"It had to happen," Choub went on, wiping his mustache on his sleeve, "some devil—may the dog have no glass of vodka in the morning—had to interfere! . . . Really, as if for a joke . . . I looked out the window on purpose as I sat inside: a wonder of a night! Clear, snow shining in the moonlight. Everything bright as day. The moment I step out the door—it's pitch-dark!"

Choub spent a long time grumbling and swearing, all the while pondering what to decide. He was dying to chatter about all sorts of nonsense at the deacon's, where, without any doubt, the headman was already sitting, and the visiting bass, and the tar dealer Mikita, who went off to the Poltava market every two weeks and cracked such jokes that good people held their sides from laughter.

Choub could already picture mentally the spiced vodka standing on the table. All this was tempting, it's true; but the darkness of the night reminded him of the laziness so dear to all Cossacks. How good it would be to lie on the stove now, with his knees bent, calmly smoking his pipe and listening, through an entrancing drowsiness, to the carols and songs of the merry lads and girls coming in crowds to the windows. He would, without any doubt, have decided on the latter if he had been alone, but now for the two of them it would not be so boring or scary to walk through the dark night, and he did not really want to appear lazy or cowardly before the others. Having finished swearing, he again turned to the chum:

"So there's no moon, chum?"

"No."

"It's odd, really! Give me a pinch. Fine snuff you've got there, chum! Where do you get it?"

"The devil it's fine," replied the chum, closing the birchbark pouch all covered with pinpricked designs. "It wouldn't make an old hen sneeze!"

"I remember," Choub went on in the same way, "the late tavern keeper Zozulia once brought me some snuff from Nezhin. Ah, what snuff that was! such good snuff! So, then, chum, what are we going to do? It's dark out."

"Let's stay home, then, if you like," said the chum, grasping the door handle.

If the chum hadn't said it, Choub would certainly have decided to stay home, but now something seemed to tug at him to do the contrary.

"No, chum, let's go! It's impossible, we have to go!"

Having said that, he was already annoyed with himself for it. He very much disliked dragging himself anywhere on such a night; but it was a comfort to him that he himself had purposely wanted it and was not doing as he had been advised.

The chum, showing not the least vexation on his face, like a man to whom it was decidedly all the same whether he stayed home or dragged himself out, looked around, scratched his shoulders with the butt of his whip, and the two chums set out on their way.

Now LET'S HAVE a look at what the beautiful daughter was doing, left alone. Oksana had not yet turned seventeen, but already in almost all the world, on this side of Dikanka and on the other, the talk was of nothing but her. The young lads, one and all, declared that there had never been, nor ever would be, a better girl in the village. Oksana knew and heard all that was said about her, and was capricious, as beauties will be. If she had gone about not in a checkered wraparound and a woolen apron, but in some sort of capote, she would have sent all her maids scurrying. The lads chased after her in droves, but, losing patience, gradually dropped out and turned to others less spoiled. The blacksmith alone persisted and would not leave off his wooing, though he was treated no better than the rest.

After her father left, she spent a long time dressing up and putting on airs before a small tin-framed mirror, and couldn't have enough of admiring herself. "Why is it that people decided to praise my prettiness?" she said as if distractedly, so as to chat with herself about something. "People lie, I'm not pretty at all." But in the mirror flashed her fresh face, alive in its child's youngness, with shining dark eyes and an inexpressibly lovely smile which burned the soul through, and all at once proved the opposite. "Are my dark eyebrows and eyes," the beauty went on, not letting go of the mirror, "so pretty that they have no equal in the world? What's so pretty about this upturned nose? and these cheeks? and lips? As if my dark braids are pretty! Ugh! they could be frightening in the evening: they twist and twine around my head like long snakes. I see now that I'm not pretty at all!" and then, holding the mirror further away from her face, she exclaimed: "No, I am pretty! Ah, how pretty! A wonder! What joy I'll bring to the one whose wife I become! How my husband will admire me! He won't know who he is. He'll kiss me to death."

"A wonderful girl!" the blacksmith, who had quietly come in, whispered, "and so little boasting! She's been standing for an hour looking in the mirror and hasn't had enough, and she even praises herself aloud!"

"Yes, lads, am I a match for you? Just look at me," the pretty little coquette went on, "how smooth my step is; my shirt is embroidered with red silk. And what ribbons in my hair! You won't see richer galloons ever! All this my father bought so that the finest fellow in the world would marry me!" And, smiling, she turned around and saw the blacksmith . . .

She gave a cry and stopped sternly in front of him.

The blacksmith dropped his arms.

It's hard to say what the wonderful girl's dusky face expressed: sternness could be seen in it, and through the sternness a certain mockery of the abashed blacksmith; and a barely noticeable tinge of vexation also spread thinly over her face; all this was so mingled and so indescribably pretty that to kiss her a million times would have been the best thing to do at that moment.

"Why have you come here?" So Oksana began speaking. "Do you want to be driven out the door with a shovel? You're all masters at sidling up to us. You instantly get wind of it when our fathers aren't home. Oh, I know you! What, is my chest ready?"

"It will be ready, my dear heart, it will be ready after the holiday. If you knew how I've worked on it: for two nights I didn't leave the smithy. Not a single priest's daughter will have such a chest. I trimmed it with such iron as I didn't even put on the chief's gig when I went to work in Poltava. And how it will be painted! Go all around the neighborhood with your little white feet and you won't find the like of it! There will be red and blue flowers all over. It will glow like fire. Don't be angry with me! Allow me at least to talk, at least to look at you!"

"Who's forbidding you—talk and look at me!"

Here she sat down on the bench and again looked in the mirror and began straightening the braids on her head. She looked at her neck, at her new silk-embroidered shirt, and a subtle feeling of self-content showed on her lips and her fresh cheeks, and was mirrored in her eyes.

"Allow me to sit down beside you!" said the blacksmith.

"Sit," said Oksana, keeping the same feeling on her lips and in her pleased eyes.

"Wonderful, darling Oksana, allow me to kiss you!" the encouraged blacksmith said and pressed her to him with the intention of snatching a kiss; but Oksana withdrew her cheeks, which were a very short distance from the blacksmith's lips, and pushed him away.

"What more do you want? He's got honey and asks for a spoon! Go away, your hands are harder than iron. And you smell of smoke. I suppose you've made me all sooty."

Here she took the mirror and again began to preen herself.

"She doesn't love me," the blacksmith thought to himself, hanging his head. "It's all a game for her. And I stand before her like a fool, not taking my eyes off her. And I could just go on standing before her and never take my eyes off her! A wonderful girl! I'd give anything to find out what's in her heart, whom she loves! But, no, she doesn't care about anybody. She admires her own self; she torments poor me; and I'm blind to the world from sorrow; I love her as no one in the world has ever loved or ever will love."

"Is it true your mother's a witch?" said Oksana, and she laughed; and the blacksmith felt everything inside him laugh. It was as if this laughter echoed all at once in his heart and in his quietly aroused nerves, and at the same time vexation came over his soul that it was not in his power to cover this so nicely laughing face with kisses.

"What do I care about my mother? You are my mother, and my father, and all that's dear in the world. If the tsar summoned me and said: 'Blacksmith Vakula, ask me for whatever is best in my kingdom, and I will give it all to you. I'll order a golden smithy made for you, and you'll forge with silver hammers.' I'd say to the tsar: 'I don't want precious stones, or a golden smithy, or all your kingdom: better give me my Oksana!'"

"See how you are! Only my father is nobody's fool. You'll see if he doesn't marry your mother," Oksana said with a sly smile. "Anyhow, the girls are not here . . . what could that mean? It's long since time for caroling. I'm beginning to get bored."

"Forget them, my beauty."

"Ah, no! they'll certainly come with the lads. We'll have a grand party. I can imagine what funny stories they'll have to tell!"

"So you have fun with them?"

"More fun than with you. Ah! somebody's knocking; it must be the lads and girls."

"Why should I wait anymore?" the blacksmith said to himself. "She taunts me. I'm as dear to her as a rusty horseshoe. But if so, at least no other man is going to have the laugh on me. Just let me see for certain that she likes somebody else more than me—I'll teach him . . ."

The knocking at the door and the cry of "Open!" sounding sharply in the frost interrupted his reflections.

"Wait, I'll open it myself," said the blacksmith, and he stepped into the front hall, intending in his vexation to give a drubbing to the first comer.

IT WAS FREEZING, and up aloft it got so cold that the devil kept shifting from one hoof to the other and blowing into his palms, trying to warm his cold hands at least a little. It's no wonder, however, that somebody would get cold who had knocked about all day in hell, where, as we know, it is not so cold as it is here in winter, and where, a chef's hat on his head and standing before the hearth like a real cook, he had been roasting sinners with as much pleasure as any woman roasts sausages at Christmas.

The witch herself felt the cold, though she was warmly dressed; and so, arms up and leg to one side, in the posture of someone racing along on skates, without moving a joint, she descended through the air, as if down an icy slope, and straight into the chimney.

The devil followed after her in the same fashion. But since this beast is nimbler than any fop in stockings, it was no wonder that at the very mouth of the chimney he came riding down on his lover's neck, and the two ended up inside the big oven among the pots.

The traveler quietly slid the damper aside to see whether her son, Vakula, had invited guests into the house, but seeing no one there except for some sacks lying in the middle of the room, she got out of the oven, threw off her warm sheepskin coat, straightened her clothes, and no one would have been able to tell that a minute before she had been riding on a broom.

The mother of the blacksmith Vakula was no more than forty years old. She was neither pretty nor ugly. It's hard to be pretty at such an age. Nevertheless, she knew so well how to charm the gravest of Cossacks over to herself (it won't hurt to observe in passing that they couldn't care less about beauty) that she was visited by the headman, and the deacon Osip Nikiforovich (when his wife wasn't home, of course), and the Cossack Korniy Choub, and the Cossack Kasian Sverbyguz. And, to do her credit, she knew how to handle them very skillfully. It never occurred to any one of them that he had a rival. If on Sunday a pious muzhik or squire, as the Cossacks call themselves, wearing a cloak with a hood, went to church—or, in case of bad weather, to the tavern—how could he not stop by at Solokha's, to eat fatty dumplings with sour cream and chat in a warm cottage with a talkative and gregarious hostess? And for that purpose the squire would make a big detour before reaching the tavern, and called it "stopping on the way." And when Solokha would go to church on a feast day, putting on a bright gingham shift with a gold-embroidered blue skirt and a nankeen apron over it, and if she were to stand just by the right-hand choir, the deacon was sure to cough and inadvertently squint in that direction; the headman would stroke his mustache, twirl his topknot around his ear, and say to the man standing next to him, "A fine woman! A devil of a woman!"

Solokha nodded to everyone, and everyone thought she was nodding to him alone. But anyone who liked meddling into other people's affairs would have noticed at once that Solokha was most amiable with the Cossack Choub. Choub was a widower. Eight stacks of wheat always stood in front of his house. Two yoke of sturdy oxen always stuck their heads from the wattle shed outside and mooed whenever they saw a chummy cow or their fat bull uncle coming. A bearded goat climbed on the roof and from there bleated in a sharp voice, like a mayor, teasing the turkey hens who strutted about the yard and turning his back whenever he caught sight of his enemies, the boys who made fun of his beard. In Choub's chests there were quantities of linen, fur coats, old-style jackets with gold braid—his late wife had liked dressing up. In his kitchen garden, besides poppies, cabbages, and sunflowers, two plots of tobacco were planted every year. All this Solokha thought it not superfluous to join to her own property, reflecting beforehand on the order that would be introduced into it once it passed into her hands, and she redoubled her benevolence toward old Choub. And to keep Vakula from getting round his daughter and laying hands on it all for himself, thus certainly preventing any mixing in on her part, she resorted to the usual way of all forty-year-old hens: making Choub and the blacksmith quarrel as often as possible. Maybe this keenness and cunning were responsible for the rumors started here and there by the old women, especially when they'd had a drop too much at some merry gathering, that Solokha was in fact a witch; that the Kizyakolupenko lad had seen she had a tail behind no longer than a spindle; that just two weeks ago Thursday she had crossed the road as a black cat; that the priest's wife once had a sow run in, crow like a rooster, put Father Kondrat's hat on her head, and run back out.

It so happened that as the old women were discussing it, some cowherd by the name of Tymish Korostyavy came along. He didn't fail to tell how in the summer, just before the Peter and Paul fast,[3] as he lay down to sleep in the shed, putting some straw under his head, he saw with his own eyes a witch with her hair down, in nothing but a shirt, start milking the cows, and he was so spellbound he couldn't move; after milking the cows, she came up to him and smeared something so vile on his lips that he spent the whole next day spitting. But all this was pretty doubtful, because no one but the Sorochintsy assessor could see a witch. And so all the notable Cossacks waved their hands on hearing this talk. "The bitches are lying!" was their usual response.

Having climbed out of the oven and straightened her clothes, Solokha, like a good housekeeper, began tidying up and putting things in order, but she didn't touch the sacks: "Vakula brought them in, let him take them out!" Meanwhile the devil, as he was flying into the chimney, had looked around somehow inadvertently and seen Choub arm in arm with his chum, already far from his cottage. He instantly flew out of the oven, crossed their path, and began scooping up drifts of frozen snow on all sides. A blizzard arose. The air turned white. A snowy net swirled back and forth, threatening to stop up the walkers' eyes, mouths, and ears. Then the devil flew back down the chimney, firmly convinced that Choub and his chum would turn back, find the blacksmith, and give him such a hiding that it would be long before he was able to take his brush and paint any offensive caricatures.

IN FACT, AS soon as the blizzard arose and the wind began cutting right into their eyes, Choub showed repentance and, pulling his ear-flapped hat further down on his head, treated himself, the devil, and the chum to abuse. However, this vexation was a pretense. Choub was very glad of the blizzard. The distance to the deacon's was eight times longer than they had already gone. The travelers turned back. The wind was blowing from behind them; but they could see nothing through the sweeping snow.

"Wait, chum! I don't think this is the right way," Choub said after a short while. "I don't see any houses. Ah, what a blizzard! Go to that side a little, chum, maybe you'll find the road, and meanwhile I'll search over here. It was the evil one prompted us to drag around in such a storm! Don't forget to holler if you find the road. Eh, what a heap of snow the devil's thrown in my face!"

The road, however, could not be seen. The chum went to one side and, wandering back and forth in his high boots, finally wandered right into the tavern. This find made him so happy that he forgot everything and, shaking off the snow, went into the front hall, not the least concerned about his chum who was left outside. Choub, meanwhile, thought he had found the road; he stopped and began shouting at the top of his lungs, but seeing that his chum didn't appear, he decided to go on by himself. He walked a little and saw his own house. Drifts of snow lay around it and on the roof. Clapping his hands, frozen in the cold, he began knocking at the door and shouting commandingly for his daughter to open.

"What do you want here?" the blacksmith cried sternly, coming out.

Choub, recognizing the blacksmith's voice, stepped back a little. "Ah, no, it's not my house," he said to himself, "the blacksmith wouldn't come to my house. Again, on closer inspection, it's not the blacksmith's either. Whose house could it be? There now! I didn't recognize it! It's lame Levchenko's, who recently married a young wife. He's the only one who has a house like mine. That's why it seemed a bit odd to me that I got home so soon. However, Levchenko is now sitting at the deacon's, that I know. Why, then, the blacksmith? . . . Oh-ho-ho! he comes calling on the young wife. That's it! Very well! . . . now I understand everything."

"Who are you and why are you hanging around the door?" the blacksmith, coming closer, said more sternly than before.

"No, I won't tell him who I am," thought Choub. "He may give me a thrashing for all I know, the cursed bastard!" and, altering his voice, he replied:

"It's me, good man! I've come to your windows to sing some carols for your amusement."

"Go to the devil with your carols!" Vakula cried angrily. "Why are you standing there? Clear out right now, do you hear?"

Choub himself was already of that sensible intention; but he found it vexing to have to obey the blacksmith's orders. It seemed some evil spirit nudged his arm, forcing him to say something contrary.

"Really, why are you shouting so?" he said in the same voice. "I want to sing carols, that's all!"

"Oh-ho! there's no stopping you with words! . . ." Following these words, Choub felt a most painful blow to his shoulder.

"So, I see you're already starting to fight!" he said, retreating a little.

"Away, away!" the blacksmith cried, awarding Choub another shove.

"What's with you!" said Choub, in a voice that expressed pain, vexation, and timorousness. "I see you fight seriously, and painfully, too!"

"Away, away with you!" the blacksmith shouted and slammed the door.

"What a brave one!" Choub said, left alone outside. "Try going near him! Just look at the big jackanapes! You think I can't get justice against you? No, my dear, I'll go, and go straight to the commissar. You'll learn about me! I don't care that you're a blacksmith and a painter. If I could see my back and shoulders, I suppose they'd be black and blue. He must have beaten me badly, the devil's son! A pity it's cold and I don't want to take my coat off! You wait, fiendish blacksmith, may the devil smash up you and your smithy, I'll set you dancing! So there, you cursed gallowsbird! He's not at home now, though. I suppose Solokha is sitting there alone. Hm . . . it's not so far from here—why not go! No one else would come in such weather. Maybe it'll be possible . . . Ohh, what a painful beating that cursed blacksmith gave me!"

Here Choub rubbed his back and set out in the other direction. The pleasantness waiting ahead in the meeting with Solokha lessened the pain somewhat and made him insensible to the frost itself, which crackled in all the streets, not muffled by the blizzard's whistling. At times his face, on which the snowstorm soaped the beard and mustache more deftly than any barber tyrannically seizing his victim by the nose, acquired a half sweet look. And yet, had it not been for the snow that criss-crossed everything before the eyes, you could long have seen Choub stopping, rubbing his back, saying, "A painful beating that cursed blacksmith gave me!" and moving on again.

WHILE THE NIMBLE fop with the tail and the goat's beard was flying out of the chimney and back into it, the little pouch that hung on a strap at his side, in which he had put the stolen moon, somehow accidentally caught on something in the oven and came open, and the moon seized the opportunity and, flying out of the chimney of Solokha's house, rose smoothly into the sky. Everything lit up. It was as if there had been no blizzard. The snow gleamed in wide, silvery fields and was all sprinkled with crystal stars. The frost seemed to grow warmer. Crowds of lads and girls appeared with sacks. Songs rang out, and it was a rare house that had no carolers crowding before it.

Wondrously the moon shines! It's hard to describe how good it is to jostle about on such a night with a bunch of laughing and singing girls and lads ready for every joke and prank that a merrily laughing night can inspire. It's warm under your thick sheepskin;

your cheeks burn still brighter with the frost; and the evil one himself pushes you into mischief from behind.

A crowd of girls with sacks barged into Choub's house and surrounded Oksana. Shouts, laughter, stories deafened the blacksmith. Interrupting each other, they all hastened to tell the beauty some new thing, unloaded their sacks and boasted about the loaves, sausages, and dumplings, of which they had already collected plenty for their caroling. Oksana seemed perfectly pleased and happy; she chatted, now with this girl, now with that, and laughed all the while. With some vexation and envy the blacksmith looked on at their merriment, and this time he cursed caroling, though he used to lose his mind over it.

"Ah, Odarka!" the merry beauty said, turning to one of the girls, "you have new booties! Oh, what pretty ones! and with gold! You're lucky, Odarka, you have a man who buys everything for you; and I don't have anyone to get me such nice booties."

"Don't grieve, my darling Oksana!" the blacksmith picked up. "It's a rare young lady who wears such booties as I'll get for you."

"You?" Oksana said, giving him a quick and haughty glance. "I'd like to see where you're going to get booties such as I could wear on my feet. Unless you bring me the ones the tsaritsa wears."

"See what she wants!" the crowd of girls shouted, laughing.

"Yes," the beauty proudly continued, "you'll all be witnesses: if the blacksmith Vakula brings me the very booties the tsaritsa wears, I give my word that I'll marry him at once."

The girls took the capricious beauty with them.

"Laugh, laugh!" said the blacksmith, following them out. "I'm laughing at my own self! I think, and can't decide what's become of my reason. She doesn't love me—so, God be with her! As if Oksana's the only one in the world. Thank God, there are lots of nice girls in the village besides her. And what is this Oksana? She'd never make a good housewife; she's only good at dressing herself up. No, enough, it's time to stop playing the fool."

But just as the blacksmith was preparing to be resolute, some evil spirit carried before him the laughing image of Oksana, saying mockingly: "Get the tsaritsa's booties for me, blacksmith, and I'll marry you!" Everything in him was stirred, and he could think of nothing but Oksana.

Crowds of carolers, the lads separately and the girls separately, hastened from one street to another. But the blacksmith walked along without seeing anything or taking part in the merriment that he used to love more than anyone else.

THE DEVIL MEANWHILE was indulging himself in earnest at Solokha's: kissed her hand, mugging like an assessor at a priest's daughter, pressed his hand to his heart, sighed, and said straight out that if she did not agree to satisfy his passions and reward him in the customary way, he was ready for anything: he'd throw himself in the water and send his soul straight to hellfire. Solokha was not so cruel, and besides, the devil, as is known, acted in cahoots with her. She did like seeing a crowd dangling after her, and she was rarely without company; however, she had thought she would spend that evening alone, because all the notable inhabitants of the village had been invited for kutya at the deacon's. But everything turned out otherwise: the devil had just presented his demand when suddenly the voice of the stalwart headman was heard. Solokha ran to open the door, and the nimble devil got into one of the sacks lying there.

The headman, after shaking the snow off the earflaps of his hat and drinking the glass of vodka that Solokha handed him, said that he had not gone to the deacon's on account of the blizzard, and seeing a light in her house, had stopped by, intending to spend the evening with her.

Before the headman finished speaking, there came a knocking at the door and the voice of the deacon.

"Hide me somewhere," the headman whispered. "I don't want to meet the deacon right now."

Solokha thought for a long time where to hide such a stout guest; she finally chose the biggest sack of coal; she dumped the coal into a barrel, and the stalwart headman got into it, mustache, head, earflaps, and all.

The deacon came in, grunting and rubbing his hands, and said that none of his guests had come, and that he was heartily glad of this opportunity to *sport* a little at her place and the blizzard did not frighten him. Here he came closer to her, coughed, smiled, touched her bare, plump arm with his long fingers, and uttered with an air that showed both slyness and self-satisfaction:

"And what have you got here, magnificent Solokha?" And having said it, he jumped back slightly.

"How—what? An arm, Osip Nikiforovich!" replied Solokha.

"Hm! an arm! heh, heh, heh!" said the deacon, heartily pleased with his beginning, and he made a tour of the room.

"And what have you got here, dearest Solokha?" he uttered with the same air, having accosted her again and taken her lightly by the neck, and jumping back in the same way.

"As if you can't see, Osip Nikiforovich!" replied Solokha. "A neck, and on that neck a necklace."

"Hm! a necklace on the neck! heh, heh, heh!" And the deacon made another tour of the room, rubbing his hands.

"And what have you got here, incomparable Solokha? . . ." Who knows what the deacon would have touched this time with his long fingers, but suddenly there came a knocking at the door and the voice of the Cossack Choub.

"Ah, my God, an extraneous person!" the frightened deacon cried. "What now, if someone of my station is found here? . . . It'll get back to Father Kondrat! . . ."

But the deacon's real apprehensions were of another sort: he feared still more that his better half might find out, who even without that had turned his thick braid into a very thin one with her terrible hand.

"For God's sake, virtuous Solokha," he said, trembling all over. "Your kindness, as it says in the Gospel of Luke, chapter thir—th— Knocking! By God, there's knocking! Oh, hide me somewhere!"

Solokha poured the coal from another sack into the barrel, and the none-too-voluminous deacon got in and sat down at the bottom, so that another half sack of coal could have been poured on top of him.

"Good evening, Solokha!" said Choub, coming in. "Maybe you

weren't expecting me, eh? it's true you weren't? maybe I'm interfering with you? . . ." Choub went on, putting a cheerful and significant look on his face, which let it be known beforehand that his clumsy head was toiling in preparation for cracking some sharp and ingenious joke. "Maybe you've been having fun here with somebody? . . . Maybe you've already hidden somebody away, eh?" And, delighted with this last remark, Choub laughed, inwardly triumphant that he alone enjoyed Solokha's favors. "Well, Solokha, now give me some vodka. I think my throat got frozen in this cursed cold. What a night before Christmas God has sent us! When it struck, Solokha, do you hear, when it struck—eh, my hands are quite numb, I can't unbutton my coat!—when the blizzard struck . . ."

"Open up!" a voice came from outside, accompanied by a shove at the door.

"Somebody's knocking," Choub said, breaking off.

"Open up!" the cry came, louder than before.

"It's the blacksmith!" said Choub, clutching his earflaps. "Listen, Solokha, put me wherever you like; not for anything in the world do I want to show myself to that cursed bastard, may the devil's son get himself blisters as big as haystacks under each eye!"

Solokha, frightened, rushed about in panic and, forgetting herself, gestured for Choub to get into the same sack where the deacon was already sitting. The poor deacon didn't even dare to show his pain by coughing or grunting when the heavy fellow sat almost on his head and stuck his frozen boots on both sides of his temples.

The blacksmith came in without saying a word or taking off his hat and all but collapsed on the bench. He was noticeably in very low spirits.

Just as Solokha was closing the door after him, someone knocked again. This was the Cossack Sverbyguz. This one could not be hidden in a sack, because it would have been impossible to find such a sack. He was more corpulent than the headman and taller than Choub's chum. And so Solokha led him out to the kitchen garden to hear all that he had to tell her.

The blacksmith looked distractedly around the corners of the room, catching from time to time the far-resounding songs of the carolers. He finally rested his eyes on the sacks: "Why are these sacks lying here? They should have been taken out long ago. I've grown all befuddled on account of this stupid love. Tomorrow's a feast day, and there's all this trash lying around the house. I must take them to the smithy."

Here the blacksmith crouched down by the huge sacks, tied them tightly, and was about to haul them onto his shoulders. But it was obvious that his thoughts were wandering God knows where, otherwise he would have heard Choub hiss when his hair got caught by the rope that tied the sack and the stalwart headman begin to hiccup quite audibly.

"Can it be that this worthless Oksana will never get out of my head?" the blacksmith said. "I don't want to think about her, yet I do, and, as if on purpose, about nothing but her. What makes the thought come into my head against my will? Why the devil do these sacks seem heavier than before! There must be something in them besides coal. Fool that I am! I forgot that everything seems heavier to me now. Before, I used to be able to bend and unbend a copper coin or a horseshoe with one hand, and now I can't lift a sack of coal. Soon the wind will knock me down. No," he cried, cheering up after a pause, "what a woman I am! I won't let anybody laugh at me! Let it even be ten sacks, I'll lift them all." And he briskly hauled sacks onto his shoulders that two strong men would have been unable to carry. "This one, too," he went on, picking up the small one, at the bottom of which the devil lay curled up. "I think I put my tools in it." Having said which, he left the house whistling the song:

No bothering with a wife for me.

Noisier and noisier sounded the songs and shouts in the streets. The crowds of jostling folk were increased by those coming from neighboring villages. The lads frolicked and horsed around freely. Often amidst the carols one could hear some merry song made up on the spot by some young Cossack. Then suddenly one of the crowd, instead of a carol, would roar a New Year's song at the top of his lungs:

Humpling, mumpling!
Give me a dumpling,
A big ring of sausage,
A bowl full of porridge!

Loud laughter would reward the funny man. A little window would be raised, and the lean arm of an old woman—they were the only ones to stay inside now with the grave fathers—would reach out with a sausage or a piece of pie. Lads and girls held up their sacks, trying to be the first to catch the booty. In one spot the lads came from all sides and surrounded a group of girls: noise, shouts, one threw a snowball, another grabbed a sack with all sorts of things in it. Elsewhere the girls caught a lad, tripped him and sent him flying headlong to the ground together with his sack. It seemed they were ready to make merry all night long. And the night, as if on purpose, glowed so luxuriantly! And the glistening snow made the moonlight seem whiter still.

The blacksmith stopped with his sacks. He imagined he heard Oksana's voice and thin laughter in the crowd of girls. Every fiber of him twitched: flinging the sacks to the ground so that the deacon on the bottom groaned with pain and the headman hiccuped with his whole gullet, he trudged on, the small sack on his shoulder, with the crowd of lads that was following the crowd of girls in which he thought he had heard Oksana's voice.

"Yes, it's she! standing like a tsaritsa, her black eyes shining! A handsome lad is telling her something; it must be funny, because she's laughing. But she's always laughing." As if inadvertently, himself not knowing how, the blacksmith pushed through the crowd and stood next to her.

"Ah, Vakula, you're here! Good evening!" said the beauty with the very smile that all but drove Vakula out of his mind. "Well, did you get a lot for your caroling? Eh, such a little sack! And the booties that the tsaritsa wears, did you get them? Get me the booties and I'll marry you!" She laughed and ran off with the crowd.

The blacksmith stood as if rooted to the spot. "No, I can't; it's more than I can bear . . ." he said at last. "But, my God, why is she so devilishly pretty? Her eyes, and her speech, and everything—it just burns me, burns me . . . No, I can't stand it anymore! It's time to put an end to it all: perish my soul, I'll go and drown myself in a hole in the ice and pass out of the picture!"

Here, with a resolute step, he went on, caught up with the crowd, came abreast of Oksana, and said in a firm voice:

"Farewell, Oksana! Seek whatever suitor you like, fool whomever you like; but you won't see any more of me in this world."

The beauty looked surprised, wanted to say something, but the blacksmith waved his hand and ran away.

"Where to, Vakula?" called the lads, seeing the blacksmith running.

"Farewell, brothers!" the blacksmith called out in reply. "God willing, we'll see each other in the next world; but we're not to carouse together anymore in this one. Farewell, don't remember any evil of me! Tell Father Kondrat to serve a panikhida[4] for my sinful soul. I didn't paint the candles for the icons of Saint Nicholas and the Mother of God, it's my fault, I got busy with worldly things. Whatever goods you find in my chest, they all go to the church! Farewell!"

After saying which, the blacksmith went off at a run with the sack on his back.

"He's cracked in the head!" said the lads.

"A lost soul!" an old woman passing by mumbled piously. "I'll go and tell them the blacksmith has hanged himself!"

MEANWHILE VAKULA, HAVING run through several streets, stopped to catch his breath. "Where am I running, in fact?" he thought, "as if all is lost. I'll try one more way: I'll go to Paunchy Patsiuk, the Zaporozhets.[5] They say he knows all the devils and can do whatever he likes. I'll go, my soul will perish anyway!"

At that the devil, who had lain for a long time without moving, leaped for joy inside the sack; but the blacksmith, supposing he'd caused this movement by somehow catching the sack with his arm, punched it with his hefty fist, gave it a toss on his shoulder, and went off to Paunchy Patsiuk.

This Paunchy Patsiuk had indeed been a Zaporozhets once; but whether he had been driven out of the Zaporozhye or had run away on his own, no one knew. He had been living in Dikanka for a long time—ten years, maybe fifteen. At first he had lived like a real Zaporozhets: didn't work, slept three-quarters of the day, ate like six mowers, and drank nearly a whole bucket at one gulp; there was room enough for it all, however, because Patsiuk, though short, was of quite stout girth. Besides, the balloon trousers he wore were so wide that, however long a stride he took, his legs were completely invisible, and it looked as though a wine barrel was moving down the street. Maybe that was why they nicknamed him "Paunchy." A few days after his arrival in the village, everybody already knew he was a wizard. If anyone was sick with something, he at once called in Patsiuk; and Patsiuk had only to whisper a few words and it was as if the illness was taken away. If it happened that a hungry squire got a fish bone caught in his throat, Patsiuk could hit him in the back with his fist so skillfully that the bone would go where it belonged without causing any harm to the squire's throat. Of late he had rarely been seen anywhere. The reason for that was laziness, perhaps, or else the fact that it was becoming more difficult each year for him to get through the door. So people had to go to him themselves if they had need of him.

The blacksmith opened the door, not without timidity, and saw Patsiuk sitting on the floor Turkish fashion before a small barrel with a bowl of noodles standing on it. This bowl was placed, as if on purpose, at the level of his mouth. Without lifting a finger, he bent his head slightly to the bowl and sipped up the liquid, occasionally catching noodles in his teeth.

"No," Vakula thought to himself, "this one's lazier than Choub: he at least eats with a spoon, but this one won't even lift his arm!"

Patsiuk must have been greatly occupied with his noodles, because he seemed not to notice at all the coming of the blacksmith, who, as he stepped across the threshold, gave him a very low bow.

"I've come for your kindness, Patsiuk," Vakula said, bowing again.

Fat Patsiuk raised his head and again began slurping up noodles.

"They say, meaning no offense . . ." the blacksmith said, plucking up his courage, "I mention it not so as to insult you in any way—that you have some kinship with the devil."

Having uttered these words, Vakula became frightened, thinking he had expressed himself too directly and hadn't softened his strong words enough, and, expecting Patsiuk to seize the barrel with the bowl and send it straight at his head, he stepped aside a little and shielded himself with his sleeve, so that the hot liquid from the noodles wouldn't splash in his face.

But Patsiuk shot him a glance and again began slurping up noodles. The heartened blacksmith ventured to continue.

"I've come to you, Patsiuk, may God grant you all good things in abundance, and bread proportionately!" The blacksmith knew how to put in a fashionable word now and then; he had acquired the knack in Poltava, while he was painting the chief's wooden fence. "My sinful self is bound to perish! nothing in the world helps! Come what may, I must ask for help from the devil himself. Well, Patsiuk?" said the blacksmith, seeing his invariable silence, "what am I to do?"

"If it's the devil you need, then go to the devil!" replied Patsiuk, without raising his eyes and continuing to pack away the noodles.

"That's why I came to you," replied the blacksmith, giving him a low bow. "Apart from you, I don't think anybody in the world knows the way to him."

Not a word from Patsiuk, who was finishing the last of the noodles.

"Do me a kindness, good man, don't refuse!" the blacksmith insisted. "Some pork, or sausage, or buckwheat flour—well, or linen, millet, whatever there may be, if needed . . . as is customary among good people . . . we won't be stingy. Tell me at least, let's say, how to find the way to him?"

"He needn't go far who has the devil on his back," Patsiuk pronounced indifferently, without changing his position.

Vakula fixed his eyes on him as if he had the explanation of these words written on his forehead. "What is he saying?" his face inquired wordlessly; and his half-open mouth was ready to swallow the first word like a noodle. But Patsiuk kept silent.

Here Vakula noticed there were no longer either noodles or

barrel before the man; instead, two wooden bowls stood on the floor, one filled with dumplings, the other with sour cream. His thoughts and eyes involuntarily turned to these dishes. "Let's see how Patsiuk is going to eat those dumplings," he said to himself. "He surely won't want to lean over and slurp them up like noodles, and it's not the right way—a dumpling has to be dipped in sour cream first."

No sooner had he thought it than Patsiuk opened his mouth wide, looked at the dumplings, and opened his mouth still wider. Just then a dumpling flipped out of the bowl, plopped into the sour cream, turned over on the other side, jumped up, and went straight into Patsiuk's mouth. Patsiuk ate it and again opened his mouth, and in went another dumpling in the same way. He was left only with the work of chewing and swallowing.

"See what a marvel!" thought the blacksmith, opening his mouth in surprise, and noticing straightaway that a dumpling was going into his mouth as well and had already smeared his lips with sour cream. Pushing the dumpling away and wiping his lips, the blacksmith began to reflect on what wonders happen in the world and what clever things a man could attain to by means of the unclean powers, observing at the same time that Patsiuk alone could help him. "I'll bow to him again, and let him explain it to me . . . Though, what the devil! today is a *hungry* kutya,[6] and he eats dumplings, non-lenten dumplings! What a fool I am, really, standing here and heaping up sins! Retreat! . . ." And the pious blacksmith rushed headlong from the cottage.

However, the devil, who had been sitting in the sack and rejoicing in anticipation, couldn't stand to see such a fine prize slip through his fingers. As soon as the blacksmith put the sack down, he jumped out and sat astride his neck.

A chill crept over the blacksmith; frightened and pale, he did not know what to do; he was just about to cross himself . . . But the devil, leaning his doggy muzzle to his right ear, said:

"It's me, your friend—I'll do anything for a friend and comrade! I'll give you as much money as you like," he squealed into his left ear. "Oksana will be ours today," he whispered, poking his muzzle toward his right ear again.

The blacksmith stood pondering.

"Very well," he said finally, "for that price I'm ready to be yours!"

The devil clasped his hands and began bouncing for joy on the blacksmith's neck. "Now I've got you, blacksmith!" he thought to himself. "Now I'll take revenge on you, my sweet fellow, for all your paintings and tall tales against devils! What will my comrades say now, when they find out that the most pious man in the whole village is in my hands?" Here the devil laughed with joy, thinking how he was going to mock all the tailed race in hell, and how furious the lame devil would be, reputed the foremost contriver among them.

"Well, Vakula!" the devil squealed, still sitting on his neck, as if fearing he might run away, "you know, nothing is done without a contract."

"I'm ready!" said the blacksmith. "With you, I've heard, one has to sign in blood; wait, I'll get a nail from my pocket!" Here he put his arm behind him and seized the devil by the tail.

"See what a joker!" the devil cried out, laughing. "Well, enough now, enough of these pranks!"

"Wait, my sweet fellow!" cried the blacksmith, "and how will you like this?" With these words he made the sign of the cross and the devil became as meek as a lamb. "Just wait," he said, dragging him down by the tail, "I'll teach you to set good people and honest Christians to sinning!" Here the blacksmith, without letting go of the tail, jumped astride him and raised his hand to make the sign of the cross.

"Have mercy, Vakula!" the devil moaned pitifully. "I'll do anything you want, anything, only leave my soul in peace—don't put the terrible cross on me!"

"Ah, so that's the tune you sing now, you cursed German! Now I know what to do. Take me on your back this minute, do you hear? Carry me like a bird!"

"Where to?" said the rueful devil.

"To Petersburg, straight to the tsaritsa!"

And the blacksmith went numb with fear, feeling himself rising into the air.

• • •

FOR A LONG time Oksana stood pondering the blacksmith's strange words. Something inside her was already telling her she had treated him too cruelly. What if he had indeed decided on something terrible? "Who knows, maybe in his sorrow he'll make up his mind to fall in love with another girl and out of vexation call her the first beauty of the village? But, no, he loves me. I'm so pretty! He wouldn't trade me for anyone; he's joking, pretending. Before ten minutes go by, he'll surely come to look at me. I really am too stern. I must let him kiss me, as if reluctantly. It will make him so happy!" And the frivolous beauty was already joking with her girlfriends.

"Wait," said one of them, "the blacksmith forgot his sacks. Look, what frightful sacks! He doesn't go caroling as we do: I think he's got whole quarters of lamb thrown in there; and sausages and loaves of bread probably beyond count. Magnificent! We can eat as much as we want all through the feast days."

"Are those the blacksmith's sacks?" Oksana picked up. "Let's quickly take them to my house and have a better look at what he's stuffed into them."

Everyone laughingly accepted this suggestion.

"But we can't lift them!" the whole crowd suddenly cried, straining to move the sacks.

"Wait," said Oksana, "let's run and fetch a sled, we can take them on a sled."

And the crowd ran to fetch a sled.

The prisoners were very weary of sitting in the sacks, though the deacon had made himself a big hole with his finger. If it hadn't been for the people, he might have found a way to get out; but to get out of a sack in front of everybody, to make himself a laughingstock . . . this held him back, and he decided to wait, only groaning slightly under Choub's uncouth boots. Choub himself had no less of a wish for freedom, feeling something under him that was terribly awkward to sit on. But once he heard his daughter's decision, he calmed down and no longer wanted to get out, considering that to reach his house one would have to walk at least a hundred paces, maybe two. If he got out, he would have to straighten his clothes, button his coat, fasten his belt—so much work! And the hat with earflaps had stayed at Solokha's. Better let the girls take him on a sled. But it happened not at all as Choub expected. Just as the girls went off to fetch the sled, the skinny chum was coming out of the tavern, upset and in low spirits. The woman who kept the tavern was in no way prepared to give him credit; he had waited in hopes some pious squire might come and treat him; but, as if on purpose, all the squires stayed home like honest Christians and ate kutya in the bosom of their families. Reflecting on the corruption of morals and the wooden heart of the Jewess who sold the drink, the chum wandered into the sacks and stopped in amazement.

"Look what sacks somebody's left in the road!" he said, glancing around. "There must be pork in them. Somebody's had real luck to get so much stuff for his caroling! What frightful sacks! Suppose they're stuffed with buckwheat loaves and lard biscuits—that's good enough. If it's nothing but flatbread, that's already something: the Jewess gives a dram of vodka for each flatbread. I'll take it quick, before anybody sees me." Here he hauled the sack with Choub and the deacon onto his shoulders, but felt it was too heavy. "No, it's too heavy to carry alone," he said, "but here, as if on purpose, comes the weaver Shapuvalenko. Good evening, Ostap!"

"Good evening," said the weaver, stopping.

"Where are you going?"

"Dunno, wherever my legs take me."

"Help me, good man, to carry these sacks! Somebody went caroling and then dropped them in the middle of the road. We'll divide the goods fifty-fifty."

"Sacks? And what's in the sacks, wheat loaves or flatbread?"

"I suppose there's everything in them."

Here they hastily pulled sticks from a wattle fence, put a sack on them, and carried it on their shoulders.

"Where are we taking it? to the tavern?" the weaver asked as they went.

"That's what I was thinking—to the tavern. But the cursed Jewess won't believe us, she'll think we stole it; besides, I just came from the tavern. We'll take it to my place. No one will be in our way: my wife isn't home."

"You're sure she's not home?" the prudent weaver asked.

"Thank God, we've still got some wits left," said the chum, "the devil if I'd go where she is. I suppose she'll be dragging about with the women till dawn."

"Who's there?" cried the chum's wife, hearing the noise in the front hall produced by the two friends coming in with the sack, and she opened the door.

The chum was dumbfounded.

"There you go!" said the weaver, dropping his arms.

The chum's wife was a treasure of a sort not uncommon in the wide world. Like her husband, she hardly ever stayed home but spent almost all her days fawning on some cronies and wealthy old women, praised and ate with great appetite, and fought with her husband only in the mornings, which was the one time she occasionally saw him. Their cottage was twice as old as the local scrivener's balloon trousers, the roof lacked straw in some places. Only remnants of the wattle fence were to be seen, because no one ever took a stick along against dogs when leaving the house, intending to pass by the chum's kitchen garden instead and pull one out of his fence. Three days would go by without the stove being lit. Whatever the tender spouse wheedled out of good people she hid the best she could from her husband, and she often arbitrarily took his booty if he hadn't managed to drink it up in the tavern. The chum, despite his perennial sangfroid, did not like yielding to her, and therefore almost always left the house with two black eyes, and his dear better half trudged off to tell the old women about her husband's outrages and the beatings she suffered from him.

Now, you can picture to yourself how thrown off the weaver and the chum were by her unexpected appearance. Setting the sack down, they stepped in front of it, covering it with their coat skirts; but it was too late: the chum's wife, though she saw poorly with her old eyes, nevertheless noticed the sack.

"Well, that's good!" she said, with the look of an exultant hawk. "It's good you got so much for your caroling! That's what good people always do; only, no, I suspect you picked it up somewhere. Show me this minute! Do you hear? Show me your sack right this minute!"

"The hairy devil can show it to you, not us," said the chum, assuming a dignified air.

"What business is it of yours?" said the weaver. "We got it for caroling, not you."

"No, you're going to show it to me, you worthless drunkard!" the wife exclaimed, hitting the tall chum on the chin with her fist and going for the sack.

But the weaver and the chum valiantly defended the sack and forced her to retreat. Before they had time to recover, the spouse came running back to the front hall, this time with a poker in her hands. She nimbly whacked her husband on the hands and the weaver on the back with the poker, and was now standing beside the sack.

"What, we let her get to it?" said the weaver, coming to his senses.

"Eh, what do you mean we let her—why did you let her?" the chum said with sangfroid.

"Your poker must be made of iron!" the weaver said after a short silence, rubbing his back. "My wife bought a poker at the fair last year, paid twenty-five kopecks—it's nothing . . . doesn't even hurt . . ."

Meanwhile the triumphant spouse, setting a tallow lamp on the floor, untied the sack and peeked into it. But her old eyes, which had made out the sack so well, must have deceived her this time.

"Eh, there's a whole boar in there!" she cried out, clapping her hands for joy.

"A boar! do you hear, a whole boar!" the weaver nudged the chum. "It's all your fault!"

"No help for it!" the chum said, shrugging.

"No help? Don't stand there, let's take the sack from her! Come on! Away with you! away! it's our boar!" the weaver shouted, bearing down on her.

"Get out, get out, cursed woman! It's not your goods!" the chum said, coming closer.

The spouse again took hold of the poker, but just then Choub climbed out of the sack and stood in the middle of the hall, stretching, like a man who has just awakened from a long sleep.

The chum's wife gave a cry, slapping her skirts, and they all involuntarily opened their mouths.

"Why did she say a boar, the fool! That's not a boar!" said the chum, goggling his eyes.

"See what a man got thrown into the sack!" said the weaver, backing away in fear. "Say what you like, you can even burst, but it's the doing of the unclean powers. He wouldn't even fit through the window!"

"It's my chum!" cried the chum, looking closer.

"And who did you think it was?" said Choub, smiling. "A nice trick I pulled on you, eh? And you probably wanted to eat me as pork? Wait, I've got good news for you: there's something else in the sack—if not a boar, then surely a piglet or some other live thing. Something's been moving under me all the time."

The weaver and the chum rushed to the sack, the mistress of the house seized it from the other side, and the fight would have started again if the deacon, seeing there was nowhere to hide, hadn't climbed out of the sack.

"Here's another one!" the weaver exclaimed in fright. "Devil knows how this world . . . it makes your head spin . . . not sausages or biscuits, they throw people into sacks!"

"It's the deacon!" said Choub, more astonished than anyone else. "Well, now! that's Solokha for you! putting us into sacks . . . That's why she's got a house full of sacks . . . Now I see it all: she had two men sitting in each sack. And I thought I was the only one she . . . That's Solokha for you!"

THE GIRLS WERE a bit surprised to find one sack missing. "No help for it, this one will be enough for us," Oksana prattled. They all took hold of the sack and heaved it onto the sled.

The headman decided to keep quiet, reasoning that if he shouted for them to untie the sack and let him out, the foolish girls would run away, thinking the devil was sitting in it, and he would be left out in the street maybe till the next day.

The girls, meanwhile, all took each other's hands and flew like the wind, pulling the sled over the creaking snow. Many of them sat on the sled for fun; some got on the headman himself.

The headman resolved to endure everything. They finally arrived, opened the doors to the house and the front hall wide, and with loud laughter dragged the sack inside.

"Let's see what's in it," they all shouted and hastened to untie the sack.

Here the hiccups that had never ceased to torment the headman all the while he was sitting in the sack became so bad that he started hicking and coughing very loudly.

"Ah, somebody's in there!" they all cried and rushed out of the house in fear.

"What the devil! Why are you running around like crazy?" said Choub, coming in the door.

"Ah, Papa!" said Oksana, "there's somebody in the sack!"

"In the sack? Where did you get this sack?"

"The blacksmith left them in the middle of the road," they all said at once.

"Well," Choub thought to himself, "didn't I say so? . . ."

"What are you so afraid of?" he said. "Let's see. Now, then, my man, never mind if we don't call you by your full name—get out of the sack!"

The headman got out.

"Ah!" cried the girls.

"The headman was in it, too," Choub said to himself in perplexity, looking him up and down, "fancy that! . . . Eh! . . ." He could say nothing more.

The headman was no less confused himself and did not know how to begin.

"Must be cold out?" he said, addressing Choub.

"A bit nippy," Choub replied. "And, if I may ask, what do you grease your boots with, mutton fat or tar?"

He had not meant to say that, he had meant to ask: "How did you, the headman, get into this sack?" but, without knowing why himself, he had said something completely different.

"Tar's better!" said the headman. "Well, good-bye, Choub!" And, pulling down his earflaps, he walked out of the house.

"Why did I ask so stupidly what he greases his boots with!" Choub said, looking at the door through which the headman had gone. "That's Solokha! putting such a man into a sack! . . . A devil of a woman! Fool that I am . . . but where's that cursed sack?"

"I threw it in the corner, there's nothing else in it," said Oksana.

"I know these tricks—nothing else in it! Give it to me; there's another one sitting in it! Shake it out well . . . What, nothing? . . . Cursed woman! And to look at her—just like a saint, as if she never put anything non-lenten near her lips."

But let us leave Choub to pour out his vexation at leisure and go back to the blacksmith, because it must already be past eight o'clock outside.

AT FIRST VAKULA found it frightening when he rose to such a height that he could see nothing below and flew like a fly right under the moon, so that if he hadn't ducked slightly he would have brushed it with his hat. However, in a short while he took heart and began making fun of the devil. He was extremely amused by the way the devil sneezed and coughed whenever he took his cypress-wood cross from his neck and put it near him. He would purposely raise his hand to scratch his head, and the devil, thinking he was about to cross him, would speed up his flight. Everything was bright aloft. The air was transparent, all in a light silvery mist. Everything was visible; and he could even observe how a sorcerer, sitting in a pot, raced past them like the wind; how the stars gathered together to play blindman's buff; how a whole swarm of phantoms billowed in a cloud off to one side; how a devil dancing around the moon took his hat off on seeing the mounted blacksmith; how a broom came flying back, having just served some witch . . . they met a lot more trash. Seeing the blacksmith, all stopped for a moment to look at him and then rushed on their way again. The blacksmith flew on, and suddenly Petersburg, all ablaze, glittered before him. (It was lit up for some occasion.) The devil, flying over the toll gate, turned into a horse, and the blacksmith saw himself on a swift racer in the middle of the street.

My God! the clatter, the thunder, the glitter; four-story walls loomed on both sides; the clatter of horses' hooves and the rumble of wheels sounded like thunder and echoed on four sides; houses grew as if rising from the ground at every step; bridges trembled;

carriages flew by; cabbies and postilions shouted; snow swished under a thousand sleds flying on all sides; passers-by pressed against and huddled under houses studded with lamps, and their huge shadows flitted over the walls, their heads reaching the chimneys and roofs. The blacksmith looked about him in amazement. It seemed to him that the houses all turned their countless fiery eyes on him and stared. He saw so many gentlemen in fur-lined coats that he didn't know before whom to doff his hat. "My God, so much nobility here!" thought the blacksmith. "I think each one going down the street in a fur coat is another assessor, another assessor! And the ones driving around in those wonderful britzkas with windows, if they're not police chiefs, then they're surely commissars, or maybe even higher up." His words were interrupted by a question from the devil: "Shall we go straight to the tsaritsa?" "No, it's scary," thought the blacksmith. "The Zaporozhtsy who passed through Dikanka in the fall are staying here somewhere. They were coming from the Setch[7] with papers for the tsaritsa. I'd better talk it over with them."

"Hey, little Satan, get in my pocket and lead me to the Zaporozhtsy."

The devil instantly shrank and became so small that he easily got into Vakula's pocket. And before Vakula had time to look around, he found himself in front of a big house, went up the stairs, himself not knowing how, opened a door, and drew back slightly from the splendor on seeing the furnished room; then he took heart somewhat, recognizing the same Cossacks who had passed through Dikanka sitting cross-legged on silk divans in their tarred boots and smoking the strongest tobacco, the kind known as rootstock.

"Good day, gentlemen! God be with you! So this is where we meet again!" said the blacksmith, going closer and bowing to the ground.

"Who's that man there?" the one sitting right in front of the blacksmith asked another sitting further away.

"You don't recognize me?" said the blacksmith. "It's me, Vakula, the blacksmith! When you passed through Dikanka in the fall, you stayed—God grant you all health and long life—for nearly two days. And I put a new tire on the front wheel of your kibitka then!"

"Ah," said the first Cossack, "this is that same blacksmith who paints so well. Greetings, landsman, what brings you here?"

"Oh, I just came for a look around. They say . . ."

"Well, landsman," the Cossack said, assuming a dignified air and wishing to show that he, too, could speak Russian, "it's a beeg city, eh?"

The blacksmith did not want to disgrace himself and look like a greenhorn; what's more, as we had occasion to see earlier, he, too, was acquainted with literate language.

"A grand province!" he replied with equanimity. "No disputing it: the houses are plenty big, there's good paintings hanging everywhere. A lot of houses have an extremity of letters in gold leaf written on them. Wonderful proportions, there's no disputing it!"

The Zaporozhtsy, hearing the blacksmith express himself so fluently, drew very favorable conclusions about him.

"We'll talk more with you later, landsman; right now we're on our way to the tsaritsa."

"To the tsaritsa? Be so kind, masters, as to take me with you!"

"You?" the Cossack said, with the air of a tutor talking to his four-year-old charge who is begging to be put on a real, big horse. "What will you do there? No, impossible." With that, his face assumed an imposing mien. "We, brother, are going to discuss our own affairs with the tsaritsa."

"Take me!" the blacksmith persisted. "Beg them!" he whispered softly to the devil, hitting the pocket with his fist.

Before he got the words out, another Cossack spoke up:

"Let's take him, brothers!"

"All right, let's take him!" said the others.

"Get dressed the same as we are."

The blacksmith was just pulling on a green jacket when the door suddenly opened, and a man with gold braid came in and said it was time to go.

Again it seemed a marvel to the blacksmith, as he raced along in the huge carriage rocking on its springs, when four-storied houses raced backward past him on both sides, and the street, rumbling, seemed to roll under the horses' hooves.

"My God, what light!" the blacksmith thought to himself. "Back home it's not so bright at noontime."

The carriages stopped in front of the palace. The Cossacks got out, went into the magnificent front hall, and started up the brilliantly lit stairway.

"What a stairway!" the blacksmith whispered to himself. "It's a pity to trample it underfoot. Such ornaments! See, and they say it's all tall tales! the devil it's tall tales! my God, what a banister! such workmanship! it's fifty roubles' worth of iron alone."

After climbing the stairs, the Cossacks passed through the first hall. The blacksmith followed them timidly, afraid of slipping on the parquet floor at every step. They passed through three halls, and the blacksmith still couldn't stop being amazed. On entering the fourth, he inadvertently went up to a painting that hung on the wall. It was of the most pure Virgin with the Child in her arms. "What a painting! what wonderful art!" he thought. "It seems to be speaking! it seems alive! And the holy Child! He clasps his little hands and smiles, poor thing! And the colors! oh, my God, what colors! I bet there's not a kopeck's worth of ochre; it's all verdigris and crimson, and the blue is so bright! Great workmanship! and the ground must have been done in white lead. But, astonishing as the painting is, this brass handle," he went on, going up to the door and feeling the latch, "is worthy of still greater astonishment. What perfect finish! I bet German blacksmiths made it all, and for a very dear price . . ."

The blacksmith would probably have gone on reasoning for a long time, if a lackey with galloons hadn't nudged his arm, reminding him not to lag behind. The Cossacks passed through two more halls and stopped. Here they were told to wait. In the hall there was a group of generals in gold-embroidered uniforms. The Cossacks bowed on all sides and stood in a cluster.

A minute later a rather stout man of majestic height, wearing a hetman's[8] uniform and yellow boots, came in, accompanied by a whole retinue. His hair was disheveled, one eye was slightly askew, his face showed a certain haughty grandeur, all his movements betrayed a habit of command. The generals who had all been pacing up and down quite arrogantly in their golden uniforms began bustling about and bowing low and seemed to hang on his every word and even his slightest gesture, so as to rush at once and fulfill it. But the hetman did not pay any attention, barely nodded his head, and went up to the Cossacks.

The Cossacks all gave a low bow.

"Are you all here?" he asked with a drawl, pronouncing the words slightly through his nose.

"All here, father!" the Cossacks replied, bowing again.

"You won't forget to speak the way I taught you?"

"No, father, we won't forget."

"Is that the tsar?" the blacksmith asked one of the Cossacks.

"Tsar, nothing! it's Potemkin[9] himself," the man replied.

Voices came from the other room, and the blacksmith did not know where to look from the multitude of ladies entering in satin dresses with long trains and the courtiers in gold-embroidered caftans and with queues behind. He saw only splendor and nothing more. Suddenly the Cossacks all fell to the ground and cried out in one voice:

"Have mercy, mother, have mercy!"

The blacksmith, seeing nothing, also zealously prostrated himself on the floor.

"Get up!" a voice imperious and at the same time pleasant sounded above them. Some of the courtiers bustled about and nudged the Cossacks.

"We won't get up, mother! we won't! we'd rather die than get up!" the Cossacks cried.

Potemkin was biting his lips. Finally he went over himself and whispered commandingly to one of the Cossacks. They got up.

Here the blacksmith also ventured to raise his head and saw standing before him a woman of small stature, even somewhat portly, powdered, with blue eyes, and with that majestically smiling air which knew so well how to make all obey and could belong only to a woman who reigns.

"His Highness promised to acquaint me today with one of my

peoples whom I have not yet seen," the lady with the blue eyes said as she studied the Cossacks with curiosity. "Are you being kept well here?" she continued, coming nearer.

"Thank you, mother! The victuals are good, though the lamb hereabouts is not at all like in our Zaporozhye—but why not take what comes? . . ."

Potemkin winced, seeing that the Cossacks were saying something completely different from what he had taught them . . .

One of the Cossacks, assuming an air of dignity, stepped forward:

"Have mercy, mother! Why would you ruin loyal people? How have we angered you? Have we joined hands with the foul Tartar? Have we made any agreements with the Turk? Have we betrayed you in deed or in thought? Why, then, the disgrace? First we heard that you had ordered fortresses built everywhere for protection against us; then we heard that you wanted to *turn us into carabinieri*[10]; now we hear of new calamities. In what is the Zaporozhye army at fault? that it brought your troops across the Perekop and helped your generals to cut down the Crimeans? . . ."[11]

Potemkin kept silent and with a small brush casually cleaned the diamonds that studded his hands.

"What, then, do you want?" Catherine asked solicitously.

The Cossacks looked meaningly at one another.

"Now's the time! The tsaritsa is asking what we want!" the blacksmith said to himself and suddenly fell to the ground.

"Your Imperial Majesty, punish me not, but grant me mercy! Meaning no offense to Your Imperial Grace, but what are the booties you're wearing made of? I bet not one cobbler in any country of the world can make them like that. My God, if only my wife could wear such booties!"

The empress laughed. The courtiers also laughed. Potemkin frowned and smiled at the same time. The Cossacks began nudging the blacksmith's arm, thinking he had lost his mind.

"Get up!" the empress said benignly. "If you want so much to have such shoes, it's not hard to do. Bring him my most expensive shoes at once, the ones with gold! Truly, this simple-heartedness pleases me very much! Here," the empress went on, directing her eyes at a middle-aged man with a plump but somewhat pale face, who was standing further off than the others and whose modest caftan with big mother-of-pearl buttons showed that he did not belong to the number of the courtiers, "you have a subject worthy of your witty pen!"[12]

"You are too gracious, Your Imperial Majesty. Here at least a La Fontaine[13] is called for," the man with the mother-of-pearl buttons replied, bowing.

"I tell you in all honesty, I still love your *Brigadier* to distraction. You read remarkably well! However," the empress went on, turning to the Cossacks, "I've heard that in the Setch you never marry."

"How so, mother! You know yourself a man can't live without a wife," replied the same Cossack who had spoken with the blacksmith, and the blacksmith was surprised to hear this Cossack, who had such a good knowledge of literate language, talk with the tsaritsa as if on purpose in the coarsest way, usually called muzhik speech. "Clever folk!" he thought to himself. "He's surely doing it for a reason."

"We're not monks," the Cossack went on, "but sinful people. We fall for non-lenten things, as all honest Christendom does. Not a few among us have wives, though they don't live with them in the Setch. There are some who have wives in Poland; there are some who have wives in the Ukraine; there are even some who have wives in Turkey."

Just then the shoes were brought to the blacksmith.

"My God, what an adornment!" he cried joyfully, seizing the shoes. "Your Imperial Majesty! If the shoes on your feet are like this, and Your Honor probably even wears them to go ice skating, then how must the feet themselves be! I bet of pure sugar, at least!"

The empress, who did in fact have very shapely and lovely feet, could not help smiling at hearing such a compliment from the lips of a simple-hearted blacksmith, who, in his Zaporozhye outfit, could be considered a handsome fellow despite his swarthy complexion.

Gladdened by such favorable attention, the blacksmith was just going to question the tsaritsa properly about everything—was it true that tsars eat only honey and lard, and so on—but feeling the Cossacks nudging him in the ribs, he decided to keep quiet. And when the empress, turning to the elders, began asking how they lived in the Setch and what their customs were, he stepped back, bent to his pocket, and said softly, "Get me out of here, quick!" and suddenly found himself beyond the toll gate.

"HE DROWNED! BY God, he drowned! May I never leave this spot if he didn't drown!" the weaver's fat wife babbled, standing in the middle of the street amidst a crowd of Dikanka women.

"What, am I some kind of liar? did I steal anybody's cow? did I put a spell on anybody, that you don't believe me?" shouted a woman in a Cossack blouse, with a violet nose, waving her arms. "May I never want to drink water again if old Pereperchikha didn't see the blacksmith hang himself with her own eyes!"

"The blacksmith hanged himself? just look at that!" said the headman, coming out of Choub's house, and he stopped and pushed closer to the talking women.

"Why not tell us you'll never drink vodka again, you old drunkard!" replied the weaver's wife. "A man would have to be as crazy as you are to hang himself! He drowned! drowned in a hole in the ice! I know it as well as I know you just left the tavern."

"The hussy! see what she reproaches me with!" the woman with the violet nose retorted angrily. "You'd better shut up, you jade! Don't I know that the deacon comes calling on you every evening?"

The weaver's wife flared up.

"The deacon what? Calls on whom? How you lie!"

"The deacon?" sang out the deacon's wife, in a rabbitskin coat covered with blue nankeen, pushing her way toward the quarreling women. "I'll show you a deacon! who said deacon?"

"It's her the deacon comes calling on!" said the woman with the violet nose, pointing at the weaver's wife.

"So it's you, you bitch!" said the deacon's wife, accosting the weaver's wife. "So it's you, you hellcat, who blow fog in his eyes and give him unclean potions to drink so as to make him come to you?"

"Leave me alone, you she-devil!" the weaver's wife said, backing away.

"You cursed hellcat, may you never live to see your children! Pfui! . . ." and the deacon's wife spat straight into the weaver's wife's eyes.

The weaver's wife wanted to respond in kind, but instead spat into the unshaven chin of the headman, who, in order to hear better, had edged right up to the quarreling women.

"Agh, nasty woman!" cried the headman, wiping his face with the skirt of his coat and raising his whip. That gesture caused everyone to disband, cursing, in all directions. "What vileness!" he repeated, still wiping himself. "So the blacksmith is drowned! My God, and what a good painter he was! What strong knives, sickles, and plows he could forge! Such strength he had! Yes," he went on, pondering, "there are few such people in our village. That's why I noticed while I was still sitting in that cursed sack that the poor fellow was really in bad spirits. That's it for your blacksmith—he was, and now he's not! And I was just going to have my piebald mare shod! . . ."

And, filled with such Christian thoughts, the headman slowly trudged home.

Oksana was confused when the news reached her. She trusted little in Pereperchikha's eyes, or in women's talk; she knew that the blacksmith was too pious to dare destroy his soul. But what if he had left with the intention of never coming back to the village? There was hardly such a fine fellow as the blacksmith anywhere else! And he loved her so! He had put up with her caprices longest! All night under her blanket the beauty tossed from right to left, from left to right—and couldn't fall asleep. Now, sprawled in an enchanting nakedness which the dark of night concealed even from herself, she scolded herself almost aloud; then, calming down, she resolved not to think about anything—and went on thinking. And she was burning all over; and by morning she was head over heels in love with the blacksmith.

Choub expressed neither joy nor grief at Vakula's lot. His thoughts were occupied with one thing: he was simply unable to forget Solokha's perfidy and, even in his sleep, never stopped abusing her.

Morning came. Even before dawn the whole church was filled

with people. Elderly women in white head scarves and white flannel blouses piously crossed themselves just at the entrance to the
church. Ladies in green and yellow vests, and some even in dark
blue jackets with gold curlicues behind, stood in front of them.
Young girls with a whole mercer's shop of ribbons wound round
their heads, and with beads, crosses, and coin necklaces on their
necks, tried to make their way still closer to the iconostasis.[14] But
in front of them all stood the squires and simple muzhiks with
mustaches, topknots, thick necks, and freshly shaven chins, almost
all of them in hooded flannel cloaks, from under which peeked
here a white and there a blue blouse. All the faces, wherever you
looked, had a festive air. The headman licked his chops, imagining
himself breaking his fast with sausage; the young girls' thoughts
were of going ice skating with the lads; the old women whispered
their prayers more zealously than ever. You could hear the Cossack
Sverbyguz's bowing all over the church. Only Oksana stood as
if not herself: she prayed, and did not pray. There were so many
different feelings crowding in her heart, one more vexing than
another, one more rueful than another, that her face expressed
nothing but great confusion; tears quivered in her eyes. The girls
couldn't understand the reason for it and didn't suspect that the
blacksmith was to blame. However, Oksana was not the only one
concerned about the blacksmith. The parishioners all noticed that
it was as if the feast was not a feast, as if something was lacking. As
luck would have it, the deacon, after his journey in the sack, had
grown hoarse and croaked in a barely audible voice; true, the visiting singer hit the bass notes nicely, but it would have been much
better if the blacksmith had been there, who, whenever the "Our
Father" or the "Cherubic Hymn" was sung, always went up to the
choir and sang out from there in the same way they sing in Poltava.
Besides, he was the one who did the duties of the church warden.
Matins were already over; after matins, the liturgy . . . Where,
indeed, had the blacksmith disappeared to?

STILL MORE SWIFTLY in the remaining time of night did the
devil race home with the blacksmith. Vakula instantly found himself by his cottage. Just then the cock crowed. "Hold on!" he cried,

snatching the devil by the tail as he was about to run away. "Wait, friend, that's not all—I haven't thanked you yet." Here, seizing a switch, he measured him out three strokes, and the poor devil broke into a run, like a muzhik who has just been given a roasting by an assessor. And so, instead of deceiving, seducing, and duping others, the enemy of the human race was duped himself. After which, Vakula went into the front hall, burrowed under the hay, and slept until dinnertime. Waking up, he was frightened when he saw the sun already high. "I slept through matins and the liturgy!"—and the pious blacksmith sank into dejection, reasoning that God, as a punishment for his sinful intention of destroying his soul, must have sent him a sleep that kept him from going to church on such a solemn feast day. However, having calmed himself by deciding to confess it to the priest the next week and to start that same day making fifty bows a day for a whole year, he peeked into the cottage; but no one was home. Solokha must not have come back yet. He carefully took the shoes from his bosom and again marveled at the costly workmanship and the strange adventure of the past night; he washed, dressed the best he could, putting on the clothes he got from the Cossacks, took from his trunk a new hat of Reshetilovo astrakhan with a blue top, which he had not worn even once since he bought it while he was in Poltava; he also took out a new belt of all colors; he put it all into a handkerchief along with a whip and went straight to Choub.

Choub goggled his eyes when the blacksmith came in, and didn't know which to marvel at: that the blacksmith had resurrected, or that the blacksmith had dared to come to him, or that he had got himself up so foppishly as a Zaporozhye Cossack. But he was still more amazed when Vakula untied the handkerchief and placed before him a brand-new hat and a belt such as had never been seen in the village, and himself fell at his feet and said in a pleading voice:

"Have mercy, father! don't be angry! here's a whip for you: beat me as much as your soul desires, I give myself up; I repent of everything; beat me, only don't be angry! You were once bosom friends with my late father, you ate bread and salt together and drank each other's health."

Choub, not without secret pleasure, beheld the blacksmith—who did not care a hoot about anyone in the village, who bent copper coins and horseshoes in his bare hands like buckwheat pancakes—this same blacksmith, lying at his feet. So as not to demean himself, Choub took the whip and struck him three times on the back.

"Well, that's enough for you, get up! Always listen to your elders! Let's forget whatever was between us! So, tell me now, what do you want?"

"Give me Oksana for my wife, father!"

Choub thought a little, looked at the hat and belt; it was a wonderful hat and the belt was no worse; he remembered the perfidious Solokha and said resolutely:

"Right-o! Send the matchmakers!"

"Aie!" Oksana cried out, stepping across the threshold and seeing the blacksmith, and with amazement and joy she fastened her eyes on him.

"Look, what booties I've brought you!" said Vakula, "the very ones the tsaritsa wears!"

"No! no! I don't need any booties!" she said, waving her hands and not taking her eyes off him. "Even without the booties, I . . ." She blushed and did not say any more.

The blacksmith went up to her and took her hand; the beauty looked down. Never yet had she been so wondrously pretty. The delighted blacksmith gently kissed her, her face flushed still more, and she became even prettier.

A BISHOP OF blessed memory was driving through Dikanka, praised the location of the village, and, driving down the street, stopped in front of a new cottage.

"And to whom does this painted cottage belong?" His Reverence asked of the beautiful woman with a baby in her arms who was standing by the door.

"To the blacksmith Vakula," said Oksana, bowing to him, for it was precisely she.

"Fine! fine work!" said His Reverence, studying the doors and windows. The windows were all outlined in red, and on the doors everywhere there were mounted Cossacks with pipes in their teeth.

But His Reverence praised Vakula still more when he learned that he had undergone a church penance and had painted the entire left-hand choir green with red flowers free of charge. That, however, was not all: on the wall to the right as you entered the church, Vakula had painted a devil in hell, such a nasty one that everybody spat as they went by; and the women, if a child started crying in their arms, would carry it over to the picture and say, "See what a caca's painted there!" and the child, holding back its tears, would look askance at the picture and press against its mother's breast.

The Terrible Vengeance

I

NOISE AND THUNDER at the end of Kiev: Captain Gorobets is celebrating his son's wedding. Many people have gathered as the captain's guests. In the old days people liked to eat well, better still did they like to drink, and better still did they like to make merry. On his bay steed came the Zaporozhets Mikitka,[1] straight from a wild spree on the Pereshlai field, where he kept the Polish noblemen drunk on red wine for seven days and seven nights. There came also the captain's sworn brother, Danilo Burulbash, with his young wife, Katerina, and his one-year-old son, from the other shore of the Dnieper, where he had a farmstead between two hills. The guests marveled at Mistress Katerina's white face, her eyebrows black as German velvet, her fancy woolen dress and light blue silken shirt, her boots with silver-shod heels; but still more they marveled that her old father had not come with her. For one year only had he been living across the Dnieper, but for twenty-one he had vanished without a word and had returned to his daughter when she was already married and had borne a son. He surely could have told of many wonders. How could he not after having lived for so long in foreign lands! There everything is different: the people are not the same, and there are no churches of Christ . . . But he had not come.

The guests were offered hot spiced vodka with raisins and plums and a round wedding loaf on a big platter. The musicians got to the bottom of it, where money had been baked in, and, quieting down for a while, laid aside their cymbals, violins, and tambourines. Meanwhile the young women and girls, wiping their lips with embroidered handkerchiefs, again stepped out from their rows; and the lads, arms akimbo, proudly looking about, were ready to rush to meet them—when the old captain brought out two icons to bless the young couple. These icons had come to him from an honorable monk, the elder Varfolomey. Their casings were not rich, they did not shine with silver or gold, but no unclean powers dared to touch anyone who had them in the house. Raising the icons aloft, the captain was about to say a short prayer . . . when the children who were playing on the ground suddenly cried out in fright; following them, the people backed away, and all pointed their fingers in fear at a Cossack who stood in their midst. Who he was, no one knew. But he had already done a fine Cossack dance and managed to make the crowd around him laugh. Yet when the captain raised the icons, his whole face suddenly changed: his nose grew and bent to one side, his eyes, green now instead of brown, leaped, his lips turned blue, his chin trembled and grew sharp as a spear, a fang shot from his mouth, a hump rose behind his head, and the Cossack was—an old man.

"It's him! It's him!" people in the crowd cried, pressing close to each other.

"The sorcerer has appeared again!" cried the mothers, snatching up their children.

Majestically and dignifiedly the captain stepped forward and said in a loud voice, setting the icons against him:

"Vanish, image of Satan, there is no place for you here!" And, hissing and snapping his teeth like a wolf, the strange old man vanished.

There arose, arose noisily, like the sea in bad weather, a murmuring and talking among the folk.

"What is this sorcerer?" asked the young and unseasoned people.

"There'll be trouble!" said the old ones, wagging their heads.

And everywhere, all over the captain's wide yard, they began gathering in clusters and listening to stories about the strange sorcerer. But they almost all said different things, and no one could tell anything for certain about him.

A barrel of mead was rolled out into the yard, and not a few buckets of Greek wine were brought. All became merry again. The musicians struck up; the girls, the young women, the dashing Cossacks in bright jackets broke into a dance. Ninety- and hundred-year-olds got tipsy and also started to dance, recalling the years that had not vanished in vain. They feasted till late into the night, and they feasted as no one feasts any longer. The guests began to disperse, but few went home: many stayed the night in the captain's wide yard; still more Cossacks fell asleep, uninvited, under the benches, on the floor, by their horses, near the barn; wherever a drunken Cossack head staggered to, there he lay and snored for all Kiev to hear.

II

It shone quietly over all the world: the moon rose from behind the hill. It covered the hilly bank of the Dnieper as with precious, snow-white damask muslin, and the shade sank still deeper into the pine thicket.

In the middle of the Dnieper floated a boat. Two lads sat in the bow, their black Cossack hats cocked, and the spray from under their oars flew in all directions like sparks from a tinderbox.

Why are the Cossacks not singing? They do not talk of księdzy[2] going all over the Ukraine rebaptising people as Catholics; nor of the two-day battle with the Horde at the Salt Lake.[3] How can they sing, how can they talk of daring deeds: their master Danilo has fallen into thought, and the sleeve of his red flannel jacket, hanging out of the boat, trails in the water; their mistress Katerina quietly rocks the baby without taking her eyes off him, and a gray dust of water sprays over the linen covering her fancy dress.

Fair is the sight from the midst of the Dnieper of the high hills, the broad meadows, and the green forest! Those hills are not hills: they have no foot; they are sharp-peaked at both bottom and top;

under them and over them is the tall sky. Those woods standing on the slopes are not woods; they are hair growing on the shaggy head of the old man of the forest. Under it his beard washes in the water, and under his beard and over his hair—the tall sky. Those meadows are not meadows: they are a green belt tied in the middle of the round sky, and the moon strolls about in both the upper and the lower half.

Master Danilo looks to neither side, he looks at his young wife.

"What is it, my young wife, my golden Katerina, have you fallen into sadness?"

"I have not fallen into sadness, my master Danilo! I am frightened by the strange stories about the sorcerer. They say he was born so frightful . . . and from an early age no child wanted to play with him. Listen, Master Danilo, to what frightening things they say: as if he always imagined that everyone was laughing at him. He would meet some man on a dark evening, and at once it would seem to him that he had opened his mouth and bared his teeth. And the next day the man would be found dead. I felt strange, I felt frightened when I heard these stories," said Katerina, taking out a handkerchief and wiping the face of the baby asleep in her arms. She had embroidered the handkerchief with red silk leaves and berries.

Master Danilo said not a word and began looking to the dark side, where far beyond the forest an earthen rampart blackened and an old castle rose from behind the rampart. Three wrinkles all at once creased his brow; his left hand stroked his gallant mustache.

"It is not so frightening that he is a sorcerer," he said, "as that he is an evil guest. Why this whim of dragging himself here? I've heard that the Polacks want to build some sort of fortress to cut off our way to the Zaporozhye. Only let it be true . . . I'll scatter the devil's nest if I hear so much as a rumor that he has any sort of den there. I'll burn the old sorcerer so that the crows have nothing to peck at. Besides, I think he has no lack of gold and other goods. Here is where the devil lives. If he has gold . . . Now we're going to pass the crosses—it's the cemetery! here his unclean forebears rot. They say they were all ready to sell themselves to Satan, souls and tattered jackets, for money. If indeed he has gold, there's no point in delaying now: war can't always bring . . ."

"I know what you are plotting. No good does the encounter with him promise me. But you are breathing so hard, you look so stern, your eyes are so grim under their scowling brows! . . ."

"Silence, woman!" Danilo said angrily. "Whoever deals with you becomes a woman himself. Lad, give me a light for my pipe!" Here he turned to one of the oarsmen, who knocked hot ashes from his pipe and transferred them to his master's pipe. "Frightening me with a sorcerer!" Master Danilo went on. "A Cossack, thank God, fears neither devils nor księdzy. Much good there'd be if we started listening to our wives. Right, lads? Our wife is a pipe and a sharp saber!"

Katerina fell silent, looking down into the slumbering water; and the wind sent ripples over the water, and the whole Dnieper silvered like a wolf's fur in the night.

The boat swung and began to hug the wooded bank. On the bank a cemetery could be seen: decrepit crosses crowded together. Guelder rose does not grow among them, there is no green grass, only the moon warms them from its heavenly height.

"Do you hear cries, my lads? Someone's calling us for help!" said Master Danilo, turning to his oarsmen.

"We hear the cries, and they seem to come from that direction," the lads said together, pointing to the cemetery.

But all grew still. The boat swung and began to round the jutting bank. Suddenly the oarsmen lowered their oars and stared fixedly. Master Danilo also stopped: fear and chill cut into their Cossack fibers.

The cross on one tomb swayed and out of it quietly rose a withered dead man. Beard down to his waist; claws on his fingers, long, longer than the fingers themselves. Quietly he raised his arms. His whole face twisted and trembled. He obviously suffered terrible torment. "I can't breathe! I can't breathe!" he moaned in a wild, inhuman voice. Like a knife blade his voice scraped at the heart, and the dead man suddenly sank under the ground. Another cross swayed, and again a dead man came out, still taller, still more terrible than the first; all overgrown, beard down to his knees, and still longer, bony nails. Still more wildly he cried: "I can't breathe!" and sank under the ground. A third cross swayed, a third dead man rose. It seemed as if nothing but bones rose high over the ground. Beard down to his very heels; fingers with long claws stuck into the ground. Terribly he stretched his arms upwards, as if trying to reach the moon, and cried out as if someone were sawing at his yellow bones . . .

The baby asleep in Katerina's arms gave a cry and woke up. The mistress herself gave a cry. The oarsmen dropped their hats into the Dnieper. The master himself shook.

Suddenly it all disappeared as if it had never been; nevertheless, the lads did not take up their oars for a long time.

Anxiously did Burulbash look at his young wife, who fearfully rocked the crying baby in her arms; he pressed her to his heart and kissed her on the brow.

"Don't be afraid, Katerina! Look, there's nothing!" he said, pointing all around. "It's the sorcerer trying to frighten people, so that no one gets into his unclean nest. He'll only frighten women with that! Give my son here!" With these words, Master Danilo raised his son to his lips. "What, Ivan, you're not afraid of sorcerers? No, papa, he says, I'm a Cossack. Enough, then, stop crying! We'll go home! we'll go home—mother will feed you porridge, put you to bed in your cradle, and sing:

> *Lullay, lullay, lullay,*
> *Lullay, little son, lullay,*
> *Grow up, grow up wise,*
> *Win glory in the Cossacks' eyes*
> *And punish their enemies.*

Listen, Katerina, it seems to me your father doesn't want to live in accord with us. He arrived sullen, stern, as if he's angry . . . Well, if you're displeased, then why come? He didn't want to drink to Cossack freedom, he didn't rock the baby in his arms! First I wanted to confide everything in my heart to him, but it didn't come out, and my speech stumbled. No, his is not a Cossack's heart! Cossack hearts, when they meet, never fail to go out to each other! What, my sweet lads, it's soon the shore? Well, I'll give you new hats. To you, Stetsko, I'll give a velvet one with gold. I took it from a Tartar, along with his head. I got all his gear; only his soul I let go free. Well, tie up! Here, Ivan, we've come home and you keep on crying! Take him, Katerina!"

They all got out. A thatched roof showed from behind the hill: the ancestral mansion of Master Danilo. Beyond it another hill, then a field, and then you could walk for a hundred miles and not find even one Cossack.

III

Master Danilo's farmstead lies between two hills, in a narrow valley that runs down to the Dnieper. His mansion is not tall: a cottage by the looks, like those of simple Cossacks, and only one room in it; but there is enough space inside for him, and his wife, and the old serving woman, and ten choice youths. There are oak shelves up on the walls all around. They are laden with bowls and pots for eating. There are silver goblets among them and glasses trimmed with gold—gifts or the plunder of war. Below them hang costly muskets, sabers, harquebuses, lances. Willingly or unwillingly they were passed on from Tartars, Turks, and Polacks; and so they are not a little nicked. Looking at them, Master Danilo recalled his battles as if by banners. Along the wall, smoothly hewn oak benches. Next to them, before the stove seat,[4] a cradle hangs on ropes put through a ring screwed into the ceiling. The floor of the room is beaten smooth and covered with clay. On the benches Master Danilo sleeps with his wife. On the stove seat sleeps the old serving woman. In the cradle the little baby sports and is lulled to sleep. On the floor the youths lie side by side. But it is better for a Cossack to sleep on the level ground under the open sky; he needs no down or feather beds; he puts fresh hay under his head and sprawls freely on the grass. It delights him to wake up in the middle of the night, to gaze at the tall, star-strewn sky and shiver from the cool of the night that refreshes his Cossack bones. Stretching and murmuring in his sleep, he lights his pipe and wraps himself tighter in his warm sheepskin.

It was not early that Burulbash woke up after the previous day's merrymaking, and when he did wake up, he sat in the corner on the bench and began to sharpen a new Turkish saber he had taken in trade; and Mistress Katerina started to embroider a silken towel with gold. Suddenly Katerina's father came in, angry, scowling, with an outlandish pipe in his teeth, approached his daughter, and began to question her sternly: What was the reason for her coming home so late?

"About such things, father-in-law, you should ask me, not her! The husband is answerable, not the wife. That's how it is with us, meaning no offense to you!" said Danilo, without quitting his occupation. "Maybe there, in infidel lands, it's different—I wouldn't know."

Color came to the father-in-law's stern face, and his eyes glinted savagely.

"Who, if not a father, is to look after his daughter!" he muttered to himself. "I ask you, then: Where were you dragging about till late in the night?"

"Now you're talking, dear father-in-law! To that I will tell you that I'm long past the age of being swaddled by women. I can seat a horse. I can wield a sharp saber with my hand. I can do a thing or two besides . . . I can answer to no one for what I do."

"I see, Danilo, I know, you want a quarrel! Whoever hides himself must have evil things on his mind."

"Think what you like," said Danilo, "and I'll think, too. Thank God, I've never yet been part of any dishonorable thing; I've always stood for the Orthodox faith and the fatherland—not like some vagabonds who drag about God knows where while Orthodox people are fighting to the death, and then come down to reap where they haven't sown. They're not even like the Uniates[5]: they never peek inside a church of God. It's they who should be questioned properly about where they drag about."

"Eh, Cossack! you know . . . I'm a bad shot: from a mere two hundred yards my bullet pierces the heart. I'm an unenviable swordsman: what I leave of a man is smaller than the grains they cook for porridge."

"I'm ready," said Master Danilo, briskly passing his saber through the air, as though he knew what he had been sharpening it for.

"Danilo!" Katerina cried loudly, seizing his arm and clinging to it. "Bethink yourself, madman! Look who you are raising your hand against! Father, your hair is white as snow, yet you flare up like a senseless boy!"

"Wife!" Master Danilo cried menacingly, "you know I don't like that. Mind your woman's business!"

The sabers clanged terribly; iron cut against iron, and sparks poured down like dust over the Cossacks. Weeping, Katerina went to her own room, threw herself down on the bed, and stopped her ears so as not to hear the saber blows. But the Cossacks did not fight so poorly that she could stifle the blows. Her heart was about to burst asunder. She felt the sound go through her whole body: clang, clang. "No, I can't bear it, I can't bear it . . . Maybe the red blood already spurts from his white body. Maybe my dear one is weakening now—and I lie here!" All pale, scarcely breathing, she went out to the room.

Steadily and terribly the Cossacks fought. Neither one could overpower the other. Now Katerina's father attacks—Master Danilo retreats. Master Danilo attacks—the stern father retreats, and again they are even. The pitch of battle. They swing . . . ough! the sabers clang . . . and the blades fly clattering aside.

"God be thanked!" said Katerina, but she cried out again when she saw the Cossacks take hold of muskets. They checked the flints, cocked the hammers.

Master Danilo shot—and missed. The father aimed . . . He is old, his sight is not so keen as the young man's, yet his hand does not tremble. A shot rang out . . . Master Danilo staggered. Red blood stained the left sleeve of his Cossack jacket.

"No!" he cried, "I won't sell myself so cheaply. Not the left arm but the right is the chief. I have a Turkish pistol hanging on the wall; never once in my life has it betrayed me. Come down from the wall, old friend! do me service!" Danilo reached out.

"Danilo!" Katerina cried in despair, seizing his hands and throwing herself at his feet. "I do not plead for myself. There is only one end for me: unworthy is the wife who lives on after her husband. The Dnieper, the cold Dnieper will be my grave . . . But look at your son, Danilo, look at your son! Who will shelter the poor child? Who will care for him? Who will teach him to fly on a black steed, to fight for freedom and the faith, to drink and carouse like a Cossack? Perish, my son, perish! Your father does not want to know you! Look how he turns his face away. Oh! I know you now! you're a beast, not a man! you have the heart of a wolf and the soul of a sly vermin. I thought you had a drop of pity in you, that human feeling burned in your stony body. Madly was I mistaken. It will bring you joy. Your bones will dance for joy in your coffin when they hear the impious Polack beasts throw your son into the flames, when your son screams under knives and scalding water. Oh, I know you! You will be glad to rise from your coffin and fan the fire raging under him with your hat!"

"Enough, Katerina! Come, my beloved Ivan, I will kiss you! No, my child, no one will touch even one hair on your head. You will grow up to be the glory of your fatherland; like the wind you will fly in the forefront of the Cossacks, a velvet hat on your head, a sharp saber in your hand. Father, give me your hand! Let us forget what has happened between us. Whatever wrong I did you, the fault was mine. Why won't you give me your hand?" Danilo said to Katerina's father, who stood in one spot, his face expressing neither anger nor reconciliation.

"Father!" Katerina cried out, embracing and kissing him. "Do not be implacable. Forgive Danilo: he will not upset you anymore!"

"For your sake only do I forgive him, my daughter!" he said, kissing her, with a strange glint in his eyes. Katerina gave a slight start: the kiss seemed odd to her, as did the strange glint in his eyes. She leaned her elbow on the table, at which Master Danilo sat bandaging his wounded arm and thinking now that it was wrong and not like a Cossack to ask forgiveness when one was not guilty of anything.

IV

There was a glimmer of daylight but no sun: the sky was louring and a fine rain sprinkled the fields, the forests, the wide Dnieper. Mistress Katerina woke up, but not joyfully: tears in her eyes, and all of her confused and troubled.

"My beloved husband, dear husband, I had a strange dream!"

"What dream, my sweet mistress Katerina?"

"I dreamed—it was truly strange, and so alive, as if I was awake—I dreamed that my father is that same monster we saw at the captain's. But I beg you, don't believe in dreams. One can see all sorts of foolishness! It was as if I was standing before him, trembling all over, frightened, and every word he said made all my fibers groan. If only you had heard what he said . . ."

"What was it he said, my golden Katerina?"

"He said, 'Look at me, Katerina, I am handsome! People should not say I am ugly. I will make you a fine husband. See what a look is in my eyes!' Here he aimed his fiery eyes at me, I gave a cry and woke up."

"Yes, dreams tell much truth. However, do you know that things are not so quiet behind the hill? It seems the Polacks have begun to show up again. Gorobets has sent to tell me not to be caught napping. He needn't worry, though; I'm not napping as it is. My lads cut down twelve big trees for barricades last night. The Pospolitstvo[6] will be treated to lead plums, and the gentlemen will dance under our knouts."

"Does my father know about it?"

"Your father is a weight on my neck! I still can't figure him out. He must have committed many sins in foreign lands. What, indeed, can be the reason? He's lived here for nearly a month and has never once made merry like a good Cossack! He refused to drink mead! do you hear, Katerina, he refused to drink the mead I shook out of the Jews in Brest. Hey, lad!" cried Master Danilo. "Run to the cellar, my boy, and fetch me some Jewish mead! . . . He doesn't even drink vodka! Confound it! I don't think, Mistress Katerina, that he believes in Christ the Lord either! Eh? What do you think?"

"God knows what you're saying, Master Danilo!"

"It's strange, Mistress!" he went on, taking the clay mug from the Cossack. "Even the foul Catholics fall for vodka; only the Turks don't drink. Well, Stetsko, did you have a good sup of mead in the cellar?"

"Just a taste, Master!"

"Lies, you son of a bitch! look at the flies going for your mustache! I can see by your eyes that you downed half a bucket! Eh,

Cossacks! such wicked folk! ready for anything for a comrade, but he'll take care of the liquor all by himself. I haven't been drunk for a long time—eh, Mistress Katerina?"

"Long, you say! And the last time . . ."

"Don't worry, don't worry, I won't drink more than a mug! And here comes a Turkish abbot squeezing in the door!" he said through his teeth, seeing his father-in-law stooping to enter.

"What is this, my daughter!" the father said, taking off his hat and straightening his belt, from which hung a saber studded with wondrous stones. "The sun is already high, and you have no dinner ready."

"Dinner is ready, my father, we will serve it now! Get out the pot with the dumplings!" said Mistress Katerina to the old serving woman who was wiping the wooden bowls. "Wait, I'd better take it out myself," Katerina went on, "and you call the lads."

Everyone sat on the floor in a circle: the father facing the icon corner, Master Danilo to the left, Mistress Katerina to the right, and the ten trusty youths in blue and yellow jackets.

"I don't like these dumplings!" said the father, having eaten a little and putting down the spoon. "They have no taste!"

"I know," Master Danilo thought to himself, "you prefer Jewish noodles."

"Why, my father-in-law," he went on aloud, "do you say the dumplings have no taste? Are they poorly prepared? My Katerina makes such dumplings as even a hetman[7] rarely gets to eat. There's no need to be squeamish about them. It's Christian food! All God's saints and holy people ate dumplings."

Not a word from the father. Master Danilo also fell silent.

A roast boar with cabbage and plums was served.

"I don't like pork," said Katerina's father, raking up the cabbage with his spoon.

"Why would you not like pork?" said Danilo. "Only Turks and Jews don't like pork."

The father frowned even more sternly.

Milk gruel was all the old father ate, and instead of vodka he sipped some black water from a flask he kept in his bosom.

After dinner, Danilo fell into a mighty hero's sleep and woke up only toward evening. He sat down and began writing letters to the Cossack army; and Mistress Katerina, sitting on the stove seat, rocked the cradle with her foot. Master Danilo sits and looks with his left eye at his writing and with his right eye out the window. And from the window the gleam of the distant hills and the Dnieper can be seen. Beyond the Dnieper, mountains show blue. Up above sparkles the now clear night sky. But it is not the distant sky or the blue forest that Master Danilo admires: he gazes at the jutting spit of land on which the old castle blackens. He fancied that light flashed in a narrow window of the castle. But all is quiet. He must have imagined it. Only the muted rush of the Dnieper can be heard below, and on three sides, one after the other, the echo of momentarily awakened waves. The river is not mutinous. He grumbles and murmurs like an old man: nothing pleases him; everything has changed around him; he is quietly at war with the hills, forests, and meadows on his banks, and carries his complaint against them to the Black Sea.

Now a boat blackened on the wide Dnieper, and again something as if flashed in the castle. Danilo whistled softly, and at his whistle the trusty lad came running.

"Quick, Stetsko, take your sharp saber and your musket and follow me."

"You're going out?" asked Mistress Katerina.

"I'm going out, wife. I must look around everywhere to see if all is well."

"But I'm afraid to stay by myself. I'm so sleepy. What if I have the same dream? I'm not even sure it was a dream—it was so lifelike."

"The old woman will stay with you; and in the front hall and outside Cossacks are sleeping!"

"The old woman is already asleep, and I somehow do not trust the Cossacks. Listen, Master Danilo, lock me in my room and take the key with you. I won't be so afraid then. And let the Cossacks lie outside my door."

"So be it!" said Danilo, wiping the dust from his musket and pouring powder into the pan.

The trusty Stetsko already stood dressed in full Cossack gear.

Danilo put on his astrakhan hat, closed the window, latched the door, locked it, and quietly went out through the yard, between his sleeping Cossacks, into the hills.

The sky was almost completely clear. A fresh wind barely wafted from the Dnieper. If it had not been for the moaning of a gull from far off, all would have been mute. But then there seemed to come a rustling . . . Burulbash and his trusty servant quietly hid behind the thorn bush that covered a felled tree. Someone in a red jacket, with two pistols and a sword at his side, was going down the hill.

"It's my father-in-law!" said Master Danilo, peering at him from behind the bush. "Where is he going at this hour, and why? Stetsko! don't gape, watch with all your eyes for which path master father will take." The man in the red jacket went right down to the bank and turned toward the jutting spit of land. "Ah! it's there!" said Master Danilo. "So, Stetsko, he's dragging himself straight to the sorcerer's hole."

"Yes, surely nowhere else, Master Danilo! otherwise we'd see him on the other side. But he disappeared near the castle."

"Wait, let's get out and then follow in his tracks. There must be something to it. No, Katerina, I told you your father was a bad man; he does nothing in the Orthodox way."

Master Danilo and his trusty lad flitted out on the jutting bank. Now they were no longer visible. The forest fastness around the castle hid them. The upper window lit up with a soft light. The Cossacks stand below thinking how to climb inside. No gates or doors are to be seen. There must be a way from the courtyard; but how to get in there! From far off the clank of chains and the running of dogs can be heard.

"Why think for so long!" said Master Danilo, seeing a tall oak tree by the window. "Stay here, lad! I'll climb the oak; from it one can look right in the window."

Here he took off his belt, laid his sword down so that it would not clank, and, seizing the branches, climbed up the tree. The window was still lit. Sitting on a branch just by the window, holding on to the tree with his arm, he looks: there is no candle in the room, yet it is light. Odd signs on the walls. Weapons hung up, all strange, such as are not worn by Turks, or Crimeans, or Polacks, or

Christians, or the gallant Swedish people. Under the ceiling, bats flit back and forth, and their shadows flit over the doors, the walls, the floor. Now the door opens without a creak. Someone comes in wearing a red jacket and goes straight to a table covered with a white cloth. "It's he, it's my father-in-law!" Master Danilo climbed down a little lower and pressed himself closer against the tree.

But the man had no time to see whether anyone was looking in the window or not. He came in gloomy, in low spirits, pulled the cloth from the table—and suddenly a transparent blue light poured softly through the room. Only the unmingled waves of the former pale golden light played and plunged as if in a blue sea, and stretched out like streaks in marble. Here he put a pot on the table and began throwing some herbs into it.

Master Danilo looked and no longer saw him in a red jacket; instead, wide balloon trousers appeared on him, such as Turks wear; pistols in the belt; on his head some wondrous hat all covered with writing neither Russian nor Polish. He looked at his face—the face, too, began to change: the nose grew long and hung over the lips; the mouth instantly stretched to the ears; a tooth stuck out of the mouth, bent to one side, and there stood before him the same sorcerer who had appeared at the captain's wedding. "True was your dream, Katerina!" thought Burulbash.

The sorcerer began walking around the table, the signs on the wall began to change more quickly, and the bats plunged down lower, then up, back and forth. The blue light grew thinner and thinner, and seemed to go out completely. And now the room shone with a faint rosy light. The wondrous light seemed to flow into all corners with a soft tinkling, then suddenly vanished, and it was dark. Only a noise was heard, as if wind were playing at a quiet hour of the evening, whirling over the watery mirror, bending the silver willows still lower to the water. And it seems to Master Danilo that the moon is shining in the room, the stars roam, the dark blue sky flashes dimly, and the cool night air even breathes in his face. And it seems to Master Danilo (here he began feeling his mustache to see if he was asleep) that it is no longer the sky but his own bedroom that he sees: his Tartar and Turkish sabers hang on the walls; around the walls are shelves, and on the shelves dishes

and household utensils; on the table, bread and salt; a cradle hanging . . . but instead of icons, terrible faces look out; on the stove
seat . . . but a thickening mist covered everything and it became
dark again. And again with an odd tinkling the whole room lit up
with a rosy light, and again the sorcerer stood motionless in his
strange turban. The sounds grew stronger and denser, the thin rosy
light grew brighter, and something white, like a cloud, hovered
in the room; and it seems to Master Danilo that the cloud is not
a cloud but a woman standing there; only what is she made of?
Is she woven of air? Why is she standing without touching the
ground or leaning on anything, and the rosy light shines through
her and the signs flash on the wall? Now she moves her transparent
head slightly: her pale blue eyes shine faintly; her hair falls in waves
over her shoulders like a light gray mist; her lips show pale red, like
the barely visible red light of dawn pouring through the transparent white morning sky; her eyebrows are faintly dark . . . Ah! it's
Katerina! Here Danilo felt as if his limbs were bound; he tried to
speak, but his lips moved soundlessly.

The sorcerer stood motionless in his place.

"Where have you been?" he asked, and she who stood before
him fluttered.

"Oh, why did you summon me?" she moaned softly. "It was so
joyful for me. I was in the place where I was born and lived for fifteen years. Oh, how good it is there! How green and fragrant that
meadow where I played as a child: the wildflowers are the same,
and our cottage, and the kitchen garden! Oh, how my kind
mother embraced me! What love was in her eyes! She caressed me,
kissed me on my lips and cheeks, combed out my blond braid with
a fine-toothed comb . . . Father!" here she fixed the sorcerer with
her pale eyes, "why did you kill my mother?"

The sorcerer shook his finger at her menacingly.

"Did I ask you to speak of that?" And the airy beauty trembled.
"Where is your mistress now?"

"My mistress Katerina is asleep now, and I was glad of that, I
took off and flew away. I've long wished to see Mother. I was suddenly fifteen. I became all light as a bird. Why have you summoned
me?"

"Do you remember everything I told you yesterday?" the sorcerer asked, so softly that it was barely audible.

"I remember, I remember; but there's nothing I wouldn't give to forget it! Poor Katerina! There's much she doesn't know of what her soul knows."

"It's Katerina's soul," thought Master Danilo; but he still dared not move.

"Repent, father! Isn't it terrible that after each of your murders the dead rise from their graves?"

"You're at your same old thing again!" the sorcerer interrupted menacingly. "I'll have my way, I'll make you do what I want. Katerina will love me! . . ."

"Oh, you're a monster and not my father!" she moaned. "No, you will not have your way! It's true you've acquired the power, by your unclean magic, of summoning a soul and tormenting it; but only God alone can make it do what is pleasing to Him. No, never while I am in her body will Katerina venture upon an ungodly deed. Father, the Last Judgment is near! Even if you were not my father, still you would never make me betray my beloved, faithful husband. Even if my husband were not faithful and dear to me, I still would not betray him, because God does not like perjured and faithless souls."

Here she fixed her pale eyes on the window outside which Master Danilo was sitting and stopped motionless . . .

"Where are you looking? Whom do you see there?" cried the sorcerer.

The airy Katerina trembled. But Master Danilo was long since on the ground and, together with his trusty Stetsko, was making his way toward his hills. "Terrible, terrible!" he repeated to himself, feeling some timorousness in his Cossack heart, and soon he was walking through his courtyard, where the Cossacks were still fast asleep, except for the one who sat on guard and smoked his pipe. The sky was all strewn with stars.

V

"How well you did to awaken me!" said Katerina, wiping her eyes with the embroidered sleeve of her nightdress and looking her husband up and down as he stood before her. "Such a terrible dream I had! How I gasped for breath! Ohh! . . . I thought I was dying . . ."

"What dream—did it go like this?" And Burulbash began to tell his wife everything he had seen.

"How did you find it out, my husband?" asked Katerina, amazed. "But no, much of what you tell is unknown to me. No, I did not dream that father had killed my mother, and I saw nothing of the dead men. No, Danilo, you're not telling it right. Ah, how terrible my father is!"

"No wonder there's much you didn't see. You don't know the tenth part of what your soul knows. Do you know that your father is an antichrist?[8] Last year, when I was going together with the Polacks against the Crimeans (I still joined with that faithless people then), the superior of the Bratsky Monastery—he's a holy man, wife—told me that an antichrist has the power to summon the soul out of any person; and the soul goes about freely when the person falls asleep, and it flies with the archangels around God's mansion. From the first your father's face did not appeal to me. If I had known you had such a father, I would not have married you; I would have left you and not taken sin upon my soul by relating myself to the race of an antichrist."

"Danilo!" Katerina said, covering her face with her hands and sobbing, "am I guilty of anything before you? Have I betrayed you, my beloved husband? How have I brought your wrath upon me? Haven't I served you faithfully? Did I ever say anything against it when you came home drunk from your young men's feasting? Didn't I give birth to a dark-browed son for you? . . ."

"Don't weep, Katerina, I know you now and will not abandon you for anything. All the sins lie upon your father."

"No, don't call him my father! He's no father to me. God is my witness, I renounce him, I renounce my father! He's an antichrist, an apostate! If he were to perish, to drown—I would not reach out to save him. If he were to grow parched from some secret herb, I would not give him water to drink. You are my father!"

VI

In a deep cellar at Master Danilo's, locked with three locks, the sorcerer sits bound in iron chains; away over the Dnieper, his demonic castle is burning, and waves, red as blood, splash and surge around the ancient walls. It is not for sorcery, not for deeds of apostasy, that the sorcerer sits in the deep cellar. God will be the judge of that. He sits there for secret treachery, for conspiring with the enemies of the Russian Orthodox land to sell the Ukrainian people to the Catholics and burn Christian churches. Grim is the sorcerer: a thought dark as night is in his head. He has only one day left to live, and tomorrow he will bid the world farewell. Tomorrow execution awaits him. And what awaits him is no easy execution: it would be more merciful to boil him alive in a cauldron, or flay him of his sinful hide. Grim is the sorcerer, and he hangs his head. Perhaps he is repentant before the hour of his death; only his sins are not such as God will forgive. Above him is a narrow window with iron bars for a sash. Clanking his chains, he gets himself to the window to see whether his daughter is passing by. She is meek as a dove, she does not remember evil, she might take pity on her father . . . But no one is there. Below runs a road; no one moves along it. Further down, the Dnieper carouses; he has no care for anyone: he storms, and it is gloomy for the prisoner to hear his monotonous noise.

Now someone appears on the road—it is a Cossack! The prisoner sighs deeply. Again all is deserted. Now someone comes down in the distance . . . A green cloak billows . . . a golden headdress blazes . . . It is she! He leans still closer to the window. Now she is drawing near . . .

"Katerina! daughter! take pity on me, have mercy! . . ."

She is mute, she does not want to listen, she does not even turn her eyes toward the prison, she has already passed by, already disappeared. The whole world is deserted. Gloomy is the noise of the Dnieper. Melancholy settles into the heart. But does the sorcerer know this melancholy?

Day draws toward evening. The sun has already set. It is already gone. It is already evening: cool; somewhere an ox is lowing; sounds come wafting from somewhere—it must be people returning from work and being merry; a boat flashes on the Dnieper . . . who cares about the prisoner! A silver crescent gleams in the sky. Now someone walks down the road from the opposite direction. It is hard to make anything out in the darkness. Katerina is coming back.

"Daughter, for Christ's sake! even fierce wolf cubs will not tear their own mother! Daughter, at least glance at your criminal father!" She does not listen and walks on. "Daughter, for the sake of your unfortunate mother! . . ." She stops. "Come and receive my last word!"

"Why do you cry out to me, apostate? Do not call me daughter! There is no relation between us. What do you want from me for the sake of my unfortunate mother?"

"Katerina! My end is near: I know your husband wants to tie me to a mare's tale and send me across the fields, or maybe he'll invent a still more terrible execution . . ."

"Is there any punishment in the world that matches your sins? Wait for it; no one is going to intercede for you."

"Katerina! It is not execution that frightens me but the torments in the other world . . . You are innocent, Katerina, your soul will fly around God in paradise; but the soul of your apostate father will burn in eternal fire, and that fire will never go out; it will flare up more and more; no drop of dew falls, no wind breathes . . ."

"It is not in my power to lighten that punishment," said Katerina, turning away.

"Katerina! Stay for one word more: you can save my soul. You don't know yet how good and merciful God is. Have you heard about the Apostle Paul, what a sinful man he was? But then he repented and became a saint."

"What can I do to save your soul?" said Katerina. "Is it for me, a weak woman, to think about it?"

"If I manage to get out of here, I will abandon everything. I will repent: I will go to the caves, put a harsh hair shirt on my body, pray to God day and night. Not just non-lenten fare, but even fish will not pass my lips! I will spread out no clothes when I go to bed! And I will keep praying and praying! And if divine mercy does not lift from me at least a hundredth part of my sins, I will bury myself up to the neck in the ground, or immure myself in a stone wall; I will take neither food nor drink, and I will die; and I will give all my goods to the monks, so that they can serve panikhidas[9] for me for forty days and forty nights."

Katerina fell to thinking.

"Even if I were to open the door, I cannot remove your chains."

"I fear no chains," he said. "You say they have chained my arms and legs? No, I blew smoke in their eyes and held out dry wood to them instead of my arm. Here I am, look, there's not a chain on me now!" he said, stepping into the middle. "I would not fear these walls either and would pass through them, but your husband himself does not know what sort of walls they are. A holy monk built them, and no unclean power can take a prisoner out of here without unlocking it with the same key the saint used to lock his cell. I'll dig the same sort of cell for myself, when I, an unheard-of sinner, am released from here."

"Listen, I'll let you out. But what if you deceive me," said Katerina, stopping outside the door, "and instead of repenting, again become the devil's brother?"

"No, Katerina, I have not long to live now. My end is near, even without execution. Do you think I would give myself up to eternal torment?"

The locks clanged.

"Farewell! May the merciful God preserve you, my child!" said the sorcerer, kissing her.

"Do not touch me, unheard-of sinner, go quickly! . . ." said Katerina. But he was no longer there.

"I let him out!" she said, frightened and gazing wildly at the walls. "What will I tell my husband now? I'm lost. All that's left for me is to bury myself alive in the grave!" And, sobbing, she nearly fell onto the stump where the prisoner had been sitting. "Yet I saved a soul," she said softly. "I did a deed pleasing to God. But my husband . . . It's the first time I've deceived him. Oh, how terrible, how hard it will be to tell him a lie. Someone's coming! It's him! my husband!" she cried desperately and fell to the ground, unconscious.

VII

"It's me, my daughter! It's me, my dear heart!" Katerina heard, coming to her senses, and saw before her the old serving woman. The woman, bending down, seemed to whisper something, stretching her withered hand over her and sprinkling her with cold water.

"Where am I?" Katerina said, getting up and looking around. "Before me the Dnieper rushes, behind me the hills . . . where have you brought me to, woman?"

"Not brought you to, but brought you from, carried you out in my arms from the stuffy cellar. I locked it with the key, so that you don't get in trouble with Master Danilo."

"Where is the key?" said Katerina, glancing at her belt. "I don't see it."

"Your husband untied it so as to go and look at the sorcerer, my child."

"To go and look? . . . Woman, I'm lost!" cried Katerina.

"May God preserve us from that, my child! Only keep silent, my little mistress, and no one will find out anything!"

"He's escaped, the cursed antichrist! Did you hear, Katerina? He's escaped!" said Master Danilo, coming up to his wife. His eyes flashed fire; his saber, clanking, shook at his side.

His wife went dead.

"Did someone let him out, my beloved husband?" she said, trembling.

"Someone did, you're right; but that someone was the devil. Look, there's a log bound in the irons instead of him. God has made it so that the devil doesn't fear Cossack hands! If any one of my Cossacks had so much as the thought in his head, and I learned of it . . . I wouldn't be able to find a punishment fit for him!"

"And if it was me? . . ." Katerina said involuntarily and stopped, frightened.

"If it was you who thought of it, then you wouldn't be my wife. I'd sew you up in a sack and drown you in the very middle of the Dnieper! . . ."

Katerina's breath was taken away, and she fancied her hair was separating from her head.

VIII

On the border road, in a tavern, Polacks have been gathering and feasting for two days. There are not a few of the scum. They must have come for some raid: some of them have muskets; spurs jingle, sabers rattle. The nobles make merry and boast, talking about their unheard-of deeds, mocking Orthodoxy, calling the Ukrainian people their slaves, twisting their mustaches imposingly and imposingly sprawling on the benches with their heads thrown back. They have a ksiądz with them. Only, the ksiądz is of the same ilk and does not even look like a Christian priest: he drinks and carouses with them and says shameful things with his infidel tongue. The servants do not yield to them in anything: the sleeves of their tattered jackets shoved back, they strut about as if they are something special. They play cards and slap each other on the nose with the cards. They have got other men's wives to come with them. Shouting, fighting! . . . The nobles are rowdy, they pull tricks: grab the Jew by his beard, paint a cross on his infidel brow; shoot blanks at their wenches and dance the Cracovienne with their infidel priest. Never has there been such temptation in the Russian land, not even from the Tartars. It must be that God destined her to suffer this disgrace for her sins! Amidst the general bedlam you can hear them talking about Master Danilo's farmstead beyond the Dnieper, about his beautiful wife . . . Not for anything good has this band gathered!

IX

Master Danilo is sitting at the table in his room, leaning on his elbow and thinking. Mistress Katerina is sitting on the stove seat, singing a song.

"I feel somehow sad, my wife!" said Master Danilo. "There's an ache in my head and an ache in my heart. Something is weighing me down. It must be that my death is straying somewhere nearby."

"Oh, my beloved husband!" thought Katerina, "lean your head on me! Why are you nursing such black thoughts in yourself?" But she did not dare to say it. Bitter it was for her, the guilty one, to accept her husband's caresses.

"Listen, my wife!" said Danilo, "do not abandon our son when I am no more. You'll get no happiness from God if you abandon him, either in this world or in the next. Hard will it be for my bones to rot in the damp earth; but harder still will it be for my soul."

"What are you saying, my husband! Did you not mock us weak women? And now you talk like a weak woman yourself. You must live for a long time yet."

"No, Katerina, my soul senses that death is near. It's growing sad in the world. Evil times are coming. Ah, I remember, I remember the years; they certainly will not come back! He was still alive, the honor and glory of our army, old Konashevich![10] The Cossack regiments pass as if before my eyes now! It was a golden time, Katerina! The hetman sat on a black steed. A mace gleamed in his hand; around him his hired troops; on both sides stirred a red sea of Zaporozhtsy. The hetman started to speak—all stood as if rooted. The old fellow wept as he began to recall for us the deeds and battles of old. Ah, if you knew, Katerina, what slaughter we did then on the Turks! You can still see the scar on my head. Four bullets went through me in four places. Not one of the wounds has healed completely. How much gold we brought home then! Cossacks scooped up precious stones with their hats. What steeds, if you knew, Katerina, what steeds we drove away with us! Ah, I'll never fight like that again! It seems I'm not old yet, and my body is hale;

yet the Cossack sword drops from my hand, I live with nothing to do and don't know myself what I live for. There's no order in the Ukraine: colonels and captains bicker among themselves like dogs. There's no chief over them all. Our nobility have changed everything according to Polish custom, they've adopted their slyness . . . sold their souls by accepting the Unia. Jewry oppresses the poor people. Oh, time, time! past time! where have you gone, my years? . . . Go to the cellar, lad, and fetch me a crock of mead! I'll drink for the old life and the years gone by!"

"How shall we receive our guests, Master? Polacks are coming from the meadow side!" said Stetsko, entering the house.

"I know what they're coming for," said Danilo, getting up from his seat. "Saddle your horses, my trusty servants! harness up! draw your sabers! don't forget to bring some lead buckwheat! We must receive our guests with honor!"

But before the Cossacks had time to mount their horses and load their muskets, the Polacks, like leaves falling from the trees in autumn, were scattered over the hillside.

"Eh, there's a few here to be reckoned with!" said Master Danilo, looking at the fat nobles bobbing imposingly in the front on their gold-harnessed horses. "Looks like we'll have one more round of famous carousing! Sport yourself, Cossack soul, for the last time! Carouse, lads, here's a holiday for us!"

And there was sport on the hills. The feast feasted: swords swing, bullets fly, horses whinny and stamp. The head goes mad from the shouting; the eyes go blind from the smoke. All is confusion. But a Cossack can sense which is friend and which foe; a bullet whistles—a dashing rider tumbles from his horse; a saber swishes—a head rolls on the ground, its tongue muttering incoherent words.

But you can see the red top of Master Danilo's Cossack hat in the throng; the golden belt over his blue jacket flashes before your eyes; the mane of his black horse flows in a whirl. Like a bird he flashes here and there; he shouts and brandishes his Damascus saber, and slashes from the right shoulder and from the left. Slash, Cossack! carouse, Cossack, as your brave heart pleases! but do not stop to gaze at the golden harness and jackets! trample gold and precious stones under your feet! Stab, Cossack! carouse, Cossack!

but look back: the infidel Polacks are already setting fire to the cottages and driving the frightened cattle away. And like a whirlwind Master Danilo turns back, and now the hat with the red top flashes near the cottages and the throng around him thins out.

Not for one hour, not for two hours, does the battle between Polacks and Cossacks go on. Not many are left of the one or the other. But Master Danilo does not tire: he knocks some out of the saddle with his long lance, and his brave horse tramples the unseated ones. Now the courtyard is clearing, now the Polacks begin to scatter; now the Cossacks strip the golden jackets and rich harness from the slain; now Master Danilo prepares for the pursuit, he looks around to gather his men . . . and boils with rage: Katerina's father appears to him. There he stands on the hill, aiming a musket at him. Danilo urges his horse straight for the man . . . Cossack, you are going to your ruin! . . . The musket boomed—and the sorcerer disappeared over the hill. Only trusty Stetsko caught a flash of the red coat and strange hat. The Cossack staggered and fell to the ground. Trusty Stetsko rushed to his master—his master lay stretched on the ground, his bright eyes closed. Scarlet blood frothed on his breast. But he must have sensed his faithful servant near. Slowly he raised his eyelids and flashed his eyes: "Farewell, Stetsko! Tell Katerina not to abandon our son! You, too, my trusty servants, do not abandon him!" and he fell silent. The Cossack soul flew out of his noble body; his lips turned blue. The Cossack slept, never to awake.

Weeping, the trusty servant beckoned to Katerina: "Come, Mistress, come: your master is done carousing. He's lying drunk as can be on the damp earth. It will be a long time before he's sober!"

Katerina clasped her hands and fell like a sheaf on the dead body. "My husband, is it you lying here with your eyes closed? Get up, my beloved falcon, reach your arm out! arise! glance at least once at your Katerina, move your lips, speak at least one word . . . But you are silent, silent, my bright master! You are blue as the Black Sea. Your heart does not beat! Why are you so cold, my master? It must be that my tears are not hot, they cannot warm you! It must be that my weeping is not loud, it does not awaken you! Who will lead your regiments now? Who will race on your black steed, hallooing loudly and brandishing a saber before the Cossacks? Cossacks, Cossacks! where is your honor and glory? Your honor and glory lie with closed eyes on the damp earth. Bury me, then, bury me together with him! Pour earth on my eyes! press maple boards to my white breast! I have no more need for my beauty!"

Katerina weeps and grieves; and the distance is all clouding with dust: old Captain Gorobets is galloping to the rescue.

X

Wondrous is the Dnieper in calm weather, when freely and smoothly he races his full waters through forests and hills. No rippling, no roaring. You look and do not know if his majestic breadth is moving or not, and you fancy he is all molded of glass, as if a blue mirror roadway, of boundless width, of endless length, hovers and meanders over the green world. It is a delight then for the hot sun to look down from on high and plunge its rays into the chill of the glassy waters and for the coastal forests to be brightly reflected in them. Green-curled! they crowd to the waters together with the wildflowers and, bending down, gaze into them and cannot have enough of it, enough of admiring their own bright image, and they smile to it and greet it, nodding their branches. But into the middle of the Dnieper they dare not look: no one except the sun and the blue sky looks there. Rare is the bird that flies to the middle of the Dnieper! Magnificent! no river in the world can equal him. Wondrous is the Dnieper, too, on a warm summer night, when everything falls asleep—man, beast, and bird—and God alone grandly surveys heaven and earth and grandly shakes his robes. Stars pour from his robes. Stars burn and shine over the world, and all are reflected at once in the Dnieper. All of them the Dnieper holds in his dark bosom. Not one escapes him, unless it goes out in the sky. The black forest studded with sleeping crows and the hills broken up since ancient times, hanging over, strain to cover him at least with their long shadows—but in vain! There is nothing in the world that can cover the Dnieper. Blue, deep blue, he goes flowing smoothly through the night as through the day, visible as far off as the human eye can see. Languidly pressing himself closer to the banks from the night's chill, he sends a silver ripple over his surface, and it flashes like the strip of a Damascus saber; and, deep blue, he sleeps again. Wondrous is the Dnieper then, too, and there is no river in the world to equal him! But when dark blue clouds pass mountain-like across the sky, and the black forest sways to its roots, the oaks creak, and lightning, ripping through the clouds, lights up all the world at once—then terrible is the Dnieper! Watery peaks roar as they beat against the hills, and withdraw with a shining and moaning, and weep and dissolve far away. So a Cossack's old mother grieves as she sends her son off to the army. Rakish and daring he rides on his black steed, arms akimbo and hat cocked; and she runs weeping after him, clings to his stirrup, snatches at his bridle, and wrings her hands over him and dissolves in bitter tears.

Savagely black between the battling waves are the charred stumps and stones on the jutting bank. A boat, pulling in, knocks against the bank, rising and falling. Who among the Cossacks has made so bold as to go in a boat while the old Dnieper is angry? He must not know that he swallows men like flies.

The boat pulls in, and from it steps the sorcerer. He is unhappy; he is bitter about the wake the Cossacks held for their slain master. The Polacks paid no small fee: forty-four nobles, with all their harness and jackets, cut to pieces, along with thirty-three servants; the rest rounded up with their horses as prisoners to be sold to the Tartars.

Down the stone steps he descended, between the charred stumps, to where he had a dugout shelter deep in the ground. He went in quietly, without creaking the door, placed a pot on the cloth-covered table, and with his long hands began throwing some unknown herbs into it; he took a mug made of some strange wood, scooped up some water, and began pouring it out, moving his lips and performing incantations. A rosy light appeared in the room; and terrible was it then to look into his face: it seemed bloody, only the deep wrinkles showed black on it, and his eyes were as if on fire. Impious sinner! his beard had long since turned gray, his face was furrowed with wrinkles, he was all dried up, yet he still carried out his godless design. A white cloud came to hover in the middle of the room, and something resembling joy flashed in his face. But why did he suddenly stand motionless, mouth gaping, not daring to stir, and why did the hair bristle on his head? In the cloud before him some strange face shone. Unasked, unbidden, it had come to visit him; it grew more distinct and fixed its gaze on him. Its features, its brows, eyes, lips—all were unfamiliar to him. He had never seen it in his life. And it seemed there was little in it that was terrible, yet an invincible horror came over him. And the strange, unfamiliar head kept looking at him fixedly through the cloud. Now the cloud was gone; yet the unknown features showed still more sharply, and the keen eyes would not tear themselves away from him. The sorcerer turned white as a sheet. He cried out in a wild voice not his own and overturned the pot . . . Everything vanished.

XI

"Calm yourself, my beloved sister!" said old Captain Gorobets. "Dreams seldom tell the truth."

"Lie down, sister!" his young daughter-in-law said. "I'll send for an old woman, a fortuneteller, and she'll pour out a flurry for you."[11]

"Have no fear," said his son, grasping his saber, "no one will harm you."

Gloomily, with dull eyes, Katerina gazed at them all and could find no words. "I myself arranged for my own ruin," she thought. "I let him go." At last she said:

"He won't leave me in peace! For ten days now I've been with you in Kiev, and my grief has not lessened at all. I thought I might at least quietly raise my son for revenge . . . Terrible, terrible he looked in my dream! God forbid that you should see him, too! My heart is still pounding. 'I will stab your baby, Katerina,' he shouted, 'if you do not marry me!'" and, bursting into sobs, she rushed to the cradle, and the frightened baby reached out his arms and cried.

The captain's son seethed and blazed with wrath, hearing this talk. Captain Gorobets himself became furious.

"Let him try coming here, the cursed antichrist; he'll taste whether there's strength in an old Cossack's arms. God sees," he said, lifting up his clairvoyant eyes, "did I not fly to give my brother Danilo a hand? His holy will! I found him already lying on a cold bed, where many a Cossack lay. Still, was his wake not magnificent? Did we let even one Polack go alive? Calm yourself, my child! No one will dare to harm you, unless I and my son are no more."

Having spoken, the old captain went over to the cradle, and the baby, seeing the red pipe with its silver trim and the pouch with the gleaming tinderbox hanging from his belt, reached out to him and laughed.

"He'll take after his father," said the old captain, removing the pipe and handing it to him. "He's still in the cradle and already wants to smoke a pipe."

Katerina quietly sighed and began to rock the cradle. They all decided to spend the night together, and soon afterwards they fell asleep. Katerina, too, fell asleep.

Out in the yard and inside the house everything was quiet; only the Cossacks standing guard were not asleep. Suddenly Katerina gave a cry and woke up, and after her everyone woke up. "He's been slain, he's been stabbed!" she cried as she rushed to the cradle.

They all stood around the cradle, frozen with fear, seeing the dead baby lying in it. No one uttered a sound, not knowing what to think of the unheard-of evildoing.

XII

Far from the Ukrainian land, past Poland, beyond the populous city of Lemberg, stretch rows of high-peaked mountains. Mountain after mountain, like a chain of stone, they push back the earth to right and left and clothe it in thick stone to keep the loud and stormy sea from seeping through. Chains of stone stretch to Wallachia and the region of the Seven Cities, and stand in a massive horseshoe between the Galician and Hungarian peoples. There are no such mountains in our parts. The eye dares not survey them; no human foot has stepped on the tops of some.

Strange, too, is their look: Is it that the eager sea overflowed its shores in a storm, heaved up its shapeless waves in a whirl, and they, petrified, remained motionless in air? Is it that heavy clouds dropped down from the sky and encumbered the earth with themselves? for they are also gray in color, and a white peak glistens and sparkles in the sun. Up to the Carpathian Mountains you still hear Russian speech, and just beyond them familiar words can be heard here and there; but then the faith is no longer the same and the speech is no longer the same. There lives the not inconsiderable Hungarian people; they ride horses, wield sabers, and drink no worse than the Cossacks; and they do not stint in producing gold coins from their pockets to pay for harness and costly caftans. Great vast lakes lie between the mountains. They are still as glass and, mirror-like, reflect the bare tops of the mountains and the green at their feet.

But who is it, in the dark of night, whether the stars shine or not, that comes riding on a huge black horse? What knight of inhuman stature gallops below the mountains, above the lakes, reflected with his gigantic horse in the still waters, his endless shadow flitting terribly over the mountains? Plate-armor gleaming, lance on his shoulder, saber clanking against his saddle, helmet pulled down, black mustache, eyes closed, eyelashes lowered—he sleeps. And, asleep, he holds the reins; and behind him on the same horse sits a child page, who also sleeps, and asleep holds on to the knight. Who is he, where is he going, and why? Who knows? Not for one day, not for two days, has he been crossing the mountains. Day breaks, the sun rises, he is not to be seen; only now and then the mountain people notice a long shadow flitting over the mountains, though the sky is clear and there is not a cloud in it. But as soon as night brings darkness, he is visible again and is reflected in the lakes, and behind him, trembling, rides his shadow. He has already crossed many mountains and gone up Krivan. There is no higher mountain in the Carpathians; like a tsar it rises above the rest. Here steed and rider have stopped, and sunk still deeper into sleep, and the clouds have descended and covered him.

XIII

"Sh . . . hush, woman! don't knock so, my baby's fallen asleep. For a long time my son cried, but now he's asleep. I'll go to the forest, woman! Why are you staring at me like that? You're terrible: iron tongs reach out from your eyes . . . such long ones, ohh! they burn like fire! You must be a witch! Oh, if you're a witch, vanish from here! you'll steal my son. He's so muddle-headed, this captain: he thinks I like living in Kiev. No, my husband is here, and my son—who is going to look after the house? I left so quietly, not a cat or a dog heard me. You want to grow young, woman? It's not hard at all, you only have to dance. Look how I dance . . ." And having uttered these incoherent words, Katerina started rushing about, looking crazily from side to side, her hands on her hips. She stamped her feet with a shriek; her silver-shod heels rang without time or measure. Unbraided black tresses scattered over her white neck. Like a bird she flew without stopping, waving her arms and nodding, and it seemed she would either drop strengthless to the ground or fly out of this world.

The old nurse stood by sorrowfully, and tears filled her deep wrinkles; heavy stone lay on the hearts of the trusty lads as they watched their mistress. She was already quite weak and lazily tapped her feet in one spot, thinking she was dancing the Turtledove. "And I have a necklace, boys!" she said, stopping at last, "and you don't . . . Where is my husband?" she suddenly cried out, snatching a Turkish dagger from her belt. "Oh! this isn't the kind of knife I need." Here tears and anguish showed on her face. "My father's heart is far away: this won't reach it. His heart is forged of iron. A witch forged it for him in hellfire. Why doesn't my father come? Doesn't he know it's time to put a knife in him? He must want me to come myself . . ." And she broke off with a strange laugh. "A funny story came into my head: I remembered how they were burying my husband. They buried him alive . . . How I wanted to laugh! . . . Listen, listen!" And instead of speaking, she began to sing a song:

A blood-drenched cart is driving by,
In that cart a Cossack lies,
Pierced his heart, empty his glance,
In his right hand he holds a lance,
And from this lance the blood runs down,
A river of blood pours on the ground.
Above the stream a maple bows,
Above the maple caws a crow.
Over the Cossack his mother cries.
Don't weep, mother, dry your eyes!
For your son has wed a wife,
The fairest young girl of his life.
In the wide field a house of clay,
No windows to let in the day.
And that's the end of all our song.
The fish and crayfish did a dance . . .
And if you don't love me, may your mother catch a chill!

So all songs had become confused in her. For a day, for two days, she has been living in her house, will hear nothing about Kiev, and does not pray, flees from people, and wanders from morning till late at night in the dark oak groves. Sharp twigs scratch her white face and shoulders; the wind tousles her unbraided tresses; old leaves rustle under her feet—she pays no heed to anything. At the hour when the sunset is fading and the stars have not yet appeared, the moon does not shine, but it is already frightening to walk in the forest: unbaptized children clamber up the trees, clutching at the branches; they sob, guffaw, roll in a tangle on the road and in the spreading nettles; maidens who destroyed their souls run out of the Dnieper's waves one after another; the hair streams from their green heads onto their shoulders, water runs loudly burbling down their long hair onto the ground; and a maiden shines through the water as through a shirt of glass; her lips smile strangely, her cheeks flush, her eyes lure one's soul out . . . she would burn up with love, she would kiss you to death . . . Flee, Christian man! her mouth is ice, her bed the cold water; she will tickle you all over and drag you into the river. Katerina pays no heed to anyone; the madwoman has no fear of water nymphs, she runs about late at night with her knife out, searching for her father.

Early in the morning a visitor arrived, of comely appearance, in a red jacket, and inquired about Master Danilo; he hears it all, wipes his tearful eyes with his sleeve, and heaves his shoulders. Says he went to war together with the late Burulbash; together they fought the Crimeans and the Turks; would never have expected that such would be the end of Master Danilo. The visitor tells of many other things and wishes to see Mistress Katerina.

At first Katerina did not listen to anything the visitor said; in the end she began to listen as if reasonably to his words. He talked of having lived together with Master Danilo as brother with brother; of hiding from the Crimeans once under a dam . . . Katerina kept listening, not taking her eyes off him.

"She'll come round!" the lads thought, looking at her. "This visitor will cure her! She's already listening reasonably!"

The visitor meanwhile began telling how Master Danilo had told him, in a moment of frank conversation: "Look here, brother Koprian, if by the will of God I'm no longer in this world, take my wife and let her be your wife . . ."

Katerina pierced him terribly with her eyes. "Ah!" she cried out, "it's him! it's my father!" and she rushed at him with her knife.

He fought for a long time, trying to tear the knife away from her. At last he tore it away, swung—and a terrible deed was done: a father killed his mad daughter.

The amazed Cossacks were about to fall upon him; but the sorcerer had already leaped on his horse and vanished from sight.

XIV

An unheard-of wonder appeared near Kiev. All the nobles and hetmans gathered to marvel at this wonder: the ends of the earth suddenly became visible far away. The Liman showed blue in the distance, and beyond the Liman spread the Black Sea. Experienced men recognized the Crimea, rising mountain-like from the sea, and the swampy Sivash. To the left could be seen the Galician land.[12]

"And what is that?" the assembled folk inquired of the old people, pointing to the gray and white peaks showing far away in the sky and looking more like clouds.

"Those are the Carpathian Mountains!" said the old people. "There are some among them on which the snow never melts and the clouds perch and stay overnight."

Here a new marvel appeared: the clouds flew off of the highest mountain, and on its peak appeared a mounted man, in full knightly armor, with his eyes shut, and he could be seen as if he were standing up close to them.

Here, from among the folk marveling with fear, one leaped on his horse and, looking wildly around, as if trying to see whether anyone was pursuing him, hastily rode off as fast as his horse could go. It was the sorcerer. Why was he so frightened? Staring in fear at the wondrous knight, he had recognized his face as the same one that had appeared to him unbidden as he performed his incantations. He himself could not understand why everything in him became confused at this sight, and, fearfully looking back, he raced his horse on until evening overtook him and the stars peeped out. Here he turned toward home, perhaps to inquire of the unclean powers what this marvel was. He was just about to jump his horse over a narrow stream that branched out across his path, when the speeding horse suddenly stopped, turned its muzzle to him, and—oh, wonder!—laughed! Two rows of white teeth flashed terribly in the darkness. The hair on the sorcerer's head stood on end. He cried out wildly, wept frenziedly, and urged his horse straight on to Kiev. He fancied that everything on all sides rushed to catch him: around him the dark forest trees, as if alive, wagging their black beards and reaching out long branches, tried to strangle him; the stars seemed to run ahead of him, pointing the sinner out to everyone; the road itself, he fancied, raced after him. The desperate sorcerer flew to Kiev, to the holy places.

XV

A hermit sat alone in his cave before a lamp, not taking his eyes from the holy book. It was already many years since he had shut himself away in his cave. He had already made himself a coffin out of boards in which he slept instead of a bed. The holy elder closed his book and began to pray . . . Suddenly a man of strange, terrible appearance rushed in. At first the holy hermit was astonished and recoiled on seeing this man. He was trembling all over like an aspen leaf; his eyes rolled wildly; a terrible fire poured fearfully from his eyes; his ugly face filled the soul with trembling.

"Father, pray! pray!" he cried desperately, "pray for a lost soul!" and he collapsed on the ground.

The holy hermit crossed himself, took out the book, opened it—and recoiled in horror, letting the book fall.

"No, unheard-of sinner, there is no mercy for you! Flee from here! I cannot pray for you!"

"No?" the sinner shouted like a madman.

"Look: the holy letters of the book are filled with blood. Never has there been such a sinner in the world!"

"You mock me, Father!"

"Go, cursed sinner! I do not mock you! Fear is coming over me. It is not good for a man to be with you!"

"No, no! you mock me, do not say . . . I see your mouth stretch: the two rows of your old teeth are showing white! . . ."

And, like one crazed, he rushed at the holy hermit and killed him.

Something groaned deeply, the groaning went across the field into the forest. From beyond the forest rose dry, bony arms with long claws; they shook and vanished.

And now he felt no fear, he felt nothing. Everything seemed somehow vague to him. There was a ringing in his ears and in his head, as from drunkenness; and everything before his eyes appeared covered with cobwebs. Leaping on his horse, he headed straight for Kanev, thinking to go from there through Cherkassy to the Tartars, right to the Crimea, himself not knowing why. He rode for one day, for another, but there was no Kanev. It was the right road; it should have been here long ago, but Kanev was nowhere to be seen. Church tops gleamed in the distance. But that was not Kanev, it was Shumsk. The sorcerer was astonished to see that he had gone in a completely different direction. He urged his horse back to Kiev, and a day later a city appeared—not Kiev but Galich,

a city still further from Kiev than Shumsk, and not far now from
the Hungarians. Not knowing what to do, he turned his horse
back again, but again felt he was going ever further in the contrary
direction. No man in the world could tell what was in the sorcerer's
soul; and if anyone had looked into it and seen what went on there,
he would not have slept the whole night long and would never
have laughed again. It was not anger, or fear, or wicked vexation.
There is no word in the world that could name it. He was burnt,
scorched, he would have trampled the whole world under his
horse's hooves, or taken the whole country from Kiev to Galich, its
people and all, and drowned it in the Black Sea. But it was not from
anger that he would have done so; no, he did not know why himself. He shuddered all over when just ahead of him the Carpathian
Mountains appeared, and tall Krivan, its crown covered with a gray
cloud as with a cap; and his horse raced on and was already roaming
in the mountains. All at once the clouds cleared, and before him in
terrible majesty appeared the rider . . . The sorcerer tries to stop, he
pulls hard at the reins; the horse whinnies wildly, tossing its mane
and racing toward the knight. Now the sorcerer fancies that everything in him is frozen, that the motionless rider stirs and all at once
opens his eyes; he sees the sorcerer racing toward him and laughs.
Like thunder the wild laughter spilled over the mountains and rang
in the sorcerer's heart, shaking everything within it. He fancied
someone strong got into him and went about inside him, hammer-
ing on his heart and nerves . . . so terribly did this laughter resound
in him!

The rider seized the sorcerer with a terrible hand and lifted him
up in the air. Instantly the sorcerer died and opened his eyes after
death. But he was now a dead man and had the gaze of a dead
man. Neither the living nor the resurrected have such a terrible
gaze. He rolled his dead eyes in all directions and saw dead men rising from Kiev, from the land of Galicia, and from the Carpathians,
their faces as like his as two drops of water.

PALE, PALE, ONE taller than another, one bonier than another,
they stood around the rider, who held this terrible plunder in his
hand. The knight laughed once more and threw him down into

the abyss. And all the dead men leaped down into the abyss, picked the dead man up, and sank their teeth into him. Yet another, taller than all of them, more terrible than all of them, wanted to rise out of the earth; but he could not, he had not the strength to do it, so great had he grown in the ground; and if he had done it, he would have overturned the Carpathians, the Seven Cities, and the land of the Turks; he stirred just slightly, and the quaking from it went all over the world. And many houses fell. And many people were crushed.

A swishing is often heard in the Carpathians, the sound as of a thousand mill wheels turning in the water. It is the dead men gnawing the dead man, in the abyss without issue, which no man has ever seen, fearing to pass near it. It happens not seldom in the world that the earth shakes from one end to the other: learned people say it is because somewhere by the sea there is a mountain out of which flames burst and burning rivers flow. But the old men who live in Hungary and the land of Galicia know better and say that the earth shakes because there is a dead man grown great and huge in it who wants to rise.

XVI

In the town of Glukhov people gathered around the old bandore player and listened for an hour as the blind man played his bandore. No bandore player had ever sung such wonderful songs or sung them so well. First he sang about the old hetmans, about Sagaidachny and Khmelnitsky.[13] Times were different then: the Cossacks were in their glory; their steeds trampled down their enemies, and no one dared to mock them. The old man sang merry songs, too, and kept glancing around at the people as if he could see; and his fingers, with little bone picks attached to them, flew like flies over the strings, and it seemed the strings played of themselves; and the people around him, the old ones with their heads hanging, and the young ones looking up at the old man, dared not even whisper to one another.

"Wait," said the old man, "I'll sing to you about a deed of yore."
The people moved closer still, and the blind man sang:

Under Master Stepan,[14] prince of the Seven Cities—and the prince of the Seven Cities was also king of the Polacks—there lived two Cossacks, Ivan and Petro. They lived as brother lives with brother. "Look, Ivan, whatever you gain, it's all half and half: when one of us is merry, the other is merry; when one of us grieves, we both grieve; if one of us gets some plunder, the plunder's divided in two; if one falls into captivity, the other sells everything and pays the ransom, or else he, too, goes into captivity." And truly, whatever the Cossacks got, they divided everything in two; and if they stole cattle or horses, they divided everything in two.

King Stepan made war on the Turks. For three weeks he fought the Turks and was still unable to drive them off. And the Turks had a pasha, one who with a dozen janissaries could cut down a whole regiment. So King Stepan announced that if some brave man could be found who would bring him this pasha dead or alive, he would pay him alone as much as he paid his whole army. "Let's go after the pasha, brother!" said brother Ivan to Petro. And the Cossacks went, one in one direction, the other in another.

Petro might still have caught him or he might not have, but Ivan already came back leading the pasha to the king himself with a noose around his neck. "Brave fellow!" said King Stepan and ordered that he be paid as much as the whole army; and he ordered that he be given lands wherever he himself chose and as much cattle as he wanted. As soon as Ivan got his payment from the king, that same day he divided everything equally between himself and Petro. Petro took half of the king's pay, but he could not bear that Ivan should be so honored by the king, and he kept revenge hidden deep in his heart.

The two knights went to the lands granted by the king, beyond the Carpathians. The Cossack Ivan seated his son on his horse and tied him to himself. It was dark—they were still riding. The child fell asleep, and Ivan himself began to doze. Do not doze, Cossack, the mountain roads are dangerous! . . . But a Cossack's horse is such that it knows its way everywhere, never stumbles and never trips. Between the mountains is a chasm; no one has ever seen the bottom of this chasm; as far as the earth is from the sky, so far is it to the bottom of this chasm. On the very edge of this chasm runs the road—two men can ride abreast on it, but three never. The horse with the dozing Cossack began to step carefully. Petro rode beside him all atremble and holding his breath for joy. He looked around and pushed his sworn brother into the chasm. And into the chasm fell the horse with the Cossack and the child.

But the Cossack seized hold of a branch and only the horse fell to the bottom. He began to climb out, his son on his back; there was still a short way to go, he raised his eyes and saw that Petro was aiming his lance at him so as to push him back. "Righteous God, better not to have raised my eyes than to see my own brother aiming a lance to push me back . . . My dear brother! pierce me with the lance, if such is my lot, but take my son! How is the innocent child to blame, that he should die such an evil death?" Petro laughed and pushed him with the lance, and Cossack and child both fell to the bottom. Petro took all the property for himself and began to live like a pasha. No one had such herds of horses as Petro. Nowhere had so many sheep and rams been seen. And Petro died.

When Petro died, God summoned the souls of the two brothers, Petro and Ivan, for judgment. "This man is a great sinner!" God said. "Ivan! I will not easily find a punishment for him; you choose how he shall be punished!" Ivan thought for a long time, devising the punishment, and said at last: "This man did me a great offense: he betrayed his brother like Judas and deprived me of my honorable name and my descen-

dants on earth. And a man without an honorable name and
descendants is like a grain of wheat cast into the ground and
lost there for nothing. No sprouts—no one will even know
that the seed was sown.

"Make it so, God, that his descendants have no happiness
on earth! that the last one of the family be such an evildoer as
the world has never seen! that after each of his evil deeds his
grandparents and great-grandparents, finding no peace in the
coffin, and suffering torments unknown to the world, rise
out of their graves! And that the Judas Petro be unable to rise,
and suffer still greater torments from that, and eat dirt in a
frenzy and writhe under the ground!

"And when the hour comes that fulfills the measure of this
man's evildoings, raise me, God, on my horse, from that chasm
up to the highest mountain, and let him come to me, and I
will hurl him from that mountain into the deepest chasm, and
let all the dead men, his grandfathers and great-grandfathers,
wherever they lived when alive, be drawn from all ends of the
earth to gnaw on him for the torments he caused them, and
gnaw on him eternally, and I will rejoice looking at his torment! And let the Judas Petro be unable to rise from the
ground, and let him strain to gnaw, but gnaw only on himself,
and let his bones keep growing bigger, that through this his
pain may become greater. This torment will be the most terrible for him: for there is no greater torment for a man than to
desire revenge and be unable to get it."

"Terrible is the punishment you have devised, man!" said
God. "Let it all be as you have said, but you, too, will sit there
eternally on your horse, and as long as you sit there on your
horse, there will be no Kingdom of Heaven for you!" And it
all happened as was said: to this day a wondrous knight stands
on horseback in the Carpathians, gazing on the dead men
gnawing the dead man in the bottomless chasm, and he feels

the dead man lying under the ground growing and gnawing his own bones in terrible torment and shaking all the earth terribly . . .

The blind man finished his song; he began to strum on the strings again; he began to sing funny little verses about Khoma and Yerema, about Stklyar Stokoza . . . but old and young still could not come to their senses and stood for a long time, their heads bowed, pondering the terrible deed that had happened in olden times.

IVAN FYODOROVICH SHPONKA
AND HIS AUNT

THERE WAS A story to do with this story: it was told us by Stepan Ivanovich Kurochka, who used to come over from Gadyach. You should know that my memory's rotten beyond words: tell me something or not, it's all the same. Just like pouring water through a sieve. Knowing this fault of mine, I asked him purposely to write it down in a notebook. Well, God grant him good health, he was always kind to me, he did write it down. I put it into a little desk; I think you know it well: it's the one in the corner as you come in . . . Ah, I forgot, you've never been to my place. My old woman, whom I've lived with for some thirty years now, never learned to read in all her born days—may as well admit it. So I noticed she was baking pirozhki[1] on some paper. Her pirozhki, my gentle readers, are amazingly good; you won't eat better pirozhki anywhere. I looked at the underside of one and saw some writing. My heart as if knew it. I went to the desk—not even half a notebook left! The rest of the pages she'd torn out for her pies! What could I do? you can't start fighting in old age!

Last year I happened to pass through Gadyach. Before we reached the town, I purposely tied a knot so that I wouldn't forget to ask Stepan Ivanovich about it. Not only that, but I made myself a promise—as soon as I sneezed in town, I'd remember him. All in vain. I passed through the town, and I sneezed, and I blew my nose in my handkerchief, yet I forgot everything; and I remembered only when I was some six miles beyond the town gates. Nothing to be done, I had to publish it without the end. However, if anyone really wishes to know what happened further on in the story, he need only go on purpose to Gadyach and ask Stepan Ivanovich. He'll tell it again with great pleasure, maybe even from beginning to end. He lives not far from the stone church. There's a little lane right there: you just turn down the lane and it's the second or third gate. Or better still: when you see a tall striped pole in the yard, and a fat woman in a green skirt comes out to meet you (he leads a bachelor's life, there's no harm in saying), then it's his yard. Or else you may meet him in the market, where he spends every morning till nine o'clock choosing fish and vegetables for his table and talking with Father Antip or the Jew tax farmer.[2] You'll recognize him at once, because nobody but he has printed duck trousers and a yellow nankeen frock coat. Here's another token for you: he always waves his arms as he walks. The local assessor, the late Denis Petrovich, always used to say when he saw him in the distance: "Look, look, there goes the windmill."

I
IVAN FYODOROVICH SHPONKA

It's four years now that Ivan Fyodorovich Shponka has been retired and living on his farmstead in Vytrebenki. When he was still Vaniusha, he studied at the Gadyach regional high school, and, it must be said, he was a most well-behaved and diligent boy. The teacher of Russian grammar, Nikifor Timofeevich Participle, used to say that if everyone in the class was as diligent as Shponka, he wouldn't have to bring in the maple ruler, with which, as he confessed himself, he was weary of rapping lazybones and pranksters on the knuckles. His notebook was always clean, neatly ruled, never a blot anywhere. He always sat placidly, his arms folded and his eyes fixed on the teacher, and he never hung scraps of paper on the back of the comrade in front of him, never carved on the bench or played *squash your granny* before the teacher came. Whenever anyone needed a penknife to sharpen his pen, he immediately turned to Ivan Fyodorovich, knowing that he always had a penknife with him; and Ivan Fyodorovich, then simply Vaniusha, would take it from the little leather case tied to the buttonhole of his gray frock coat, and asked only that they not scrape the pen with the sharp edge, assuring them that the dull edge was meant for that. Such good behavior soon attracted the attention of the Latin teacher himself, whose mere cough in the front hall, which preceded the thrusting of his frieze overcoat and pockmark-adorned face through the doorway, inspired fear in the whole class. This terrible teacher, who always had two bundles of birch switches on the lectern and half his auditors on their knees, made Ivan Fyodorovich his monitor, though there were many in the class of much greater ability.

Here we cannot omit one occasion which influenced his entire life. One of the students he had charge of as monitor, in order to incline him to put down a *scit*[3] on his record, though he didn't know a scrap of the lesson, brought a buttered pancake to class wrapped in paper. Ivan Fyodorovich, though he had a bent for justice, was hungry just then and unable to resist temptation: he took the pancake, stood a book in front of him, and began to eat. And he was so occupied with it that he didn't even notice the deathly silence that suddenly fell over the class. He came to his senses with horror only when the dreaded hand, reaching out from the frieze overcoat, seized him by the ear and dragged him into the middle of the classroom. "Give the pancake here! Give it here, I tell you, scoundrel!" said the terrible teacher. Then he seized the buttery pancake with his fingers and flung it out the window, strictly forbidding the boys running around in the yard to pick it up. After which he beat Ivan Fyodorovich most painfully on the hands. And rightly so: it was the fault of the hands, they and not any other part of the body had done the taking. Be that as it may, the timidity inseparable from him to begin with increased still more. Perhaps this very event was the reason why he never had any wish to enter the civil service, seeing from experience that it was not always possible to keep the lid on things.

He was approaching fifteen when he passed into the second class, where, instead of the short catechism and the four rules of arithmetic, he started on the full-length one, the book on the duties of man, and fractions. But seeing that the further into the forest, the thicker grow the trees, and receiving news that his papa had bid the world farewell, he stayed on for another two years and then, with his mother's consent, joined the P—— infantry regiment.

The P—— infantry regiment was not at all of the sort to which many infantry regiments belong; and, even though it was mostly quartered in villages, it was nevertheless on such a footing that it would not yield to certain cavalry regiments. The majority of the officers drank vymorozki[4] and knew how to pull Jews by their sidelocks no worse than the hussars; several of them even danced the mazurka, and the colonel of the P—— regiment never missed an opportunity of mentioning it when talking with someone in society. "I have many," he used to say, patting himself on the belly after each word, "who dance the mazurka, sir. A good many, sir. A great many." To better show readers the cultivation of the P—— infantry regiment, we shall add that two of the officers gambled terribly at faro and would lose uniform, visored cap, greatcoat, sword knot, and underwear to boot—something not always found even among cavalrymen.

The company of such comrades, however, by no means diminished Ivan Fyodorovich's timidity. And since he did not drink vymorozki, preferring a glass of vodka before dinner and supper, and did not dance the mazurka or play faro, he naturally always had to stay alone. And so, while the others would go in hired carriages to visit small landowners, he sat at home and exercised himself in occupations dear only to a meek and kindly soul: polishing his buttons, reading a fortune-telling book, setting mousetraps in the corners of his room, and, finally, taking off his uniform and lying in bed. On the other hand, there was no one in the regiment more disciplined than Ivan Fyodorovich. And he commanded his platoon so well that the company commander always held him up as an example. For that, in a short time, eleven years after being made ensign, he was promoted to sub-lieutenant.

In the course of that time, he received the news that his mother had died; and his aunt, his mother's sister, whom he knew only because she used to bring him dried pears and her own very tasty homemade gingerbreads when he was a child, and even sent them to Gadyach (she was on bad terms with his mother and therefore Ivan Fyodorovich had not seen her later)—this aunt, out of the goodness of her heart, undertook to manage his small estate, of which she duly informed him in a letter. Ivan Fyodorovich, being fully confident of his aunt's reasonableness, began to carry on with his service as before. Another in his place, on receiving such rank, would have grown very proud; but pride was completely unknown to him, and having become a sub-lieutenant, he was the very same Ivan Fyodorovich that he had been in the rank of ensign. Staying on for four years after this event so remarkable for him, he was preparing to set out from Mogilev province for Great Russia with his regiment when he received a letter with the following content:

My gentle nephew, Ivan Fyodorovich,
I am sending you underwear—five pairs of cotton socks and four shirts of fine linen—and I also want to discuss business with you: since you are already of a not unimportant rank, which I think you know yourself, and are already of such age that it is time you took up the management of your estate, there is no longer any need for you to serve in the army. I am old now and cannot look after everything on your estate; and indeed I have much to reveal to you personally besides. Come, Vaniusha. In anticipation of the true pleasure of seeing you,
I remain your most loving aunt
Vasilisa Tsupchevska

A strange turnip has grown in our kitchen garden—more like a potato than a turnip.

Within a week of receiving this letter, Ivan Fyodorovich wrote in reply:

My dear madam, Aunt Vasilisa Kashporovna!

I thank you very much for sending me the underwear. My socks especially were very old, so that my orderly had to darn them four times, which made them very tight. As to your opinion about my service, I fully agree with you and sent in my resignation two days ago. As soon as I am discharged, I will hire a carriage. I was unable to fulfill your prior request concerning the wheat seed, the hard Siberian variety: there is none such to be found in all Mogilev province. The pigs here are fed on homebrew mash mixed with a little flat beer.

With the utmost respect, my dear madam aunt, I remain your nephew

Ivan Shponka

At last Ivan Fyodorovich was discharged with the rank of sub-lieutenant, hired a Jew for forty roubles to take him from Mogilev to Gadyach, and sat himself in the kibitka just at the time when the trees became clothed in young, still sparse leaves, all the earth greened brightly with fresh green, and all the fields smelled of spring.

II
THE ROAD

Nothing remarkable happened on the road. They traveled for a little over two weeks. Ivan Fyodorovich might have arrived sooner, but the pious Jew kept his sabbath on Saturdays and, covering himself with his horse blanket, prayed all day long. However, Ivan Fyodorovich, as I have had occasion to observe before, was the sort of man who would not allow himself to be bored. During that time, he would open his suitcase, take out his linen, examine it well to see if it was properly laundered, properly folded, would carefully remove a piece of fluff from the new uniform, already made without epaulettes, and would put it all back in the best way. Generally speaking, he did not like reading books; and if he ever peeked into the fortune-telling book, it was because he liked meeting familiar things there, already read several times. So a townsman goes to his club every day, not in order to hear anything new there, but to meet those friends with whom from time immemorial he has been used to chatting in the club. So an official takes great pleasure in reading the directory several times a day, not for the sake of any diplomatic undertakings, but because he delights exceedingly in seeing names in print. "Ah! Ivan Gavrilovich So-and-so!" he repeats to himself in a muted voice. "Ah! and here I am! Hm! . . ." And the next day he rereads it, again with the same exclamations.

After two weeks of traveling, Ivan Fyodorovich reached a village some seventy miles from Gadyach. It was a Friday. The sun had long set when, with kibitka and Jew, he drove into the inn.

This inn was in no way different from others built in small villages. The traveler is usually treated zealously to hay and oats there, as if he were a post-horse. But if he should wish to have a meal such as decent people ordinarily have, he must keep his appetite intact for the next occasion. Ivan Fyodorovich, knowing all that, had provided himself beforehand with two strings of bagels and a sausage, and, having ordered a glass of vodka, which is never lacking in any inn, began on his supper, sitting on a bench in front of an oak table planted permanently in the clay floor.

In the meantime there came the noise of a britzka. The gates creaked, but for a long time no britzka drove into the yard. A loud voice was quarreling with the old woman who ran the inn. "I'll drive in," Ivan Fyodorovich heard, "but if a single bedbug bites me in your house, I'll beat you, by God, I'll beat you, you old witch! And I'll pay you nothing for the hay!"

A minute later the door opened and in came, or, rather, heaved himself, a fat man in a green frock coat. His immobile head rested on a short neck that seemed fatter still because of his double chin. Even by the look of him, he seemed to be one of those people who never rack their brains over trifles and whose whole life goes swimmingly.

"Greetings to you, my dear sir!" he said, seeing Ivan Fyodorovich.

Ivan Fyodorovich made a wordless bow.

"And may I ask with whom I have the honor of speaking?" the fat arrival went on.

Under such interrogation, Ivan Fyodorovich involuntarily got up from his seat and stood at attention, something he ordinarily did when his colonel asked him a question.

"Retired Sub-lieutenant Ivan Fyodorovich Shponka," he replied.

"And dare I ask to what parts you are traveling?"

"To my own farmstead, sir—Vytrebenki."

"Vytrebenki!" the stern interrogator exclaimed. "Allow me, my dear, dear sir, allow me!" he kept repeating as he approached him, waving his arms as if someone were hindering him or as if he were pushing his way through a crowd, and, coming close, he took Ivan Fyodorovich into his embrace and planted a kiss first on his right cheek, then on the left, and then again on the right. Ivan Fyodorovich liked this kissing very much, because the stranger's big cheeks felt like soft pillows on his lips.

"Allow me, my dear sir, to introduce myself!" the fat man went on. "I am a landowner in the same Gadyach district and your neighbor. I live in the village of Khortyshche, no more than four miles from your farmstead of Vytrebenki. My name is Grigory Grigorievich Storchenko. Without fail, without fail, my dear sir, I don't even want to know you unless you come to visit the village of Khortyshche. I'm hurrying off on an errand now . . . And what is this?" he said in a mild voice to the entering lackey, a boy in a long Cossack blouse with patches on the elbows, who with a perplexed mien was placing bundles and boxes on the table. "What is this? What?" and Grigory Grigorievich's voice was imperceptibly becoming more and more menacing. "Did I tell you to put it here, my gentle? did I tell you to put it here, scoundrel? Didn't I tell you to heat the chicken up first, you cheat? Get out!" he cried, stamping his foot. "Wait, you mug! where's the hamper with the bottles? Ivan Fyodorovich!" he said, pouring some liquor into a glass, "a little cordial if you please?"

"By God, sir, I can't . . . I've already had occasion . . ." Ivan Fyodorovich said, faltering.

"I won't hear of it, my dear sir!" the landowner raised his voice, "I won't hear of it! I'm not moving from this spot until you try . . ."

Ivan Fyodorovich, seeing it was impossible to refuse, drank it off, not without pleasure.

"This is a chicken, my dear sir," the fat Grigory Grigorievich went on, cutting it up in the wooden box with a knife. "I must tell you that my cook, Yavdokha, is fond of a nip now and then, and so it often comes out too dry. Hey, boy!" here he turned to the boy in the Cossack blouse, who was bringing in a featherbed and pillows, "make my bed up on the floor in the middle of the room! See that you pile the hay a bit higher under the pillow! And pull a tuft of hemp from the woman's spinning to stop my ears for the night! You should know, my dear sir, that I've been in the habit of stopping my ears for the night ever since that cursed time when a cockroach got into my left ear in a Russian tavern. The cursed Russians, as I found out later, even eat cabbage soup with cockroaches in it. It's impossible to describe what happened to me: such a tickling in my ear, such a tickling . . . you could just climb the wall! A simple old woman helped me when I got back to our parts. And how, do you think? Merely by whispering some spell on it. What do you say about these medical men, my dear sir? I think they simply fool and befuddle us. Some old woman knows twenty times better than all these medical men."

"Indeed, sir, what you say is perfectly true. In fact, some old . . ." Here he stopped, as if unable to find the appropriate word.

It will do no harm if I say that generally he was not lavish with words. Maybe the reason was his timidity, or maybe it was the wish to express himself more beautifully.

"Give that hay a real good shaking!" Grigory Grigorievich said to his lackey. "The hay here is so vile you have to keep watching for twigs. Allow me, my dear sir, to wish you a good night! We won't see each other tomorrow: I'll be setting out before dawn. Your Jew will keep his sabbath, because tomorrow's Saturday, and so there's no need for you to get up early. And don't forget my request. I don't even want to know you unless you come to the village of Khortyshche."

Here Grigory Grigorievich's valet pulled his frock coat and boots off him, replacing them with a dressing gown, and Grigory Grigorievich tumbled into bed, and it looked as if one huge feather-erbed were lying on another.

"Hey, boy! where are you off to, scoundrel! Come here, straighten my blanket! Hey, boy, pile up some hay under my head! and, say, have the horses been watered yet? More hay! here, under this side! and straighten the blanket nicely, scoundrel! Like that! more! ah! . . ."

Here Grigory Grigorievich sighed another time or two and sent a terrible nose-whistling all over the room, occasionally letting out such snores that the old woman snoozing on the stove bench[5] would wake up and suddenly look all around her, but, seeing nothing, would calm down and go back to sleep.

When Ivan Fyodorovich woke up the next day, the fat landowner was no longer there. This was the only remarkable event that befell him on the road. Three days later he was nearing his farmstead.

He felt his heart pound hard when the windmill peeked out, its sails turning, and when, as the Jew drove his nags up the hill, a row of pussy willows appeared down below. A pond gleamed vividly and brightly through them, breathing freshness. Here he once used to swim, in this very pond he used to wade with other boys, up to his neck in the water, hunting for crayfish. The kibitka rode up the dam, and Ivan Fyodorovich saw the same little thatch-roofed old house; the same apple and cherry trees he used to climb on the sly. As soon as he drove into the yard, dogs of all sorts came running from every side: brown, black, gray, spotted. Some threw themselves, barking, under the horses' hooves, others ran behind, noticing that the axle was greased with lard; one stood by the kitchen, covering a bone with his paw and howling at the top of his voice; another barked from a distance as he ran back and forth wagging his tail, as if to say: "Look, good Christian folk, what a wonderful young fellow I am!" Boys in dirty shirts came running to see. A sow, strolling in the yard with sixteen piglets, raised her snout with an inquisitive air and grunted louder than usual. In the yard there were many canvases with wheat, millet, and oats drying in the sun. On the roof there were also many varieties of herbs drying: chicory, hawkweed, and others.

Ivan Fyodorovich was so busy gazing at it all that he came to his senses only when the spotted dog bit the Jew on the calf as he was getting down from the box. The people of the household came running, including the cook, one woman, and two girls in woolen shirts, and after the first exclamations—"Why, it's our young master!"—announced that the aunt was in the kitchen garden planting sweet corn together with the girl Palashka and the coachman Omelko, who often carried out the duties of gardener and watchman. But the aunt, who had seen the bast-covered kibitka from far off, was already there. And Ivan Fyodorovich was amazed when she all but picked him up, as if he couldn't believe this was the aunt who had written to him about her illness and decrepitude.

III
THE AUNT

Aunt Vasilisa Kashporovna was then about fifty years old. She had never been married, and she used to say that her maidenly life was dearer to her than anything. However, as far as I can recall, no one had ever offered to marry her. The reason for that was that all men felt some sort of timidity in her presence and simply could not get up the courage to propose to her. "Vasilisa Kashporovna has quite a character!" her wooers used to say, and they were perfectly right, because Vasilisa Kashporovna could make anyone feel lower than grass. The drunken miller, who had been good for absolutely nothing at all, she managed, through her own manly pulling of his topknot every day, without any extraneous remedies, to turn not into a man but into pure gold. She was of almost gigantic height and of corresponding build and strength. It seemed that nature had committed an unpardonable error in having arranged for her to wear a dark brown housecoat with little ruffles on weekdays and with a red cashmere shawl on Easter Sunday and her name day, whereas the most becoming things would have been a dragoon's mustache and jackboots. On the other hand, her occupations corresponded perfectly to her appearance: she rowed the boat herself, handling the oars more skillfully than any fisherman; she hunted game; she stood over the mowers all the while they worked; she knew the exact number of melons and watermelons in her patch; she took a toll of five kopecks per cart from those passing over her dam; she climbed the trees to shake down the pears; she gave beatings to her vassals with her terrible hand, and with the same awesome hand offered a glass of vodka to the deserving. Almost simultaneously she cursed, dyed yarn, ran the kitchen, made kvass, cooked jam with honey; she bustled all day and had time for everything. The result was that Ivan Fyodorovich's little estate, which, according to the latest census, consisted of eighteen souls,[6] flourished in the full sense of the word. Besides, she loved her nephew all too ardently and carefully saved every kopeck for him.

On his homecoming, Ivan Fyodorovich's life decidedly changed and took a totally different path. It seemed as if nature had created him precisely for managing an eighteen-soul estate. The aunt herself noticed that he was going to make a good proprietor, though, all the same, she did not yet allow him to enter into all branches of management. "He's still a young lad," she used to say, despite the fact that Ivan Fyodorovich was just shy of forty, "he can't know everything!"

However, he was constantly present in the fields beside the reapers and mowers, and this brought inexplicable delight to his meek soul. The swinging in unison of a dozen or more shining scythes; the swish of grass falling in orderly rows; the occasional pealing song of the women reapers, now merry as the welcoming of guests, now melancholy as parting; the calm, clear evenings—and what evenings! how free and fresh the air! how everything comes alive then: the steppe turns red and blue and glows with flowers; quails, bustards, gulls, grasshoppers, thousands of insects, and from them comes whistling, buzzing, chirring, crying, and suddenly a harmonious chorus; and it's all never silent for a moment! And the sun is going down and disappearing. Oh! how fresh and good! In the fields, now here, now there, cookfires are started, with cauldrons over them, and around the cauldrons mustached mowers sit; steam rises from the dumplings. The dusk turns gray . . . It's hard to say what went on inside Ivan Fyodorovich then. When he joined the mowers, he would forget to sample their dumplings, which he liked very much, and stand motionless in one spot, his eyes following a gull vanishing in the sky, or counting the shocks of harvested grain that studded the field.

Before too long there was talk everywhere of Ivan Fyodorovich being a great manager. The aunt was utterly overjoyed with her nephew and never missed an opportunity to boast about him. One day—this was after the harvest was over and, namely, at the end of July—Vasilisa Kashporovna, taking Ivan Fyodorovich by the hand, said with a mysterious air that she now wished to talk with him about a matter that had long occupied her.

"You know, gentle Ivan Fyodorovich," so she began, "that there are eighteen souls on your farmstead; that is according to the census, however, while without it one might count as many as twenty-four. But that's not the point. You know the woods behind our pasture, and you must know the wide meadow beyond that same woods: it measures a little less than fifty acres, and there's so much grass that you could sell more than a hundred roubles' worth a year, especially if, as people say, a cavalry regiment is to be stationed here."

"Of course I know it, Auntie—the grass is very good."

"I know myself that it's very good, but do you know that in reality all that land is yours? Why do you pop your eyes so? Listen, Ivan Fyodorovich! Do you remember Stepan Kuzmich? What am I saying—remember! How could you! You were so little then, you couldn't even say his name! I remember, when I came, just before St. Philip's,[7] I picked you up, and you almost ruined my whole dress. Fortunately, I handed you over to the nanny Matryona just in time. Such a nasty boy you were then! . . . But that's not the point. All the land beyond our farmstead, and the village of Khortyshche itself, belonged to Stepan Kuzmich. Even before you came into the world, I must tell you, he started visiting your mother—true, at times when your father wasn't home. Not that I say it in reproach of her! God rest her soul!—though the dear departed was always unfair to me. But that's not the point. Be that as it may, only Stepan Kuzmich left you a deed of gift for that very estate I've been talking about. But, just between us, your late mother was of a most whimsical character. The devil himself, Lord forgive me the vile word, wouldn't have been able to understand her. What she did with that deed, God alone knows. I simply think it's in the hands of that old bachelor Grigory Grigorievich Storchenko. That fat-bellied rogue got the whole estate. I'm ready to stake God knows what that he concealed the deed."

"Allow me to say, Auntie—isn't that the Storchenko I became acquainted with at the posting station?"

Here Ivan Fyodorovich told of his encounter.

"Who knows about him!" the aunt replied, after pondering a little. "Maybe he's not a scoundrel. True, it's only six months since he moved here to live, not long enough to get to know the man. The old woman, his mother, is a very sensible woman, I've heard, and a great expert at pickling cucumbers, they say. Her serf girls make excellent rugs. But since you say he was nice to you, go and see him! Maybe the old sinner will listen to his conscience and give back what doesn't belong to him. You're welcome to take the britzka, only those cursed children pulled all the nails out in the rear. The coachman Omelko must be told to tack the leather down all over."

"What for, Auntie? I'll take the dogcart you sometimes go hunting in."

At that the conversation ended.

IV
THE DINNER

At dinnertime Ivan Fyodorovich drove into the village of Khortyshche and turned a bit timid as he began to approach the master's house. This house was long and covered not with a thatched roof, such as many neighboring landowners had, but with wood. The two barns in the yard also had wooden roofs; the gates were of oak. Ivan Fyodorovich was like that dandy who, having come to a ball, looks around and sees that everyone is dressed more smartly than he is. Out of deference, he stopped his cart by the barn and went on foot to the porch.

"Ah! Ivan Fyodorovich!" cried the fat Grigory Grigorievich, who was walking about the yard in a frock coat but with no tie, waistcoat, or suspenders. However, even this outfit seemed to burden his corpulent girth, because he was sweating profusely. "Why, you said you'd just greet your aunt and come straight over, and then you didn't!" After which words, Ivan Fyodorovich's lips met with the same familiar pillows.

"It's mostly the cares of the estate . . . I've come for a moment, sir, on business, as a matter of fact . . ."

"For a moment? Now, that won't do. Hey, boy!" cried the fat host, and the same boy in the Cossack blouse ran out from the kitchen. "Tell Kasian to lock the gates at once, do you hear, lock them tight! And unharness the gentleman's horses this minute! Please go in, it's so hot here my shirt's soaking wet."

Ivan Fyodorovich, having gone in, resolved not to lose any time, and, despite his timidity, to attack resolutely.

"My aunt had the honor . . . she told me that a deed of gift from the late Stepan Kuzmich . . ."

It's hard to describe what a disagreeable look these words produced on the vast face of Grigory Grigorievich.

"By God, I can't hear a thing!" he replied. "I must tell you, I once had a cockroach sitting in my left ear. Those cursed Russians breed cockroaches everywhere in their cottages. No pen can describe what a torment it was. Tickle, tickle, tickle. An old woman helped me with the simplest remedy . . ."

"I wanted to say . . ." Ivan Fyodorovich ventured to interrupt, seeing that Grigory Grigorievich deliberately meant to divert their talk to other things, "that the late Stepan Kuzmich's will mentions, so to speak, a deed of gift . . . according to which, sir, there is owing to me . . ."

"I know, it's your aunt who's managed to talk you up. It's a lie, by God, a lie! My uncle never made any deed of gift. True, there's mention of some deed in the will, but where is it? No one has produced it. I'm telling you this because I sincerely wish you well. By God, it's a lie!"

Ivan Fyodorovich fell silent, considering that, indeed, it may only have been his aunt's imagination.

"And here comes mama with my sisters!" said Grigory Grigorievich, "which means dinner is ready. Come along!" Whereupon he dragged Ivan Fyodorovich by the arm to a room with a table on which vodka and appetizers stood.

At the same time a little old lady came in, short, a veritable coffee pot in a bonnet, with two young ladies, one fair and one dark. Ivan Fyodorovich, being a well-bred cavalier, went up to kiss the old lady's hand first, and then the hands of the two young ladies.

"This is our neighbor, mama, Ivan Fyodorovich Shponka!" said Grigory Grigorievich.

The old lady looked intently at Ivan Fyodorovich, or perhaps it only seemed that she did. Anyhow, she was kindness itself. It seemed all she wanted was to ask Ivan Fyodorovich how many cucumbers they had pickled for the winter.

"Did you drink some vodka?" the little old lady asked.

"Mama, you must not have had enough sleep," said Grigory Grigorievich. "Who asks a guest whether he's had a drink? Just keep offering, and whether we've drunk or not is our business. Ivan Fyodorovich, if you please, centaury or caraway flavored, which do you prefer? What are you doing standing there, Ivan Ivanovich?" Grigory Grigorievich said, turning around, and Ivan Fyodorovich saw Ivan Ivanovich approaching the vodka in a long-skirted frock coat with an enormous standing collar that covered the nape of his neck completely, so that his head sat in the collar as in a britzka.

Ivan Ivanovich approached the vodka, rubbed his hands, examined the glass well, filled it, held it up to the light, poured all the vodka from the glass into his mouth without swallowing it, rinsed his mouth well with it, after which he swallowed it and, downing some bread with salted mushrooms, turned to Ivan Fyodorovich:

"Do I have the honor of speaking with Mr. Shponka, Ivan Fyodorovich?"

"Yes, sir," answered Ivan Fyodorovich.

"You've changed considerably, if I may say so, since the time when I first knew you. Yes, indeed," Ivan Ivanovich went on, "I remember you just so high!" Saying which, he held his hand two feet from the floor. "Your late papa, God rest his soul, was a rare man. His melons and watermelons were such as you won't find anywhere nowadays. Here, for instance," he went on, drawing him aside, "they'll serve you melons at table. What sort of melons are they? You don't even want to look at them! Would you believe it, my dear sir, he had watermelons," he said with a mysterious look, spreading his arms as if he wanted to put them around a stout tree, "by God, like that!"

"Let's go to the table!" said Grigory Grigorievich, taking Ivan Fyodorovich by the arm.

Everyone went to the dining room. Grigory Grigorievich sat in his usual place at the head of the table, covering himself with an enormous napkin and looking like the heroes that barbers portray on their signboards. Ivan Fyodorovich, blushing, sat in the place assigned to him, across from the two young ladies; and Ivan Ivanovich did not fail to place himself next to him, heartily rejoicing that he had someone with whom to share his knowledge.

"You shouldn't have taken the pope's nose, Ivan Fyodorovich! It's a turkey!" said the little old lady, addressing Ivan Fyodorovich, who at that moment was being offered a platter by a rustic waiter in a gray tailcoat with a black patch. "Take the back!"

"Mama! no one asked you to interfere!" said Grigory Grigorievich. "You may be sure our guest knows what to take himself! Take a wing, Ivan Fyodorovich, the other one, with the gizzard! Why did you take so little? Take the thigh! You with the platter, what are you gawking at? Beg! On your knees, scoundrel! Say at once: 'Ivan Fyodorovich! Take the thigh!'"

"Ivan Fyodorovich, take the thigh!" the waiter with the platter bellowed, kneeling down.

"Hm, what sort of turkey is this?" Ivan Ivanovich said in a low voice, with a disdainful look, turning to his neighbor. "This isn't how turkey ought to be! You should see my turkeys! I assure you, one of mine has more fat on it than a dozen of these. Would you believe it, my dear sir, when they walk in the yard it's even disgusting to look at them, they're so fat! . . ."

"You're lying, Ivan Ivanovich!" said Grigory Grigorievich, who had listened in on his speech.

"I'll tell you," Ivan Ivanovich went on talking to his neighbor in the same way, pretending not to have heard Grigory Grigorievich's words, "last year, when I sent them to Gadyach, I was paid fifty kopecks apiece. And even so I didn't want to sell."

"You're lying, I tell you, Ivan Ivanovich!" Grigory Grigorievich said more loudly, stressing each syllable for better clarity.

But Ivan Ivanovich, pretending it had nothing to do with him, went on in the same way, only much more softly.

"Precisely so, my dear sir, I didn't want to sell. Not a single landowner in Gadyach had . . ."

"Ivan Ivanovich! you're just stupid and nothing more," Grigory Grigorievich said loudly. "Ivan Fyodorovich knows it all better than you do and is surely not going to believe you."

Here Ivan Ivanovich became thoroughly offended, fell silent, and started packing away the turkey, even though it was not as fat as those that were disgusting to look at.

The noise of knives, spoons, and plates replaced the conversation for a time; but loudest of all was Grigory Grigorievich's sucking out of a lamb's marrowbone.

"Have you read," Ivan Ivanovich asked of Ivan Fyodorovich after a certain silence, sticking his head out of his britzka, "*Korobeinikov's*

Journey to the Holy Places?[8] A true delight for heart and soul! They don't publish such books anymore. Most regretful, I didn't notice the year."

Ivan Fyodorovich, hearing that the matter concerned a book, began assiduously serving himself sauce.

"It's truly surprising, my dear sir, when you think that a simple tradesman passed through all those places. Nearly two thousand miles, my dear sir! Nearly two thousand miles! Truly, the Lord himself granted him to visit Palestine and Jerusalem."

"So you say," said Ivan Fyodorovich, who had already heard a lot about Jerusalem from his orderly, "that he was also in Jerusalem? . . ."

"What are you talking about, Ivan Fyodorovich?" Grigory Grigorievich spoke from the other end of the table.

"I, that is, had occasion to observe that there are such remote countries in the world!" said Ivan Fyodorovich, heartily pleased to have uttered so long and difficult a sentence.

"Don't believe him, Ivan Fyodorovich!" said Grigory Grigorievich, not hearing very well. "It's all lies!"

Meanwhile dinner was over. Grigory Grigorievich went to his room, as usual, to have a little snooze; and the guests followed the old hostess and the young ladies to the living room, where the same table on which they had left the vodka when they went to dinner was, as if by some metamorphosis, covered with little dishes of various sorts of preserves and platters with watermelons, cherries, and melons.

Grigory Grigorievich's absence could be noticed in everything. The hostess became more talkative and revealed, on her own, without being asked, a lot of secrets about the making of fruit jellies and the drying of pears. Even the young ladies began to talk; but the fair one, who seemed six years younger than her sister and looked as if she was about twenty-five, was more taciturn.

But Ivan Ivanovich spoke and acted most of all. Being sure that no one would throw him off or confuse him now, he talked about cucumbers, and about planting potatoes, and about what sensible people there had been in olden times—a far cry from those of the present day!—and about how the further it went, the smarter it got, attaining to the invention of the most clever things. In short, this was one of those people who take the greatest pleasure in being occupied with soul-delighting conversation, and will talk about anything that can be talked about. If the conversation touched on important and pious subjects, Ivan Ivanovich sighed after every word, nodding his head slightly; if on estate management, he stuck his head out of his britzka and made such faces that, just looking at them, one could learn how to make pear kvass, how big were the melons he was talking about, and how fat the geese that ran in his yard.

Finally, in the evening, Ivan Fyodorovich managed with great difficulty to say good-bye; and, despite his tractability and their attempts to force him to stay the night, he held to his intention to leave, and left.

V
THE AUNT'S NEW PLOT

"Well, so, did you coax the deed out of the old villain?" With this question Ivan Fyodorovich was met by his aunt, who had been waiting impatiently for him on the porch for several hours already and finally, unable to help herself, had run out the gate.

"No, auntie!" Ivan Fyodorovich said, getting out of the cart, "Grigory Grigorievich hasn't got any deed."

"And you believed him! He's lying, curse him! There'll come a day, really, when I go and beat him up with my own hands. Oh, I'll get him to lose some of his fat! However, I must talk with our court clerk first, to see whether we can't claim it through the court . . . But that's not the point now. Well, was the dinner good?"

"Very . . . yes, auntie, quite."

"Well, so, what were the courses, tell me? The old woman knows how to run her kitchen, I know that."

"Cottage cheese cakes with sour cream, auntie. Stuffed pigeons with sauce . . ."

"And turkey with plums?" asked the aunt, being herself a great expert at preparing that dish.

"Turkey, too! . . . Quite beautiful young ladies they are, Grigory Grigorievich's sisters, especially the fair one!"

"Ah!" the aunt said and looked intently at Ivan Fyodorovich, who blushed and dropped his eyes. A new thought quickly flashed in her head. "Well, so?" she asked curiously and keenly, "what kind of eyebrows does she have?"

It will do no harm to note that, in feminine beauty, the aunt always gave first place to the eyebrows.

"Her eyebrows, auntie, are absolutely like you described yourself as having when you were young. And little freckles all over her face."

"Ah!" said the aunt, pleased with Ivan Fyodorovich's observation, though he had had no intention of paying her a compliment by it. "And what kind of dress did she have on?—though in any case it's hard now to find such sturdy fabrics as, for instance, this housecoat I'm wearing is made of. But that's not the point. Well, so, did you talk with her about anything?"

"You mean, that is . . . me, auntie? Perhaps you're already thinking . . ."

"And why not? what's so remarkable? it's God's will! Maybe it's your destiny that you and she live as a couple."

"I don't know how you can say that, auntie. It proves that you don't know me at all . . ."

"Well, now he's offended!" said the aunt. "He's still a young lad," she thought to herself, "doesn't know a thing! They should be brought together, let them get acquainted!"

Here the aunt went to have a look in the kitchen and left Ivan Fyodorovich. But from then on she thought only of seeing her nephew married soon and of fussing over little grandchildren. Nothing but wedding preparations were piling up in her head, and it could be noticed that though she now bustled over everything much more than before, all the same things went rather worse than better. Often, while cooking some pastry, which she generally never entrusted to the cook, she would forget herself and, imagining a little grandson standing by her and asking for cake, would absentmindedly hold out the best piece to him in her hand, while the yard dog, taking advantage of it, would snatch the tasty morsel and bring her out of her reverie with his loud chomping, for which he would always get beaten with the poker. She even neglected her favorite occupations and stopped going hunting, especially after she shot a crow instead of a partridge, something that had never happened to her before.

Finally, some four days later, everyone saw the britzka rolled out of the shed into the yard. The coachman Omelko, also both gardener and watchman, had been banging with the hammer since early morning, tacking down the leather and constantly driving away the dogs that licked the wheels. I consider it my duty to warn readers that this was the same britzka in which Adam drove about; and therefore, if anybody tries to pass some other one off as Adam's britzka, it will be a downright lie, and the britzka will certainly be a false one. It is totally unknown how it was saved from the flood. It must be supposed that there was a special shed for it on Noah's ark. It's a pity readers cannot have a vivid description of its appearance. Suffice it to say that Vasilisa Kashporovna was very pleased with its architecture and always expressed regret over old vehicles becoming outmoded. She liked very much the way the britzka was constructed—that is, slightly lopsided, so that its right side was much higher than the left, because, as she used to say, a man of small stature could get in on one side, and on the other a man of great stature. In any case, some five people of small stature could fit into the britzka, or three of the aunt's size.

Around midday, Omelko, having finished with the britzka, led out of the stable three horses not much younger than the britzka and began tying them to the majestic vehicle with a rope. Ivan Fyodorovich and his aunt got in, one from the left side, the other from the right, and the britzka set off. The muzhiks who happened along their way, seeing such a rich vehicle (the aunt rarely drove out in it), stopped respectfully, doffed their hats, and made low bows. About two hours later the kibitka stopped before the porch—I think there's no need to say—before the porch of Storchenko's house. Grigory Grigorievich was not at home. The old lady and the young ladies came out to the living room to meet the guests. The aunt approached with majestic step, put one leg forward with great adroitness, and said loudly:

"I am very pleased, my dear madam, to have the honor of personally paying you my respects. And along with that, allow me to thank you for your hospitality to my nephew, Ivan Fyodorovich, who has given it much praise. Your buckwheat, madam, is excellent! I saw it as I was driving up to the village. And allow me to ask, how many stacks do you get per acre?"

After which followed a general planting of kisses. And once they were settled in the living room, the old hostess began:

"Regarding the buckwheat, I am unable to tell you: that is along Grigory Grigorievich's line. I haven't occupied myself with it for a long time, and I can't—I'm too old! In olden times, I remember, we used to have buckwheat up to the waist. God knows how it is now. Though, anyhow, they say everything's better these days!" Here the old lady sighed, and an observer might have heard in this sigh the sigh of the old eighteenth century.

"I've heard, my dear madam, that your own serf girls make excellent rugs," said Vasilisa Kashporovna, thereby touching the old lady's most sensitive string. At these words she became as if animated and talk poured from her about how yarn ought to be dyed and how to prepare thread for it. From rugs the conversation quickly slipped over to the pickling of cucumbers and the drying of pears. In short, before an hour went by, the two ladies were talking as if they had known each other forever. Vasilisa Kashporovna already began saying many things to her in such a soft voice that Ivan Fyodorovich was unable to make anything out.

"But wouldn't you like to have a look?" said the old hostess, rising.

After her the young ladies and Vasilisa Kashporovna also rose, and they all moved toward the serving-girls' room. The aunt, however, gave a sign to Ivan Fyodorovich to stay and said something softly to the old lady.

"Mashenka!" the old lady said, turning to the fair girl, "stay with our guest and talk with him, so that our guest doesn't get bored!"

The fair young lady stayed and sat down on the sofa. Ivan Fyodorovich sat on his chair as if on needles, blushing and looking down; but the young lady seemed not to notice it at all and sat indifferently on the sofa, studying the windows and walls diligently or following with her eyes a cat that timorously ran under the chairs.

Ivan Fyodorovich plucked up his courage a bit and was about to begin a conversation; but it seemed he had lost all his words on the road. Not a single thought occurred to him.

The silence lasted about a quarter of an hour. The young lady went on sitting in the same way.

Finally Ivan Fyodorovich took heart.

"There's quite a lot of flies in summer, miss!" he uttered in a half-trembling voice.

"An incredible lot!" replied the young lady. "My brother specially made a swatter out of mama's old shoe, but there's still quite a lot."

Here the conversation stopped. And in no way could Ivan Fyodorovich find his tongue again.

Finally the mistress, the aunt, and the dark young lady came back. After talking a little while longer, Vasilisa Kashporovna took her leave of the old lady and the young ones, in spite of invitations to stay the night. The old lady and the girls came out to the porch to see the guests off, and for a long time still they kept bowing to the aunt and nephew peeking out of the britzka.

"Well, Ivan Fyodorovich! what did you talk about with the young miss?" the aunt asked on their way.

"Marya Grigorievna is a very modest and well-behaved girl!" said Ivan Fyodorovich.

"Listen, Ivan Fyodorovich! I want to talk seriously with you. You are, thank God, in your thirty-eighth year. You already have a good rank. It's time to think about children! You absolutely must have a wife . . ."

"What, auntie?" Ivan Fyodorovich cried out, frightened. "What, a wife? No, auntie, for pity's sake . . . You make me completely ashamed . . . I've never been married before . . . I absolutely wouldn't know what to do with her!"

"You'll find out, Ivan Fyodorovich, you'll find out," the aunt said, smiling, and thought to herself: "My, oh, my. He's still quite a young lad, doesn't know a thing!" "Yes, Ivan Fyodorovich," she said aloud, "you won't find a better wife than Marya Grigorievna. Besides, you liked her very much. I've already discussed it at length with the old woman: she's very pleased to see you as her son-in-law. True, we don't know what that sinner of a Grigorievich is going to say. But we won't consider him, just let him try and with-hold the dowry, we'll have him in court . . ."

At that moment the britzka drove into the yard and the ancient nags livened up, sensing their stalls nearby.

"Listen, Omelko! give the horses a good rest first, don't take them for water right after unharnessing, they're hot. Well, Ivan Fyodorovich," the aunt went on, climbing out, "I advise you to think it over well. I still have to run by the kitchen. I forgot to give Solokha orders for supper, and I suppose the worthless woman hasn't thought of it herself."

But Ivan Fyodorovich stood as if thunderstruck. True, Marya Grigorievna was a very nice young lady; but to get married! . . . that seemed to him so strange, so odd, that he was simply unable to think of it without fear. To live with a wife! . . . incomprehensible! He wouldn't be alone in his room, there'd be two of them every-where! . . . Sweat broke out on his face as he fell to pondering more deeply.

He went to bed earlier than usual, but despite all efforts was unable to fall asleep. At last the longed-for sleep, that universal pacifier, visited him—but what sleep! He had never had more incoherent dreams. First he dreamed that everything around him was noisy, whirling, and he is running, running, not feeling the legs under him . . . he's already at the end of his strength . . . Sud-denly somebody grabs him by the ear. "Aie! who's that?" "It's me, your wife!" some voice said noisily. And he suddenly woke up. Then he imagined that he was already married, that everything in their house was so odd, so strange: in his room, instead of a single bed, there stood a double bed. On a chair sits the wife. It's strange to him; he doesn't know how to approach her, what to say to her, and he notices that she has a goose face. Inadvertently, he turns away and sees another wife, also with a goose face. He turns another way—there stands a third wife. Behind him, one more wife. Here anguish came over him. He rushed into the garden; but it was hot in the garden. He took his hat off and saw: a wife is sitting in the hat, too. Sweat broke out on his face. He went to his pocket to get a handkerchief—there's a wife in the pocket as well; he took a wad of cotton out of his ear—there sits another wife . . . Then suddenly he was hopping on one foot, and his aunt, looking at him, said with an imposing air, "Yes, you must hop, because you're a married man now." He turns to her, but the aunt is no longer an aunt but a belfry. And he feels that someone is pulling him on a rope up the belfry. "Who is pulling me?" Ivan Fyodorovich asks pitifully. "It's me, your wife pulling you, because you're a bell." "No, I'm not a bell, I'm Ivan Fyodorovich!" he cries. "Yes, you're a bell," says the colonel of the P—— infantry regiment, passing by. Then he suddenly dreamed that his wife was not a person at all but some sort of woolen fabric; that he was in Mogilev, going into a shop. "What kind of fabric would you like?" says the shopkeeper. "Take some wife, it's the most fashionable fabric! very good quality! everybody makes frock coats from it now." The shopkeeper measures and cuts the wife. Ivan Fyodorovich takes it under his arm and goes to a tailor, a Jew. "No," says the Jew, "this is poor fabric! Nobody makes frock coats from it . . ."

In fear and beside himself, Ivan Fyodorovich woke up. He was streaming with cold sweat.

As soon as he got up in the morning, he at once appealed to the fortune-telling book, at the end of which one virtuous bookseller, in his rare kindness and disinterestedness, had placed an abbreviated interpretation of dreams. But there was absolutely nothing in it even faintly resembling such an incoherent dream.

Meanwhile, in the aunt's head a totally new plot was hatching, which you will hear about in the next chapter.

OLD WORLD LANDOWNERS

I LIKE VERY much the modest life of those solitary proprietors of remote estates who in Little Russia are usually known as the old world and who, like decrepit, picturesque little houses, are so nicely mottled and so completely the opposite of a new, smooth building whose walls have not yet been washed by rain, whose roof is not yet covered with green mold, and whose porch does not yet show its red bricks through missing plaster. I like sometimes to descend for a moment into the realm of this remarkably solitary life, where not one desire flies over the paling that surrounds the small yard, over the wattle fence that encloses the garden filled with apple and plum trees, over the village cottages surrounding it, slumped to one side, in the shade of pussy willows, elders, and pear trees. The life of their modest owners is quiet, so quiet that for a moment you forget yourself and think that the passions, desires, and restlessness produced by the evil spirit who troubles the world do not exist at all, and that you saw them only in a splendid, shining dream. From here I can see a low house with a gallery of small, blackened wooden posts running all the way round it, so that it would be possible in time of hail and thunder to close the shutters without getting wet by rain. Behind it, a fragrant bird cherry, whole rows of low fruit trees drowning in the purple of cherries and the ruby sea of plums covered with a leaden bloom; a branching maple in the shadow of which a rug has been spread for resting on; in front of the house, a vast yard of low, fresh grass, with a beaten path from the barn to the kitchen and from the kitchen to the master's quarters; a long-necked goose drinking water with her young, downy-soft goslings; the paling hung with strings of dried pears and apples and with rugs airing out; a cart full of melons standing by the barn; an unharnessed ox lying lazily beside it—all this has an inexplicable charm for me, perhaps because I no longer see it, and because everything we are parted from is dear to us. Be that as it may, even as my britzka drove up to the porch of this little house, my soul would assume a remarkably pleasant and calm state; the horses would trot merrily to the porch, the coachman would most calmly climb down from the box and fill his pipe as if he had come to his own house; the very barking set up by the phlegmatic Rustys, Rovers, and Fidos was pleasant to my ears. But most of all I liked the owners of these modest corners themselves, the little old men, the little old women who came solicitously to meet me. Their faces come back to me even now, in the noise and crowd, amid fashionable tailcoats, and then suddenly I am overcome by reverie and have visions of the past. On their faces there was always written such kindness, such cordiality and pure-heartedness, that you would unwittingly renounce all your bold dreams, at least for a short while, and pass imperceptibly into lowly bucolic life.

To this day I cannot forget an old couple from times past, who, alas, are no more, yet my soul is still filled with pity and my feelings are strangely wrung when I imagine myself coming again some day to their former, now-deserted dwelling and seeing a cluster of tumbledown cottages, an untended pond, an overgrown ditch in the place where the little low house used to stand—and nothing more. Sad! I feel sad beforehand! But let us turn to the story.

Afanasy Ivanovich Tovstogub and Pulkheria Ivanovna, the Tovstogub wife, as the neighboring peasants called her, were the old folk I was beginning to tell about. If I were a painter and wanted to portray Philemon and Baucis[1] on canvas, I would never choose any other original than them. Afanasy Ivanovich was sixty years old, Pulkheria Ivanovna fifty-five. Afanasy Ivanovich was tall, always went about in a sheepskin coat covered with camlet, sat hunched over, and almost always smiled, whether talking or merely listening. Pulkheria Ivanovna was rather serious, she hardly ever laughed, but there was so much kindness written in her face and eyes, so much readiness to treat you to the best of everything they had, that you would surely have found a smile much too sugary on her kind face. The pattern of light wrinkles on their faces was so pleasant that an artist would surely have stolen it. By it one seemed able to read their whole life, the serene, calm life led by old, native-born, simple-hearted and yet wealthy families, who are always such a contrast to those low Little Russians who push their way up from tar-makers and dealers, fill the courts and government offices like locusts, rip the last kopeck out of their own compatriots, flood Petersburg with pettifoggers, finally make some fortune, and to their last name, which ends in o, solemnly add the letter v.[2] No, like all the ancient and native-born families of Little Russia, they bore no resemblance to these despicable and pathetic creatures.

It was impossible to look at their mutual love without sympathy. They never spoke to each other informally but always with respect, as Afanasy Ivanovich and Pulkheria Ivanovna. "Was it you who went through the seat of the chair, Afanasy Ivanovich?" "No matter, don't be angry, Pulkheria Ivanovna, it was me." They never had children, and therefore all their affection was focused on themselves. Once, when he was young, Afanasy Ivanovich had served in the volunteer cavalry, later he became a staff major, but that was very long ago, a bygone thing, Afanasy Ivanovich himself hardly ever recalled it. Afanasy Ivanovich had married at the age of thirty, when he was a fine fellow and wore an embroidered uniform; he had even abducted Pulkheria Ivanovna rather adroitly when her relations refused to give her to him; but of that, too, he remembered very little, or at least never spoke.

All these long-past, extraordinary events were replaced by a quiet and solitary life, by those drowsy and at the same time harmonious reveries which you experience sitting on a village balcony overlooking the garden, when a wonderful rain makes a luxuriant splashing on the leaves, pouring down in bubbling streams and casting a drowsy spell over your limbs, and meanwhile a rainbow steals from behind the trees and like a half-ruined arch shines with its seven muted colors in the sky. Or when you are rocked by a carriage bobbing between green shrubs, and a steppe quail throbs, and fragrant grass together with wildflowers and ears of wheat poke through the doors of the carriage, striking you pleasantly on the hands and face.

He always listened with a pleasant smile to the guests who came to see him, and sometimes spoke himself, but mainly to ask questions. He was not one of those old people who make a nuisance of themselves, eternally praising the old days or denouncing the new. On the contrary, in questioning you, he showed great curiosity and concern for the circumstances of your own life, its successes and failures, which always interest all kindly old men, though it somewhat resembled the curiosity of a child who, while talking to you, studies your watch fob. In those moments his face, one might say, breathed kindness.

The rooms of the house in which our old folk lived were small, low, such as one meets among old world people. In each room there was an enormous stove that took up almost a third of it. These rooms were terribly warm, because Afanasy Ivanovich and Pulkheria Ivanovna were both very fond of warmth. The fireboxes were all in the front hall, which was always filled nearly to the ceiling with the straw customarily used instead of wood in Little Russia. The crackling of this burning straw and its light made the front hall very pleasant on a winter evening, when ardent youths, chilled in the pursuit of some swarthy beauty, came running in clapping their hands. The walls of the rooms were adorned with several paintings, big and small, in old-fashioned narrow frames. I'm certain that the hosts themselves had long forgotten their content, and if some had been taken away, they surely would not have noticed it. There were two large oil portraits. One of them represented some bishop, the other Peter III.[3] The Duchess of La Vallière,[4] stained by flies, looked out from a narrow frame.

Around the windows and over the door there were many small pictures, such as one somehow gets used to regarding as spots on the wall and therefore simply does not look at. The floors in almost all the rooms were of clay, but it was beaten down so neatly and kept so clean, as surely no parquet is kept in any rich house where a drowsy gentleman in livery lazily does the sweeping.

Pulkheria Ivanovna's room was all filled with chests, boxes, little boxes, and little chests. A multitude of little bundles and bags with flower, vegetable, and watermelon seeds hung on the walls. A multitude of balls of yarn of various colors, of scraps from old dresses made in the course of half a century, was tucked into the corners of the chests and between them. Pulkheria Ivanovna was a great manager and collected everything, sometimes without knowing of what use it would be later.

But the most remarkable thing in the house was the singing doors. As soon as morning came, the singing of the doors sounded throughout the house. I'm unable to say why they sang—whether it was the fault of rusty hinges, or the workman who made them concealed some secret in them—but the remarkable thing was that each door had its own special voice: the door to the bedroom sang in the highest treble, the dining room door in a hoarse bass, while the one in the front hall produced some strange cracked and at the same time moaning sound, so that, listening attentively, one could finally hear quite clearly: "My, oh, my, how cold I am!" I know that many people dislike this sound very much; but I have a great love for it, and if I happen now to hear the occasional creaking of a door, it immediately smells of the village to me, of the low little room lit by a candle in an old-fashioned candlestick, of supper already set on the table, of the dark May night gazing at the laid table through the open window from the garden, of the nightingale showering the garden, the house, and the distant river with his trills, of the fright and rustling of the branches . . . and, God, what a long string of memories comes to me then!

The chairs in the room were wooden, massive, as is usual with old-time things; they all had high, carved backs, natural, with no varnish or paint; they were not even upholstered, and somewhat resembled the chairs on which bishops sit to this day. Triangular tables in the corners, a rectangular one in front of the sofa, and a mirror in a narrow gilt frame with carved leaves, which flies had covered with black specks, a rug in front of the sofa with birds looking like flowers and flowers looking like birds—these were about all the furnishings in the unpretentious house where my old couple lived.

The female serfs' quarters were crowded with young and not-so-young girls in striped shirts, whom Pulkheria Ivanovna sometimes gave some trifles to sew or set to sorting out berries, but who mostly slept and raided the kitchen. Pulkheria Ivanovna considered it necessary to keep them in the house and strictly supervised their morals. But, to her great astonishment, before a few months went by, one of her girls would grow much plumper at the waist, and this would seem the more astonishing since there were almost no bachelors in the place, except perhaps for the houseboy, who went around barefoot in a gray short-tailed coat and whenever he wasn't eating was sure to be asleep. Pulkheria Ivanovna usually reprimanded the guilty girl and gave strict orders that no such thing should happen again. On the windowpanes a terrible number of flies pinged, overwhelmed completely by the heavy basso of a bumblebee, occasionally accompanied by the piercing shrieks of wasps; but as soon as the candles were brought in, the whole throng would go to sleep and cover the ceiling like a black cloud.

Afanasy Ivanovich took very little care of the management, though all the same he did sometimes go out to the mowers and reapers and watched their work quite closely; the whole burden of government lay on Pulkheria Ivanovna. Pulkheria Ivanovna's management consisted in a ceaseless locking and unlocking of the storehouse, in pickling, drying, and stewing a numberless multitude of fruits and plants. Her house was the perfect likeness of a chemical laboratory. Under the apple tree a fire was forever burning, and the iron tripod was never without a cauldron or copper pot on it, for preserves, jellies, fruit pastes made with honey, sugar, and I don't remember what else. Under another tree the coachman was forever distilling vodka in a copper still, with peach leaves, bird-cherry flowers, centaury, cherry pits, and by the end of the process was quite unable to move his tongue, pouring out such nonsense that Pulkheria Ivanovna could not understand a thing and would send him to the kitchen to sleep. So much of this stuff was cooked, pickled, and dried that Pulkheria Ivanovna would finally have drowned the yard in it—because she liked to prepare things for laying away beyond what she counted on using—if a good half of it hadn't been eaten by the household serf girls, who would get into the storehouse and gorge themselves so terribly that they would spend whole days afterwards groaning and complaining about their stomachs.

As for the tillage and other aspects of management that lay outside the household, Pulkheria Ivanovna had little opportunity of entering into them. The steward, together with the village headman, stole unmercifully. They made a custom of entering their master's forests as if they were their own; they built a lot of sleds and sold them at the local fair; besides that, they sold all the big oak trees to the neighboring Cossacks to be cut down for their mills. Only once did Pulkheria Ivanovna have a wish to inspect her forests. For that purpose a droshky was harnessed with enormous leather aprons which, as soon as the coachman snapped the reins and the horses, veterans of the old militia,[5] started from their place, filled the air with strange noises, so that one could suddenly hear a flute, a tambourine, and a drum; every little nail and iron staple set up such a clangor that even out at the mills one could hear the mistress leaving her yard, though it was nearly a mile and a half away. Pulkheria Ivanovna could not fail to notice the terrible devastation in the forest and the loss of the oaks, which she knew to have been hundreds of years old when she was a child.

"Why is it, Nichipor," she said, addressing her steward, who was right there, "that with you the oaks have grown so sparse? Look out that the hair on your head doesn't grow sparse, too."

"Why sparse?" the steward replied. "They perished! Perished just like that—thunder beat them down, worms gnawed at them—they perished, ma'am, perished."

Pulkheria Ivanovna, thoroughly satisfied with that answer, went home and gave instructions to double the watch in the garden on her Spanish cherries and the big winter bergamots.

Those worthy rulers, the steward and the headman, thought it quite unnecessary to bring all the flour into the master's own barn and that half was enough; in the end, even the half that was delivered was either moldy or damp and had been rejected at the fair. But however much the steward and the headman stole, however much everyone in the household stuffed his face, from the housekeeper to the pigs, who consumed a terrible quantity of plums and apples, and often shoved the trees with their snouts to shake down a whole rain of fruit; however much the sparrows and crows pecked up; however much all the household people took as presents to their kin in other villages, even stealing old linen and yarn from the storerooms, all of which returned to the universal source, that is, the tavern; however much visitors, their phlegmatic coachmen and lackeys stole—the blessed earth produced everything in such abundance, and Afanasy Ivanovich and Pulkheria Ivanovna needed so little, that all this terrible plundering seemed to go entirely unnoticed in their management.

The two old folk, as was the ancient custom of old world landowners, liked very much to eat. As soon as day broke (they always rose early) and the doors started their discordant concert, they would be at the table having coffee. After having his coffee, Afanasy Ivanovich would go out to the front door and, shaking his handkerchief, say, "Shoo, shoo! Off the porch, geese!" In the yard he would usually run into the steward. He would enter into his usual conversation with him, ask in great detail about the work, and come out with such observations and instructions as would astonish anyone with his extraordinary knowledge of management; and a newcomer would not even dare think it possible to steal from such a keen-sighted master. But his steward was not gun-shy, he knew how to answer and, even more so, how to handle his job.

After that, Afanasy Ivanovich would go back in and, approaching Pulkheria Ivanovna, would say:

"Well, now, Pulkheria Ivanovna, isn't it time we had a little bite of something?"

"What could we have now, Afanasy Ivanovich?—unless it was shortcake with lard, or poppyseed pirozhki,[6] or maybe some pickled mushrooms?"

"Why not the mushrooms, or else the pirozhki?" Afanasy Ivanovich would reply, and a tablecloth with pirozhki and mushrooms would suddenly appear.

An hour before dinner, Afanasy Ivanovich would have another snack, drink an old-fashioned silver cup of vodka, followed by mushrooms, various dried fish, and so on. Dinner was served at twelve noon. Besides platters and sauce boats, there stood on the table a multitude of pots with sealed lids to keep some savory dishes of old-fashioned cookery from losing their flavor. At dinner the conversation was about subjects most closely related to dining.

"It seems to me," Afanasy Ivanovich would say, "that this kasha[7] is a wee bit burnt—don't you think so, Pulkheria Ivanovna?"

"No, Afanasy Ivanovich, put more butter on it, then it won't seem burnt, or else pour some mushroom sauce on it."

"Why not?" Afanasy Ivanovich would say, holding out his plate, "let's try it and see."

After dinner Afanasy Ivanovich would have a little hour of rest, after which Pulkheria Ivanovna would bring a sliced watermelon and say:

"Here, Afanasy Ivanovich, taste what a good watermelon it is."

"Never mind that it's red inside, Pulkheria Ivanovna," Afanasy Ivanovich would say, accepting a none-too-small slice, "sometimes it's no good even when it's red."

But the watermelon would immediately disappear. After that Afanasy Ivanovich would also eat a few pears and go for a walk in the garden with Pulkheria Ivanovna. On returning home, Pulkheria Ivanovna would go about her duties, and he would sit under the gallery roof facing the yard and watch the storehouse ceaselessly revealing and covering its insides, and the serf girls jostling each other, bringing heaps of all sorts of stuff in and out in wooden boxes, sieves, trays, and other containers for fruit. A little later he would send for Pulkheria Ivanovna or go to her himself and say:

"What is there that I might eat, Pulkheria Ivanovna?"

"What is there?" Pulkheria Ivanovna would say, "unless I go and tell them to bring you some berry dumplings that I asked them to keep specially for you?"

"That's nice," Afanasy Ivanovich would answer.

"Or maybe you'd like some custard?"

"That's good," Afanasy Ivanovich would answer. After which it would all be brought at once and duly eaten up.

Before supper Afanasy Ivanovich would again snack on something or other. At nine-thirty supper was served. After supper they would all go to bed again, and a general silence would settle over this active yet quiet little corner. The room in which Afanasy Ivanovich and Pulkheria Ivanovna slept was so hot that it was a rare person who could spend any length of time in it. But on top of that, for even greater warmth, Afanasy Ivanovich slept on the stove,[8] though the intense heat often made him get up several times during the night and pace the room. Sometimes Afanasy Ivanovich groaned as he walked. Then Pulkheria Ivanovna would ask:

"Why are you groaning, Afanasy Ivanovich?"

"God knows, Pulkheria Ivanovna, feels like I've got a bit of a stomachache," Afanasy Ivanovich would say.

"Hadn't you better eat something, Afanasy Ivanovich?"

"I don't know if that would be good, Pulkheria Ivanovna! Anyhow, what might I eat?"

"Some buttermilk, or stewed dried pears?"

"Why not, just so as to try it?" Afanasy Ivanovich would say.

A sleepy serf girl would go and rummage in the cupboards, and Afanasy Ivanovich would eat a little plateful, after which he usually said:

"There, that feels better."

Sometimes, when the weather was clear and the rooms were well heated, Afanasy Ivanovich got merry and liked to poke fun at Pulkheria Ivanovna and talk about something different.

"And if our house suddenly caught fire, Pulkheria Ivanovna," he would say, "what would we do then?"

"God preserve us from that!" Pulkheria Ivanovna would say, crossing herself.

"Well, but supposing our house caught fire, where would we go then?"

"God knows what you're saying, Afanasy Ivanovich! How could our house burn down? God won't let it."

"Well, but what if it did burn down?"

"Well, then we'd move into the kitchen wing. You could take the housekeeper's little room for a while."

"And if the kitchen wing burned down, too?"

"Now, really! God wouldn't permit such a thing as both house and kitchen burning down at once! Well, then we'd have the storehouse till the new house was built."

"And if the storehouse burns down as well?"

"God knows what you're saying! I don't even want to listen to you! It's a sin to say it, and God punishes that sort of talk."

But Afanasy Ivanovich, pleased at having poked fun at Pulkheria Ivanovna, would smile, sitting on his chair.

But for me the old folk seemed most interesting when they were having guests. Then everything in their house acquired a different air. These good people, one might say, lived for their guests. The very best they had was all brought out. They vied with each other in trying to treat you to everything their farm had produced. But the most pleasant thing for me was that they were obliging without being cloying. This ready cordiality was so meekly expressed on their faces, was so becoming in them, that willy-nilly you would agree to their requests. It proceeded from the clear, serene simplicity of their kind and artless souls. This cordiality was a far cry from what you're treated to by a clerk in a government office who owes his success to you, calls you his benefactor, and cowers at your feet. A guest was never allowed to leave the same day: he absolutely had to spend the night.

"You can't set out so late on such a long journey!" Pulkheria Ivanovna always said (the guest usually lived two or three miles away).

"Of course not," Afanasy Ivanovich would say, "who knows what may happen: robbers may fall upon you, or some other bad men."

"God preserve us from robbers!" Pulkheria Ivanovna would say.

"Why talk of such things before going to bed at night? Robbers or no robbers, it's dark, it's not good at all to go. And your coachman, I know your coachman, he's so weak and small, any nag can beat him; and besides, he's surely tipsy by now and sleeping somewhere."

And the guest absolutely had to stay. However, evening in a low, warm room, cordial, warming, and lulling conversation, steaming hot food served on the table, always nourishing and expertly cooked, would be his reward. I can see Afanasy Ivanovich as if it were right now, sitting hunched on a chair, smiling his usual smile and listening to the guest with attention and even pleasure! Often the talk ran to politics. The guest, who also very rarely left his estate, frequently offered his surmises with an important look and a mysterious expression on his face, saying that the French had secretly agreed with the English to turn Bonaparte loose on Russia again, or else simply talked of war being imminent, and then Afanasy Ivanovich often said, as if not looking at Pulkheria Ivanovna:

"I'm thinking of going to war myself. Why shouldn't I go to war?"

"He's off again!" Pulkheria Ivanovna would interrupt. "Don't believe him," she would say, addressing the guest. "How can he go to war, old as he is? The first soldier will shoot him down! By God, he will! He'll just take aim and shoot him down."

"So what," Afanasy Ivanovich would say, "I'll shoot him down, too."

"Just hear him talk!" Pulkheria Ivanovna would pick up. "How can he go to war? His pistols got rusty long ago sitting in the closet. You should see them: the way they are, the powder will blow them up before they do any shooting. He'll hurt his hands, and disfigure his face, and stay crippled forever."

"So what," Afanasy Ivanovich would say, "I'll buy myself a new weapon. I'll take a saber or a Cossack lance."

"He makes it all up. It just comes into his head and he starts talking," Pulkheria Ivanovna would pick up vexedly. "I know he's joking, but even so, it's unpleasant to listen. He always says something like that, sometimes you listen and listen, and then you get scared."

But Afanasy Ivanovich, pleased to have given Pulkheria Ivanovna a little fright, would be laughing as he sat hunched on his chair.

To me Pulkheria Ivanovna was most entertaining at the moments when she was treating a guest to hors d'œuvres.

"This," she would say, unstopping a decanter, "is vodka infused with yarrow and sage. If someone has an ache in the shoulder blades or the lower back, it's a great help. This one is with centaury: if you have a ringing in the ears or blotches on your face, it's a great help. And this one's distilled with peach stones; here, take a glass, what a wonderful smell! If someone bumps the corner of a cupboard or a table as he's getting out of bed and gets a lump on his forehead, it's enough just to drink one little glass before dinner and it will go away as if by magic, that same minute, as if he'd never had it."

This was followed by the same kind of report on other decanters, that almost all of them had some healing properties. Having loaded the guest with all this pharmacy, she would lead him to a multitude of plates.

"These are mushrooms with thyme! These are with cloves and walnuts! A Turkish woman taught me how to pickle them, back when we still had Turkish prisoners.[9] She was such a nice woman, it didn't even show that she confessed the Turkish faith. She went about just as we do, only she didn't eat pork, said it was somehow forbidden by their law. These are mushrooms with black currant leaves and nutmeg! And these are big gourds done in vinegar: it's the first time I've tried it, I don't know how they came out, it's Father Ivan's secret. First you spread some oak leaves in a small barrel, then put in some pepper and saltpeter, and some hawkweed flowers, too—you just take the flowers and spread them stems up. And these are pirozhki! cheese pirozhki! with poppyseed juice! And these are the ones Afanasy Ivanovich likes best, with cabbage and buckwheat."

"Yes," added Afanasy Ivanovich, "I like them very much. They're tender and slightly tart."

Generally, Pulkheria Ivanovna was in exceptionally good spirits whenever they had guests. A kindly old woman! She belonged entirely to her guests. I loved visiting them, and though I overate terribly, as all their visitors did, and though it was very bad for me, nevertheless I was always glad to go there. However, I think that the very air of Little Russia may possess some special quality that aids digestion, because if anyone here tried to eat like that, he would undoubtedly wind up lying not in his bed but on the table.[10]

Kindly old folk! But my narrative is approaching a very sad event which changed the life of this peaceful corner forever. This event will seem the more striking because it proceeded from a quite unimportant incident. But, in the strange order of things, it is always insignificant causes that give birth to great events, and, vice versa, great undertakings have ended in insignificant consequences. Some conqueror gathers all the forces of his state, spends several years making war, his generals cover themselves with glory, and finally it all ends with the acquisition of a scrap of land on which there isn't even room enough to plant potatoes; while, on the other hand, two sausage makers from two towns start fighting over nothing, other towns get involved in the quarrel, then villages and hamlets, then the whole country. But let's drop this reasoning: it's out of place here. Besides, I don't like reasoning that remains mere reasoning.

Pulkheria Ivanovna had a little gray cat that almost always lay curled up at her feet. Pulkheria Ivanovna sometimes patted her and tickled her neck with her finger, which the pampered cat arched as high as she could. It cannot be said that Pulkheria Ivanovna loved her all that much, she was simply attached to her, being used to seeing her all the time. Afanasy Ivanovich, however, often poked fun at this attachment:

"I don't know what you find in a cat, Pulkheria Ivanovna. What good is it? If you had a dog, it would be a different matter: a dog you can take hunting, but what good is a cat?"

"Be quiet, Afanasy Ivanovich," Pulkheria Ivanovna would say, "you just like to talk, that's all. Dogs are untidy, dogs make a mess, dogs break everything, but cats are gentle creatures, they won't do anyone any harm."

However, cats and dogs were all the same for Afanasy Ivanovich; he just said it to poke a little fun at Pulkheria Ivanovna.

Behind their garden was a big woods that had been wholly spared by their enterprising steward—perhaps because the sound of the ax would have come to Pulkheria Ivanovna's ears. It was dense, overgrown, the old tree trunks were covered with rampant hazel bushes and looked like shaggy pigeon legs. This woods was inhabited by wild cats. Wild forest cats should not be confused with those dashing fellows who run over the rooftops of houses. City dwellers, despite their tough character, are far more civilized than the inhabitants of the forests. The latter, on the contrary, are grim and savage folk; they always go about thin, scrawny, meowing in coarse, untrained voices. They sometimes dig subterranean passages under barns and steal lard; they even come right into the kitchen, suddenly jumping through an open window when they notice that the cook has gone out to the bushes. Lofty feelings are generally unknown to them; they live by plunder and kill young sparrows right in their nests. These cats spent a long time sniffing at Pulkheria Ivanovna's meek little cat through a hole under the barn and finally lured her away, as a troop of soldiers lures away a foolish peasant girl. Pulkheria Ivanovna noticed the cat's disappearance and sent people to look for her, but the cat was not to be found. Three days passed; Pulkheria Ivanovna felt sorry, then finally forgot all about it. One day when, after inspecting her kitchen garden, she was coming back with fresh cucumbers she had picked for Afanasy Ivanovich with her own hand, her hearing was struck by a most pitiful meowing. She said, as if instinctively: "Kitty, kitty!" and suddenly out of the weeds came her gray cat, thin, scrawny; it was clear that she had had nothing in her mouth for several days. Pulkheria Ivanovna kept calling her, but the cat stood in front of her, meowing and not daring to come near; it was clear that she had grown quite wild in the meantime. Pulkheria Ivanovna went on ahead of her, still calling the cat, who timorously followed her as far as the fence. Finally, seeing old familiar places, she went inside. Pulkheria Ivanovna at once ordered that she be given milk and meat, and, sitting before her, delighted in the greed with which her poor favorite ate piece after piece and lapped up the milk. The gray fugitive got fat before her eyes and no longer ate so greedily. Pulkheria Ivanovna reached out to pat her, but the ungrateful thing must have grown too used to the predatory cats, or picked up romantic ideas about love in poverty being better than any mansion, since the wild cats were dirt poor; be that as it may, she jumped out the window, and none of the servants could catch her.

The old woman fell to pondering. "It's my death come for me!" she said to herself, and nothing would distract her. All day she was sad. In vain did Afanasy Ivanovich joke and try to find out why she was suddenly so sorrowful: Pulkheria Ivanovna either would not reply or her replies failed totally to satisfy Afanasy Ivanovich. The next day she looked noticeably thinner.

"What's wrong, Pulkheria Ivanovna? You're not sick?"

"No, I'm not sick, Afanasy Ivanovich! I want to announce a special event to you: I know that I will die this summer; my death has already come for me!"

Afanasy Ivanovich's mouth twisted somehow painfully. He tried, however, to overcome the sad feeling in his soul, and said with a smile:

"God knows what you're saying, Pulkheria Ivanovna! You must have drunk peach vodka instead of your usual decoction of herbs."

"No, Afanasy Ivanovich, I didn't drink peach vodka," said Pulkheria Ivanovna.

And Afanasy Ivanovich felt sorry that he had poked fun at Pulkheria Ivanovna, and he looked at her and a tear hung on his eyelash.

"I ask you to carry out my will, Afanasy Ivanovich," said Pulkheria Ivanovna. "When I die, bury me by the church fence. Put my gray dress on me, the one with little flowers on a brown background. Don't put the satin dress on me, the one with the raspberry stripes: a dead woman doesn't need such a dress. What's the good of it? And you could use it: make a fancy dressing gown out of it for when guests come, so that you can look decent when you receive them."

"God knows what you're saying, Pulkheria Ivanovna!" said Afanasy Ivanovich. "Death's a long way off, and you're already frightening us with such talk."

"No, Afanasy Ivanovich, I know now when my death will be.

But don't grieve over me: I'm already an old woman and have lived enough. You're old, too, we'll soon see each other in the next world."

But Afanasy Ivanovich wept like a baby.

"It's sinful to cry, Afanasy Ivanovich! Don't sin and make God angry with your sorrow. I'm not sorry to die. One thing I'm sorry about," a deep sigh interrupted her speech for a moment, "I'm sorry I don't know who to leave you with, who will take care of you when I die. You're like a little child: whoever looks after you must love you."

Here such deep, such devastating heart's pity showed on her face that I think no one could have looked on her at that moment with indifference.

"Watch out, Yavdokha," she said, addressing the housekeeper, whom she had sent for on purpose, "when I die, you must look after the master, cherish him like your own eye, like your own child. See that they cook what he likes in the kitchen. Always give him clean linen and clothes; dress him decently when there happen to be guests, or else he may come out in an old dressing gown, because even now he often forgets which are feast days and which are ordinary. Don't take your eyes off him, Yavdokha, I'll pray for you in the other world, and God will reward you. So don't forget, Yavdokha. You're old now, you don't have long to live, you mustn't heap sin on your soul. If you don't look after him, you won't be happy in this life. I'll ask God personally not to give you a good end. You'll be unhappy yourself, and your children will be unhappy, and none of your posterity will have God's blessing in anything."

The poor old woman! At that moment she was thinking neither of the great moment ahead of her, nor of her soul, nor of her future life; she was thinking only of her poor companion with whom she had spent her life and whom she was leaving orphaned and unprotected. With extraordinary efficiency, she arranged everything in such a way that afterwards Afanasy Ivanovich would not notice her absence. Her certainty of imminent death was so strong and her state of mind was so set on it that, in fact, a few days later she lay down and could no longer take any food. Afanasy

Ivanovich turned all attention and never left her bedside. "Maybe you'll eat something, Pulkheria Ivanovna?" he would say, looking anxiously in her eyes. But Pulkheria Ivanovna would not say anything. Finally, after a long silence, she made as if to say something, moved her lips—and her breath flew away.

Afanasy Ivanovich was completely amazed. The thing seemed so wild to him that he did not even weep. With dull eyes he gazed at her as if not understanding what this corpse could mean.

The dead woman was laid on the table, dressed in the dress she herself had appointed, with her hands crossed and a candle placed in them—he looked at it all insensibly. Many people of various ranks filled the yard, many guests came to the funeral, long tables were set up in the yard; kutya,[11] liqueurs, pies covered them in heaps; the guests talked, wept, gazed at the deceased, discussed her qualities, looked at him—but he viewed it all strangely. The deceased was finally taken up and borne away, people flocked behind, and he, too, followed her. The priests were in full vestments, the sun shone, nursing infants wept in their mothers' arms, larks sang, children in smocks ran and frolicked on the road. Finally the coffin was placed over the hole, he was told to go up and kiss the dead woman for the last time; he went up, kissed her, tears came to his eyes, but some sort of insensible tears. The coffin was lowered down, the priest took the spade and threw in the first handful of earth, in a deep, drawn-out chorus the reader and two sextons sang "Memory Eternal"[12] under the clear, cloudless sky, the workmen took up their spades, and earth now covered the hole smoothly—at that moment he made his way to the front; everyone parted, allowing him to pass, wishing to know his intentions. He raised his eyes, looked around dully, and said: "Well, so you've buried her already! What for?!" He stopped and did not finish his speech.

But when he returned home, when he saw that his room was empty, that even the chair on which Pulkheria Ivanovna used to sit had been taken away—he wept, wept hard, wept inconsolably, and tears poured in streams from his lusterless eyes.

That was five years ago. What grief is not taken away by time? What passion will survive an unequal battle with it? I knew a

man in the bloom of his still youthful powers, filled with true nobility and virtue, I knew him when he was in love, tenderly, passionately, furiously, boldly, modestly, and before me, almost before my
eyes, the object of his passion—tender, beautiful as an angel—was
struck down by insatiable death. I never saw such terrible fits of
inner suffering, such furious, scorching anguish, such devouring
despair as shook the unfortunate lover. I never thought a man
could create such a hell for himself, in which there would be no
shadow, no image, nothing in the least resembling hope . . . They
tried to keep an eye on him; they hid all instruments he might
have used to take his own life. Two weeks later he suddenly mastered himself: he began to laugh, to joke; freedom was granted
him, and the first thing he did with it was buy a pistol. One day his
family was terribly frightened by the sudden sound of a shot. They
ran into the room and saw him lying with his brains blown out. A
doctor who happened to be there, whose skill was on everyone's
lips, saw signs of life in him, found that the wound was not quite
mortal, and the man, to everybody's amazement, was healed. The
watch on him was increased still more. Even at table they did not
give him a knife and tried to take away from him anything that
he might strike himself with; but a short while later he found a
new occasion and threw himself under the wheels of a passing carriage. His arm and leg were crushed; but again they saved him. A
year later I saw him in a crowded room; he sat at the card table
gaily saying "*Petite ouverte,*"[13] keeping one card turned down, and
behind him, leaning on the back of his chair, stood his young wife,
who was sorting through his chips.

As I said, five years had passed since Pulkheria Ivanovna's death
when I visited those parts and stopped at Afanasy Ivanovich's
farmstead to call on my old neighbor, with whom I once used to
spend the days pleasantly and always ate too much of the excellent
food prepared by the cordial hostess. As I drove up to the place, the
house seemed twice as old to me, the peasant cottages lay completely on their sides—no doubt just like their owners; the paling
and wattle fence were completely destroyed, and I myself saw the
cook pulling sticks out of it for kindling the stove, when she had
only to go two extra steps to get to the brushwood piled right

there. With sadness I drove up to the porch; the same Rustys and Rovers, blind now or with lame legs, began barking, raising their wavy tails stuck with burrs. An old man came out to meet me. It was he! I recognized him at once; but he was now twice as hunched as before. He recognized me and greeted me with the same familiar smile. I followed him inside; everything there seemed as before, but I noticed a strange disorder in it all, some tangible absence of something or other; in short, I sensed in myself those strange feelings that come over us when for the first time we enter the dwelling of a widower whom we had known before inseparable from his lifelong companion. These feelings are like seeing before us a man we had always known in good health, now lacking a leg. The absence of the solicitous Pulkheria Ivanovna could be seen in everything: at the table one of the knives was lacking a handle; the dishes were no longer prepared with the same artfulness. I did not want to ask about the management and was even afraid to look at the farm works.

When we sat down to eat, a serf girl covered Afanasy Ivanovich with a napkin—and it was very well she did, because otherwise he would have spilled sauce all over his dressing gown. I tried to entertain him by telling him various bits of news; he listened with the same smile, but at times his look was completely insensible, and thoughts did not wander but vanished into it. Often he would raise a spoonful of kasha and, instead of putting it into his mouth, put it to his nose; instead of stabbing a piece of chicken with his fork, he stabbed the decanter, and then the serf girl would take his hand and guide it to the chicken. Sometimes we had to wait several minutes for the next dish. Afanasy Ivanovich would notice it himself and say, "Why are they so long in bringing the food?" But I could see through the chink of the door that the boy who served the food gave no thought to it at all and was asleep with his head on the bench.

"This is the dish," Afanasy Ivanovich said when we were served mnishki[14] with sour cream, "this is the dish," he went on, and I noticed that his voice was beginning to tremble and a tear was about to come from his leaden eyes, while he made every effort to hold it back, "this is the dish that the la——, the la——, the late . . ." and all at once the tears poured down. His hand fell on the plate, the plate overturned, fell off and broke, sauce got all over him; he sat insensibly, insensibly holding his spoon, and like a stream, like a ceaselessly flowing fountain, the tears poured down in torrents onto the napkin covering him.

"God!" I thought, looking at him, "five years of all-destroying time—already an insensible old man, an old man whose life seems never to have been disturbed by a single strong feeling of the soul, whose whole life seems to have consisted entirely of sitting on a high-backed chair, of eating little dried fish and pears, and of good-natured storytelling—and such a long, burning sorrow! And which is stronger in us—passion or habit? Or do all our strong impulses, all the whirlwind of our desires and boiling passions, come merely from our bright youth and seem deep and devastating only because of that?" Be it as it may, just then all our passions seemed childish to me compared with this long, slow, almost insensible habit. Several times he attempted to pronounce the dead woman's name, but halfway through it his calm and ordinary face became convulsively disfigured, and I was struck to the heart by his childlike weeping. No, these were not the tears usually shed so generously by old folk describing their pitiful situation and misfortunes to you; neither were they the tears they weep over a glass of punch—no! these were tears that flowed without the asking, of themselves, stored up in the bitter pain of an already cold heart.

He did not live long after that. I learned of his death recently. It's strange, however, that the circumstances of his end had some resemblance to the death of Pulkheria Ivanovna. One day Afanasy Ivanovich decided to take a little stroll in the garden. As he was slowly walking down the path with his usual unconcern, having no thoughts at all, a strange incident occurred with him. He suddenly heard someone behind him say in a rather distinct voice: "Afanasy Ivanovich!" He turned around, but there was absolutely no one there; he looked in all directions, peeked into the bushes—no one anywhere. It was a calm day and the sun was shining. He pondered for a moment; his face somehow livened up, and he finally said: "It's Pulkheria Ivanovna calling me!"

It has undoubtedly happened to you that you hear a voice calling you by name, something simple people explain by saying that a soul is longing for the person and calling him, and after that comes inevitable death. I confess I have always feared this mysterious call. I remember hearing it often in childhood: sometimes my name would suddenly be distinctly spoken behind me. Usually, at the moment, it was a most clear and sunny day; not a leaf stirred on any tree in the garden, there was a dead silence, even the grasshoppers would stop chirring at that moment; not a soul in the garden; yet I confess that if night, most furious and stormy, with all the inferno of the elements, had overtaken me alone amid an impenetrable forest, I would not have been as frightened of it as of this terrible silence amid a cloudless day. Usually I would flee from the garden then, breathless and in the greatest fear, and would calm down only when I happened to meet somebody whose look would drive away this terrible heart's desert.

He submitted wholly to his soul's conviction that Pulkheria Ivanovna was calling him; he submitted with the will of an obedient child; he wasted away, coughed, dwindled like a candle, and finally went out the way a candle does when there is nothing left to feed its poor flame. "Lay me next to Pulkheria Ivanovna" was all he said before he died.

His wish was fulfilled and he was buried near the church, beside Pulkheria Ivanovna's grave. There were fewer guests at the funeral, but just as many simple folk and beggars. The master's house was now completely empty. The enterprising steward, together with the village headman, dragged over to their own cottages all the remaining old things and junk that the housekeeper had not managed to steal. Soon some distant relation arrived from God knows where, the heir to the whole estate, who before that had served as a lieutenant in I don't remember which regiment, a terrible reformer. He noted at once the utter disorder and neglect in matters of management; he resolved to root it out, to correct it without fail, and to introduce order in everything. He bought six fine English sickles, nailed a special number on each cottage, and finally managed so well that in six months the estate was taken into custody. This wise custody (consisting of a former assessor and some staff captain in a faded uniform) did not take long putting an end to all the chickens and eggs. The cottages, which lay nearly on the ground, collapsed completely; the peasants took to drinking hard and were counted mostly as runaways. The actual owner himself, who incidentally lived quite peaceably with his custody and drank punch with it, rarely visited his estate and never stayed long. To this day he goes to all the fairs in Little Russia, inquires thoroughly into the prices of various major products that are sold wholesale, such as flour, hemp, honey and so on, but buys only small trifles such as little flints, a nail for cleaning his pipe, and generally anything that doesn't go beyond a wholesale price of one rouble.

VIY*

As soon as the booming seminary bell that hung by the gates of the Bratsky Monastery in Kiev rang out in the morning, crowds of schoolboys and seminarians[1] came hurrying from all over the city. Grammarians, rhetoricians, philosophers, and theologians, notebooks under their arms, trudged to class. The grammarians were still very small; as they walked they pushed each other and quarreled among themselves in the thinnest trebles; their clothes were almost all torn or dirty, and their pockets were eternally full of various sorts of trash, such as knucklebones, whistles made from feathers, unfinished pieces of pie, and occasionally even a little sparrow that, by chirping suddenly amidst the extraordinary silence of the classroom, would procure for its patron a decent beating on both hands, and sometimes the cherrywood rod. The rhetoricians walked more sedately: their clothes were often perfectly intact, but instead their faces were almost always adorned with some rhetorical trope: one eye completely closed, or a big

---

*Viy is a colossal creation of folk imagination. This name is applied by people in Little Russia to the chief of the gnomes, whose eyelids reach to the ground. The whole story is a popular legend. I did not wish to change it in any way and tell it almost as simply as I heard it. (Author's note.)

bubble instead of a lip, or some other mark; these swore by God and talked among themselves in tenors. The philosophers dropped a whole octave lower: there was nothing in their pockets except strong, coarse tobacco. They kept nothing stashed away and ate whatever came along on the spot; the smell of pipes and vodka sometimes spread so far around them that a passing artisan would stand for a long time sniffing the air like a hound.

The marketplace at that time was usually just beginning to stir, and women with bagels, rolls, watermelon seeds, and poppyseed cakes tugged those who had them by their coattails of thin broadcloth or some sort of cotton.

"Young sirs! Young sirs! Here! Here!" they said on all sides. "There are good bagels, poppyseed cakes, twists, rolls! Fine ones, by God! with honey! homemade!"

Another woman, holding up something long made of twisted dough, cried:

"Here's an icicle, young sirs! Buy an icicle!"

"Don't buy anything from that one! Look how foul she is—her nose is awful and her hands are dirty . . ."

But they were afraid to pester the philosophers and theologians, because the philosophers and theologians liked to sample things, and always by the handful.

On reaching the seminary, the whole crowd settled by classes in low-ceilinged but rather spacious rooms with small windows, wide doors, and dirty desks. The classroom would suddenly be filled with the hum of many voices: the monitors listened to their charges, the ringing treble of a grammarian would fall in tune with the jingling of the windowpanes in the small windows, the glass echoing with almost the same sound; from the corner came the low buzz of a rhetorician whose mouth and thick lips ought to have belonged to philosophy at the least. He buzzed in a bass, and from afar all you heard was: boo, boo, boo, boo . . . The monitors, as they heard the lessons, looked with one eye under the desk, where a roll or dumpling or pumpkin seeds stuck out of their subordinate's pocket.

If all this learned crowd managed to come a little earlier, or if they knew that the professors would be later than usual, then, with universal agreement, a battle would be planned, and in this battle everyone had to take part, even the censors, whose duty was to look after the order and morals of all the student estate. Usually two theologians decided how the battle would go: whether each class should stand separately for itself, or they should divide themselves into two halves, the boarders and the seminary. In any case, it was the grammarians who would begin it first, but as soon as the rhetoricians mixed in, they would flee and stand on higher ground to watch the battle. Then philosophy with long black mustaches would step forth, and finally theology in terrible ballooning trousers and with the thickest necks. The usual end was that theology would beat them all, and philosophy, rubbing its sides, would be hustled into class, where it settled down to rest at the desks. A professor who had once taken part in such battles himself, on entering the classroom, would know at once from his students' flushed faces that it had been a fine battle, and while he gave the rhetorics a knuckle-rapping, in another class another professor would be applying the wooden slats to the hands of philosophy. With the theologians it was done in a totally different way: each was allotted, as the professor of theology put it, a measure of "big peas," dealt out with a short leather whip.

For feast days and solemnities, the boarders and seminarians went around visiting houses with miracle plays. Sometimes they performed a comedy, and on such occasions some theologian, nearly as tall as the Kiev belfry, would always distinguish himself playing Herodias or the wife of the Egyptian courtier Potiphar.[2] As a reward they might get a length of linen, or a sack of millet, or half a boiled goose, or the like.

All these learned folk, both seminary and boarders, while living in some sort of hereditary hostility among themselves, had extremely poor means of obtaining food and were at the same time extraordinarily voracious; so that to count how many dumplings each of them gobbled up at supper would have been a quite impossible task; and therefore the voluntary donations of wealthy citizens were never enough. Then a senate comprised of philoso-

phers and theologians would send out the grammarians and rhetoricians, under the leadership of one philosopher—and would
sometimes join them itself—sacks over their shoulders, to lay waste
people's kitchen gardens. And pumpkin gruel would appear in the
school. The senators ate so much melon and watermelon that
the monitors would hear two lessons instead of one from them the
next day: one proceeding from the mouth, the other growling in
the senatorial stomach. Boarders and seminary wore what looked
like some sort of long frock coats which reached *heretofore,* a tech-
nical term meaning below the heels.

The most solemn event for the seminary was vacation, beginning with the month of June, when the boarders used to be sent
home. Then the whole high road would be covered with grammarians, philosophers, and theologians. Whoever did not have his
own refuge would go to one of his friends. Philosophers and theologians would go *on conditions*—that is, they would undertake to
teach or prepare the children of wealthy people for school, and
would earn a new pair of boots by it and occasionally enough for a
frock coat. This whole crowd would string along together like a
Gypsy camp, cook kasha[3] for themselves, and sleep in the fields.
Each dragged a sack on his back with a shirt and a pair of foot-
rags. The theologians were especially thrifty and neat: to avoid
wearing out their boots, they would take them off, hang them on a
stick, and carry them over their shoulder, especially when there
was mud. Then, rolling their trousers to the knee, they would go
splashing fearlessly through the puddles. As soon as they caught
sight of a farmstead, they would turn off the high road and,
approaching a cottage that looked better kept than the others,
would line up in front of the windows and begin a full-throated
hymn. The cottager, some old Cossack peasant, would listen to
them for a long time, leaning on both arms, then weep very
bitterly and say, turning to his wife: "Wife! what these students
are singing must be something very intelligent; bring out some
lard for them and whatever else we've got!" And a whole bowl
of dumplings would be poured into a sack. A decent hunk of
lard, a few white loaves, and sometimes even a trussed-up chicken

would go in as well. Fortified with these supplies, the grammarians, rhetoricians, philosophers, and theologians would continue on their way. However, the further they went, the smaller the crowd became. Almost all of them would have reached home, leaving only those whose parental nests were further away than the others.

Once during such a journey three students turned off the high road in order to provide themselves with victuals at the first farmstead they happened upon, because their sack had long been empty. These were: the theologian Khalyava, the philosopher Khoma Brut, and the rhetorician Tiberiy Gorobets.

The theologian was a tall, broad-shouldered man, and of an extremely strange character: whatever lay near him he was sure to steal. On other occasions his character was extremely glum, and when he got drunk he would hide in the weeds, and it would cost the seminary enormous efforts to find him there.

The philosopher Khoma Brut was of a merry disposition. He liked very much to lie about and smoke his pipe. When he drank, he was sure to hire musicians and dance the trepak. He often got a taste of the "big peas," but with perfectly philosophical indifference, saying what will be, will be.

The rhetorician Tiberiy Gorobets did not yet have the right to grow a mustache, drink vodka, and smoke a pipe. All he had was his topknot,[4] and therefore his character was not much developed at that time; but judging by the big bumps on the forehead with which he often came to class, one could suppose he would make a fine warrior. The theologian Khalyava and the philosopher Khoma often pulled him by the topknot as a sign of their patronage and employed him as their deputy.

It was already evening when they turned off the high road. The sun had just gone down and the warmth of the day was still in the air. The theologian and the philosopher walked along silently smoking their pipes; the rhetorician Tiberiy Gorobets knocked the heads off burdocks growing on the roadside with a stick. The road went among stands of oak and hazel bushes that dotted the meadows. The plain was occasionally disrupted by slopes and small hills, green and round as cupolas. A field of ripening grain showed in two places, making it known that some village must soon appear. But it was more than an hour since they had passed the strips of grain and no dwelling had come along yet. Twilight was already darkening the sky, and only in the west was there a pale remnant of vermilion radiance.

"What the devil!" said the philosopher Khoma Brut. "It certainly looked as if there'd be a farmstead."

The theologian said nothing; he looked around, then put his pipe back in his mouth, and they all went on their way.

"By God!" the philosopher said, stopping again. "It's as dark as the devil's fist."

"Maybe there'll be some farm further on," said the theologian, without releasing his pipe.

Meanwhile, however, it was already night, and a rather dark night at that. Clouds made it gloomier still, and by all tokens neither stars nor moon were to be expected. The students noticed that they had lost their way and for a long while had not been walking on the road.

The philosopher, after feeling in all directions with his feet, at last said abruptly:

"But where's the road?"

The theologian pondered silently and observed:

"Yes, it's a dark night."

The rhetorician stepped to one side and tried to feel for the road on all fours, but his hands kept ending up in fox holes. Everywhere there was nothing but steppe where it seemed no one passed. The travelers made another effort to move forward a bit, but everywhere was the same wilderness. The philosopher tried shouting, but his voice was completely muffled on all sides and met no response. Only a little later came a faint wailing that resembled the howling of a wolf.

"Well, what do we do now?" said the philosopher.

"Why, we stay and spend the night in the fields!" said the theologian, and he went to his pocket to get his tinderbox and light up his pipe again. But the philosopher could not agree to that. He had always been in the habit of packing away a ten-pound hunk of bread and some four pounds of lard before going to bed and this time felt a sort of unbearable solitude in his stomach. Besides, for all his merry disposition, the philosopher was somewhat afraid of wolves.

"No, Khalyava, we can't," he said. "What, lie down and stretch out like some dog without fortifying ourselves? Let's try again, maybe we'll happen onto some dwelling and manage to get at least a glass of vodka for the night."

At the word *vodka* the theologian spat to one side and observed: "Sure, there's no point staying in the fields."

The students went on and, to their greatest joy, fancied they heard a distant barking. Figuring out the direction, they listened, set off more cheerfully and, after going a little further, saw a light.

"A farmstead! By God, a farmstead!" said the philosopher.

His anticipation did not disappoint him: in a short while they indeed saw a small farmstead that consisted of just two cottages sharing the same yard. There was light in the windows. A dozen plum trees stuck up by the paling. Peeking through cracks in the boards of the gates, the students saw a yard filled with ox carts. Just then stars appeared here and there in the sky.

"Watch out, brothers, don't hang back! We must get a night's lodging at all costs!"

The three learned men knocked at the gate with one accord and shouted:

"Open up!"

The door of one cottage creaked, and a minute later the students saw before them an old woman in a sheepskin coat.

"Who's there?" she cried with a muffled cough.

"Let us in for the night, granny. We've lost our way. It's as bad out in the fields as it is in a hungry belly."

"And what sort of folk are you?"

"We're harmless folk: the theologian Khalyava, the philosopher Brut, and the rhetorician Gorobets."

"Can't do it," the old woman grumbled. "I've got a yard full of people, and every corner of the cottage is taken. Where will I put you? And such big and hefty folk at that! My cottage will fall apart if I take in the likes of you. I know these philosophers and theologians. Once you start taking in those drunkards, there soon won't be any house. Away! Away with you! There's no room for you here!"

"Have mercy, granny! Can it be that Christian souls must perish for no reason at all? Put us up wherever you like. And if we somehow do something or other—let our arms wither, and whatever else God only knows. There!"

The old woman seemed to soften a little.

"Very well," she said, as if considering, "I'll let you in. Only I'll make you all sleep in different places, for my heart won't be at peace if you lie together."

"That's as you will, we won't object," replied the students.

The gates creaked and they went into the yard.

"Well, granny," said the philosopher, following the old woman, "and what if, as they say . . . by God, it's as if wheels are turning in my stomach. We haven't had a sliver in our mouths since morning."

"See what he's after!" the old woman said. "I've got nothing, nothing like that, and I didn't start the stove all day."

"And tomorrow," the philosopher went on, "we'll pay for it all, well and good, in cash. Yes," he went on softly, "the devil of a cent you'll get!"

"Go on, go on! and be content with what you've got. Such tender young sirs the devil's brought us!"

The philosopher Khoma became utterly despondent at these words. But suddenly his nose caught the scent of dried fish. He glanced at the trousers of the theologian walking beside him and saw an enormous fish tail sticking out of his pocket: the theologian had already managed to snatch a whole carp off a wagon. And since he had done it not for any profit but simply from habit, and, having forgotten his carp completely, was looking around for something else to filch, not intending to overlook even a broken wheel, the philosopher Khoma put his hand into his pocket as if it were his very own and pulled out the carp.

The old woman got the students installed: the rhetorician was put in the cottage, the theologian was shut up in an empty closet, the philosopher was assigned to the sheep pen, also empty.

The philosopher, left alone, ate the carp in one minute, examined the wattled sides of the pen, shoved his foot into the curious snout that a pig had poked through from the next pen, and rolled over on his other side in order to fall into a dead sleep. Suddenly the low door opened and the old woman, stooping down, came into the pen.

"Well, granny, what do you want?" said the philosopher.

But the old woman came toward him with outspread arms.

"Oh-ho!" thought the philosopher. "Only no, dearie, you're obsolete!" He moved slightly further off, but again the old woman unceremoniously came toward him.

"Listen, granny," said the philosopher, "it's a fast period,[5] and I'm the sort of man who won't break his fast even for a thousand gold roubles."

But the old woman kept spreading her arms and grasping for him without saying a word.

The philosopher became frightened, especially when he noticed that her eyes flashed with some extraordinary light.

"Granny! what is it? Go, go with God!" he cried.

But the old woman did not say a word and kept grabbing for him with her arms.

He jumped to his feet, intending to flee, but the old woman stood in the doorway, fixing her flashing eyes on him, and again began to come toward him.

The philosopher wanted to push her away with his hands, but noticed to his astonishment that his arms would not rise, nor would his legs move; with horror he discovered that the sound of his voice would not even come from his mouth: the words stirred soundlessly on his lips. He heard only how his own heart was beating; he saw how the old woman came up to him, folded his arms, bent his neck, jumped with catlike quickness onto his back, struck him on the side with a broom, and he, leaping like a saddle horse, carried her on his back. All this happened so quickly that the philosopher barely managed to recover his senses and seize both his knees with his hands in an effort to stop his legs; but, to his great amazement, they kept moving against his will and performed leaps quicker than a Circassian racer. When they passed the farmstead, and a smooth hollow opened out before them, and the coal-black forest spread out to one side, only then did he say to himself: "Oh-oh, this is a witch!"

A reverse crescent moon shone in the sky. The timid midnight radiance lay lightly as a transparent blanket and steamed over the earth. Forest, meadows, sky, valleys—all seemed to be sleeping with open eyes. Not a flutter of wind anywhere. There was something damply warm in the night's freshness. The shadows of trees and bushes, like comets, fell in sharp wedges over the sloping plain. Such was the night when the philosopher Khoma Brut galloped with an incomprehensible rider on his back. He felt some languid, unpleasant, and at the same time sweet feeling coming into his heart. He lowered his head and saw that the grass, which was almost under his feet, seemed to be growing deep and distant and that over it was water as transparent as a mountain spring, and the grass seemed to be at the deep bottom of some bright, transparent sea; at least he clearly saw his own reflection in it, together with the old woman sitting on his back. He saw some sun shining there instead of the moon; he heard bluebells tinkle, bending their heads. He saw a water nymph swim from behind the sedge; her back and leg flashed, round, lithe, made all of a shining and quivering. She turned toward him, and her face, with its light, sharp, shining eyes, with its soul-invading song, now approached him, was already at the surface, then, shaking with sparkling laughter, withdrew—and then she turned over on her back, and the sun shone through her nebulous breasts, matte as unglazed porcelain, at the edges of their white, tenderly elastic roundness. Water covered them in tiny bubbles like beads. She trembles all over and laughs in the water . . .

Is he seeing it, or is he not? Is he awake or asleep? But what now? Wind or music: ringing, ringing, and whirling, and approaching, and piercing the soul with some unbearable trill . . .

"What is it?" thought the philosopher Khoma Brut, looking down, as he raced on at top speed. Sweat streamed from him. He felt a demonically sweet feeling, he felt some piercing, some languidly terrible pleasure. It often seemed to him as if his heart were no longer there at all, and in fear he would clutch at it with his hand. Exhausted, bewildered, he began to recall all the prayers he ever knew. He ran through all the exorcisms against spirits—and suddenly felt some relief; he felt his step beginning to become lazier, the witch held somehow more weakly to his back. Thick grass touched him, and he no longer saw anything extraordinary in it. The bright crescent shone in the sky.

"All right, then!" thought the philosopher Khoma, and he began saying exorcisms almost aloud. Finally, quick as lightning, he jumped from under the old woman and in his turn leaped on her back. With her small, quick step the old woman ran so fast that the rider could hardly catch his breath. The earth just flashed beneath him. Everything was clear in the moonlight, though the moon was not full. The valleys were smooth, but owing to the speed everything flashed vaguely and confusedly in his eyes. He snatched up a billet lying in the road and started beating the old woman as hard as he could with it. She let out wild screams; first they were angry and threatening, then they turned weaker, more pleasant, pure, and then soft, barely ringing, like fine silver bells, penetrating his soul. A thought flashed inadvertently in his head: Is this really an old woman? "Oh, I can't take any more!" she said in exhaustion and fell to the ground.

He got to his feet and looked into her eyes: dawn was breaking and the golden domes of the Kievan churches shone in the distance. Before him lay a beauty with a disheveled, luxurious braid and long, pointy eyelashes. Insensibly, she spread her bare white arms and moaned, looking up with tear-filled eyes.

Khoma trembled like a leaf on a tree: pity and some strange excitement and timidity, incomprehensible to himself, came over him; he broke into a headlong run. His heart beat uneasily on the way, and he was quite unable to explain to himself this strange new feeling that had come over him. He no longer wanted to go around to the farmsteads and hastened back to Kiev, pondering this incomprehensible incident as he went.

There were almost no students in the city: they had all gone to the farmsteads, either on conditions, or simply without any conditions, because on Little Russian farmsteads one can eat dumplings, cheese, sour cream, fritters as big as a hat, without paying a penny. The big, sprawling house where the boarders lodged was decidedly empty, and thoroughly as the philosopher searched in all the corners, even feeling in all the holes and crannies under the roof, nowhere did he find a piece of bacon or at least an old knish—things usually stashed away by the boarders.

However, the philosopher soon found a solution to his troubles: he strolled, whistling, through the marketplace three times or so, exchanged winks at the very end with some young widow in a yellow cap who sold ribbons, lead shot, and wheels—and that same day was fed wheat dumplings, chicken . . . in a word, there was no counting what lay before him on the table, set in a small clay house amid cherry trees. That same evening the philosopher was seen in the tavern: he was lying on a bench smoking his pipe, as was his custom, and in front of everybody tossed a gold piece to the Jew tavern keeper. Before him stood a mug. He looked at people coming and going with coolly contented eyes and no longer gave any thought to his extraordinary incident.

MEANWHILE, THE RUMOR spread everywhere that the daughter of one of the richest Cossack chiefs, whose farmstead was some thirty-five miles from Kiev, had come home from a walk one day all beaten up, had barely managed to reach her father's house, was now lying near death, and before her dying hour had expressed the wish that the prayers at her deathbed and for three days after her death be read by one of the Kievan seminarians: Khoma Brut. The philosopher learned it from the rector himself, who summoned him specially to his room and announced that he must hasten on his way without delay, that the eminent chief had specially sent people and a cart for him.

The philosopher gave a start from some unaccountable feeling which he could not explain to himself. A dark foreboding told him that something bad lay in store for him. Not knowing why himself, he announced directly that he would not go.

"Listen, *domine* Khoma!"[6] said the rector (on certain occasions he spoke very courteously with his subordinates), "the devil if anyone's asking you whether you want to go or not. I'm telling you only this, that if you keep standing on your mettle and being clever, I'll order you whipped with young birch rods on the back and other parts—so well that you won't need to go to the steam-baths."

The philosopher, scratching lightly behind his ear, walked out without saying a word, intending to trust to his legs at the first opportunity. Deep in thought, he was going down the steep steps to the poplar-ringed courtyard when he stopped for a minute, hearing quite clearly the voice of the rector giving orders to his house-keeper and someone else, probably one of those the chief had sent to fetch him.

"Thank your master for the grain and eggs," the rector was say-ing, "and tell him that as soon as the books he wrote about are ready, I'll send them at once. I've already given them to the scribe for copying. And don't forget, dear heart, to tell the master that I know there are good fish to be had on his farmstead, especially sturgeon, which he can send whenever there's a chance: at the markets here it's expensive and no good. And you, Yavtukh, give the lads a glass of vodka. And tie up the philosopher, otherwise he'll take off."

"Why, that devil's son!" the philosopher thought to himself, "he's got wind of it, the long-legged slicker!"

He went down the steps and saw a kibitka, which at first he took for a granary on wheels. Indeed, it was as deep as a brick kiln. This was an ordinary Krakow vehicle such as Jews hire, fifty of them squeezing in along with their goods, to carry them to every town where their noses smell a fair. He was awaited by some six stalwart and sturdy Cossacks, no longer young men. Jackets of fine flannel with fringe showed that they belonged to a considerable and wealthy owner. Small scars bespoke their having once been to war, not without glory.

"No help for it! What will be, will be!" the philosopher thought to himself and, addressing the Cossacks, said loudly:

"Greetings, friends and comrades!"

"Greetings to you, master philosopher!" some of the Cossacks replied.

"So I'm supposed to get in there with you? A fine wagon!" he went on, climbing in. "Just hire some musicians and you could dance in it!"

"Yes, a commensurate vehicle!" said one of the Cossacks, getting up on the box along with the coachman, who had a rag wrapped around his head instead of his hat, which he had already left in the tavern. The other five, together with the philosopher, climbed deep inside and settled on sacks filled with various purchases made in town.

"I'd be curious to know," said the philosopher, "if this wagon were to be loaded, for example, with certain goods—salt, say, or iron wedges—how many horses would it need?"

"Yes," the Cossack on the box said after some silence, "it would need a sufficient number of horses."

After which satisfactory answer, the Cossack considered he had the right to keep silent the rest of the way.

The philosopher had a great desire to find out in more detail who this chief was, what sort of character he had, what this rumor was about his daughter, who had come home in such an extraordinary fashion and was now dying, and whose story was now connected with his own, how it was with them and what went on in the house? He addressed them with questions; but the Cossacks must also have been philosophers, because they said nothing in reply, lay on the sacks and smoked their pipes. Only one of them addressed the coachman sitting on the box with a brief order: "Keep an eye out, Overko, you old gawk. When you get near the tavern, the one on the Chukhrailovsky road, don't forget to stop, and wake me and the other lads up if we happen to fall asleep." After that he fell rather loudly asleep. However, these admonitions were quite superfluous, because as soon as the gigantic wagon approached the tavern on the Chukhrailovsky road, everybody shouted with one voice: "Stop!" Besides, Overko's horses were already so used to it that they themselves stopped in front of every tavern. Despite the hot July day, everybody got out of the wagon and went into the low, dingy room where the Jew tavern keeper rushed with signs of joy to welcome his old acquaintances. Under his coat skirts the Jew brought several pork sausages and, having placed them on the table, immediately turned away from this Talmud-forbidden fruit. They all settled around the table. A clay mug appeared in front of each guest. The philosopher Khoma had to take part in the general feasting. And since people in Little Russia, once they get a bit merry, are sure to start kissing each other or weeping, the whole place was soon filled with kissing: "Well, now, Spirid, give us a smack!" "Come here, Dorosh, till I embrace you!"

One Cossack who was a bit older than the others, with a gray mustache, rested his cheek on his hand and began sobbing his heart out over his having no father or mother and being left all alone in the world. Another was a great reasoner and kept comforting him, saying: "Don't cry, by God, don't cry! What's this now . . . God, He knows how and what it is." The one named Dorosh became extremely inquisitive and, addressing himself to the philosopher Khoma, kept asking him:

"I'd like to know what they teach you at the seminary—the same as what the deacon reads in church, or something else?"

"Don't ask!" drawled the reasoner. "Let it all be as it has been. God, He knows how it should be; God knows everything."

"No," Dorosh went on, "I want to know what's written in those books. Maybe something completely different from the deacon's."

"Oh, my God, my God!" the esteemed mentor said to that. "What on earth are you talking about? God's will decided it so. It's all as God gave it, they can't go changing it."

"I want to know all what's written there. I'll go to the seminary, by God, I will! What do you think, that I can't learn? I'll learn all of it, all of it!"

"Oh, my God, my goddy God! . . ." the comforter said and lowered his head to the table, because he was quite unable to hold it up on his shoulders any longer.

The other Cossacks talked about landowners and why the moon shines in the sky.

The philosopher Khoma, seeing such a disposition of minds, decided to take advantage of it and slip away. First he addressed the gray-haired Cossack who was grieving over his father and mother:

"What's there to cry about, uncle," he said, "I'm an orphan myself! Let me go free, lads! What do you need me for?"

"Let's set him free!" some replied. "He's an orphan. Let him go where he likes."

"Oh, my God, my goddy God!" the comforter said, raising his head. "Free him! Let him go!"

And the Cossacks were going to take him to the open fields themselves, but the one who showed his curiosity stopped them, saying:

"Hands off! I want to talk to him about the seminary. I'm going to the seminary myself . . ."

Anyhow, this escape could hardly have been accomplished, because when the philosopher decided to get up from the table, his legs turned as if to wood, and he began to see so many doors in the room that it was unlikely he could have found the real one.

Only in the evening did this company all remember that they had to be on their way. Scrambling into the wagon, they drove off, urging their horses on and singing a song, the words and meaning of which could hardly be made out. After spending the better half of the night rambling about, constantly losing the way, which they knew by heart, they finally descended a steep hill into a valley, and the philosopher noticed a palisade or wattle fence stretching along the sides, low trees and roofs peeking from behind them. This was the big settlement belonging to the chief. It was long past midnight; the sky was dark and small stars flashed here and there. There was no light in any of the huts. Accompanied by the barking of a dog, they drove into the yard. On both sides thatch-roofed sheds and cottages could be seen. One of them, in the middle, directly facing the gates, was bigger than the rest and seemed to be the owner's dwelling. The wagon stopped before something like a small shed, and our travelers went to sleep. The philosopher, however, wanted to look the master's mansion over a little; but however wide he opened his eyes, he could see nothing clearly: instead of the house, he saw a bear; the chimney turned into a rector. The philosopher waved his hand and went to sleep.

When the philosopher woke up, the whole house was astir: during the night the master's daughter had died. Servants ran to and fro in a flurry. Some old woman cried. A crowd of the curious looked through the fence into the master's yard, as if there was anything to be seen there.

The philosopher began leisurely to examine the places he had been unable to make out at night. The master's house was a small, low building such as was commonly built in Little Russia in the old days. It had a thatched roof. The sharp and high little pediment, with a small window resembling an upturned eye, was painted all over with blue and yellow flowers and red crescents. It was held up by oak posts, the upper half rounded and the lower hexagonal, with fancy turning at the tops. Under this pediment was a small porch with benches on both sides. At the ends of the house were shed roofs on the same sort of posts, some of them twisted. A tall pear tree with a pyramidal top and trembling leaves greened in front of the house. Several barns stood in two rows in the yard, forming a sort of wide street leading to the house. Beyond the barns, toward the gates, the triangles of two cellars stood facing each other, also roofed with thatch. The triangular wall of each was furnished with a door and painted over with various images. On one of them a Cossack was portrayed sitting on a barrel, holding a mug over his head with the inscription: "I'll Drink It All." On the other, a flask, bottles, and around them, for the beauty of it, an upside-down horse, a pipe, tambourines, and the inscription: "Drink—the Cossack's Delight." From the loft of one of the barns, through an enormous dormer window, peeked a drum and some brass trumpets. By the gates stood two cannon. Everything showed that the master of the house liked to make merry and that the yard often resounded with the noise of feasting. Outside the gates were two windmills. Behind the house ran the gardens; and through the treetops one could see only the dark caps of chimneys hiding in the green mass of cottages. The entire settlement was situated on a wide and level mountain ledge. To the north everything was screened off by a steep mountain, the foot of which came right down to the yard. Looked at from below, it seemed steeper still, and on its high top the irregular stems of skimpy weeds stuck out here and there, black against the bright sky. Its bare and clayey appearance evoked a certain despondency. It was all furrowed with gullies and grooves left by rain. In two places, cottages were stuck to its steep slope; over one of them an apple tree, propped by small stakes and a mound of dirt at its roots, spread its branches broadly. Windfallen apples rolled right down into the master's yard. From the top a road wound down all over the mountain and in its descent went past the yard into the settlement. When the philosopher measured its terrible steepness and remembered the previous day's journey, he decided that either the master's horses were very smart or the Cossacks' heads were very strong to have managed, even in drunken fumes, not to tumble down head first along with the boundless wagon and the baggage. The philosopher stood on the highest point of the yard, and when he turned and looked in the opposite direction, he was presented with a totally different sight. The settlement, together with the slope, rolled down onto a plain. Vast meadows opened out beyond the reach of sight; their bright greenery became darker in the distance, and whole rows of villages blued far off, though they were more than a dozen miles away. To the right of these meadows, mountains stretched and the distant, barely noticeable strip of the Dnieper burned and darkled.

"Ah, a fine spot!" said the philosopher. "To live here, to fish in the Dnieper and the ponds, to take a net or a gun and go hunting for snipe and curlew! Though I suppose there's also no lack of bustards in these meadows. Quantities of fruit can be dried and sold in town or, even better, distilled into vodka—because no liquor can touch vodka made from fruit. And it also wouldn't hurt to consider how to slip away from here."

He noticed a small path beyond the wattle fence, completely overgrown with weeds. He mechanically stepped onto it, thinking at first only of taking a stroll, and then of quietly blowing out between the cottages into the meadows, when he felt a rather strong hand on his shoulder.

Behind him stood the same old Cossack who had grieved so bitterly yesterday over the death of his mother and father and his own loneliness.

"You oughtn't to be thinking, master philosopher, about skipping from the farmstead!" he said. "It's not set up here so as you can run away; and the roads are bad for walking. Better go to the master: he's been waiting for you a long time in his room."

"Let's go! Why not? . . . It's my pleasure," said the philosopher, and he followed after the Cossack.

The chief, an elderly man with a gray mustache and an expression of gloomy sorrow, was sitting at a table in his room, his head propped in both hands. He was about fifty years old; but the deep despondency on his face and a sort of wasted pallor showed that his soul had been crushed and destroyed all of a sudden, in a single moment, and all the old gaiety and noisy life had disappeared forever. When Khoma came in together with the old Cossack, he took away one of his hands and nodded slightly to their low bow.

Khoma and the Cossack stopped respectfully by the door.

"Who are you, and where from, and of what estate, good man?" the chief said, neither kindly nor sternly.

"I'm the philosopher Khoma Brut, a student."

"And who was your father?"

"I don't know, noble sir."

"And your mother?"

"I don't know my mother, either. Reasonably considering, of course, there was a mother; but who she was, and where from, and when she lived—by God, your honor, I don't know."

The chief paused and seemed to sit pondering for a moment.

"And how did you become acquainted with my daughter?"

"I didn't become acquainted, noble sir, by God, I didn't. I've never had any dealings with young ladies in all my born days. Deuce take them, not to say something improper."

"Then why was it none other than you, precisely, that she appointed to read?"

The philosopher shrugged his shoulders:

"God knows how to explain that. It's a known fact that masters sometimes want something that even the most literate man can't figure out. And as the saying goes: 'Hop faster, mind the master!'"

"And you wouldn't happen to be lying, mister philosopher?"

"May lightning strike me right here if I'm lying."

"If you'd lived only one little minute longer," the chief said sadly, "I'd surely have learned everything. 'Don't let anybody read over me, daddy, but send to the Kiev seminary at once and bring the student Khoma Brut. Let him pray three nights for my sinful soul. He knows . . .' But what he knows, I didn't hear. She, dear soul, could only say that, and then she died. Surely, good man, you must be known for your holy life and God-pleasing deeds, and maybe she heard about you."

"Who, me?" the student said, stepping back in amazement. "Me, a holy life?" he said, looking the chief straight in the eye. "God help you, sir! Indecent though it is to say, I went calling on the baker's wife on Holy Thursday itself."

"Well . . . surely you were appointed for some reason. You'll have to start the business this same day."

"To that, your honor, I'd reply . . . of course, anybody versed in Holy Scripture could commensurably . . . only here it would call for a deacon, or at least a subdeacon. They're smart folk and know how it's done, while I . . . And I haven't got the voice for it, and myself I'm—devil knows what. Nothing to look at."

"That's all very well, only I'll do everything my little dove told me to do, I won't leave anything out. And once you've prayed over her properly for three nights, starting today, I'll reward you. Otherwise—I wouldn't advise even the devil himself to make me angry."

The chief uttered these last words with such force that the philosopher fully understood their meaning.

"Follow me!" said the chief.

They stepped out to the front hall. The chief opened the door to another room opposite the first. The philosopher stopped in the hall for a moment to blow his nose and then with some unaccountable fear crossed the threshold. The whole floor was covered with red cotton cloth. In the corner, under the icons, on a high table, lay the body of the dead girl, on a cover of blue velvet adorned with gold fringe and tassels. Tall wax candles twined with guelder rose stood at her head and feet, shedding their dim light, lost in the brightness of day. The face of the dead girl was screened from him by the disconsolate father, who sat before her, his back to the door. The philosopher was struck by the words he heard:

"I'm not sorry, my darling daughter, that you, to my sorrow and grief, have left the earth in the flower of your youth, without living out your allotted term. I'm sorry, my little dove, that I do not know who it was, what wicked enemy of mine, that caused your death. And if I knew of anyone who might only think of insulting you or just of saying something unpleasant about you, I swear to

God he would never see his children again, if he happened to be as old as I am, or his father and mother, if he was still a young man; and his body would be thrown to the birds and beasts of the steppe. But woe is me, my wild marigold, my little quail, my bright star, that I must live out the rest of my life with no delight, wiping the tears with my coattails as they flow from my aged eyes, while my enemy rejoices and laughs secretly at the feeble old man . . ."

He stopped, and the reason for it was the rending grief that resolved itself in a whole flood of tears.

The philosopher was moved by such inconsolable sorrow. He coughed and gave a muffled grunt, wishing thereby to clear his voice a little.

The chief turned and pointed to the place at the dead girl's head, before a small lectern on which some books lay.

"I can do the three nights' work somehow," thought the philosopher, "and the master will fill both my pockets with gold coins for it."

He approached and, clearing his throat once more, began to read, paying no attention to anything around him and not daring to look into the dead girl's face. A deep silence settled in. He noticed that the chief had left. Slowly he turned his head to look at the dead girl, and . . .

A shudder ran through his veins: before him lay a beauty such as there had never been on earth. It seemed that facial features had never before been assembled into such sharp yet harmonious beauty. She lay as if alive. Her brow, beautiful, tender, like snow, like silver, seemed thoughtful; her eyebrows—night amid a sunny day, thin, regular—rose proudly over her closed eyes, and her eyelashes, falling pointy on her cheeks, burned with the heat of hidden desires; her mouth—rubies about to smile . . . Yet in them, in these same features, he saw something terribly piercing. He felt his soul begin to ache somehow painfully, as if, in the whirl of merriment and giddiness of a crowd, someone suddenly struck up a song about oppressed people. The rubies of her mouth seemed to make the blood scald his heart. Suddenly something terribly familiar showed in her face.

"The witch!" he cried out in a voice not his own, looked away, turned pale, and began reading his prayers.

It was the very witch he had killed.

When the sun began to set, the dead girl was taken to the church. The philosopher supported the black-draped coffin with one shoulder, and on that shoulder he felt something cold as ice. The chief himself walked in front, bearing the right side of the dead girl's cramped house. The blackened wooden church, adorned with green moss and topped by three conical cupolas, stood desolate almost at the edge of the village. One could see it was long since any service had been celebrated in it. Candles burned before almost every icon. The coffin was placed in the middle, right in front of the altar. The old chief kissed the dead girl once more, made a prostration, and walked out together with the bearers, ordering the philosopher to be given a good meal and taken to the church after supper. Going into the kitchen, all those who had carried the coffin started touching the stove, something people in Little Russia have the custom of doing after they see a dead body.

The hunger that the philosopher began to feel just then made him forget all about the deceased for a few moments. Soon all the household servants began gradually to gather in the kitchen. The kitchen of the chief's house was something like a club, to which everything that inhabited the yard flowed, including the dogs, who came right up to the door wagging their tails for bones and scraps. Wherever anyone might be sent, on whatever errand, he would always stop at the kitchen first, to rest on a bench for a moment and smoke a pipe. The bachelors who lived in the house and paraded around in Cossack blouses all lay about here for almost the whole day, on the benches, under the benches, on the stove—in short, wherever they could find a comfortable place to lie. Besides, everybody was forever forgetting something in the kitchen—a hat, a knout for stray dogs, or the like. But the most numerous gathering was at suppertime, when the horseherd came after rounding up all his horses, and the cowherd after bringing the cows home for milking, and all the rest who were not to be seen in the course of the day. During supper, loquacity would come to the most taciturn tongues. Here everything was usually talked about: someone who was having new trousers made for himself . . . and what was inside the earth . . . and someone who had seen a wolf . . . There were numerous *bonmotists*[7] here, of whom there is no lack among the people of Little Russia.

The philosopher sat down with the others in a wide circle under the open sky in front of the kitchen porch. Soon a woman in a red cap stuck herself out the door holding a hot pot of dumplings with both hands, and placed it in the midst of those ready to eat. Each of them took a wooden spoon from his pocket, or some, lacking a spoon, a splinter of wood. As soon as the mouths began to move a bit more slowly and the wolfish appetite of the whole gathering subsided a little, many began to talk. The talk naturally had to turn to the dead girl.

"Is it true," said one young shepherd, who had stuck so many buttons and brass badges on his leather pipe strap that he looked like a mercer's shop, "is it true that the young miss, not to speak ill of her, kept company with the unclean one?"

"Who? The young miss?" said Dorosh, already known to our philosopher. "But she was a downright witch! I'll swear she was a witch!"

"Enough, enough, Dorosh!" said another, the one who had shown such readiness to give comfort during the trip. "God help them, it's none of our business. No point in talking about it."

But Dorosh was not at all disposed to be silent. He had only just gone to the cellar with the steward on some necessary business and, after bending a couple of times to two or three barrels, had come out extremely cheerful and talking nonstop.

"What do you want? For me to keep quiet?" he said. "But she rode on me, on me myself! By God, she did!"

"And what, uncle," said the young shepherd with the buttons, "are there some tokens you can tell a witch by?"

"No," answered Dorosh. "There's no way to tell. Read through all the psalters, you still won't be able to tell."

"You can, too, Dorosh. Don't say that," said the same comforter. "Not for nothing did God give everybody a special trait. People who've got some learning say witches have little tails."

"When a woman's old, she's a witch," the gray-haired Cossack said coolly.

"Ah, you're a good lot, too!" picked up the woman, who was just then pouring fresh dumplings into the emptied pot. "Real fat boars!"

The old Cossack, whose name was Yavtukh but who was nick-named Kovtun, showed a smile of pleasure on his lips, seeing that his words had struck the old woman to the quick; and the cowherd let out such dense laughter as if two bulls, facing each other, had bellowed at once.

The beginning conversation awakened an irrepressible desire and curiosity in the philosopher to learn more in detail about the chief's deceased daughter. And therefore, wishing to bring him back to the former matter, he addressed his neighbor with these words:

"I wanted to ask, why is it that all the folk sitting here over sup-per consider the young miss a witch? What, did she cause some evil or put a hex on somebody or other?"

"There were all kinds of things," replied one of the seated men, with a smooth face extremely like a shovel.

"And who doesn't remember the huntsman Mikita, or that . . ."

"And what about the huntsman Mikita?" said the philosopher.

"Wait! I'll tell about the huntsman Mikita," said Dorosh.

"I'll tell about Mikita," said the herdsman, "because he was my chum."

"I'll tell about Mikita," said Spirid.

"Let him! Let Spirid tell it!" shouted the crowd.

Spirid began:

"You, mister philosopher Khoma, didn't know Mikita. Ah, what a rare man he was! He knew every dog like his own father, so he did. The present huntsman Mikola, who's sitting third down from me, can't hold a candle to him. He also knows his business, but next to Mikita he's trash, slops."

"You're telling it good, really good!" said Dorosh, nodding approvingly.

Spirid went on:

"He'd spot a rabbit quicker than you could take a pinch of snuff.

He'd whistle: 'Here, Robber! Here, Racer!' and be off at full speed
on his horse, and there'd be no telling whether he was ahead of the
dog or the dog ahead of him. He'd toss off a pint of rotgut as if
it had never been there. A fine huntsman he was! Only in more
recent days he started staring at the young miss all the time. Either
he was really smitten, or she'd put a spell on him, only it was the
end of the man, he went all soft, turned into devil knows what—
pah! it's even indecent to say it."

"Good," said Dorosh.

"The young miss would no sooner glance at him than he'd drop
the bridle, call Robber Grouchy, stumble all over, and do God
knows what. Once the young miss came to the stable where he
was grooming a horse. 'Mikitka,' she says, 'let me lay my little leg
on you.' And he, the tomfool, gets all happy. 'Not only your little
leg,' he says, 'you can sit right on me.' The young miss lifted up her
leg, and when he saw her bare leg, white and plump, the charm,
he says, just stunned him. He bent his back, the tomfool, grabbed
her bare legs with both hands, and went galloping like a horse
all over the fields. And he couldn't tell anything about where
they rode, only he came back barely alive, and after that he got all
wasted, like a chip of wood. And once, when they came to the stable, instead of him there was just a heap of ashes and an empty
bucket lying there: he burned up, burned up of his own self. And
what a huntsman he was, you won't find another like him in the
whole world."

When Spirid finished his story, talk came from all sides about
the merits of the former huntsman.

"And have you heard about Shepchikha?" said Dorosh, addressing Khoma.

"No."

"Oh-ho! Then it's clear they don't teach you much sense there
in your seminary. Well, listen! In our settlement there's a Cossack
named Sheptun. A good Cossack! He likes to steal or tell a lie
sometimes without any need, but . . . a good Cossack! His place
isn't far from here. At this same time as we're now having supper,
Sheptun and his wife finished eating and went to bed, and since
the weather was fine, Shepchikha slept outside and Sheptun inside

on a bench; or, no, it was Shepchikha inside on a bench and Sheptun outside . . ."

"And not on a bench, Shepchikha lay on the floor," the woman
picked up, standing in the doorway, her cheek propped on her
hand.

Dorosh looked at her, then at the floor, then at her again, and
after a pause said:

"When I pull your underwear off in front of everybody, it won't
be so nice."

This warning had its effect. The old woman fell silent and did
not interrupt anymore.

Dorosh went on.

"And in a cradle that hung in the middle of the hut lay their
one-year-old baby—I don't know whether of male or female sex.
Shepchikha lay there, and then she heard a dog scratching outside
the door and howling so loud you just wanted to flee the house.
She got frightened—for women are such foolish folk that you
could stick your tongue out at her behind the door at night and
she'd have her heart in her mouth. 'Anyhow,' she thinks, 'why
don't I go and hit the cursed dog in the snout, maybe it'll stop
howling.' And taking her poker, she went to open the door. As
soon as it was slightly open, the dog darted between her legs and
went straight for the baby's cradle. Shepchikha saw that it was no
longer a dog but the young miss. And if it had been the young miss
looking the way she knew her, it would have been nothing; but
there was this one thing and circumstance: that she was all blue and
her eyes were burning like coals. She grabbed the baby, bit its
throat, and began drinking its blood. Shepchikha only cried out,
'Ah, evil thing!' and fled. But she saw that the front doors were
locked. She ran to the attic. The foolish woman sat there trembling, and then she saw that the young miss was coming to the
attic. She fell on the foolish woman and started biting her. It was
morning before Sheptun got his wife out of there, blue and bitten
all over. And the next day the foolish woman died. That's what
arrangements and temptations can happen! Though she's the master's progeny, all the same a witch is a witch."

After this story, Dorosh looked around smugly and poked his forefinger into his pipe, preparing to fill it with tobacco. The material about the witch became inexhaustible. Each in turn hastened to tell something. The witch drove right up to the door of one man's house in the form of a haystack; she stole another's hat or pipe; cut off the braids of many village girls; drank several buckets of blood from others.

At last the whole company came to their senses and saw that they had been talking too much, because it was already quite dark outside. They all began trudging off to sleep, putting themselves either in the kitchen, or in the sheds, or in the middle of the yard.

"Well, now, Mr. Khoma, it's time we went to the deceased," said the gray-haired Cossack, turning to the philosopher, and the four of them, Spirid and Dorosh included, went to the church, swinging their knouts at the dogs, of which there were a great many and which angrily bit at their sticks.

The philosopher, though he had fortified himself with a good mug of vodka, secretly felt timorousness creeping over him as they drew near the lighted church. The tales and strange stories he had heard helped to affect his imagination still more. The darkness under the paling and trees began to thin; the place was becoming more bare. They finally stepped past the decrepit church fence into the small yard, beyond which there were no trees and nothing opened out but empty fields and meadows swallowed by the darkness of night. Together with Khoma, the three Cossacks climbed the steep steps of the porch and went into the church. Here they left the philosopher, having wished him a successful performance of his duty, and locked the door on him as the master had ordered.

The philosopher remained alone. First he yawned, then stretched himself, then blew on both hands, and finally looked around. In the middle stood the black coffin. Candles flickered before dark icons. Their light illumined only the iconostasis[8] and, faintly, the middle of the church. The far corners of the vestibule were shrouded in darkness. The tall, ancient iconostasis showed a profound decrepitude; its openwork, covered in gold, now gleamed only in sparks. The gilding had fallen off in some places, and was quite blackened in others; the faces of the saints, completely darkened, looked somehow gloomy. The philosopher glanced around once more.

"Why," he said, "what's frightening about it? No man can get in here, and against the dead and visitors from the other world I've got such prayers that, once I've read them, they'll never lay a finger on me. Nothing to it," he said with a wave of the hand, "let's read!"

Going up to the choir, he saw several bundles of candles.

"That's good," thought the philosopher, "I must light up the whole church so that it's bright as day. Ah, too bad I can't smoke my pipe in God's church!"

And he began sticking wax candles to all the ledges, lecterns, and icons, not stinting in the least, and soon the whole church was filled with light. Only the darkness above seemed to become deeper, and the dark images looked more gloomily from the old carved frames on which gold gleamed here and there. He went up to the coffin, timidly looked into the dead girl's face, and could not help shutting his eyes with a slight start.

Such terrible, dazzling beauty!

He turned and wanted to step away; but with strange curiosity, with the strange, self-contradictory feeling that will not leave a man especially in a time of fear, he could not refrain from glancing at her as he went, and then, with the same feeling of trepidation, glancing once more. Indeed, the deceased girl's sharp beauty seemed frightful. Perhaps she even would not have struck him with such panic terror if she had been slightly ugly. But there was in her features nothing dull, lusterless, dead. The face was alive, and it seemed to the philosopher that she was looking at him through closed eyes. It even seemed to him that a tear rolled from under her right eyelash, and when it stopped on her cheek, he made out clearly that it was a drop of blood.

He hastily went over to the choir, opened the book and, to cheer himself up, began reading in his loudest voice. His voice struck the wooden walls of the church, long silent and deaf. Solitary, without echo, it poured in a low bass into the utterly dead silence and seemed a little wild even to the reader himself.

"What's there to be afraid of?" he thought to himself meanwhile. "She won't get up from her coffin, because she'll be afraid of God's word. Let her lie there! And what kind of Cossack am I if I'm scared? So I drank a bit—that's why it seems so frightening. If I could take some snuff—ah, fine tobacco! Nice tobacco! Good tobacco!"

And yet, as he turned each page, he kept glancing sidelong at the coffin, and an involuntary feeling seemed to whisper to him: "Look, look, she's going to get up, she's going to rise, she's going to peek out of the coffin!"

But there was a deathly silence. The coffin stood motionless. The candles poured out a whole flood of light. Terrible is a lit-up church at night, with a dead body and not a living soul!

Raising his voice, he began singing in various voices, trying to stifle the remnants of his fear. Yet he turned his eyes to the coffin every other moment, as if asking the inadvertent question: "What if she rises, what if she gets up?"

But the coffin did not stir. If only there was a sound, some living being, even the chirp of a cricket in the corner! There was just the slight sizzle of some remote candle and the faint spatter of wax dripping on the floor.

"Well, what if she gets up? . . ."

She raised her head . . .

He gazed wildly and rubbed his eyes. But she was indeed no longer lying but sitting up in the coffin. He turned his eyes away, then again looked with horror at the coffin. She's standing up . . . she's walking through the church with her eyes closed, constantly spreading her arms as if wishing to catch someone.

She was walking straight toward him. In fear he drew a circle around himself. With an effort he began reading prayers and reciting the incantations that had been taught him by one monk who had seen witches and unclean spirits all his life.

She stood almost on the line itself; but it was clearly beyond her power to cross it, and she turned all blue, like someone dead for several days. Khoma did not have the courage to look at her. She was frightful. She clacked her teeth and opened her dead eyes. But, seeing nothing, she turned in the other direction with a fury that showed in her twitching face and, spreading her arms, clutched with them at every pillar and corner, trying to catch Khoma. Finally she stopped, shook her finger, and lay down in her coffin.

The philosopher still could not come to his senses and kept glancing fearfully at the witch's cramped dwelling. Finally the coffin suddenly tore from its place and with a whistle began flying all through the church, crossing the air in every direction. The philosopher saw it almost over his head, but at the same time he saw that it could not enter the circle he had drawn, so he stepped up his incantations. The coffin crashed down in the middle of the church and remained motionless. The corpse again rose up from it, blue, turning green. But just then came the distant crowing of a cock. The corpse sank back into the coffin and the coffin lid slammed shut.

The philosopher's heart was pounding and sweat streamed from him; but, encouraged by the crowing of the cock, he quickly finished reading the pages he ought to have read earlier. At daybreak he was relieved by the beadle and gray-haired Yavtukh, who on this occasion performed the duties of a church warden.

Having gone to lie down, the philosopher was unable to fall asleep for a long time, but fatigue overcame him and he slept till dinner. When he woke up, all the events of the night seemed to have happened in a dream. To bolster his strength, he was given a pint of vodka. At dinner he quickly relaxed, contributed observations on this and that, and ate a rather mature pig almost by himself. However, he did not venture to speak of his experiences in the church, from some feeling unaccountable to himself, and, to the questions of the curious, replied: "Yes, there were all sorts of wonders." The philosopher was one of those people in whom, once they have been fed, an extraordinary philanthropy awakens. Pipe in his teeth, he lay looking at them all with extraordinarily sweet eyes and kept spitting to the side.

After dinner the philosopher was in the highest spirits. He managed to walk about the whole village and make the acquaintance of nearly everybody; he was even chased out of two cottages; one comely young wench gave him a decent whack on the back with a shovel when he decided to feel and find out what kind of material her blouse and kirtle were made of. But the closer it came to evening, the more pensive the philosopher grew. An hour before supper, almost all the household people would gather to play *kasha* or *kragli*—a variety of skittles in which long sticks are used instead of balls and the winner has the *right to ride on his partner's back.* Then the game would become very interesting for the spectator: often the cowherd, broad as a pancake, got astride the swineherd, puny, short, consisting of nothing but wrinkles. Another time the cowherd would bend his back and Dorosh would jump onto it, always saying: "Hey, what a hefty bull!" Those who were more sober-minded sat by the kitchen porch. They had an extremely serious air as they smoked their pipes, even when the young people laughed heartily over some witticism of the cowherd or Spirid. In vain did Khoma try to take part in this fun: some dark thought, like a nail, was lodged in his head. Over supper, hard though he tried to cheer himself up, fear kindled in him as darkness spread over the sky.

"Well, our time has come, mister student!" the familiar gray-haired Cossack said to him, getting up from his place together with Dorosh. "Let's go to work."

Khoma was again taken to the church in the same way; again he was left alone, and the door was locked on him. No sooner was he left alone than timorousness began once more to creep into his breast. Again he saw the dark icons, the gleaming frames, and the familiar black coffin standing in menacing silence and immobility in the middle of the church.

"Well," he said, "this marvel doesn't make me marvel now. It's only frightening the first time. Yes! it's only a little frightening the first time, and then it's not frightening anymore, not frightening at all."

He hastened to the choir, drew a circle around himself, spoke several incantations, and began reading loudly, resolved not to raise his eyes from the book or pay attention to anything. He had been reading for about an hour already, and had begun to weary and to cough a little. He took a snuff bottle from his pocket and, before taking a pinch, timorously turned his gaze to the coffin. His heart went cold.

The corpse was already standing before him, right on the line, fixing her dead green eyes on him. The student shuddered and felt a chill run through all his veins. Dropping his eyes to the book, he began reading his prayers and exorcisms louder and heard the corpse clack her teeth again and wave her arm, wishing to seize him. But, looking out of the corner of one eye, he saw that the corpse was trying to catch him in the wrong place and evidently could not see him. She was growling hollowly, and began to utter dreadful words with her dead lips; they spluttered hoarsely, like the gurgling of boiling pitch. He could not have said what they meant, but something dreadful was contained in them. The philosopher fearfully realized that she was reciting incantations.

Wind swept through the church at these words, and there was a noise as of a multitude of fluttering wings. He heard wings beating against the glass of the church windows and their iron frames, heard claws scratching iron with a rasping noise and countless powers banging on the doors, trying to break in. His heart pounded heavily all the while; shutting his eyes, he kept reading incantations and prayers. At last something suddenly whistled far away. It was the distant crowing of a cock. The exhausted philosopher stopped and rested his soul.

Those who came to relieve the philosopher found him barely alive. He was leaning back against the wall, goggle-eyed, and stared fixedly at the Cossacks who where shaking him. They practically carried him out and had to support him all the way. Coming to the master's yard, he roused himself and asked to be given a pint of vodka. After drinking it, he smoothed the hair on his head and said:

"There's all sorts of trash in this world! And such horrors happen as—oh, well . . ." At that the philosopher waved his hand.

The circle that had gathered around him hung their heads on hearing such words. Even the young boy whom all the servants considered their rightful representative when it came to such matters as cleaning the stables or toting water, even this poor boy also stood gaping.

Just then a not entirely old wench passed by in a tight-fitting apron that displayed her round and firm shape, the old cook's assistant, a terrible flirt, who always found something to pin to her cap—a bit of ribbon, or a carnation, or even a scrap of paper if there was nothing else.

"Greetings, Khoma!" she said, seeing the philosopher. "Ai-yai-yai! what's happened to you?" she cried out, clasping her hands.

"What do you mean, foolish woman?"

"Ah, my God! But you've gone all gray!"

"Oh-oh! And it's the truth she's telling!" said Spirid, studying him intently. "You've really gone all gray like our old Yavtukh."

On hearing this, the philosopher rushed headlong to the kitchen, where he had noticed a triangular piece of mirror glued to the wall and stained by flies, in front of which forget-me-nots, periwinkles, and even a garland of marigolds were stuck, showing that it was intended for the stylish flirt's toilette. He saw with horror the truth of their words: half of his hair had indeed turned white.

Khoma Brut hung his head and gave himself over to reflection.

"I'll go to the master," he said finally, "tell him everything, and explain that I don't want to read anymore. Let him send me back to Kiev right now."

In such thoughts, he directed his steps toward the porch of the master's house.

The chief was sitting almost motionless in his room; the same hopeless sorrow that the philosopher had met on his face earlier remained there still. Only his cheeks were much more sunken than before. It was clear that he had taken very little food, or perhaps not touched anything at all. His extraordinary pallor gave him a sort of stony immobility.

"Greetings, poor lad," he said, seeing Khoma, who stood hat in hand in the doorway. "Well, how is it with you? Everything fine?"

"Fine, fine indeed. Such devilish goings-on, I'd like to just grab my hat and flee wherever my legs will take me."

"How's that?"

"It's your daughter, sir . . . Reasonably considering, of course, she's of noble birth; nobody will maintain the contrary; only, not to anger you by saying so, God rest her soul . . ."

"What about my daughter?"

"She's had some dealings with Satan. Giving me such horrors that I can't read any scriptures."

"Read, read! It was not for nothing that she called you. She was worried about her soul, my little dove, and wished to drive away all wicked thoughts by prayer."

"Have it your way, sir—by God, it's too much for me!"

"Read, read!" the chief went on in the same admonitory voice. "You've got one night left now. You'll do a Christian deed, and I'll reward you."

"Rewards or no rewards . . . As you like, sir, only I won't read!" Khoma said resolutely.

"Listen, philosopher!" said the chief, and his voice grew strong and menacing, "I don't like these notions. You can do that in your seminary, but not with me: I'll give you such a thrashing as your rector never gave. Do you know what a good leather whip is?"

"How could I not!" said the philosopher, lowering his voice. "Everybody knows what a leather whip is: an insufferable thing in large quantities."

"Yes. Only you still don't know what a scotching my boys can deliver!" the chief said menacingly, getting to his feet, and his face acquired an imperious and ferocious expression that revealed all his unbridled character, only temporarily lulled by sorrow. "First they'll scotch you for me, then douse you with vodka, then start over. Go, go! do your business! If you don't, you won't get up; if you do—a thousand pieces of gold!"

"Oh-ho-ho! Some customer!" the philosopher thought, going out. "No joking with this one. Just you wait, brother: I'll cut and run so fast your dogs will never catch me."

And Khoma resolved to escape without fail. He only waited till the time after dinner, when the household people all had the habit of getting into the hay under the sheds and producing, open-mouthed, such a snoring and piping that the yard came to resemble a factory. This time finally came. Even Yavtukh stretched out in the sun, his eyes closed. In fear and trembling, the philosopher quietly went to the garden, from where it seemed to him it would be easier and less conspicuous to escape into the fields. This garden, as commonly happens, was terribly overgrown and thus highly conducive to any secret undertaking. Except for one path beaten down on household necessity, the rest was hidden by thickly spreading cherry trees, elders, burdock that stuck its tall stalks with clingy pink knobs way up. Hops covered the top of this whole motley collection of trees and bushes like a net, forming a roof above them that spread over to the wattle fence and hung down it in twining snakes along with wild field bluebells. Beyond the wattle fence that served as a boundary to the garden, there spread a whole forest of weeds which no one seemed to be interested in, and a scythe would have broken to pieces if it had decided to put its blade to their thick, woody stems.

As the philosopher went to step over the wattle fence, his teeth chattered and his heart pounded so hard that it frightened him. The skirt of his long chlamys seemed stuck to the ground, as if someone had nailed it down. As he was stepping over, it seemed to him that some voice rattled in his ears with a deafening whistle: "Where to, where to?" The philosopher flitted into the weeds and broke into a run, constantly stumbling over old roots and crushing moles underfoot. He could see that once he got through the weeds, all he had to do was run across a field, beyond which darkled a thicket of blackthorn, where he reckoned he would be safe, and passing through which he supposed he would come to the road straight to Kiev. He ran across the field at once and wound up amid the dense blackthorns. He got through the blackthorns, leaving pieces of his frock coat on every sharp thorn in lieu of a toll, and found himself in a small hollow. A pussy willow spread its hanging branches almost to the ground. A small spring shone pure as silver. The philosopher's first business was to lie down and drink his fill, because he felt unbearably thirsty.

"Good water!" he said, wiping his mouth. "I could rest here."

"No, better keep running. You might have somebody after you."

These words came from above his ears. He turned: before him stood Yavtukh.

"Yavtukh, you devil!" the philosopher thought to himself. "I could just take you by the legs and . . . and beat your vile mug in, and whatever else you've got, with an oak log."

"You oughtn't to have made such a detour," Yavtukh went on.

"Much better to take the path I did: straight past the stables. And it's too bad about the frock coat. Good broadcloth. How much did you pay per yard? Anyhow, we've had a nice walk, it's time for home."

The philosopher, scratching himself, trudged after Yavtukh. "The accursed witch will give me a hot time now," he thought. "Though what's with me, really? What am I afraid of? Am I not a Cossack? I did read for two nights, God will help with the third. The accursed witch must have done a good deal of sinning for the unclean powers to stand by her like that."

These reflections occupied him as he entered the master's yard. Having encouraged himself with such observations, he persuaded Dorosh, who, through his connection with the steward, occasionally had access to the master's cellar, to fetch a jug of rotgut, and the two friends, sitting under the shed, supped not much less than half a bucket, so that the philosopher, suddenly getting to his feet, shouted: "Musicians! We must have musicians!"—and, without waiting for the musicians, broke into a trepak in the cleared spot in the middle of the yard. He danced until it came time for the afternoon snack, when the household people, standing in a circle around him, as is usual in such cases, finally spat and went away, saying, "Look how long the man's been dancing!" Finally the philosopher went right to sleep, and only a good dousing with cold water could wake him up for supper. Over supper he talked about what a Cossack is and how he should not be afraid of anything in the world.

"It's time," said Yavtukh, "let's go."

"Bite on a nail, you accursed hog!" thought the philosopher, and getting to his feet, said:

"Let's go."

On the way, the philosopher constantly glanced to right and left and tried to talk a little with his guides. But Yavtukh kept mum; Dorosh himself was untalkative. The night was infernal. Far off a whole pack of wolves howled. And even the dogs' barking was somehow frightening.

"Seems like it's something else howling—that's not a wolf," said Dorosh.

Yavtukh kept mum. The philosopher found nothing to say.

They approached the church and stepped in under its decrepit vaults, which showed how little the owner of the estate cared about God and his own soul. Yavtukh and Dorosh withdrew as before, and the philosopher remained alone. Everything was the same. Everything had the same menacingly familiar look. He paused for a minute. In the middle, as ever, stood the motionless coffin of the terrible witch. "I won't be afraid, by God, I won't be afraid!" he said, and, again drawing a circle around himself, he began recalling all his incantations. The silence was dreadful; the candles flickered, pouring light all over the church. The philosopher turned one page, then another, and noticed that he was not reading what was in the book at all. In fear he crossed himself and began to sing. This cheered him somewhat: the reading went ahead, and pages flashed by one after another. Suddenly . . . amidst the silence . . . the iron lid of the coffin burst with a crack and the dead body rose. It was still more horrible than the first time. Its teeth clacked horribly, row against row; its lips twitched convulsively and, with wild shrieks, incantations came rushing out. Wind whirled through the church, icons fell to the floor, broken glass dropped from the windows. The doors tore from their hinges, and a numberless host of monsters flew into God's church. A terrible noise of wings and scratching claws filled the whole church. Everything flew and rushed about, seeking the philosopher everywhere.

Khoma's head cleared of the last trace of drunkenness. He just kept crossing himself and reading prayers at random. And at the same time he heard the unclean powers flitting about him, all but brushing him with the tips of their wings and repulsive tails. He did not have the courage to look at them closely; he only saw the whole wall occupied by a huge monster standing amidst its own tangled hair as in a forest; through the web of hair two eyes stared horribly, the eyebrows raised slightly. Above it in the air there was something like an immense bubble, with a thousand tongs and scorpion stings reaching from its middle. Black earth hung on them in lumps. They all looked at him, searching, unable to see him, surrounded by the mysterious circle.

"Bring Viy! Go get Viy!" the words of the dead body rang out.

And suddenly there was silence in the church; the wolves' howling could be heard far away, and soon heavy footsteps rang out in the church; with a sidelong glance he saw them leading in some squat, hefty, splay-footed man. He was black earth all over. His earth-covered legs and arms stuck out like strong, sinewy roots. Heavily he trod, stumbling all the time. His long eyelids were lowered to the ground. With horror Khoma noticed that the face on him was made of iron. He was brought in under the arms and put right by the place where Khoma stood.

"Lift my eyelids, I can't see!" Viy said in a subterranean voice— and the entire host rushed to lift his eyelids.

"Don't look!" some inner voice whispered to the philosopher. He could not help himself and looked.

"There he is!" Viy cried and fixed an iron finger on him. And all that were there fell upon the philosopher. Breathless, he crashed to the ground and straightaway the spirit flew out of him in terror.

A cockcrow rang out. This was already the second cockcrow; the gnomes had missed the first. The frightened spirits rushed pellmell for the windows and doors in order to fly out quickly, but nothing doing: and so they stayed there, stuck in the doors and windows. When the priest came in, he stopped at the sight of such disgrace in God's sanctuary and did not dare serve a panikhida[9] in such a place. So the church remained forever with monsters stuck in its doors and windows, overgrown with forest, roots, weeds, wild blackthorn; and no one now can find the path to it.

WHEN RUMORS OF this reached Kiev and the theologian Khalyava heard, finally, that such had been the lot of the philosopher Khoma, he fell to thinking for a whole hour. In the meantime great changes had happened with him. Fortune had smiled on him: upon completing his studies, he had been made bell-ringer of the tallest belfry, and he almost always went about with a bloody nose, because the wooden stairs of the belfry had been put together every which way.

"Have you heard what happened with Khoma?" Tiberiy Gorobets, by then a philosopher and sporting a fresh mustache, said, coming up to him.

"It's what God granted him," said the ringer Khalyava. "Let's go to the tavern and commemorate his soul!"

The young philosopher, who had come into his rights with the passion of an enthusiast, so that his trousers and frock coat and even his hat gave off a whiff of spirits and coarse tobacco, instantly expressed his readiness.

"Khoma was a nice man!" said the ringer, as the lame tavern keeper set the third mug down in front of him. "A fine man! And he perished for nothing!"

"No, I know why he perished: because he got scared. If he hadn't been scared, the witch couldn't have done anything to him. You just have to cross yourself and spit right on her tail, and nothing will happen. I know all about it. Here in Kiev, the women sitting in the marketplace are all witches."

To this the ringer nodded as a sign of agreement. But, noticing that his tongue was unable to articulate a single word, he carefully got up from the table and, swaying from side to side, went off to hide himself in the remotest part of the weeds. Withal not forgetting, out of long habit, to steal an old boot sole that was lying on a bench.

The Story of How Ivan Ivanovich Quarreled with Ivan Nikiforovich

Chapter I
Ivan Ivanovich and Ivan Nikiforovich

A FINE BEKESHA[1] Ivan Ivanovich has! A most excellent one! And what fleece! Pah, damnation, what fleece! dove gray and frosty! I'll bet you anything that nobody has the like! Look at it, for God's sake—especially if he starts talking with somebody—look from the side: it's simply delicious! There's no describing it: velvet! silver! fire! Lord God! Saint Nicholas the holy wonder-worker! why don't I have a bekesha like that! He had it made for him back before Agafya Fedoseevna went to Kiev. Do you know Agafya Fedoseevna? The one who bit off the assessor's ear?

A wonderful man, Ivan Ivanovich! What a house he's got in Mirgorod! A gallery on oak posts all the way round it, with benches along it everywhere. When it gets too hot, Ivan Ivanovich throws off the bekesha and his underclothes, and relaxes on the gallery in just his shirt, watching what goes on in the yard and street. What apples and pears he's got right under his windows! Just open the window—the branches burst into the room. That's all in front of the house; but you should see what he's got in his gar-

den! What hasn't he got in it! Plums, cherries, black cherries, all
kinds of vegetables, sunflowers, cucumbers, melons, beans—even
a threshing floor and a smithy.

A wonderful man, Ivan Ivanovich! He has a great love of melons. They're his favorite food. As soon as he finishes dinner and
goes out to the gallery in nothing but his shirt, he immediately
tells Gapka to bring two melons. Then he cuts them up himself,
collects the seeds in a special piece of paper, and begins to eat.
Then he tells Gapka to bring the inkpot and himself, with his own
hand, writes on the paper with the seeds: "This melon was eaten
on such-and-such date." If there was some guest at the time, then:
"with the participation of so-and-so."

The late judge of Mirgorod always looked at Ivan Ivanovich's
house with admiration. Yes, it's not a bad little house at all. I like
the way rooms and hallways have been added on to it, so that if
you look at it from afar you see only roofs sitting one on top of the
other, looking very much like a plateful of pancakes, or, better
still, like the kind of fungus that grows on trees. Anyhow, the roofs
are all thatched with rushes; a willow, an oak, and two apple trees
lean on them with their spreading branches. Small windows with
whitewashed openwork shutters flash between the trees and even
run out to the street.

A wonderful man, Ivan Ivanovich! The Poltava commissary also
knows him! Dorosh Tarasovich Pukhivochka, whenever he comes
from Khorol, always stops to see him. And the archpriest, Father
Pyotr, who lives in Koliberda, whenever he has a half-dozen guests
gathered, always says he knows of no one who fulfills his Christian
duty or knows how to live so well as Ivan Ivanovich.

God, how time flies! By then ten years had gone by since he was
left a widower. He had no children. Gapka has children and they
often run about in the yard. Ivan Ivanovich always gives each of
them a bagel, or a slice of melon, or a pear. Gapka carries the keys
to his storerooms and cellars; the keys to the big trunk in his bedroom and the middle storeroom Ivan Ivanovich keeps himself, and
he doesn't like to let anyone into them. Gapka, a healthy girl, goes
about in an apron and has fresh calves and cheeks.

And what a pious man Ivan Ivanovich is! Every Sunday he puts on his bekesha and goes to church. On entering, Ivan Ivanovich, after bowing in all directions, usually installs himself in the choir and sings along very well in a bass voice. And when the service is over, Ivan Ivanovich simply can't refrain from going up to every beggar. He might not want to occupy himself with something so boring if he weren't prompted to it by his natural kindness.

"Greetings, poor dear!" he usually says, having sought out a most crippled woman in a ragged dress made all of patches. "Where are you from, dear?"

"I come from a farmstead, good sir. It's three days since I've had anything to eat or drink. My own children drove me out!"

"Poor thing, why have you come here?"

"Just to beg alms, good sir, if someone would give me enough to buy bread."

"Hm! so it's bread you want?" Ivan Ivanovich usually asks.

"How can I not? I'm hungry as a dog."

"Hm!" Ivan Ivanovich usually replies. "Then maybe you'd also like some meat?"

"Whatever your honor gives me I'll be pleased with."

"Hm! so meat is better than bread?"

"A hungry person can't be choosy. Whatever your honor gives me, it's all good."

At that the old woman usually holds out her hand.

"Well, go with God," Ivan Ivanovich says. "Why are you standing there? I'm not beating you!" And, after addressing the same questions to a second one, and a third, he finally goes home, or stops to have a glass of vodka with his neighbor Ivan Nikiforovich, or with the judge, or with the police chief.

Ivan Ivanovich likes it very much when someone gives him a present or a treat. That pleases him very much.

Ivan Nikiforovich is also a very good man. His yard is next to Ivan Ivanovich's yard. Never yet has the world produced such friends as they are with each other. Anton Prokofievich Pupopuz, who to this day still goes around in a brown frock coat with blue sleeves and on Sundays has dinner at the judge's, used to say that the devil himself had tied Ivan Nikiforovich and Ivan Ivanovich to each other with a piece of string. Wherever the one goes, the other gets dragged along.

Ivan Nikiforovich never married. Though there was talk that he had been married, it was a sheer lie. I know Ivan Nikiforovich very well, and I can tell you that he never even had any intention of getting married. Where on earth does all this gossip come from? Just as it got spread about that Ivan Nikiforovich was born with a tail behind. But that invention is so preposterous, as well as vile and indecent, that I don't even consider it necessary to refute it before my enlightened readers, who undoubtedly know that only witches, and a very few of them, have tails behind, and, anyhow, they belong more to the female sex than to the male.

Despite their great attachment, these rare friends were not entirely alike. Their characters can best be known by comparison: Ivan Ivanovich has an extraordinary gift for speaking with extreme pleasantness. Lord, how he speaks! The feeling can only be compared with that of someone picking through your hair or gently passing a finger over your heel. You listen and listen—and your head lolls. Pleasant! extremely pleasant! like a nap after swimming. Ivan Nikiforovich, on the contrary, is mostly silent, though if he slaps on a phrase, just hold tight: he'll trim you better than any razor. Ivan Ivanovich is tall and lean; Ivan Nikiforovich is slightly shorter, but instead expands sideways. Ivan Ivanovich's head resembles a turnip tail-down, Ivan Nikiforovich's a turnip tail-up. It's only after dinner that Ivan Ivanovich lies on the gallery in nothing but his shirt; in the evening he puts on his bekesha and goes somewhere—either to the town store, which he supplies with flour, or out to the fields to hunt quail. Ivan Nikiforovich lies on the porch all day long—if the day isn't very hot, he usually puts his back to the sun—and doesn't care to go anywhere. In the morning, if he's of a mind to, he may pass around the yard, looking over the household, and then retire again. In the old days, he would sometimes call on Ivan Ivanovich. Ivan Ivanovich is an extremely refined man and never says an improper word in decent conversation, and becomes offended at once if he hears one. Ivan Nikiforovich sometimes makes a slip; then Ivan Ivanovich usually gets up from his place and says, "Enough, enough, Ivan Nikiforovich, sooner take to the sunlight than speak such ungodly words." Ivan Ivanovich gets very angry if he finds a fly in his borscht: he's beside himself then, and he throws the plate, and it also means trouble for the host. Ivan Nikiforovich is extremely fond of bathing, and once he's in the water up to his chin, he asks that a table with a samovar also be put in the water, and he likes very much to drink his tea in such coolness. Ivan Ivanovich shaves twice a week, Ivan Nikiforovich once. Ivan Ivanovich is extremely inquisitive. God forbid you should begin telling him something and not finish! And if he's displeased with something, he lets it be known at once. It's very hard to tell by the look of him whether Ivan Nikiforovich is pleased or angry; he may be glad of something, but he doesn't show it. Ivan Ivanovich is of a somewhat timorous character; Ivan Nikiforovich, on the contrary, has such wide gathered trousers that, if they were inflated, the whole yard with its barns and outbuildings could be put into them. Ivan Ivanovich has big, expressive eyes of a tobacco color and a mouth somewhat resembling the letter V; Ivan Nikiforovich has small, yellowish eyes that disappear completely between his bushy eyebrows and plump cheeks, and a nose that looks like a ripe plum. Ivan Ivanovich, when he treats you to snuff, always licks the lid of the snuff box with his tongue first, then flips it open and, offering it to you, says, if you're an acquaintance, "May I venture to ask you, my good sir, to help yourself?" and if you're not an acquaintance, "May I venture to ask you, my good sir, not having the honor of knowing your rank, name, and patronymic, to help yourself?" Whereas Ivan Nikiforovich hands you his snuff bottle and only adds: "Help yourself." Like Ivan Ivanovich, Ivan Nikiforovich has a great dislike of fleas; and therefore neither Ivan Ivanovich nor Ivan Nikiforovich ever passes a Jewish peddler without buying various jars of elixirs against these insects from him, having first given him a good scolding for confessing the Jewish faith.

However, despite certain dissimilarities, Ivan Ivanovich and Ivan Nikiforovich are both excellent people.

Chapter II
From Which Can Be Learned What Ivan Ivanovich Took a Liking to, What the Conversation Between Ivan Ivanovich and Ivan Nikiforovich Was About, and How It Ended

One morning—this was in the month of July—Ivan Ivanovich was lying on the gallery. The day was hot, the air dry and flowing in streams. Ivan Ivanovich had already managed to visit the farmstead and the mowers outside town to inquire of the muzhiks and women whence, whither, and why, got mighty tired and lay down to rest. While lying there, he spent a long time looking at the sheds, the yard, the outbuildings, the chickens running in the yard, and thought to himself, "Lord God, what a proprietor I am! Is there anything I haven't got? Fowl, outbuildings, barns, what not else; vodka of various flavors; pears and plums in the orchards; poppies, cabbage, and peas in the garden . . . What is there that I haven't got? . . . I'd like to know, what haven't I got?"

Having asked himself such a profound question, Ivan Ivanovich fell to thinking; and meanwhile his eyes sought new objects, stepped over the fence into Ivan Nikiforovich's yard, and involuntarily became occupied with a curious spectacle. A skinny woman was taking packed-away clothes out one by one and hanging them on the line for airing. Soon an old uniform top with frayed cuffs spread its sleeves in the air and embraced a brocade jacket, after which another stuck itself out, a gentleman's, with armorial buttons and a moth-eaten collar; then white twill pantaloons with stains, which had once been pulled onto Ivan Nikiforovich's legs and now might be pulled onto his fingers. After them, another pair came out to hang, looking like an inverted V. Then came a dark blue Cossack beshmet[2] that Ivan Nikiforovich had had made for himself some twenty years before, when he was preparing to join the militia and even let his mustache grow. Finally, what with one thing and another, a sword thrust itself out as well, looking like a steeple sticking up in the air. Then came the whirling skirts of something resembling a caftan of a grass-green color, with brass buttons the size of five-kopeck pieces. From behind its skirts peeked a waistcoat trimmed in gold braid, with a big cutout front. The waistcoat was soon screened by a deceased grandmother's old skirt, with pockets that could accommodate whole watermelons. All of this mixed together made up a very entertaining spectacle for Ivan Ivanovich, while the sun's rays, striking here and there on a blue or green sleeve, a red cuff or a portion of gold brocade, or sparkling on the sword steeple, turned it into something extraordinary, like those nativity scenes that itinerant hucksters take around to the farmsteads. Especially when a crowd of people, tightly packed, watches King Herod in a golden crown or Anton leading his goat; behind the stage a violin squeals; a Gypsy beats on his own lips instead of a drum, and the sun is setting, and the fresh chill of the southern night, unnoticed, clings closer and closer to the fresh shoulders and breasts of the plump farm girls.

Soon the old woman crept out of the storeroom groaning and dragging on her back an ancient saddle with torn-off stirrups, scuffed leather holsters for pistols, a saddle blanket once of a scarlet color, with gold embroidery and bronze plaques.

"Look at the foolish woman!" thought Ivan Ivanovich. "Next she'll drag Ivan Nikiforovich himself out for an airing!"

And, indeed, Ivan Ivanovich was not entirely mistaken in his surmise. About five minutes later, Ivan Nikiforovich's nankeen balloon trousers emerged and took up almost half the yard with themselves. After that she also brought out a hat and a gun.

"What does this mean?" thought Ivan Ivanovich. "I've never seen a gun at Ivan Nikiforovich's. What's he up to? He doesn't go shooting, but he keeps a gun! What does he need it for? A nice little thing, too! I've long wanted to get myself one like it. I'd really like to have that little gun; I love fooling with guns."

"Hey, you, woman!" cried Ivan Ivanovich, beckoning with his finger.

The old woman came up to the fence.

"What have you got there, granny?"

"You can see for yourself it's a gun."

"What kind of gun?"

"Who knows what kind! If it was mine, maybe I'd know what it's made of. But it's the master's."

Ivan Ivanovich stood up and began to examine the gun on all sides, forgetting to reprimand the old woman for hanging it and the sword out to air.

"Iron, you'd expect," the old woman went on.

"Hm! iron. Why iron?" Ivan Ivanovich said to himself. "And has the master had it long?"

"Long, maybe."

"A nice little thing!" Ivan Ivanovich went on. "I'll beg it from him. What use does he have for it? Or else I'll trade him something. Say, granny, is the master at home?"

"He is."

"What's he doing? lying down?"

"Lying down."

"All right, then, I'll go and see him."

Ivan Ivanovich got dressed, took his blackthorn in case of dogs, because in Mirgorod you meet more of them than of people in the streets, and went.

Though Ivan Nikiforovich's yard was next to Ivan Ivanovich's, and you could climb over the wattle fence from one to the other, Ivan Ivanovich nevertheless went via the street. From this street he had to go down a lane so narrow that if two carts, each drawn by one horse, chanced to meet in it, they'd be unable to pass each other and would stay in that position until they were seized by the rear wheels and pulled in opposite directions back out to the street. And a passer-by on foot would get himself adorned, as if with flowers, with the burrs that grew along the fences on both sides. On one side Ivan Ivanovich's shed looked onto this lane, on the other Ivan Nikiforovich's barn, gates, and dovecote.

Ivan Ivanovich went up to the gates and clanked the latch: inside, the barking of dogs arose; but the motley pack soon ran off wagging their tails, seeing that the face was a familiar one. Ivan Ivanovich crossed the yard, a colorful mixture of Indian pigeons, fed by Ivan Nikiforovich's own hand, melon and watermelon rinds, an occasional green patch, an occasional broken wheel or barrel hoop, or an urchin lying about in a dirty shirt—a picture such as painters love! The shadow of the hanging clothes covered almost the whole yard and lent it a certain coolness. The woman met him with a bow and stood gaping in her place. In front of the house was a pretty porch with a roof supported by two oak posts—unreliable protection from the sun, which at that season in Little Russia doesn't joke but leaves the walker streaming with hot sweat from head to foot. From this it may be seen how strong was Ivan Ivanovich's wish to acquire the needed object, since he decided to go out at such a time, even abandoning his usual custom of going for a walk only in the evening.

The room Ivan Ivanovich entered was completely dark, because the shutters were closed, and a ray of sunlight, passing through a hole made in the shutters, turned iridescent and, striking the opposite wall, drew on it a colorful landscape of rush roofs, trees, and the clothing hanging outside, only all of it inverted. This lent the room a sort of wondrous half-light.

"God be with you!" said Ivan Ivanovich.

"Ah! greetings, Ivan Ivanovich!" replied a voice from the corner of the room. Only then did Ivan Ivanovich notice Ivan Nikiforovich lying on a rug spread out on the floor. "Excuse me for appearing before you in my natural state."

Ivan Nikiforovich way lying there with nothing on, not even a shirt.

"Never mind. Did you have a good night's sleep, Ivan Nikiforovich?"

"I did. And you, Ivan Ivanovich?"

"I did."

"So you just got up?"

"Just got up? Lord help you, Ivan Nikiforovich! how could one sleep so late! I've just come from the fields. Wonderful crops on the way! Delightful! And the hay is so tall, soft, rich!"

"Gorpina!" cried Ivan Nikiforovich, "bring Ivan Ivanovich some vodka and pies with sour cream."

"Nice weather today."

"Don't praise it, Ivan Ivanovich. Devil take it! there's no escaping the heat!"

"You've got to go mentioning the devil. Ah, Ivan Nikiforovich! You'll remember my words, but it will be too late: you'll get it in the other world for your ungodly talk."

"How did I offend you, Ivan Ivanovich? I didn't touch your father or your mother. I don't know what I did to offend you."

"Come, come, Ivan Nikiforovich!"

"By God, I didn't offend you, Ivan Ivanovich!"

"It's strange, the quail still won't come to the whistle."

"As you wish, think whatever you like, only I didn't offend you in any way."

"I don't know why they won't come," Ivan Ivanovich said, as if not listening to Ivan Nikiforovich. "Maybe it's not the season yet, only it seems it's just the right season."

"You say the crops are good?"

"Delightful crops! Delightful!"

Whereupon silence ensued.

"What's this with you hanging out clothes, Ivan Nikiforovich?" Ivan Ivanovich finally asked.

"Yes, fine clothes, nearly new, the cursed woman almost let them rot. I'm airing them out now; fine fabric, excellent, just turn it inside out and you can wear it again."

"I liked one little thing there, Ivan Nikiforovich."

"Which?"

"Tell me, please, what use you have for that gun that's been put out to air with the clothes?" Here Ivan Ivanovich offered him some snuff. "May I venture to ask you to help yourself?"

"Never mind, you help yourself! I'll snuff my own!" At which Ivan Nikiforovich felt around and came up with a snuff bottle. "Stupid woman, so she hung the gun out, too! That Jew in Sorochintsy makes good snuff. I don't know what he puts in it, but it's so aromatic! A bit like balsam. Here, take a chew of some in your mouth. Like balsam, right? Take some, help yourself!"

"Tell me, please, Ivan Nikiforovich, going back to the gun: What are you going to do with it? You have no need for it."

"How, no need for it? What if I have occasion to shoot?"

"God help you, Ivan Nikiforovich, when are you going to shoot? Maybe after the Second Coming. As far as I know or anyone else remembers, you've never shot so much as a single duck, and your whole nature has not been fashioned by the Lord God for hunting. Your shape and posture are imposing. How can you go dragging yourself about the swamps, if your clothes, which could not decently be called by name in every conversation, are still being aired out, what then? No, you need peace, repose." (Ivan Ivanovich, as was mentioned earlier, could speak extremely picturesquely when he needed to convince somebody. How he could speak! God, how he could speak!) "Yes, and so you need suitable activities. Listen, give it to me!"

"How can I! It's an expensive gun. You won't find such a gun anywhere now. I bought it off a Turk when I was still intending to join the militia. And now I should suddenly up and give it away? How can I? It's a necessity."

"Why a necessity?"

"Why? And when robbers attack the house . . . Of course it's a necessity. Thank God, I'm at ease now and not afraid of anybody. And why? Because I know I've got a gun in the closet."

"A real good gun! Look, Ivan Nikiforovich, the lock's broken!"

"So what if it's broken? It can be fixed. It just needs to be oiled with hempseed oil to keep it from rusting."

"From your words, Ivan Nikiforovich, I don't see any friendly disposition toward me. You don't want to do anything for me as a token of good will."

"How can you say I don't show you any good will, Ivan Ivanovich? Shame on you! Your oxen graze on my steppe, and I've never once borrowed them from you. When you go to Poltava, you always ask for the loan of my cart, and what—did I ever refuse? Children from your yard climb over the fence into mine and play with my dogs, and I say nothing: let them play, so long as they don't touch anything! let them play!"

"If you don't want to give it to me, maybe we can make a trade."

"And what will you give me for it?" With that, Ivan Nikiforovich leaned on his arm and looked at Ivan Ivanovich.

"I'll give you the brown sow, the one I fattened in the pen. A fine sow! You'll see if she doesn't produce a litter for you next year."

"I don't know how you can say it, Ivan Ivanovich. What do I need your sow for? To feast the devil's memory?"

"Again! You just can't do without some devil or other! It's a sin on you, by God, it's a sin, Ivan Nikiforovich!"

"But really, Ivan Ivanovich, how can you go offering devil knows what—some sow—for a gun!"

"Why is it devil knows what, Ivan Nikiforovich?"

"What else? You can judge pretty well for yourself. Here we have a gun, a known thing; and there, devil knows what—a sow! If it wasn't you talking, I might take it in an offensive way."

"What do you find so bad in a sow?"

"Who do you really take me for? That some sow . . ."

"Sit down, sit down! I won't . . . Let the gun stay yours, let it rot and rust away standing in a corner of the closet—I don't want to talk about it anymore."

After which silence ensued.

"They say," Ivan Ivanovich began, "three kings have declared war on our tsar."

"Yes, Pyotr Fyodorovich told me. What is this war? and why?"

"It's impossible to say for certain what it's about, Ivan Nikiforovich. I suppose the kings want us all to embrace the Turkish faith."

"Some fools to want that!" said Ivan Nikiforovich, raising his head.

"You see, and our tsar declared war on them for it. No, he says, you can embrace the Christian faith!"

"And so? Ours will beat them, Ivan Ivanovich!"

"Yes, they will. So, then, Ivan Nikiforovich, don't you want to trade me your little gun?"

"I find it strange, Ivan Ivanovich: you're a man known for his learning, it seems, yet you speak like an oaf. What a fool I'd be if . . ."

"Sit down, sit down. God help it! let it perish, I won't say any more! . . ."

Just then the snack was brought in.

Ivan Ivanovich drank a glass and followed it with pie and sour cream.

"Listen, Ivan Nikiforovich, besides the sow, I'll give you two sacks of oats, since you didn't sow any oats. This year you'll need to buy oats anyway."

"By God, Ivan Ivanovich, a man has to eat a lot of peas before he talks with you." (That's nothing, Ivan Nikiforovich can come out with much better phrases.) "Has anybody ever seen a gun traded for two sacks of oats? No fear you'll go offering me your bekesha."

"But you've forgotten, Ivan Nikiforovich, that I'm also giving you the sow."

"What! a sow and two sacks of oats for a gun?"

"Why, it's not enough?"

"For a gun?"

"Of course, for a gun."

"Two sacks for a gun?"

"Not two empty sacks, but with oats; and you forgot the sow."

"Go kiss your sow! Or if you don't want to, then kiss the devil!"

"Oh, touch-me-not! You'll see, they'll lard your tongue with hot needles in the other world for such iniquitous words. After talking with you, a man has to wash his face and hands and smoke himself with incense."

"Beg pardon, Ivan Ivanovich, but a gun is a noble thing, a most curious amusement, and a pleasing adornment for a room besides . . ."

"Well, Ivan Nikiforovich, you fuss over your gun *like a fool over a fancy purse*," Ivan Ivanovich said vexedly, because he was indeed beginning to get angry.

"And you, Ivan Ivanovich, are a real *goose*."

If Ivan Nikiforovich hadn't said this word, they would have had an argument and parted friends as usual; but now something quite different happened. Ivan Ivanovich got all fired up.

"What's that you said, Ivan Nikiforovich?" he asked, raising his voice.

"I said you resemble a goose, Ivan Ivanovich!"

"How dare you, sir, forgetting all decency and respect for a man's rank and name, dishonor him with such an abusive denomination?"

"What's abusive about it? Why on earth are you waving your arms like that, Ivan Ivanovich?"

"I repeat, how dare you, contrary to all decency, call me a goose?"

"I sneeze on your head, Ivan Ivanovich! What are you clucking like that for?"

Ivan Ivanovich could no longer control himself: his lips trembled, his mouth changed its usual V shape and now resembled an O, he blinked his eyes so that it was frightening to see. This happened very rarely with Ivan Ivanovich. For this he had to be greatly angered.

"Then I declare to you," said Ivan Ivanovich, "that I do not want to know you!"

"A big thing! By God, I won't cry over that!" replied Ivan Nikiforovich.

He was lying, lying, by God! He was very upset by it.

"My foot will not cross your doorsill."

"Oh-ho-ho!" said Ivan Nikiforovich, too upset himself to know what to do and, contrary to his habit, getting to his feet. "Hey, woman! laddie!" At which there appeared from behind the door the same skinny woman and a rather short boy tangled in a long and wide frock coat. "Take Ivan Ivanovich by the arms and lead him out the door!"

"What! a gentleman?" cried Ivan Ivanovich with a feeling of pride and indignation. "Just you dare! Come on! I'll destroy you along with your stupid master! The crows won't find what's left of you!" (Ivan Ivanovich spoke with extraordinary power when his soul was shaken.)

The whole group represented a powerful picture: Ivan Nikiforovich standing in the middle of the room in all his unadorned beauty! The woman, her mouth gaping and with a most senseless and fearful look on her face! Ivan Ivanovich with one arm raised aloft, the way Roman tribunes are portrayed! This was an extraordinary moment! a magnificent spectacle! And yet there was only one spectator: this was the boy in the boundless frock coat, who stood quite calmly and cleaned his nose with his finger.

Finally Ivan Ivanovich took his hat.

"You're behaving very well, Ivan Nikiforovich! Splendid! I'll remember you for it."

"Go, Ivan Ivanovich, go! And watch out, don't cross my path: I'll punch your mug in, Ivan Ivanovich!"

"Take this for that, Ivan Nikiforovich!" replied Ivan Ivanovich, making him a fig and slamming the door behind him, which creaked hoarsely and opened again.

Ivan Nikiforovich appeared in the doorway and wanted to add something, but Ivan Ivanovich, no longer looking back, went flying out of the yard.

Chapter III
WHAT HAPPENED AFTER THE QUARREL
BETWEEN IVAN IVANOVICH
AND IVAN NIKIFOROVICH

And so these two respected men, the honor and adornment of Mirgorod, quarreled with each other! And over what? Over a trifle, over a goose. Refused to see each other, broke all ties, though before they had been known as the most inseparable of friends! Every day Ivan Ivanovich and Ivan Nikiforovich used to send to inquire after each other's health, and often talked with each other from their balconies, and said such pleasant things to each other that it was a heart's delight to listen to them. On Sundays, Ivan Ivanovich in his thick woolen bekesha and Ivan Nikiforovich in a yellow-brown nankeen jacket used to go to church all but arm in arm. And if Ivan Ivanovich, who was extremely keen-sighted, was the first to notice a puddle or some other uncleanness in the middle of the street, as sometimes happens in Mirgorod, he always said to Ivan Nikiforovich, "Be careful, don't put your foot down here, it's not a nice spot." Ivan Nikiforovich, for his part, also showed the most touching signs of friendship, and however far away he was standing, always held his hand out to Ivan Ivanovich with the snuff bottle, saying, "Help yourself!" And what excellent estates they both had! . . . And these two friends . . . When I heard about it, I was thunderstruck! For a long time I refused to believe it: good God! Ivan Ivanovich has quarreled with Ivan Nikiforovich! Such worthy people! Is there anything solid left in this world?

When Ivan Ivanovich came home, he was greatly agitated for a long time. Usually he would stop first at the stable to see if his little mare was eating her hay (Ivan Ivanovich has a grayish mare with a spot on her forehead, a very nice little horse); after that he would feed the turkeys and pigs with his own hands, and only then go inside, where he would either make wooden utensils (he knew how to fashion various objects quite skillfully out of wood, no worse than a turner), or read a book printed by Lubiy, Gariy, and Popov[3] (Ivan Ivanovich cannot remember the title, because the serf girl tore off the top part of the title page long ago while playing with the baby), or else rest on the gallery. But now he did not go about any of his usual occupations. In place of that, on meeting Gapka, he started scolding her for hanging about idly, when she was in fact carrying grain to the kitchen; he threw his stick at the cock, who came to the porch for his usual handout; and when a dirty little boy in a tattered shirt ran up to him and shouted, "Daddy, daddy, give me a gingerbread!" he threatened and stamped his feet at him so terribly that the frightened boy ran off God knows where.

Finally, however, he came to his senses and got down to his usual affairs. He had a late dinner, and it was nearly evening when he lay down to rest on the gallery. A good borscht with squab, made by Gapka, drove the morning's incident away completely. Ivan Ivanovich again began to survey his domain with pleasure. Finally his gaze rested on his neighbor's yard and he said to himself: "I haven't been to Ivan Nikiforovich's today; I must go and see him." Having said that, Ivan Ivanovich took his hat and stick and went outside; but as soon as he passed through the gate, he remembered the quarrel, spat, and turned back. Almost the same movement occurred in Ivan Nikiforovich's yard. Ivan Ivanovich saw the woman already setting her foot on the wattle fence, intending to climb into his yard, when Ivan Nikiforovich's voice

suddenly rang out: "Come back! come back! never mind!" However, Ivan Ivanovich got very bored. It was quite possible that the
two worthy men would have made peace the very next day if a
certain event in Ivan Nikiforovich's house hadn't dashed all hopes
and poured oil on the flames of enmity that were ready to die out.

In the evening of the same day, Agafya Fedoseevna arrived at
Ivan Nikiforovich's. Agafya Fedoseevna was neither a relation nor
an in-law, nor even a kuma[4] of Ivan Nikiforovich. It would seem
she had absolutely no reason for coming to visit him, and he himself was not very glad to have her; nevertheless she would come
and stay for whole weeks and sometimes longer. Then she would
take the keys, and the entire household would be in her hands.
This was very unpleasant for Ivan Nikiforovich, and yet, to his
own surprise, he obeyed her like a child, and though he sometimes
tried to object, Agafya Fedoseevna always came out on top.

I confess I don't understand why it's so arranged that women
grab us by the nose as deftly as if it were a teapot handle. Either
their hands are made for it, or our noses are no longer good for
anything. And despite the fact that Ivan Nikiforovich's nose somewhat resembled a plum, she still grabbed him by that nose and led
him around with her like a little dog. In her presence he even
changed, involuntarily, his usual way of life: he did not spend so
long lying in the sun, and if he did, it was not in his natural state
but always in a shirt and trousers, though Agafya Fedoseevna by no
means demanded it. She was not a lover of ceremony, and when
Ivan Nikiforovich had a fever, she herself, with her own hands,
rubbed him from head to foot with turpentine and vinegar. Agafya
Fedoseevna wore a cap on her head, three warts on her nose, and a
coffee-colored housecoat with little yellow flowers. Her whole
body resembled a barrel, and therefore it was as hard to find her
waist as to see your own nose without a mirror. Her legs were
short, formed after the pattern of two pillows. She gossiped, ate
boiled beets in the mornings, and cursed exceedingly well—her
face never once changing its expression during all these diverse
occupations, a thing which only women are customarily able to
display.

As soon as she came, everything turned inside out.

"Don't make peace with him, Ivan Nikiforovich, and don't apologize: he wants to ruin you, that's the sort of man he is! You don't know him yet."

The accursed woman muttered and muttered and made it so that Ivan Nikiforovich didn't even want to hear about Ivan Ivanovich.

Everything looked different now: if a neighboring dog happened to get into the yard, it was beaten with whatever came to hand; the children who climbed over the fence came back screaming, their shirts tucked up, with traces of a birching on their backsides. Even the woman herself, when Ivan Ivanovich wished to ask her about something, performed such an indecency that Ivan Ivanovich, as a man of extreme delicacy, spat and said only, "What a nasty woman! Worse than her master!"

Finally, to crown all the insults, his hateful neighbor had a goose pen built directly facing him, where they used to climb over the wattle fence, as if with the special purpose of aggravating the insult. This pen, repulsive to Ivan Ivanovich, was built with devilish speed—in a single day.

This aroused anger and a desire for revenge in Ivan Ivanovich. He did not, however, show any sign of irritation, despite the fact that the pen even occupied a portion of his land; but his heart beat so hard that it was extremely difficult for him to maintain this external calm.

So he spent the day. Night came . . . Oh, if I were a painter, I would wondrously portray all the loveliness of the night! I would portray how all Mirgorod lies sleeping; how countless stars gaze motionlessly down on it; how the visible silence resounds with the near and far-off barking of dogs; how the amorous beadle races past them and climbs over the fence with chivalrous fearlessness; how the white walls of houses enveloped in moonlight turn still whiter, the trees above them turn darker, the shadow of the trees falls blacker, the flowers and hushed grass grow more fragrant, and the crickets, indefatigable cavaliers of the night, with one accord begin their chirping songs in all corners. I would portray how, in one of these low clay cottages, a dark-browed town girl with quivering young breasts tosses on her solitary bed dreaming of a hussar's mustache and spurs while moonlight laughs on her cheeks. I would portray how the black shadow of a bat flits over the white road and settles on the white chimneys of the houses . . . But I would scarcely be able to portray Ivan Ivanovich going out that night with a saw in his hand. So many different feelings were written on his face! Softly, softly he crept close and got under the goose pen. Ivan Nikiforovich's dogs still knew nothing of the quarrel between them and therefore allowed him, as an old friend, to approach the pen, which rested entirely on four oak posts. Coming to the nearest post, he put his saw to it and began sawing. The noise produced by the saw made him look around every moment, but the thought of the offense restored his courage. The first post was sawn through; Ivan Ivanovich went on to the next. His eyes glowed and saw nothing from fear. Suddenly Ivan Ivanovich cried out and went numb: a dead man appeared to him; but he quickly recovered, seeing it was a goose stretching out its neck toward him. Ivan Ivanovich spat in indignation and began to go on with his work. The second post was sawn through: the building lurched. Ivan Ivanovich's heart began to pound so terribly when he started on the third that he interrupted his work several times; it was already more than half sawn through when the unsteady building suddenly lurched badly . . . Ivan Ivanovich barely managed to jump clear as it collapsed with a crash. Grabbing his saw, terribly frightened, he went running home and threw himself on his bed, not having the courage even to look out the window at the consequences of his dreadful deed. He fancied that Ivan Nikiforovich's entire household had gathered: the old woman, Ivan Nikiforovich, the boy in the endless frock coat—armed with pikestaffs, Agafya Fedoseevna at their head, they were all coming to devastate and destroy his house.

The whole of the next day Ivan Ivanovich spent as if in a fever. He kept imagining that in revenge for it his hateful neighbor would at the very least set fire to his house. And he therefore gave Gapka orders to keep an eye out at all times everywhere for dry straw stuck someplace or other. Finally, in order to forestall Ivan

Nikiforovich, he decided to run ahead hare-like and make a claim against him in the Mirgorod local court. What it consisted of can be found out in the next chapter.

Chapter IV
ABOUT WHAT HAPPENED IN THE OFFICE OF THE MIRGOROD LOCAL COURT

A wonderful town, Mirgorod! What buildings it has! And with thatch, or rush, or even wooden roofs; a street to the right, a street to the left, excellent wattle fences everywhere; hops twine over them, pots hang on them, from behind them the sunflower shows it sunlike head, poppies redden, fat pumpkins flash . . . Magnificent! A wattle fence is always adorned with objects that make it still more picturesque: a hanging apron, or a shift, or balloon trousers. In Mirgorod there is neither thievery nor crookery, and therefore everybody hangs up whatever he likes. When you get to the square, you're sure to stop for a while and admire the view: there is a puddle in it, an astonishing puddle! the only one like it you'll ever chance to see! It takes up almost the whole square. A beautiful puddle! The houses, big and small, which from afar might be taken for haystacks, stand around marveling at its beauty.

But to my mind there's no house better than the local courthouse. Whether it's made of oak or birch is not my affair; but it has eight windows, my dear sirs! eight windows in a row, looking right onto the square and that expanse of water of which I've already spoken and which the police chief calls a lake! It alone is painted a granite color: the rest of the houses of Mirgorod are simply whitewashed. Its roof is entirely of wood, and would even have been painted with red paint, if the oil prepared for that purpose had not been eaten, garnished with onion, by the clerks, which happened, as if by design, during a fast period, and so the roof went unpainted. The porch juts out into the square, and chickens often run about on it, because there's almost always grain or something else edible spilled on the porch, though that is not done on purpose but solely through the carelessness of the petitioners. It is divided into two halves: in one is the *office*, in the other the *jail-house*. In the half where the office is, there are two clean, white-washed rooms: one, the anteroom, is for petitioners; in the other, there's a desk adorned with ink blots, and on it a zertsalo.[5] Four oak chairs with high backs; against the walls, ironbound chests containing piles of regional calumny. On one of these chests there then stood a boot polished with wax. The office had been open since morning. The judge, a rather plump man, though somewhat thinner than Ivan Nikiforovich, with a kindly mien, in a greasy housecoat, holding a pipe and a cup of tea, was talking with the court clerk. The judge's lips were right under his nose, and he could therefore sniff his upper lip to his heart's content. This lip served him as a snuffbox, because the snuff addressed to his nose almost always spilled on it. And so, the judge was talking with the court clerk. To one side stood a barefoot girl holding a tray with teacups.

At the end of the table, the secretary was reading the decision of a case, but in such a monotonous and mournful voice that the accused himself might have fallen asleep listening to it. The judge would undoubtedly have done so before anyone else, if he hadn't entered, meanwhile, into an amusing conversation.

"I purposely tried to find out," the judge said, sipping tea from the already cold cup, "how they turn out to sing so well. I had a fine blackbird some two years ago. What then? Suddenly he went off completely. Started singing God knows what. As it continued, he got worse, turned guttural, hoarse—fit for the trash heap. And owing to a mere trifle! Here's how it happens: they get a lump under the throat, smaller than a pea. You need only prick this lump with a needle. Zakhar Prokofievich taught me that, and I'll tell you precisely how: I come to see him . . ."

"Shall I read another one, Demyan Demyanovich?" interrupted the secretary, who had already finished reading several minutes earlier.

"You read all of it? Imagine, so quickly! I didn't hear a thing! Where is it? Give it to me, I'll sign it. What else have you got?"

"The Cossack Bokitko's case concerning the stolen cow."

"Very well, read it! So, I come to see him . . . I can even tell you in detail what he treated me to. The vodka was served with a balyk[6]—one of a kind! Yes, not like our balyk, which"—here the judge clucked his tongue and smiled, while his nose sniffed from his usual snuffbox—"which our Mirgorod grocery treats us to. I didn't eat any pickled herring, because, as you yourself know, it gives me heartburn. But I did try the caviar—wonderful caviar! not to say excellent! Then I drank some peach vodka flavored with centaury. There was also saffron vodka, but, as you yourself know, I don't drink saffron vodka. It's very nice, you see: first to arouse the appetite, as they say, and then to finish . . . Ah! it's been ages, ages . . ." the judge suddenly cried out, seeing Ivan Ivanovich come in.

"God be with you! I wish you good day!" said Ivan Ivanovich, bowing to all sides with a pleasantness proper only to himself. My God, how he's able to charm everyone with his manners! Such refinement I've never seen anywhere. He knew his own worth very well, and therefore regarded general respect as his due. The judge himself offered Ivan Ivanovich a chair, and his nose drew all the snuff from his upper lip, which with him was always a sign of great pleasure.

"What may we offer you, Ivan Ivanovich?" he asked. "Would you care for a cup of tea?"

"No, thank you very much," replied Ivan Ivanovich, bowing and sitting down.

"If you please, just one little cup!" repeated the judge.

"No, thank you. You are most hospitable," Ivan Ivanovich replied, bowing and sitting down.

"One cup," repeated the judge.

"No, don't trouble yourself, Demyan Demyanovich."

With that, Ivan Ivanovich bowed and sat down.

"One little cup?"

"Oh, very well, one little cup," said Ivan Ivanovich, reaching toward the tray.

Lord God! such bottomless refinement some people have! It's impossible to describe what a pleasant impression such behavior makes!

"Wouldn't you care for another cup?"

"I humbly thank you," replied Ivan Ivanovich, placing the cup upside down on the tray and bowing.

"Be so kind, Ivan Ivanovich!"

"I can't. Thank you very much." With that, Ivan Ivanovich bowed and sat down.

"Ivan Ivanovich! be a friend, one little cup!"

"No, much obliged."

Having said this, Ivan Ivanovich bowed and sat down.

"Just one cup! one little cup!"

Ivan Ivanovich reached toward the tray and took a cup.

Pah! damnation! How some people are able, how they manage to maintain their dignity!

"Demyan Demyanovich," Ivan Ivanovich said as he finished the last sip, "I've come to you on some necessary business. I'm putting in a claim." With that, Ivan Ivanovich set down his cup and took from his pocket a sheet of official stamped paper with writing on it. "A claim against an enemy of mine, a sworn enemy."

"Who might that be?"

"Ivan Nikiforovich Dovgochkhun."

At these words the judge nearly fell off his chair.

"What are you saying!" he uttered, clasping his hands. "Ivan Ivanovich, is this you?"

"You can see for yourself it is."

"The Lord God and all his saints be with you! What! you, Ivan Ivanovich, have become enemies with Ivan Nikiforovich? Is it your lips saying so? Repeat it again! Someone must be hiding behind you and talking in your place! . . ."

"What's so incredible about it? I can't bear the sight of him; he has mortally offended me, insulted my honor."

"Most holy Trinity! how will I ever make my mother believe it now? And she, the old lady, says to me every day, when I quarrel with my sister, 'You children live like cat and dog together. Why don't you take example from Ivan Ivanovich and Ivan Nikiforovich? There are two real friends! Such friends! Such worthy people!' That's friends for you! Tell me, what was it? how?"

"It's a delicate matter, Demyan Demyanovich! impossible to put into words. Better order my petition to be read. Here, take it from this side, it's more fitting."

"Read it, Taras Tikhonovich!" said the judge, turning to the secretary.

Taras Tikhonovich took the petition and, having blown his nose with the aid of two fingers, as all court secretaries do, began to read:

"From Ivan, son of Ivan, Pererepenko, gentleman of the Mirgorod region and landowner, a petition; and on what, the points follow herewith:

"1. Known to the whole world for his iniquitous, loathsome, and beyond-all-measure law-breaking actions, the gentleman, Ivan, son of Nikifor, Dovgochkhun, on the 7th of July of the year 1810 instant, did occasion me a mortal offense, as much in reference to my personal honor as in equal measure to the humiliation and embarrassment of my rank and name. This gentleman, being of vile appearance, is likewise of an abusive character and filled with all sorts of blasphemy and abuse . . ."

Here the reader paused briefly in order to blow his nose again, and the judge pressed his hands together in awe and only kept saying to himself:

"What a glib pen! Lord God! how the man can write!"

Ivan Ivanovich asked for the reading to proceed, and Taras Tikhonovich went on:

"This gentleman, Ivan, son of Nikifor, Dovgochkhun, when I came to him with friendly offers, publicly called me by a name offensive to me and defaming to my honor, namely: *goose*, whereas it is known to the whole Mirgorod region that I have hitherto in no way ever been called, and have no intention of being called, this vile animal. And the proof of my noble origin is that the day of my birth, and equally well the baptism I received, have been recorded in the register of the Church of the Three Hierarchs.[7] A *goose*, as is known to all who are at least somewhat versed in science, cannot be recorded in a register, for a *goose* is not a person but a bird, which fact is positively known to everyone, even if they have not gone to school. But the said malignant gentleman, being

informed of all this, with no other purpose than that of occasion-
ing me an offense mortifying to my rank and estate, did abuse me
with the said vile word.

"2. This same improper and indecent gentleman also encroached
upon my familial property, received by me from my parent, of the
clerical estate, Ivan, of blessed memory, son of Onisy, Pererepenko,
by transposing, contrary to all law, a goose pen directly opposite
my porch, doing so with no other intention than that of aggravating the offense already inflicted upon me, for the said pen had
hitherto been standing in a suitable place and was still quite sturdy.
But the loathsome intent of the above-mentioned gentleman consisted solely in turning me into a witness of indecent goings-on,
for it is known that no one goes to a pen, still less to a goose pen,
on decent business. In this illegal act, the two front posts intruded
upon my own land, which I received while my parent Ivan, of
blessed memory, son of Onisy, Pererepenko, was still alive, and
which, starting from the barn, went in a straight line all the way to
where the women wash their pots.

"3. The above-depicted gentleman, whose very name and sur-
name inspire all possible loathing, nurses in his heart the wicked
intention of setting fire to me in my own house. Indubitable
tokens of which are manifest in the following: 1st, the said malignant gentleman has begun to emerge from his rooms frequently,
something he never undertook before, on account of his laziness
and the vile corpulence of his body; 2nd, in his servant's quarters,
which are adjacent to the fence surrounding my land, received by
me from my late parent, Ivan, of blessed memory, son of Onisy,
Pererepenko, a light burns every day and for an extraordinary
length of time, which is already manifest evidence, for hitherto, in
his miserly avarice, not only the tallow candle but even the night
lamp was always put out.

"And therefore I request that the said gentleman, Ivan, son of
Nikifor, Dovgochkhun, being guilty of arson, of insult to my
rank, name, and family, and of the thievish appropriation of property, and above all of the base and reprehensible appending to my
family name of the appellation *goose,* have a penalty imposed on
him, with payment of expenses and losses, and be condemned

himself as a trespasser, put in chains, and taken to jail, which decision with respect to my petition should be handed down at once
and without fail.

"Written and composed by Mirgorod landowner Ivan, son of
Ivan, Pererepenko, gentleman."

After the reading of the petition, the judge went up to Ivan
Ivanovich, took him by the button, and began speaking to him
almost like this:

"What are you doing, Ivan Ivanovich! For fear of God, drop this
petition, let it perish! (May Satan visit its dreams!) Better take Ivan
Nikiforovich by the hands, and kiss each other, and buy a bottle of
Santurin or Nikopolis, or else just make a little punch, and invite
me! We'll drink together and forget the whole thing!"

"No, Demyan Demyanovich! it is not that sort of affair," Ivan
Ivanovich said with that importance which was always so becoming to him. "Not the sort of affair that can be resolved in amicable
agreement. Good-bye! Good-bye to you, too, gentlemen!" he
went on with the same importance, addressing them all. "I hope
my petition will produce the proper effect." And he walked out,
leaving the whole office in amazement.

The judge sat without saying a word; the secretary took some
snuff; the office boys overturned the broken piece of bottle they
used as an inkstand; and the judge himself absentmindedly smeared
the puddle of ink over the table with his finger.

"What do you say to that, Dorofei Trofimovich?" said the
judge, turning to the court clerk after some silence.

"I say nothing," replied the court clerk.

"Such goings-on!" continued the judge.

Before he finished saying it, the door creaked and the front half
of Ivan Nikiforovich heaved itself into the office, while the rest
remained in the anteroom. The appearance of Ivan Nikiforovich—and, what's more, in court—seemed so extraordinary that
the judge cried out; the secretary broke off his reading. One office
boy in the frieze likeness of a half-tailcoat put a quill in his
mouth; the other swallowed a fly. Even the invalid who fulfilled
the functions of both messenger and watchman, who till then had
been standing by the door scratching under his dirty shirt with

stripes sewn to the shoulder, even this invalid gaped and stepped on somebody's foot.

"What fates bring you here? why and wherefore? How are you, Ivan Nikiforovich?"

But Ivan Nikiforovich was neither dead nor alive, because he had gotten mired in the doorway and could not make a step forward or back. In vain did the judge shout into the anteroom for someone there to shove Ivan Nikiforovich into the office from behind. There was only one petitioner in the anteroom, an old woman, who, despite all the efforts of her bony arms, could do nothing. Then one of the office boys, with fat lips, broad shoulders, a fat nose, and torn elbows, his eyes glancing about slyly and drunkenly, went up to the front part of Ivan Nikiforovich, folded his arms crosswise as if he were a child, and winked to the old invalid, who placed his knee against Ivan Nikiforovich's belly, and, despite his pitiful moans, squeezed him out into the anteroom. Then they slid back the bolts and opened the other half of the door. While they were at it, the office boy and his helper, the invalid, in their concerted efforts, spread such a strong smell with their breath that the office turned for a time into a public house.

"Did they hurt you, Ivan Nikiforovich? I'll tell my mother, she'll send you a tincture—just rub your shoulders and lower back, and it will all go away."

But Ivan Nikiforovich sank onto a chair and, apart from prolonged *oh's,* was unable to say anything. Finally, in a weak voice, barely audible from exhaustion, he uttered:

"Will you indulge?" and, taking the snuff bottle from his pocket, added, "here, help yourselves!"

"I'm very pleased to see you," answered the judge. "But, all the same, I can't imagine what made you undertake the effort and present us with such an agreeable unexpectedness."

"A petition . . ." was all Ivan Nikiforovich could utter.

"A petition? What sort?"

"A claim . . ." here breathlessness produced a long pause, "ohh! . . . a claim against a crook . . . Ivan Ivanovich Pererepenko."

"Lord! you too! Such rare friends! A claim against such a virtuous man! . . ."

"He's Satan in person!" Ivan Nikiforovich said curtly.

The judge crossed himself.

"Take the petition and read it."

"Nothing to do but read it, Taras Tikhonovich," said the judge, addressing the secretary with an air of displeasure, and his nose inadvertently sniffed his upper lip, which previously it used to do only from great pleasure. Such willfulness on the part of his nose vexed the judge still more. He took out his handkerchief and swept all the snuff from his upper lip in punishment for its insolence.

The secretary, having performed his usual start-up, which he always resorted to before beginning to read, that is, without the aid of a handkerchief, began in his usual voice, thus:

"A petition from Ivan, son of Nikifor, Dovgochkhun, gentleman of the Mirgorod region, and on what, the points follow herewith:

"1. From his hateful spite and obvious ill will, Ivan, son of Ivan, Pererepenko, who calls himself a gentleman, is causing me various losses, doing me dirt, and performing other devious and terrifying acts, and yesterday, like a robber and a thief, with axes, saws, chisels, and other metalworking tools, got into my yard during the night and with his very own hands and in blameworthy fashion did chop up my very own goose pen located therein. For which, on my part, I never gave any cause for such an illegal and marauding act.

"2. The said gentleman Pererepenko presumes upon my very life and, having kept this intention secret until the 7th day of the last month, came to me and in a friendly and cunning fashion started begging for my gun, which was in my room, offering me, with his particular niggardliness, a lot of worthless things—to wit: a brown sow and two measures of oats. But, divining his criminal intention even then, I made every effort to divert him from it; but the said crook and scoundrel, Ivan, son of Ivan, Pererepenko, did abuse me in a churlish manner, and since then has nursed an irreconcilable enmity toward me. Furthermore, the said oftmentioned violent gentleman and robber, Ivan, son of Ivan, Pererepenko, is of quite blameworthy origin: his sister was a notorious strumpet who went off with a company of chasseurs that was

quartered in Mirgorod five years ago; and she registered her husband as a peasant. His father and mother were also most lawless
people, and both were unimaginable drunkards. Yet the above-
mentioned gentleman and robber Pererepenko has exceeded all his
relations in bestial and blameworthy acts and, in the guise of piety,
does the most godless things: does not keep fasts, for on the eve of
St. Philip's Day[8] this apostate bought a lamb and ordered his lawless
wench Gapka to slaughter it the next day, explaining that he supposedly needed tallow just then for lamps and candles.

"Therefore I request that this gentleman, being a robber, a blasphemer, and a crook, already caught thieving and marauding, be
put in irons and conveyed to prison, or to the state jail, and that
there, on discretion, being stripped of his ranks and nobility, he be
given a good basting with birch rods and be sent to hard labor in
Siberia as necessary; that he be made to pay all expenses and losses,
and that a decision be forthcoming on this my petition.

"Setting hand to which petition, I am Ivan, son of Nikifor,
Dovgochkhun, gentleman of the Mirgorod region."

As soon as the secretary finished reading, Ivan Nikiforovich
took his hat and bowed, with the intention of leaving.

"What's the hurry, Ivan Nikiforovich?" the judge called after
him. "Stay a while! have some tea! Oryshko! Why are you standing
there, stupid girl, winking at the office boys? Go and bring tea!"

But Ivan Nikiforovich, frightened to have gone so far from
home and to have endured such a dangerous quarantine, had
already managed to get through the door, saying:

"Don't trouble yourself, it's my pleasure . . ." and closed it
behind him, leaving the whole office in amazement.

There was nothing to be done. Both petitions were accepted,
and the affair was about to take a rather interesting turn when one
unforeseen circumstance lent it still greater amusement. As the
judge was leaving the office in the company of the court clerk and
the secretary, while the office boys were filling a sack with the
chickens, eggs, loaves of bread, pies, knishes, and other stuff
brought by petitioners, just then a brown sow ran into the room
and, to the astonishment of those present, snatched—not a pie or
crust of bread, but Ivan Nikiforovich's petition, which lay at the

end of the table with its pages hanging down. Having snatched the paper, the brown porker ran off so quickly that none of the officials could catch her, despite the hurling of rulers and ink bottles.

This extraordinary incident caused terrible turmoil, because a copy had not even been made of it yet. The judge—that is, his secretary and the court clerk—discussed this unheard-of circumstance for a long time; the decision was finally taken to write a report about it to the police chief, since the investigation of this case belonged rather to the civil police. Report No. 389 was sent to him that same day, whereupon there took place a rather curious conversation, which readers may learn about in the next chapter.

Chapter V
WHICH CONTAINS AN ACCOUNT OF A MEETING BETWEEN TWO DISTINGUISHED PERSONS OF MIRGOROD

Ivan Ivanovich had only just finished his household chores and gone out, as usual, to lie on the gallery, when, to his unutterable astonishment, he saw something red in the gateway. It was the police chief's cuff, which, along with his collar, had acquired a polish and turned at the edges into patent leather. Ivan Ivanovich thought to himself: "That's nice, Pyotr Fyodorovich is coming for a chat," but was very astonished to see the police chief come in extremely quickly and swinging his arms, which usually happened with him quite seldom. On the police chief's uniform sat eight buttons, the ninth having been torn off during the procession for the blessing of the church some two years earlier, so that the policemen were still unable to find it, though the police chief, while receiving the daily reports of the precinct officers, always asked whether the button had been found. These eight buttons sat on him the way peasant women plant beans, one to the left, another to the right. His left leg had been shot through in the last campaign, which caused him, as he limped, to throw it so far to the side that he thereby undid almost all the labor of the right leg. The more speedily the police chief sent his infantry into action, the less it advanced. And therefore, before the police chief reached the gallery, Ivan Ivanovich had plenty of time to lose himself in conjectures as to the reason why the police chief was swinging his arms so quickly. He was the more interested as the matter seemed to be of extraordinary importance, for he even had a new sword on him.

"Greetings, Pyotr Fyodorovich!" cried Ivan Ivanovich, who, as has already been said, was very inquisitive and was simply unable to restrain his impatience at the sight of the police chief storming the porch steps, but still not raising his eyes and quarreling with his infantry, which was in no way capable of taking a step at a single try.

"I wish good day to my gentle friend and benefactor, Ivan Ivanovich!" replied the police chief.

"I ask you kindly to sit down. I see you're tired, because your wounded leg hinders . . ."

"My leg!" cried the police chief, casting one of those looks at Ivan Ivanovich that a giant casts at a pigmy or a learned pedant at a dancing master. With that he raised his leg and stamped on the floor. This brave act cost him dearly, however, because his whole body lurched and his nose pecked the railing; but the wise guardian of order didn't bat an eye, straightened himself up at once, and went to his pocket as if in order to produce his snuffbox. "About myself I may inform you, my gentle friend and benefactor, Ivan Ivanovich, that in my lifetime I've taken part in all sorts of campaigns. Yes, seriously, I have. For instance, during the campaign of eighteen-oh-seven . . . Ah, let me tell you how I once climbed a fence after a pretty little German girl." At this the police chief screwed up one eye and gave a devilishly sly smile.

"And where have you been today?" asked Ivan Ivanovich, wishing to interrupt the police chief, the sooner to bring him to the reason for his visit; he would have liked very much to ask what it was that the police chief intended to tell him; but a refined knowledge of the world presented to him all the indecency of such a question, and Ivan Ivanovich had to restrain himself and wait for the answer, his heart meanwhile pounding with extraordinary force.

"If you please, I'll tell you where I've been," answered the police chief. "First of all, I must inform you that the weather today is excellent . . ."

At these last words Ivan Ivanovich nearly died.

"But, if you please," the police chief went on. "I've come to you today on a rather important matter." Here the police chief's face and bearing adopted the same preoccupied attitude with which he had stormed the porch.

Ivan Ivanovich revived and trembled as in a fever, being prompt, as usual, to ask a question:

"What's important about it? Is it really important?"

"Only consider, if you please: first of all, I venture to inform you, my gentle friend and benefactor, Ivan Ivanovich, that you . . . for my part, I . . . please consider, it's nothing to me; but governmental considerations, governmental considerations require it: you have violated the rules of proper order! . . ."

"What are you saying, Pyotr Fyodorovich? I don't understand a thing."

"Good gracious, Ivan Ivanovich! How is it you don't understand a thing? Your own animal stole a very important official document, and after that you say you don't understand a thing!"

"What animal?"

"Your own brown sow, if you please."

"And what fault is that of mine? The court guard shouldn't leave the door open!"

"But, Ivan Ivanovich, it's your own animal—that means it's your fault."

"I humbly thank you for making me equal to a sow."

"Now, I didn't say that, Ivan Ivanovich! By God, I didn't! Please judge in pure conscience: it is known to you, beyond any doubt, that according to the official rules, unclean animals are forbidden to walk about the town, more especially the main streets of the town. You must agree it's forbidden."

"God knows what your saying! A big thing if a sow goes out in the street!"

"If you please, Ivan Ivanovich, I must inform you, if you please, if you please, this is absolutely impossible! There's no help for it.

Authority wills—we must obey. I don't argue, chickens and geese
sometimes run around in the streets and even in the square—
chickens and geese, mark you—but as for pigs and goats, I already
gave instructions last year not to allow them in the public squares.
Which instructions I ordered read aloud before all the assembled
people."

"No, Pyotr Fyodorovich, I see nothing here, except that you are
trying in every way to offend me."

"Now, that you cannot say, my most gentle friend and benefactor—that I am trying to offend you. You remember: I didn't say a
word last year when you built a roof a whole three feet higher than
the regulation measure. On the contrary, I made it seem as if I'd
ignored it completely. Believe me, my most gentle friend, even
now I would completely, so to speak . . . but my duty—in short,
responsibility demands the observance of cleanliness. Judge for
yourself, if on the main street suddenly . . ."

"Much good your main streets are! The women all go there to
throw out whatever they don't need."

"If you please, I must inform you, Ivan Ivanovich, that it is you
who are offending me! True, it does happen occasionally, but for
the most part only by the fence, the sheds, or the storehouses; but
that a sow in farrow should get into the main street, into the
square, such a thing . . ."

"What of it, Pyotr Fyodorovich! Sows are God's creatures!"

"I agree! The whole world knows that you're a learned man.
You know science and various other subjects. I never studied any
science, of course. I began learning to write longhand when I was
going on thirty. As you know, I came up from the ranks."

"Hm!" said Ivan Ivanovich.

"Yes," the police chief went on, "in the year eighteen-oh-one I
was a lieutenant in the fourth company of the forty-second regiment of chasseurs. Our company commander, be it known to you,
was Captain Yeremeev." Here the police chief poked his fingers
into the snuffbox that Ivan Ivanovich was holding open while rubbing the snuff.

Ivan Ivanovich replied:

"Hm!"

"But it is my duty," the police chief went on, "to obey the demands of the government. Do you know, Ivan Ivanovich, that someone who purloins an official document in court is subject to criminal prosecution, the same as for any other crime?"

"I know it so well that I'll also teach you, if you like. It says that about people—if you, for instance, had stolen the document—but a sow is an animal, a creature of God!"

"That's all very true, but the law says 'guilty of purloining . . .' I ask you to listen attentively: *guilty*! Here neither kind, nor sex, nor rank is mentioned—that means an animal can also be guilty. Say what you will, but before being sentenced to punishment, the animal must be presented to the police as a violator of order."

"No, Pyotr Fyodorovich!" Ivan Ivanovich objected coolly. "That will not be!"

"As you wish, only I must follow the instructions of the authorities."

"Why are you trying to scare me? Really, do you want to send the one-armed soldier for me? I'll tell my serving woman to drive him out with a poker. He'll have his last arm broken."

"I wouldn't dare argue with you. In that case, if you don't want to present her to the police, make whatever use of her you please: butcher her for Christmas whenever you like, and make some hams, or just eat her. Only, if you're going to make sausages, I'll ask you to send me a couple of the ones your Gapka is so good at making, with pork blood and fat. My Agrafena Trofimovna likes them very much."

"I'll send you a couple of sausages, if you please."

"I'll be very grateful to you, my gentle friend and benefactor. Now, allow me to tell you just one word more: I've been charged by the judge, as well as by all our acquaintances, to reconcile you, so to speak, with your friend Ivan Nikiforovich."

"What! with that boor? I should be reconciled with that churl? Never! It will not be, it will not!" Ivan Ivanovich was in an extremely resolute state of mind.

"As you wish," replied the police chief, treating both his nostrils to snuff. "I wouldn't dare give advice: allow me to tell you, however, that you're quarreling now, but once you're reconciled . . ."

But Ivan Ivanovich began talking about hunting quail, which usually happened when he wanted to change the subject.

And so, having achieved no success, the police chief had to go back where he came from.

Chapter VI
FROM WHICH THE READER MAY EASILY LEARN EVERYTHING CONTAINED IN IT

Hard though they tried to conceal the matter in court, by the next day the whole of Mirgorod knew that Ivan Ivanovich's sow had stolen Ivan Nikiforovich's petition. The police chief was the first to forget himself and let it slip. When Ivan Nikiforovich was told of it, he said nothing, asking only: "Was she brown?"

But Agafya Fedoseevna, who was present, again began to get after Ivan Nikiforovich:

"What's the matter with you, Ivan Nikiforovich? You'll be laughed at like a fool if you let it pass! What kind of gentleman will you be after that! You'll be worse than the woman who sells the sweets you like so much!"

And the obstreperous woman convinced him! She found a middle-aged little man somewhere, swarthy, with blotches all over his face, in a dark blue frock coat with patched elbows—a perfect office inkpot! He tarred his boots, carried three quills behind his ear and a glass vial tied to a button with string instead of an inkpot; he ate nine pies at one go and stuffed the tenth into his pocket, and he could write so much of every sort of calumny on one sheet of stamped paper that no reader could read through it at one go without interspersing it with coughs and sneezes. This small semblance of a human being toiled, moiled, scribbled, and finally cooked up the following document:

"To the Mirgorod regional court from Ivan, son of Nikifor, Dovguchkhun, gentleman.

"Pursuant upon the said petition of mine, which came from me, Ivan, son of Nikifor, Dovgochkhun, gentleman, in conjunction with Ivan, son of Ivan, Pererepenko, gentleman, to which the same Mirgorod regional court has shown its indulgence. And this same said brazen willfulness of the brown sow, being kept secret and coming to be heard through outside persons. Since the said permissiveness and indulgence is indisputably subject to prosecution as ill-intentioned; for the said sow is a stupid animal and that much less capable of stealing a document. From which it obviously follows that the oft-mentioned sow was undoubtedly put up to it by the adversary himself, the self-styled gentleman, Ivan, son of Ivan, Pererepenko, already exposed as a robber, attempted murderer, and blasphemer. But the said Mirgorod court, with its peculiar partiality, evinced secret connivance of its person; without which connivance the said sow could in no way have been permitted to steal the document: for the Mirgorod regional court is well provided with servants, it being enough to mention just the soldier alone, who abides in the anteroom at all times, and who, though having a crippled arm and one blind eye, is of quite commensurable ability for driving a sow away and hitting her with a cudgel. From which may be trustworthily seen the connivance of the said Mirgorod regional court and the indisputable sharing of the Jewish profits from it by combining mutually. And the said aforementioned robber and gentleman, Ivan, son of Ivan, Pererepenko, is acting as a fraudulent plaintiff. Which is why I, Ivan, son of Nikifor, Dovgochkhun, gentleman, bring it to the due omniscience of the said regional court that, unless the stated petition is extracted from the brown sow or her accomplice, the gentleman Pererepenko, and a decision on it is justly made in my favor, I, Ivan, son of Nikifor, Dovgochkhun, gentleman, will file a complaint with the state court concerning the illegal connivance of the said court, with the appropriate formal transfer of the case.—Ivan, son of Nikifor, Dovgochkhun, gentleman of the Mirgorod region."

This petition had its effect: the judge, like all good people generally, was a man of a cowardly sort. He turned to the secretary. But the secretary sent a deep "Hm" through his teeth and showed on his face that indifferent and devilishly ambiguous expression which Satan alone wears when he sees at his feet a victim having recourse to him. One means remained: to reconcile the two friends. But how to set about it, if all attempts so far had proved unsuccessful? Nevertheless, they decided to try again; but Ivan Ivanovich announced directly that he did not wish to, and even became very angry. Ivan Nikiforovich, instead of a reply, turned his back and didn't say a word. Then the matter proceeded with the extraordinary rapidity for which courts are ordinarily so famous. The document was marked, recorded, assigned a number, filed, signed, all on one and the same day, and the case was put on a shelf, where it lay and lay and lay—a year, another, a third. A host of brides managed to get married; a new street was laid in Mirgorod; the judge lost a molar and two eyeteeth; Ivan Ivanovich had more kids running around the yard than ever—where they came from God only knows! Ivan Nikiforovich, to reprove Ivan Ivanovich, built a new goose pen, though a bit further away than the former one, and got himself completely built off from Ivan Ivanovich, so that these worthy people hardly ever glimpsed each other's faces—and the case went on lying, in the very best order, on the shelf, which ink blots had turned to marble.

Meanwhile there took place an extremely important event for the whole of Mirgorod.

The police chief gave a party! Where shall I get brushes and paints to portray the diversity of the gathering and the sumptuous feast? Take a watch, open it, and see what goes on inside! Awful nonsense, isn't it? And now imagine as many wheels, if not more, standing in the middle of the police chief's yard. What britzkas and carts there were! One with a wide rear and a narrow front; another with a narrow rear and a wide front. One that was both britzka and cart at the same time; another that was neither britzka nor cart; one resembling an enormous haystack or a merchant's fat wife; another a disheveled Jew or a skeleton not yet entirely free of skin; one had the perfect profile of a pipe with a chibouk; another resembled nothing at all, the image of some strange creature, perfectly ugly and extremely fantastic. From the middle of all this chaos of wheels and boxes there arose the semblance of a carriage with a room-sized window crossed with a thick frame. Coachmen in gray caftans, blouses, and hempen coats, in sheepskin hats and miscellaneous peaked caps, pipes in their hands, led unharnessed horses across the yard. What a party the police chief gave! If you like, I'll list everybody who was there: Taras Tarasovich, Evpl Akinfovich, Evtikhy Evtikhievich, Ivan Ivanovich—not that Ivan Ivanovich but the other one, Savva Gavrilovich, our Ivan Ivanovich, Elevfery Elevferievich, Makar Nazarievich, Foma Grigorievich . . . I can't go on! it's beyond me! My hand is tired of writing! And so many ladies! swarthy and fair, tall and short, some fat as Ivan Niki-forovich, some so thin it seemed each of them could have been put into the police chief's scabbard. So many hats! so many dresses! red, yellow, coffee, green, blue, new, turned, re-cut; shawls, rib-bons, reticules! Farewell, poor eyes! After this spectacle you won't be good for anything. And what a long table was stretched out! And how they all talked, what noise they made! A mill with all its millstones, wheels, gears, and mortars is nothing compared to that! I can't tell you what they talked about, but I can only think it was about many pleasant and useful things, such as: the weather, dogs, wheat, hats, stallions. Finally, Ivan Ivanovich—not that Ivan Ivanovich but the other one, who is blind in one eye—said:

"I find it strange that my right eye" (the one-eyed Ivan Ivano-vich always spoke of himself ironically) "does not see Ivan Niki-forovich, Mr. Dovgochkhun."

"He didn't want to come," said the police chief.

"How so?"

"It's already two years, God bless us, since they quarreled with each other—Ivan Ivanovich and Ivan Nikiforovich, that is—and where the one is, the other won't go for anything!"

"What are you saying?" With that the one-eyed Ivan Ivanovich raised his eyes and clasped his hands. "Well, now, if people with good eyes can't live in peace, how will I get along with my blind one!"

At these words everybody roared with laughter. Everybody liked the one-eyed Ivan Ivanovich, because the jokes he cracked were entirely in the present-day taste. Even the tall, lean man in the cotton flannel frock coat with a plaster on his nose, who till then had been sitting in the corner and had never once changed the movement of his face, even when a fly flew up his nose—this same gentleman got up from his seat and moved closer to the crowd that had formed around the one-eyed Ivan Ivanovich.

"Listen!" said the one-eyed Ivan Ivanovich, when he saw that he had a good-sized company around him. "Listen! Instead of you all now ogling my blind eye, why don't we get our two friends reconciled instead! Right now Ivan Ivanovich is talking with the women and girls—let's quietly send for Ivan Nikiforovich and push them together."

Everybody unanimously accepted Ivan Ivanovich's suggestion and decided immediately to send for Ivan Nikiforovich at home, to ask him by all means to come to dinner at the police chief's. But an important problem—whom to entrust with this important errand—threw them all into perplexity. They argued for a long time over who was most capable and skillful along diplomatic lines; finally it was unanimously decided to entrust it all to Anton Prokofievich Golopuz.[9]

But first we must acquaint the reader somewhat with this remarkable character. Anton Prokofievich was a wholly virtuous man in the full sense of the word: if one of the distinguished persons of Mirgorod gave him a neckerchief or undergarment, he thanked him; if someone flicked him slightly on the nose, he thanked him for that as well. If someone asked him, "How is it, Anton Prokofievich, that your frock coat is brown but the sleeves are light blue?" he always used to reply: "And you don't have anything like it! Just wait, it'll get worn and turn the same color all over!" And indeed, under the effect of the sun, the blue cloth began to turn brown and now matches the color of the frock coat perfectly! But the strange thing is that Anton Prokofievich was in the habit of wearing flannel clothes in the summer and nankeen in the winter. Anton Prokofievich has no house of his own. He had one once, at the edge of town, but he sold it and used the money to buy a troika of bay horses and a small britzka, in which he drove around visiting landowners. But since they were a lot of trouble, and he had to have money to buy oats besides, Anton Prokofievich traded them for a fiddle and a serving girl, with twenty-five roubles to boot. Then Anton Prokofievich sold the fiddle and traded the girl for a gold brocade tobacco pouch. And now he has a pouch such as no one else has. Owing to this pleasure, he can no longer drive around visiting estates, but has to stay in town and sleep in various houses, particularly those of the gentlemen who enjoy giving him flicks on the nose. Anton Prokofievich likes to eat well and plays a good game of "fools" and "millers." Obedience was always his element, and therefore, taking his hat and stick, he set forth immediately. But, as he walked, he began reasoning about how he might induce Ivan Nikiforovich to come to the party. The rather tough character of this otherwise worthy man made the undertaking all but impossible. And why, indeed, should he venture to come, if getting up from his bed was already a great labor for him? But, supposing he did get up, why should he go to a place where—as he undoubtedly knew—his implacable enemy was? The more Anton Prokofievich thought about it, the more obstacles he found. The day was stifling; the sun burned down; sweat streamed from him. Anton Prokofievich, though he might be flicked on the nose, was a very clever man in many respects—he simply wasn't so lucky at trading—and knew very well when he should pretend to be a fool, and sometimes proved resourceful in circumstances and on occasions when an intelligent man would scarcely have been able to wriggle his way out.

While his inventive mind was thinking up some means of convincing Ivan Nikiforovich, and he was already going bravely to meet it all, a certain unexpected circumstance left him rather bewildered. Here it will do no harm to inform the reader that Anton Prokofievich had, among other things, a pair of trousers with the strange property that, whenever he wore them, dogs always bit him on the calves. As ill luck would have it, he was wearing precisely those trousers that day. And that was why he had no sooner given himself over to reflection than his hearing was struck by terrible barking on all sides. Anton Prokofievich raised such a cry—no one could shout louder than he—that not only our woman acquaintance and the owner of the boundless frock coat ran to meet him, but even the boys from Ivan Ivanovich's yard came pouring out, and though the dogs only managed to bite one of his legs, nevertheless it greatly diminished his cheerfulness, and he approached the porch with a certain timidity.

Chapter VII
And Last

"Ah! greetings! What are you teasing the dogs for?" said Ivan Nikiforovich, seeing Anton Prokofievich, because no one ever spoke to Anton Prokofievich except jokingly.

"They can all drop dead! Who's teasing them?" replied Anton Prokofievich.

"You're lying."

"By God, I'm not! Pyotr Fyodorovich is inviting you to dinner."

"Hm!"

"Yes, by God! and he insists on it so much, I can't tell you. 'Why is it,' he says, 'that Ivan Nikiforovich avoids me like an enemy? Never stops by to chat or sit a while.'"

Ivan Nikiforovich stroked his chin.

"'If Ivan Nikiforovich doesn't come now,' he says, 'I don't know what I'll think: he must have something against me. Do me a favor, Anton Prokofievich, persuade Ivan Nikiforovich!' So what about it, Ivan Nikiforovich? Come on, there's an excellent company gathered there now!"

Ivan Nikiforovich began to scrutinize a rooster that was standing on the porch crowing his throat off.

"If you knew, Ivan Nikiforovich," the zealous deputy went on, "what sturgeon, what fresh caviar Pyotr Fyodorovich has been sent!"

At that Ivan Nikiforovich turned his head and began listening attentively.

This encouraged the deputy.

"Let's hurry. Foma Grigorievich is there, too! What's the matter?" he added, seeing that Ivan Nikiforovich went on lying in the same position. "Well, do we go or don't we?"

"I don't want to."

This "I don't want to" struck Anton Prokofievich. He thought his convincing presentation had thoroughly persuaded this otherwise worthy man, but instead he heard a resolute "I don't want to."

"And why don't you want to?" he said, almost with vexation, which appeared in him extremely rarely, even when they put burning paper on his head, something the judge and the police chief particularly enjoyed doing.

Ivan Nikiforovich took a pinch of snuff.

"As you like, Ivan Nikiforovich, but I don't know what's holding you back."

"Why should I go?" Ivan Nikiforovich said at last. "That robber will be there!" So he usually called Ivan Ivanovich.

Good God, was it so long ago that . . .

"By God, he won't! As God is holy, he won't! May I be struck by lightning on this very spot!" replied Anton Prokofievich, who was ready to swear by God ten times an hour. "Come on, Ivan Nikiforovich!"

"You're lying, Anton Prokofievich, he's there, eh?"

"No, by God, he's not! May I never leave this spot if he's there! And consider for yourself, why would I lie? May my arms and legs wither! . . . What, you still don't believe me? May I drop dead right here in front of you! May my father and mother and I myself never see the Kingdom of Heaven! You still don't believe me?"

These assurances finally set Ivan Nikiforovich perfectly at ease, and he ordered his valet in the infinite frock coat to bring his balloon trousers and nankeen jacket.

I suppose that to describe the way in which Ivan Nikiforovich put on his balloon trousers, wrapped a tie around his neck, and finally put on the nankeen jacket, which had a split under the left arm, is completely superfluous. Suffice it to say that he preserved a fitting calm all the while and made not a word of reply to Anton Prokofievich's suggestion of trading something for his Turkish tobacco pouch.

Meanwhile the gathering impatiently awaited the decisive moment when Ivan Nikiforovich would appear and the general wish that these two worthy people become reconciled would finally be fulfilled. Many were virtually certain that Ivan Nikiforovich wouldn't come. The police chief even offered to bet the one-eyed

Ivan Ivanovich that he wouldn't, but did not conclude it only because the one-eyed Ivan Ivanovich insisted that the police chief stake his shot-through leg and he his blind eye, which the police chief found highly insulting, while the company quietly laughed. No one sat at the table yet, though it was long past one o'clock— by which time, in Mirgorod, even on gala occasions, people have long been dining.

No sooner did Anton Prokofievich appear in the doorway than he was instantly surrounded by everyone. To all their questions, Anton Prokofievich shouted one resolute phrase: "He won't come." No sooner had he uttered it, and a shower of reprimands, curses, and perhaps even flicks, prepared itself to pour down on his head for his unsuccessful embassy, than the door suddenly opened and—in came Ivan Nikiforovich.

If Satan himself or a dead man had appeared, they would not have caused such amazement in the whole gathering as that into which it was thrown by Ivan Nikiforovich's unexpected arrival. And Anton Prokofievich simply dissolved, holding his sides, from the joy of having played such a trick on the whole company.

Be that as it may, but it was almost unbelievable for them all that Ivan Nikiforovich should have managed in so short a time to dress himself as befits a gentleman. Ivan Ivanovich was not there just then; he had stepped out for some reason. Having recovered from its amazement, the whole public displayed concern for Ivan Niki- forovich's health and expressed satisfaction at his having increased in girth. Ivan Nikiforovich exchanged kisses with them all, saying, "Much obliged."

Meanwhile the smell of borscht spread through the room and pleasantly tickled the nostrils of the now hungry guests. They all flocked to the dining room. A file of ladies, talkative and taciturn, skinny and fat, drew forward, and the long table rippled with all colors. I will not describe the dishes that were set on the table! I will say nothing of the mnishki[10] with sour cream, nor the tripe served with the borscht, nor the turkey with plums and raisins, nor the dish that looked very much like boots soaked in kvass, nor the sauce that was the swan song of an old-style cook—a sauce served all enveloped in a spiritous flame, which greatly amused and at the same time frightened the ladies. I will not speak of these dishes, because I much prefer eating them to holding forth on them in conversation.

Ivan Ivanovich had a great liking for fish prepared with horse-radish. He became especially occupied with this useful and nour-ishing exercise. He was removing the finest fish bones and placing them on his plate when he somehow inadvertently glanced across the table: God in heaven, how strange! Opposite him sat Ivan Nikiforovich!

At one and the same moment, Ivan Nikiforovich also glanced up! . . . No! . . . I can't . . . Give me another pen! My pen is slug-gish, lifeless, the slit is too fine for this picture! Their faces became as if petrified in an expression of amazement. Each of them beheld a long-familiar face, to which it would seem one was ready to go up instinctively, as to an unexpected friend, and hold out a snuff bottle, saying, "Help yourself" or "May I venture to ask you to help yourself"; but, along with that, the same face was terrible, like an evil omen! Sweat streamed from Ivan Ivanovich and Ivan Nikiforovich.

The people present, all who were at the table, turned mute with attention and could not tear their eyes from the former friends. The ladies, who till then had been taken up with a rather interest-ing conversation about the ways of preparing capon, suddenly broke it off. Everything became hushed! It was a picture deserving of the brush of a great painter!

Finally Ivan Ivanovich took out his handkerchief and began to blow his nose; but Ivan Nikiforovich looked around and rested his eyes on the open door. The police chief noticed this gesture at once and ordered the door tightly shut. Then each of the friends began to eat, and not once did they glance at each other again.

As soon as the dinner was over, the two former friends left their places and began looking for their hats, so as to slip away. Then the police chief winked, and Ivan Ivanovich—not that Ivan Ivanovich but the other, the one with the blind eye—stood behind Ivan Nikiforovich's back, while the police chief got behind Ivan Ivano-vich's back, and the two started shoving them from behind so as to push them together and not let go until they shook hands. Ivan

Ivanovich of the blind eye did push Ivan Nikiforovich, somewhat obliquely but still rather successfully, toward the place where Ivan Ivanovich had been standing; but the police chief's aim was way off, because he was unable to manage the willfulness of his infantry, which this time did not obey any commands and, as if on purpose, kept straying extremely far and in the completely opposite direction (which may have come from the fact that there were a great many liqueurs of all sorts on the table), so that Ivan Ivanovich fell over a lady in a red dress who, out of curiosity, had stuck herself right in the center. Such an omen did not bode any good. However, to put things right, the judge took the police chief's place and, sucking all the snuff from his upper lip into his nose, pushed Ivan Ivanovich in the other direction. This is the usual means of reconciliation in Mirgorod. It's something like playing ball. As soon as the judge pushed Ivan Ivanovich, Ivan Ivanovich of the blind eye took the firmest stand and pushed Ivan Nikiforovich, from whom the sweat poured down like rain off a roof. Though the two friends put up a strong resistance, they were nevertheless pushed together, because the two acting sides received significant reinforcement from the other guests.

Then they were surrounded tightly on all sides and were not let out until they resolved to shake hands with each other.

"God be with you, Ivan Nikiforovich and Ivan Ivanovich! Tell us in all conscience, what did you quarrel about? Wasn't it over a trifle? Aren't you ashamed before people and before God?"

"I don't know," said Ivan Nikiforovich, puffing with fatigue (one could see that he was not at all against the reconciliation), "I don't know what it was that I did to Ivan Ivanovich. Why, then, did he chop down my pen and plot to destroy me?"

"I'm not guilty of any evil designs," said Ivan Ivanovich, not turning his eyes to Ivan Nikiforovich. "I swear before God and before all of you honorable gentlemen, I did nothing to my enemy. Why, then, does he abuse me and do damage to my rank and name?"

"In what way have I done you damage, Ivan Ivanovich?" said Ivan Nikiforovich.

Another minute of talk and the long enmity would have been on the point of dying out. Ivan Nikiforovich was already going to his pocket to produce his snuff bottle and say, "Help yourself."

"Isn't it damage," Ivan Ivanovich replied, without raising his eyes, "if you, my dear sir, insult my rank and family name with a word that it is even indecent to utter here?"

"Allow me to tell you as a friend, Ivan Ivanovich" (with that, Ivan Nikiforovich touched Ivan Ivanovich's button with his finger, signifying his entire good will), "that you got offended over devil knows what—over my calling you a *goose* . . ."

Ivan Nikiforovich caught himself committing the carelessness of uttering this word; but it was already too late: the word had been uttered.

Everything went to the devil!

If the uttering of this word without any witnesses had put Ivan Ivanovich beside himself and in such a rage as God keep us from ever seeing in any man—what now, only consider, gentle readers, what now, when this deadly word was uttered in a gathering that included many ladies, before whom Ivan Ivanovich liked to be especially proper? If Ivan Nikiforovich had acted differently, if he had said *bird* instead of *goose*, things still might have been put right.

But—it was all over!

He cast a glance at Ivan Nikiforovich—and what a glance! If this glance had been endowed with executive power, it would have turned Ivan Nikiforovich to dust. The guests understood this glance and hastened to separate them. And this man, the epitome of mildness, who never passed over a beggar woman without questioning her, rushed out in a terrible fury. Such violent storms the passions can produce!

For a whole month nothing was heard of Ivan Ivanovich. He locked himself up in his house. The secret trunk was unlocked, and from the trunk were taken—what? silver roubles! old ones, his ancestral silver roubles! And these roubles passed into the soiled hands of ink-slingers. The case was transferred to the state court. And when Ivan Ivanovich received the joyful news that it was to be decided the next day, only then did he look outside and venture to leave his house. Alas! since then, the court has informed him daily for the past ten years that the case would be concluded the next day!

SOME FIVE YEARS ago I passed through the town of Mirgorod. I was traveling in bad weather. It was autumn, with its damp, melancholy days, its mud and mists. Some sort of unnatural green—the creation of dull, ceaseless rains—covered the fields and meadows with a thin net, which was as becoming as pranks to an old man or roses to an old woman. Weather affected me strongly then—I was dull when it was dull. But, despite that, as I approached Mirgorod, I felt my heart beating fast. God, so many memories! I hadn't seen Mirgorod for twelve years. Here, in touching friendship, there had then lived two singular men, two singular friends. And how many notable people had died! The judge Demyan Demyanovich was dead by then; Ivan Ivanovich, the one with the blind eye, had also bid the world farewell. I drove into the main street; poles with bunches of straw tied to their tops stood everywhere: some new project was under way! Several cottages had been demolished. The remnants of palings and wattle fences stuck up dejectedly.

It was then a feast day. I ordered my bast-covered kibitka to stop in front of the church and went in so quietly that no one turned around. True, there was no one to do so. The church was empty. Almost no people. One could see that even the most pious were afraid of the mud. The candles in that bleak, or, better to say, sickly daylight, were somehow strangely unpleasant; the dark vestibule was melancholy; the oblong windows with round glass poured down rainy tears. I stepped into the vestibule and turned to one respectable, gray-haired old man:

"If I may ask, is Ivan Nikiforovich still living?"

Just then the lamp flashed more brightly before the icon, and the light fell directly on the face of my neighbor. How surprised I was when, peering at him, I saw familiar features! It was Ivan Nikiforovich himself! But how changed he was!

"Are you well, Ivan Nikiforovich? You've aged so!"

"Yes, I've aged. I came from Poltava today," replied Ivan Niki-forovich.

"You don't say! You went to Poltava in such bad weather?"

"No help for it! The lawsuit . . ."

At that, I, too, sighed involuntarily. Ivan Nikiforovich noticed this sigh and said:

"Don't worry, I have definite information that the case will be decided in my favor next week."

I shrugged and went to find out something about Ivan Ivano-vich.

"Ivan Ivanovich is here," someone told me, "he's in the choir."

Then I saw a skinny figure. Was this Ivan Ivanovich? His face was covered with wrinkles; his hair was completely white; but the bekesha was the same. After the preliminary greetings, Ivan Ivanovich turned to me with that joyful smile which was always so becoming to his funnel-like face, and said:

"Shall I inform you of some pleasant news?"

"What news?" I said.

"My case will be decided tomorrow without fail. The court says it's certain."

I sighed still more deeply and hastened to take my leave, because I was traveling on important business, and got into my kibitka. The skinny horses, known in Mirgorod as the posthaste kind, drew away, producing with their hooves, as they sank into the gray mass of mud, a sound unpleasant to the ear. Rain poured down in streams on the Jew who sat on the box covering himself with a bast mat. Dampness penetrated me thoroughly. The melancholy town gate, with a sentry box in which an invalid sat mending his gray armor, slowly passed by. Again the same fields, in places turned up and black, in others showing green, the wet jackdaws and crows, the monotonous rain, the sky tearful and without a bright spot.—It's dull in this world, gentlemen!

PETERSBURG
TALES

Nevsky Prospect

THERE IS NOTHING better than Nevsky Prospect, at least not in Petersburg; for there it is everything. What does this street—the beauty of our capital—not shine with! I know that not one of its pale and clerical inhabitants would trade Nevsky Prospect for anything in the world. Not only the one who is twenty-five years old, has an excellent mustache and a frock coat of an amazing cut, but even the one who has white hair sprouting on his chin and a head as smooth as a silver dish, he, too, is enchanted with Nevsky Prospect. And the ladies! Oh, the ladies find Nevsky Prospect still more pleasing. And who does not find it pleasing? The moment you enter Nevsky Prospect, it already smells of nothing but festivity. Though you may have some sort of necessary, indispensable business, once you enter it you are sure to forget all business. Here is the only place where people do not go out of necessity, where they are not driven by the need and mercantile interest that envelop the whole of Petersburg. A man met on Nevsky Prospect seems less of an egoist than on Morskaya, Gorokhovaya, Liteiny, Meshchanskaya, and other streets, where greed, self-interest, and necessity show on those walking or flying by in carriages and droshkies. Nevsky Prospect is the universal communication of Petersburg. Here the inhabitant of the Petersburg or Vyborg side who has not visited his friend in Peski or the Moscow Gate[1] for several years can be absolutely certain of meeting him. No directory or inquiry office will provide such reliable information as Nevsky Prospect. All-powerful Nevsky Prospect! The only entertainment for a poor man at the Petersburg feast! How clean-swept are its sidewalks, and, God, how many feet have left their traces on it! The clumsy, dirty boot of the retired soldier, under the weight of which the very granite seems to crack, and the miniature shoe, light as smoke, of a young lady, who turns her head to the glittering shop windows as a sunflower turns toward the sun, and the clanking sword of a hope-filled sub-lieutenant that leaves a sharp scratch on it—everything wreaks upon it the power of strength or the power of weakness. What a quick phantasmagoria is performed on it in the course of a single day! How many changes it undergoes in the course of a single day and night!

Let us begin from earliest morning, when the whole of Petersburg smells of hot, freshly baked bread and is filled with old women in tattered dresses and coats carrying out their raids on churches and compassionate passers-by. At that time Nevsky Prospect is empty: the stout shop owners and their salesclerks are still asleep in their Holland nightshirts or are soaping their noble cheeks and drinking coffee; beggars gather near the pastry shops, where a sleepy Ganymede,[2] who yesterday was flying about with chocolate like a fly, crawls out, tieless, broom in hand, and tosses them stale cakes and leftovers. Down the streets trudge useful folk: Russian muzhiks pass by occasionally, hurrying to work, their boots crusted with lime that even the Ekaterininsky Canal, famous for its cleanness, would be unable to wash off. At that time it is usually unfitting for ladies to go about, because the Russian people like to express themselves in such sharp terms as they would probably not hear even in the theater. An occasional sleepy clerk will plod by, briefcase under his arm, if he has to pass Nevsky Prospect on his way to the office. One may say decidedly that at that time, that is, until twelve o'clock, Nevsky Prospect does not constitute anyone's goal, it serves only as a means: it gradually fills with people who have their own occupations, their own cares, their own vexations, and do not think about it at all. The Russian muzhik talks about his ten coppers or seven groats, the old men and women wave their arms and talk to themselves, sometimes with quite expressive gestures, but no one listens to them or laughs at them, except perhaps some urchins in hempen blouses, with empty bottles or repaired shoes in their hands, racing along Nevsky Prospect like lightning. At that time, however you may be dressed, even if you have a peaked cap on your head instead of a hat, even if your collar sticks out too far over your tie—no one will notice it.

At twelve o'clock Nevsky Prospect is invaded by tutors of all nations with their charges in cambric collars. English Joneses and French Coques walk hand in hand with the charges entrusted to their parental care and, with proper gravity, explain to them that the signs over the shops are made so that by means of them one may learn what is to be found inside the shop. Governesses, pale misses and rosy Slavs, walk majestically behind their light, fidgety girls, telling them to raise their shoulders a bit higher and straighten their backs; in short, at this time Nevsky Prospect is a pedagogical Nevsky Prospect. But the closer it comes to two o'clock, the fewer in number are the tutors, pedagogues, and children: they are finally supplanted by their loving progenitors, who hold on their arms their bright, multicolored, weak-nerved companions. Gradually their company is joined by all those who have finished their rather important domestic business, to wit: discussing the weather with their doctor, as well as a little pimple that has popped out on the nose, informing themselves about the health of their horses and children, who incidentally show great promise, reading an advertisement in the newspaper and an important article on arrivals and departures, and, finally, drinking a cup of coffee or tea; and these are joined by those on whom an enviable fate has bestowed the blessed title of official for special missions. And these are joined by those who serve in the foreign office and are distinguished by the nobility of their occupations and habits. God, how beautiful some posts and jobs are! how they elevate and delight the soul! but, alas! I am not in the civil service and am denied the pleasure of beholding my superiors' refined treatment of me. Whatever you meet on Nevsky Prospect is all filled with decency: men in long frock coats, their hands in their pockets, ladies in pink, white, and pale blue satin redingotes and hats. Here you will meet singular side-whiskers, tucked with extraordinary and amazing art under the necktie, velvety whiskers, satiny whiskers, black as sable or coal, but, alas, belonging only to the foreign office. Providence has denied black side-whiskers to those serving in other departments; they, however great the unpleasantness, must wear red ones. Here you will meet wondrous mustaches, which no pen or brush is able to portray; mustaches to which the better part of a lifetime is devoted—object of long vigils by day and by night; mustaches on which exquisite perfumes and scents have been poured, and which have been anointed with all the most rare and precious sorts of pomades, mustaches which are wrapped overnight in fine vellum, mustaches which are subject to the most touching affection of their possessors and are the envy of passers-by. A thousand kinds of hats, dresses, shawls—gay-colored, ethereal, for which their owners' affection sometimes lasts a whole two days—will bedazzle anyone on Nevsky Prospect. It seems as if a whole sea of butter-flies has suddenly arisen from the stems, their brilliant cloud un-dulating over the black beetles of the male sex. Here you will meet such waists as you have never seen in dreams: slender, narrow waists, no whit thicker than a bottle's neck, on meeting which you deferentially step aside, lest you somehow imprudently nudge them with your discourteous elbow; timidity and fear will come over your heart, lest somehow from your imprudent breath the loveliest work of nature and art should be broken. And what la-dies' sleeves you meet on Nevsky Prospect! Ah, how lovely! They somewhat resemble two airborne balloons, so that the lady would suddenly rise into the air if the man were not holding her; for raising a lady into the air is as easy and pleasant as bringing a champagne-filled glass to your lips. Nowhere do people exchange bows when they meet with such nobility and nonchalance as on Nevsky Prospect. Here you will meet that singular smile, the height of art, which may cause you sometimes to melt with pleasure, sometimes suddenly to see yourself lower than grass, and you hang your head, sometimes to feel yourself higher than the Admiralty spire,[3] and you raise it. Here you will meet people discussing a concert or the weather with an extraordinary nobility and sense of their own dignity. You will meet thousands of inconceivable characters and phenomena. O Creator! what strange characters one meets on Nevsky Prospect! There is a host of such people as, when they meet you, unfailingly look at your shoes, and, when you pass by, turn to look at your coattails. To this day I fail to understand why this happens. At first I thought they were shoe-makers, but no, that is not the case: for the most part they serve in various departments, many are perfectly well able to write an official letter from one institution to another; or else they are people occupied with strolling, reading newspapers in pastry shops—in short, they are nearly all decent people. At this blessed time, from two to three in the afternoon, when Nevsky Prospect may be called a capital in motion, there takes place a major exhibition of the best products of humanity. One displays a foppish frock coat with the best of beavers, another a wonderful Greek nose, the third is the bearer of superb side-whiskers, the fourth of a pair of pretty eyes and an astonishing little hat, the fifth of a signet ring with a talisman on his smart pinkie, the sixth of a little foot in a charming bootie, the seventh of an astonishment-arousing neck-tie, the eighth of an amazement-inspiring mustache. But it strikes three and the exhibition is over, the crowd thins out . . . At three, a new change. Suddenly spring comes to Nevsky Prospect: it gets all covered with clerks in green uniforms. Hungry titular, court, and other councillors try with all their might to put on speed. Young collegiate registrars, provincial and collegiate secretaries hasten to make use of their time and take a stroll on Nevsky Prospect with a bearing which suggests that they have not spent six hours sitting in an office. But the old collegiate secretaries, titular and court councillors walk briskly, their heads bowed: they cannot be bothered with gazing at passers-by; they are not yet completely torn away from their cares; there is a jumble in their heads and a whole archive of started and unfinished cases; for a long time, instead of a signboard, they see a carton of papers or the plump face of the office chief.

From four o'clock on, Nevsky Prospect is empty, and you will hardly meet even one clerk on it. Some seamstress from a shop runs across Nevsky Prospect, a box in her hands; some pathetic victim of a humanitarian lawyer, reduced to begging in a frieze overcoat; some visiting eccentric for whom all hours are the same; some long, tall Englishwoman with a reticule and a book in her hands; some company agent, a Russian in a half-cotton frock coat gathered at the back, with a narrow little beard, who lives all his life in a slapdash way, in whom everything moves—back and arms and legs and head—as he goes deferentially down the sidewalk; now and then a lowly artisan; you will not meet anyone else on Nevsky Prospect.

But as soon as dusk falls on the houses and streets, and the sentry, covering himself with a bast mat, climbs the ladder to light the lantern, and prints which do not dare show themselves in the daytime peek out of the low shop windows, then Nevsky Prospect again comes to life and begins to stir. Then comes that mysterious time when lamps endow everything with some enticing, wondrous light. You will meet a great many young men, mostly bachelors, in warm frock coats or overcoats. At that time there is a sense of some goal, or, better, of something resembling a goal, something extremely unaccountable; everyone's steps quicken and generally become very uneven. Long shadows flit over the walls and pavement, their heads all but reaching the Police Bridge. Young collegiate registrars, provincial and collegiate secretaries stroll about for a very long time; but the old collegiate registrars, titular councillors, and court councillors mostly stay home, either because they are married folk or because their food is very well prepared by their live-in German cooks. Here you will meet the respectable old men who strolled along Nevsky Prospect with such gravity and such amazing nobility at two o'clock. You will see them running just like young collegiate registrars to peek under the hat of a lady spotted from far off, whose thick lips and rouge-plastered cheeks are liked by so many strollers, most of all by the

salesclerks, company agents, shopkeepers, always dressed in German frock coats, who go strolling in whole crowds and usually arm
in arm.

"Wait!" Lieutenant Pirogov cried at that moment, tugging at
the young man in the tailcoat and cloak who was walking beside
him. "Did you see?"

"I did, a wonderful girl, a perfect Perugino Bianca."[4]

"But who are you talking about?"

"Her, the dark-haired one. And what eyes! God, what eyes! The
bearing, and the figure, and the shape of the face—sheer wonders!"

"I'm talking about the blonde who walked after her in the same
direction. Why don't you go after the brunette, since you liked her
so much?"

"Oh, how could I?" the young man in the tailcoat exclaimed,
blushing. "As if she were the kind to walk about Nevsky Prospect
in the evening. She must be a very noble lady," he went on, sighing, "her cloak alone is worth about eighty roubles!"

"Simpleton!" cried Pirogov, pushing him toward where the
bright cloak was fluttering. "Go on, ninny, you'll miss her! And I'll
follow the blonde."

The two friends parted.

"We know you all," Pirogov thought with a self-satisfied and
self-confident smile, sure that no beauty would be able to resist
him.

The young man in the tailcoat and cloak went with timid and
tremulous steps toward where, some distance away, the colorful
cloak was fluttering, now bathed in bright light as it approached a
street lamp, now instantly covered in darkness as it left it behind.
His heart was pounding, and he unwittingly quickened his pace.
He did not even dare dream of gaining any right to the attention
of the beauty flying off into the distance, still less to admit such a
black thought as Lieutenant Pirogov had hinted at; he merely
wished to see the house, to make note of where this lovely being
dwelt, who seemed to have flown down from heaven right onto
Nevsky Prospect and would surely fly off again no one knew

where. He flew along so quickly that he was constantly pushing staid gentlemen with gray side-whiskers off the sidewalk. This young man belonged to a class which represents quite a strange phenomenon among us and belongs as much to the citizens of Petersburg as a person who comes to us in a dream belongs to the real world. This exceptional group is highly unusual in a city in which everyone is either an official, a shopkeeper, or a German artisan. He was an artist. A strange phenomenon, is it not? A Petersburg artist! An artist in the land of snows, an artist in the land of Finns, where everything is wet, smooth, flat, pale, gray, misty. These artists do not in the least resemble Italian artists—proud, ardent, like Italy and its sky; on the contrary, they are for the most part kind and meek people, bashful, lighthearted, with a quiet love for their art, who drink tea with their two friends in a small room, who talk modestly about their favorite subject and are totally indifferent to all superfluity. He is forever inviting some old beggar woman to his place and making her sit for a good six hours, so as to transfer her pathetic, insensible expression to canvas. He paints his room in perspective, with all sorts of artistic clutter appearing in it: plaster arms and legs turned coffee-colored with time and dust, broken easels, an overturned palette, a friend playing a guitar, paint-stained walls, and an open window through which comes a glimpse of the pale Neva and poor fishermen in red shirts. They paint almost everything in dull, grayish colors—the indelible imprint of the north. Yet, for all that, they apply themselves with genuine pleasure to their work. They often nurture a genuine talent in themselves, and if the fresh air of Italy were to breathe on them, it would surely develop as freely, broadly, and vividly as a plant that has finally been brought outside into the open air. They are generally very timid: a star[5] or a thick epaulette throws them into such confusion that they unwittingly lower the price of their works. They like to play the dandy on occasion, but this dandyism always stands out in them and looks something like a patch. You will sometimes meet an excellent tailcoat on them and a dirty cloak, an expensive velvet waistcoat and a frock coat all covered with paint. Just as you will sometimes meet on their unfinished landscape a nymph painted upside down, which the artist, finding no other place, sketched on the dirty background of an old work he once delighted in painting. He never looks you straight in the eye; or if he does, it is somehow vaguely, indefinitely; he does not pierce you with the hawk's eye of an observer or the falcon's gaze of a cavalry officer. The reason for that is that he sees, at one and the same time, both your features and those of some plaster Hercules standing in his room, or else he imagines a painting of his own that he still means to produce. That is why his responses are often incoherent, not to the point, and the muddle of things in his head increases his timidity all the more. To this kind belonged the young man we have described, the artist Piskarev, shy, timid, but bearing in his soul sparks of feeling ready on the right occasion to burst into flame. With a secret tremor he hastened after his object, who had struck him so strongly, and he himself seemed to marvel at his own boldness. The unknown being to whom his eyes, thoughts, and feelings clung so, suddenly turned her head and looked at him. God, what divine features! The loveliest brow, of a dazzling whiteness, was overshadowed by beautiful, agate-like hair. They were curly, those wondrous tresses, some of which fell from under her hat onto her cheek, touched with a fine, fresh color called up by the cool of the evening. Her lips were locked on a whole swarm of the loveliest reveries. All that remains of childhood, that comes of dreaming and quiet inspiration by a lighted lamp—all this seemed to join and merge and be reflected in her harmonious lips. She glanced at Piskarev, and his heart fluttered at this glance; it was a stern glance, a sense of indignation showed on her face at the sight of such insolent pursuit; but on this beautiful face wrath itself was bewitching. Overcome with shame and timidity, he stopped, his eyes cast down; but how lose this divinity without even discovering to what holy place she had descended for a visit? Such thoughts came into the young dreamer's head, and he resolved on pursuit. But to do it without being noticed, he hung back, glanced around nonchalantly and studied the shop signs, while not losing sight of a single step the unknown lady took. Passers-by began to flit by more rarely, the street grew quieter; the beauty looked back, and it seemed to him that a slight smile flashed on her lips. He trembled all over and did not believe his eyes. No, it was the street lamp with its deceitful light showing the semblance of a smile on her face; no, it was his own dreams laughing at him. But it stopped the breath in his breast, everything in him turned into a vague trembling, all his senses were aflame, and everything before him was covered with a sort of mist. The sidewalk rushed under him, carriages with galloping horses seemed motionless, the bridge was stretched out and breaking on its arch, the house stood roof down, the sentry box came tumbling to meet him, and the sentry's halberd, along with the golden words of a shop sign and its painted scissors, seemed to flash right on his eyelashes. And all this was accomplished by one glance, by one turn of a pretty head. Unhearing, unseeing, unheeding, he raced in the light tracks of beautiful feet, himself trying to moderate the quickness of his pace, which flew in time with his heart. Sometimes doubt would come over him: Was the expression of her face indeed so benevolent?—and then he would stop for a moment, but the beating of his heart, the invincible force and agitation of all his feelings, urged him onward. He did not even notice how a four-story house suddenly rose before him, how all four rows of windows, shining with light, glared at him at once, and the railings of the entrance opposed him with their iron thrust. He saw the unknown woman fly up the steps, look back, put her finger to her lips, and motion for him to follow her. His knees trembled; his senses and thoughts were on fire; a lightning flash of joy pierced his heart with an unbearable point! No, it was no dream! God, so much happiness in one instant! such a wonderful life of two minutes!

But was it not a dream? Could it be that she, for one of whose heavenly glances he would be ready to give his whole life, to approach whose dwelling he already counted an inexplicable bliss—could it be that she had just shown him such favor and attention? He flew up the stairs. He did not feel any earthly thought; he was not heated with the flame of earthly passion, no, at that moment he was pure and chaste, like a virginal youth, still breathing the vague spiritual need for love. And that which in a depraved man would arouse bold thoughts, that same thing, on the contrary, made him still more radiant. This trust which a weak, beautiful being had shown in him, this trust imposed on him a vow of chivalric rigor, a vow slavishly to fulfill all her commands. He wished only for her commands to be all the more difficult and unrealizable, so that he could fly to overcome them with the greater effort. He had no doubt that some secret and at the same time important reason had made the unknown woman entrust herself to him, that some important services would surely be required of him, and he already felt in himself enough strength and resolve for everything.

The stairway wound around, and his quick dreams wound with it. "Watch your step!" a voice sounded like a harp and filled his veins with fresh trembling. On the dark height of the fourth floor, the unknown lady knocked at the door—it opened, and they went in together. A rather good-looking woman met them with a candle in her hand, but she gave Piskarev such a strange and insolent look that he involuntarily lowered his eyes. They went into the room. Three female figures in different corners appeared before his eyes. One was laying out cards; the second sat at a piano and with two fingers picked out some pathetic semblance of an old polonaise; the third sat before a mirror combing her long hair and never thought of interrupting her toilette at the entrance of a stranger. Some unpleasant disorder, to be met with only in the carefree room of a bachelor, reigned over all. The rather nice furniture was covered with dust; a spider had spread its web over a molded cornice; in the half-open doorway to another room, a spurred boot gleamed and the red piping of a uniform flitted: a loud male voice and female laughter rang out unrestrainedly.

God, where had he come! At first he refused to believe it and began studying the objects that filled the room more attentively; but the bare walls and curtainless windows showed no presence of a thoughtful housewife; the worn faces of these pathetic creatures, one of whom sat down almost in front of his nose and gazed at him as calmly as at a spot on someone's clothes—all this convinced him that he had come to one of those revolting havens where pathetic depravity makes its abode, born of tawdry education and the terrible populousness of the capital. One of those havens where man blasphemously crushes and derides all the pure and holy that adorns life, where woman, the beauty of the world, the crown of creation, turns into some strange, ambiguous being, where, along with purity of soul, she loses everything feminine and repulsively adopts all the mannerisms and insolence of a man, and ceases to be that weak, that beautiful being so different from us. Piskarev looked her up and down with astonished eyes, as if still wishing to make sure that it was she who had so bewitched him and swept him away on Nevsky Prospect. But she stood before him as beautiful as ever; her hair was as wonderful; her eyes seemed as heavenly. She was fresh; she was just seventeen; one could see that terrible depravity had overtaken her only recently; it had not yet dared to touch her cheeks, they were fresh and lightly tinted by a fine blush—she was beautiful.

He stood motionless before her and was about to fall into the same simple-hearted reverie as earlier. But the beauty got bored with such long silence and smiled significantly, looking straight into his eyes. Yet this smile was filled with some pathetic insolence; it was as strange and as suited to her face as an expression of piety is to the mug of a bribe-taker, or an accountant's ledger to a poet. He shuddered. She opened her pretty lips and began to say something, but it was all so stupid, so trite . . . As if intelligence left a person together with chastity. He did not want to hear any more. He was extremely ridiculous and as simple as a child. Instead of taking advantage of this favor, instead of being glad of such an occasion, as anyone else in his place would undoubtedly have been, he rushed out headlong, like a wild goat, and ran down to the street.

His head bowed, his arms hanging limp, he sat in his room like a poor man who found a priceless pearl and straightaway dropped it into the sea. "Such a beauty, such divine features—and where, in what place! . . ." That was all he was able to utter.

Indeed, pity never possesses us so strongly as at the sight of beauty touched by the corrupting breath of depravity. Let ugliness make friends with it, but beauty, tender beauty . . . in our thoughts it is united only with chastity and purity. The beauty who had so bewitched poor Piskarev was in fact a marvelous, extraordinary phenomenon. Her presence in that despicable circle seemed still more extraordinary. Her features were all so purely formed, the

whole expression of her beautiful face was marked by such nobility, that it was simply impossible to think that depravity had
stretched out its terrible claws over her. She would have been a
priceless pearl, the whole world, the whole paradise, the whole
wealth of an ardent husband; she would have been the beautiful, gentle star of an unostentatious family circle, and would have
given sweet orders with one movement of her beautiful mouth.
She would have been a divinity in a crowded hall, on the bright
parquet, in the glow of candles, the awestruck company of her
admirers lying speechless at her feet. But, alas! by the terrible will
of some infernal spirit who wishes to destroy the harmony of life,
she had been flung, with a loud laugh, into the abyss.

Filled with rending pity, he sat by a guttering candle. It was long
after midnight, the bell in the tower struck half-past, and he sat
fixed, sleepless, keeping a pointless vigil. Drowsiness, taking advantage of his fixity, was gradually beginning to come over him, the
room was already beginning to disappear, only the light of the
candle penetrated the reveries that were coming over him, when
suddenly a knock at the door made him start and come to his
senses. The door opened and a lackey in rich livery came in. Never
had rich livery visited his solitary room, and that at such an unusual hour . . . He was perplexed and looked at the entering lackey
with impatient curiosity.

"The lady whom you were pleased to visit several hours ago,"
the lackey said with a courteous bow, "bids me invite you to call
on her and sends a carriage for you."

Piskarev stood in wordless astonishment: a carriage, a liveried
lackey! . . . No, there must be some mistake here . . .

"Listen, my good fellow," he said with timidity, "you must have
come to the wrong place. The lady undoubtedly sent you for
someone else, and not for me."

"No, sir, I am not mistaken. Was is not you who kindly accompanied a lady on foot to a house on Liteiny, to a room on the
fourth floor?"

"Yes."

"Well, then, make haste if you please, the lady wishes to see you
without fail and asks you kindly to come straight to her house."

Piskarev ran down the stairs. A carriage was indeed standing outside. He got into it, the door slammed, the pavement rumbled under wheels and hooves, and the lit-up perspective of buildings with bright signboards raced past the carriage windows. On the way, Piskarev kept thinking and was unable to figure out this adventure. A private house, a carriage, a lackey in rich livery . . . he could in no way reconcile all this with the room on the fourth floor, the dusty windows, and the out-of-tune piano.

The carriage stopped in front of a brightly lit entrance, and he was struck at once: by the row of carriages, the talk of the coachmen, the brightly lit windows, and the sounds of music. The lackey in rich livery helped him out of the carriage and respectfully led the way to a front hall with marble columns, a doorman all drowned in gold, cloaks and fur coats scattered about, and a bright lamp. An airy stairway with shining banisters, perfumed with scents, raced upwards. He was already on it, he was already in the first room, frightened and drawing back at the first step from the terrible crowdedness. The extraordinary diversity of faces threw him into complete bewilderment; it seemed as if some demon had chopped the whole world up into a multitude of different pieces and mixed those pieces together with no rhyme or reason. Ladies' gleaming shoulders, black tailcoats, chandeliers, lamps, airy gauzes flying, ethereal ribbons, and a fat double bass peeking from behind the railing of a magnificent gallery—everything was splendid for him. He saw at once so many venerable old and half-old men with stars on their tailcoats, ladies who stepped so lightly, proudly, and gracefully over the parquet or sat in rows, he heard so many French and English words, moreover the young men in black tailcoats were filled with such nobility, talked or kept silent with such dignity, were so incapable of saying anything superfluous, joked so majestically, smiled so respectfully, wore such superb side-whiskers, knew so well how to display perfect hands as they straightened their ties, the ladies were so airy, so completely immersed in self-satisfaction and rapture, lowered their eyes so charmingly, that . . . but the humble air of Piskarev, who clung fearfully to a column, was enough to show that he was utterly at a loss. At that moment the crowd surrounded a group of dancers.

They raced on, wrapped in transparent Parisian creations, dresses woven of the very air; carelessly they touched the parquet with their shining little feet, and were more ethereal than if they had not touched it at all. But one among them was dressed more finely, more splendidly and dazzlingly than the rest. Inexpressible, the very finest combination of taste showed in her attire, and yet it seemed that she did not care about it at all and that it showed inadvertently, of itself. She both looked and did not look at the crowd of spectators around her, her beautiful long eyelashes lowered indifferently, and the shining whiteness of her face struck the eye still more dazzlingly when a slight shadow fell on her charming brow as she inclined her head.

Piskarev made a great effort to force his way through the crowd and get a better look at her, but, to his greatest vexation, some huge head with dark, curly hair kept getting in the way; the crowd also pressed him so much that he did not dare move forward or backward for fear he might somehow shove some privy councillor. But then he did push to the front and looked at his clothes, wishing to straighten them properly. Heavenly Creator, what was this! He had a frock coat on, and it was all covered with paint: in his haste he had even forgotten to change into decent clothes. He blushed to his ears and, dropping his glance, wanted to disappear somewhere, but there was decidedly nowhere to disappear to: court chamberlains in brilliant uniforms stood in a solid wall behind him. He wished he was far away from the beauty with the wonderful brow and eyelashes. He fearfully raised his eyes to see whether she was looking at him: God! she was standing right in front of him . . . But what is this? what is this? "It's she!" he cried almost aloud. Indeed it was she, the very same one he had met on Nevsky and followed to her house.

She raised her eyelashes meanwhile and looked at everyone with her bright eyes. "Aie, aie, aie, what beauty! . . ." was all he was able to utter with failing breath. She looked around the whole circle of people, all of whom strove to hold her attention, but her weary and inattentive eyes soon turned away and met the eyes of Piskarev. Oh, what heaven! what paradise! Grant him strength, O Creator, to bear it! Life will not contain it, it will destroy and carry off his soul! She made a sign, but not with her hand, not by inclining her head—no, but her devastating eyes expressed this sign so subtly and inconspicuously that no one could see it, yet he saw it, he understood it. The dance lasted a long time; the weary music seemed to fade and go out altogether, then it would break loose again, shriek and thunder. Finally—the end! She sat down, her bosom heaved under the thin smoke of gauze; her hand (O Creator, what a wonderful hand!) dropped on her knees, crushing her airy dress beneath it, and her dress under her hand seemed to start breathing music, and its fine lilac color emphasized still more the bright whiteness of this beautiful hand. Just to touch it—nothing more! No other desires—they are all too bold . . . He stood behind her chair, not daring to speak, not daring to breathe.

"Was it boring for you?" she said. "I was bored, too. I see that you hate me . . ." she added, lowering her long eyelashes.

"Hate you? Me? . . . I . . ." Piskarev, utterly at a loss, was about to say, and would probably have produced a whole heap of the most incoherent things, but just then a gentleman-in-waiting approached with witty and pleasant observations and a beautifully curled forelock on his head. He rather pleasantly displayed a row of rather good teeth, and each of his witticisms was a sharp nail in Piskarev's heart. At last some third person, fortunately, addressed the gentleman with some question.

"How unbearable!" she said, raising her heavenly eyes to him. "I'll go and sit at the other end of the room. Meet me there!"

She slipped through the crowd and disappeared. He shoved his way through the crowd like a madman and was already there.

Yes, it was she! She was sitting like a queen, the best of all, the most beautiful of all, and was seeking him with her eyes.

"You're here," she said softly. "I'll be frank with you: you must have thought the circumstances of our meeting strange. Could you really think that I belong to that despicable class of creatures among whom you met me? To you my actions seem strange, but I will reveal a secret to you. Will you be able," she said, fixing her eyes on him, "to keep it forever?"

"Oh, I will, I will, I will! . . ."

But just then a rather elderly man approached, spoke to her in some language unknown to Piskarev, and offered her his arm. She looked at Piskarev with imploring eyes and motioned to him to stay where he was and wait for her to come back, but he, in a fit of impatience, was unable to obey any orders, even from her lips. He started after her; but the crowd parted them. He could no longer see the lilac dress! Anxiously he went from room to room, shoving everyone he met unmercifully, but in all the rooms there were aces sitting over whist, sunk in dead silence. In one corner of the room, several elderly men argued about the advantages of military service over civil; in another, people in superb tailcoats were exchanging light remarks about a multivolume edition of a hardworking poet. Piskarev felt one elderly man of respectable appearance seize him by the button of his tailcoat and present for his judgment some quite correct observation of his, but he rudely pushed him away without even noticing that he had a rather significant decoration around his neck. He ran to the next room—she was not there either. To a third—not there. "Where is she? Give her to me! Oh, I cannot live without another look at her! I want to hear what she was going to say"—but his search was all in vain. Anxious, weary, he pressed himself into a corner and gazed at the crowd; but his strained eyes began to present everything to him in some vague way. Finally, the walls of his own room began to show clearly before him. He raised his eyes. Before him stood a candlestick with the light nearly gone out inside it; the whole candle had melted away; tallow had poured over the table.

So he had been sleeping! God, what a dream! And why wake up? why not wait one more moment: she surely would have appeared again! The unpleasant and wan light of vexatious day showed in his windows. Such gray, such dingy disorder in his room . . . Oh, how repulsive reality is! What is it compared with dreams? He undressed hastily and went to bed, wrapped in a blanket, wishing to call back the flown vision for a moment. Sleep, indeed, was not slow in coming to him, but it did not at all present him with what he would have liked to see: now a Lieutenant Pirogov would come with his pipe, now an Academy watchman, now an actual state councillor, now the head of a Finnish woman whose portrait he had painted once, and other such nonsense.

He lay in bed till noon, wishing to fall asleep; but she would not appear. If only she would show her beautiful features for a moment, if only he could hear her light footstep for a moment, if only her bare arm, bright as snow on a mountaintop, could flash before him.

Abandoning everything, forgetting everything, he sat with a crushed, hopeless look, filled only with his dream. He did not think of eating anything; without any interest, without any life, his eyes gazed out the window to the courtyard, where a dirty water-carrier was pouring water that froze in the air, and the bleating voice of a peddler quavered: "Old clothes for sale." The everyday and real struck oddly on his ear. Thus he sat till evening, when he greedily rushed to bed. For a long time he struggled with sleeplessness and finally overcame it. Again some dream, some trite, vile dream. "God, be merciful; show her to me for a moment at least, just for one moment!" Again he waited till evening, again fell asleep, again dreamed of some official who was an official and at the same time a bassoon. Oh, this was unbearable! At last she came! her head and her tresses . . . she looks . . . Oh, how brief! Again the mist, again some stupid dream.

In the end dreams became his life, and his whole life thereafter took a strange turn: one might say he slept while waking and watched while asleep. If anyone had seen him sitting silently before the empty table or walking down the street, he would certainly have taken him for a lunatic or someone destroyed by hard drinking; his gaze was quite senseless, his natural distractedness developed, finally, and imperiously drove all feeling, all movement, from his face. He became animated only with the coming of night.

Such a state unsettled his health, and his most terrible torment was that sleep finally began to desert him entirely. Wishing to salvage this his only possession, he used every means to restore it. He heard that there was a means of restoring sleep—one had only to take opium. But where to get this opium? He remembered one Persian shopkeeper who sold shawls and who, whenever they met, asked him to paint a beauty for him. He decided to go to him, supposing that he would undoubtedly have this opium. The Persian received him sitting on a couch, his legs tucked under him.

"What do you need opium for?" he asked.

Piskarev told him about his insomnia.

"Very well, I give you opium, only paint me a beauty. Must be a fine beauty! Must be with black eyebrows and eyes big as olives; and me lying beside her smoking my pipe! Do you hear? Must be a fine one! a beauty!"

Piskarev promised everything. The Persian stepped out for a minute and returned with a little pot filled with dark liquid, carefully poured some of it into another little pot and gave it to Piskarev, with instructions to take no more than seven drops in water. He greedily seized this precious pot, which he would not have given up for a heap of gold, and rushed headlong home.

On coming home, he poured a few drops into a glass of water and, having swallowed it, dropped off to sleep.

God, what joy! It's she! She again! but now with a completely different look! Oh, how nicely she sits by the window of a bright country house! Her dress breathes such simplicity as only a poet's thought is clothed in. Her hair is done . . . O Creator, how simply her hair is done, and how becoming it is to her! A short shawl lightly covers her slender neck; everything in her is modest, everything in her is—a mysterious, inexplicable sense of taste. How lovely her graceful gait! how musical the sound of her footsteps and the rustle of her simple dress! how beautiful her arm clasped round with a bracelet of hair! She says to him with tears in her eyes: "Don't despise me. I'm not at all what you take me for. Look at me, look at me more closely, and say: Am I capable of what you think?" "Oh, no, no! If anyone dares to think so, let him . . ." But he woke up, all stirred, distraught, with tears in his eyes. "It would be better if you didn't exist, didn't live in the world, but were the creation of an inspired artist! I would never leave the canvas, I would eternally gaze at you and kiss you. I would live and breathe by you, as the most beautiful dream, and then I would be happy. My desires could reach no further. I would call upon you as my guardian angel, before sleep and waking, and I would wait for you whenever I had to portray the divine and holy. But now . . . what a terrible life! What is the use of her being alive? Is the life of a madman pleasant for his relations and friends who once used to love him? God, what is our life! An eternal discord between dream and reality!" Thoughts much like these constantly occupied him. He did not think about anything, he even ate almost nothing, and impatiently, with a lover's passion, waited for evening and the desired vision. His thoughts were constantly turned to one thing, and this finally acquired such power over his whole being and imagination that the desired image came to him almost every day, always in a situation contrary to reality, because his thoughts were perfectly pure, like the thoughts of a child. Through his dreams, the object itself was somehow becoming more pure and totally transformed.

Taking opium enflamed his thoughts still more, and if anyone was ever in love to the utmost degree of madness, impetuously, terribly, destructively, stormily, he was that unfortunate man.

Of all his dreams, one was the most joyful for him: he imagined his studio, he was so happy, he sat holding the palette with such pleasure! And she was right there. She was his wife now. She sat beside him, her lovely elbow resting on the back of his chair, and looked at his work. Her eyes, languid, weary, showed the burden of bliss; everything in his room breathed of paradise; there was such brightness, such order! O Creator! she leaned her lovely head on his breast . . . He had never had a better dream. He got up after it, somehow more fresh and less distracted than before. Strange thoughts were born in his head. "It may be," he thought, "that she's been drawn into depravity by some involuntary, terrible accident; it may be that the impulses of her soul are inclined to repentance; it may be that she herself wishes to tear herself away from her terrible condition. And can one indifferently allow for her ruin, and that at a moment when it is enough just to reach out a hand to save her from drowning?" His thoughts went further still. "No one knows me," he said to himself, "and who cares about me anyway? And I don't care about them either. If she shows pure repentance and changes her life, then I'll marry her. I must marry her, and surely I'll do much better than many of those who marry their housekeepers, and often even the most despicable creatures. But my deed will be an unmercenary and perhaps even a great one. I'll restore to the world its most beautiful ornament."

Having come up with such a light-minded plan, he felt the flush of color on his face; he went to the mirror and was himself frightened by his sunken cheeks and the pallor of his face. He began to dress carefully; he washed, brushed his hair, put on a new tailcoat, a smart waistcoat, threw on a cloak, and went out. He breathed the fresh air and felt freshness in his heart, like a convalescent who has decided to go out for the first time after a long illness. His heart was pounding as he approached the street where he had not set foot since the fatal encounter.

He spent a long time looking for the house; his memory seemed to fail him. Twice he walked up and down the street, not knowing where to stop. Finally one seemed right to him. He quickly ran up the stairs, knocked at the door: the door opened, and who should come out to meet him? His ideal, his mysterious image, the original of his dreamt pictures, she by whom he lived, lived so terribly, so tormentingly, so sweetly. She herself stood before him. He trembled; he could barely keep his feet from weakness, overcome by an impulse of joy. She stood before him just as beautiful, though her eyes were sleepy, though pallor had already crept over her face, no longer so fresh—yet still she was beautiful.

"Ah!" she cried out, seeing Piskarev and rubbing her eyes (it was then already two o'clock). "Why did you run away from us that time?"

Exhausted, he sat down on a chair and gazed at her.

"And I just woke up. They brought me back at seven in the morning. I was completely drunk," she added with a smile.

Oh, better you were mute and totally deprived of speech than to utter such things! She had suddenly shown him the whole of her life as in a panorama. However, he mastered himself despite that and decided to try whether his admonitions might have an effect on her. Summoning his courage, he began in a trembling and at the same time fervent voice to present her terrible position to her. She listened to him with an attentive look and with that sense of astonishment which we show at the sight of something unexpected and strange. With a slight smile, she glanced at her friend who was sitting in the corner and who, abandoning the comb she was cleaning, also listened attentively to the new preacher.

"True, I'm poor," Piskarev said finally, after a long and instructive admonition, "but we'll work; we'll vie with each other in our efforts to improve our life. There's nothing more pleasant than to owe everything to oneself. I'll sit over my paintings, you'll sit by me, inspiring my labors, embroidering or doing some other handwork, and we won't lack for anything."

"What!" she interrupted his speech with an expression of some disdain. "I'm no laundress or seamstress that I should do any work!"

God! in these words all her low, all her contemptible life was expressed—a life filled with emptiness and idleness, the faithful companions of depravity.

"Marry me!" her friend, till then sitting silently in the corner, picked up with an impudent look. "If I was a wife, I'd sit like this!"

And with that she made some stupid grimace with her pathetic face which the beauty found very funny.

Oh, this was too much! This was more than he could bear! He rushed out, having lost all feeling and thought. His reason was clouded: stupidly, aimlessly, seeing, hearing, feeling nothing, he wandered about for the whole day. No one could say whether he slept anywhere or not; only the next day, following some stupid instinct, did he come to his apartment, pale, dreadful-looking, his hair disheveled, with signs of madness on his face. He locked himself in his room, let no one in and asked for nothing. Four days passed, and his locked room never once opened; finally a week went by, and the room still remained locked. They rushed to the door, began calling him, but there was no answer; finally they broke the door down and found his lifeless body with the throat cut. A bloody razor lay on the floor. From his convulsively spread arms and terribly disfigured appearance, it could be concluded that his hand had not been steady and that he had suffered for a long time before his sinful soul left his body.

Thus perished, the victim of a mad passion, poor Piskarev, quiet, timid, modest, childishly simple-hearted, who bore in himself a spark of talent which in time might have blazed up broadly and brightly. No one wept over him; no one could be seen by his lifeless body except the ordinary figure of a district inspector and the indifferent mien of a city doctor. His coffin was quietly taken to Okhta,[6] even without religious rites; only a soldier-sentry wept as he followed it, and that because he had drunk an extra dram of vodka. Not even Lieutenant Pirogov came to look at the body of the unfortunate wretch upon whom, while he lived, he had bestowed his lofty patronage. However, he could not be bothered with that; he was occupied with an extraordinary event. But let us turn to him.

I don't like corpses and dead men, and it always gives me an unpleasant feeling when a long funeral procession crosses my path and an invalid soldier, dressed like some sort of Capuchin, takes a pinch of snuff with his left hand because his right is occupied with a torch. My heart is always vexed at the sight of a rich catafalque and a velvet coffin; but my vexation is mixed with sadness when I see a drayman pulling the bare pine coffin of a poor man, and only some beggar woman met at an intersection plods after it, having nothing else to do.

It seems we left Lieutenant Pirogov at the point of his parting from poor Piskarev and rushing after the blonde. This blonde was a light, rather interesting little creature. She stopped in front of each shop window to gaze at the displays of belts, kerchiefs, earrings, gloves, and other trifles; she fidgeted constantly, looked in all directions, and glanced over her shoulder. "You're mine, little sweetie!" Lieutenant Pirogov repeated self-confidently as he continued his pursuit, covering his face with the collar of his overcoat lest he meet some acquaintance. But it will do no harm if we inform readers of who this Lieutenant Pirogov was.

But before we tell who this Lieutenant Pirogov was, it will do no harm if we say a thing or two about the society to which Pirogov belonged. There are officers in Petersburg who constitute a sort of middle class in society. You will always find one of them at a soiree, at a dinner given by a state or actual state councillor, who earned this rank by forty long years of labor. Several pale daughters, completely colorless, like Petersburg, some of them overripe, a tea table, a piano, dancing—all this is usually inseparable from a bright epaulette shining by a lamp, between a well-behaved blonde and the black tailcoat of a brother or a friend of the family. It is very hard to stir up these cool-blooded girls and make them laugh; it takes very great art, or, better to say, no art at all. One must speak so that it is neither too intelligent nor too funny, so that it is all about the trifles that women like. In this the gentlemen under discussion should be given their due. They have a special gift for making these colorless beauties laugh and listen. Exclamations stifled by laughter—"Ah, stop it! Aren't you ashamed to make me laugh so!"—are usually their best reward. Among the upper classes they occur very rarely, or, better to say, never. They are forced out altogether by what this society calls aristocrats; however, they are considered educated and well-bred people. They like talking about literature; they praise Bulgarin, Pushkin, and Grech, and speak with contempt and barbed wit of A. A. Orlov.[7] They never miss a single public lecture, be it on accounting or even on forestry. In the theater, whatever the play, you will always find one of them, unless they are playing some Filatkas,[8] which are highly insulting to their fastidious taste. They are constantly in the theater. For theater managers, these are the most profitable people. In plays, they especially like good poetry; they also like very much to call loudly for the actors; many of them, being teachers in government schools, or preparing students for them, in the end acquire a cabriolet and a pair of horses. Then their circle widens: they finally arrive at marrying a merchant's daughter who can play the piano, with a hundred thousand or so in cash and a heap of bearded relations. However, this honor they cannot attain before being promoted to the rank of colonel at the very least. Because our Russian beards, though still giving off a whiff of cabbage, have no wish for their daughters to marry any but generals, or colonels at the very least. These are the main features of this sort of young men. But Lieutenant Pirogov had a host of talents that belonged to him personally. He declaimed verses from *Dmitri Donskoy* and *Woe from Wit*[9] superbly well, and possessed a special art of producing smoke rings from his pipe so skillfully that he could suddenly send ten of them passing one through another. He could very pleasantly tell a joke about a cannon being one thing and a unicorn something else again. However, it is rather difficult to enumerate all the talents fate had bestowed on Pirogov.

He liked talking about some actress or dancer, but not so sharply as a young sub-lieutenant usually talks about this subject. He was very pleased with his rank, to which he had recently been promoted, and though he would occasionally say, while lying on the sofa: "Ah, ah! vanity, all is vanity! So what if I'm a lieutenant?"—secretly he was very flattered by this new dignity; in conversation he often tried to hint at it indirectly, and once, when he ran across some scrivener in the street who seemed impolite to him, he immediately stopped him and in a few but sharp words gave him to know that before him stood a lieutenant and not some other sort of officer. He tried to expound it the more eloquently as two good-looking ladies were just passing by. Generally, Pirogov showed a passion for all that was fine, and he encouraged the artist Piskarev; however, this may have proceeded from his great desire to see his masculine physiognomy in a portrait. But enough about Pirogov's qualities. Man is such a wondrous being that it is never possible to count up all his merits at once. The more you study him, the more new particulars appear, and their description would be endless.

And so Pirogov would not cease his pursuit of the unknown lady, entertaining her now and then with questions to which she replied sharply, curtly, and with some sort of vague sounds. Through the dark Kazan gate they entered Meshchanskaya Street, the street of tobacco and grocery shops, of German artisans and Finnish nymphs. The blonde ran more quickly and fluttered through the gates of a rather dingy house. Pirogov followed her. She ran up the narrow, dark stairway and went in at a door, through which Pirogov also boldly made his way. He found himself in a big room with black walls and a soot-covered ceiling. There was a heap of iron screws, locksmith's tools, shiny coffeepots and candlesticks on the table; the floor was littered with copper and iron shavings. Pirogov realized at once that this was an artisan's dwelling. The unknown lady fluttered on through a side door. He stopped to think for a moment, but, following the Russian rule, resolved to go ahead. He entered a room in no way resembling the first, very neatly decorated, showing that the owner was a German. He was struck by an extraordinarily strange sight.

Before him sat Schiller—not the Schiller who wrote *Wilhelm Tell* and the *History of the Thirty Years' War,* but the well-known Schiller, the tinsmith of Meshchanskaya Street. Next to Schiller stood Hoffmann—not the writer Hoffmann, but a rather good cobbler from Ofitserskaya Street, a great friend of Schiller's.[10] Schiller was drunk and sat on a chair stamping his foot and heatedly saying something. All this would not have been so surprising to Pirogov, but what did surprise him was the extremely strange posture of the figures. Schiller was sitting, his rather fat nose stuck out and his head raised, while Hoffmann was holding him by this nose with two fingers and waggling the blade of his cobbler's knife just above the surface of it. Both personages were speaking in German, and therefore Lieutenant Pirogov, whose only German was "*Gut Morgen,*" was able to understand nothing of this whole story. Schiller's words, however, consisted of the following:

"I don't want, I have no need of a nose!" he said, waving his arms. "For this one nose I need three pounds of snuff a month. And I pay in the Russian vile shop, because the German shop doesn't have Russian snuff, I pay in the Russian vile shop forty kopecks for each pound; that makes one rouble twenty kopecks; twelve times one rouble twenty kopecks makes fourteen roubles forty kopecks. Do you hear, Hoffmann my friend? For this one nose, fourteen roubles forty kopecks! Yes, and on feast days I snuff rappee, because I don't want to snuff Russian vile tobacco on feast days. I snuff two pounds of rappee a year, two roubles a pound. Six plus fourteen—twenty roubles forty kopecks on snuff alone. That's highway robbery! I ask you, Hoffmann my friend, is it not so?" Hoffmann, who was drunk himself, answered in the affirmative. "Twenty roubles forty kopecks! I'm a Swabian German; I have a king in Germany. I don't want a nose! Cut my nose off! Here's my nose!"

And had it not been for the sudden appearance of Lieutenant Pirogov, there is no doubt that Hoffmann would have cut Schiller's nose off just like that, because he was already holding his knife in such a position as if he were about to cut out a shoe sole.

Schiller found it extremely vexing that an unknown, uninvited person had suddenly hindered them so inopportunely. Despite his being under the inebriating fumes of beer and wine, he felt it somewhat indecent to be in the presence of an outside witness while looking and behaving in such a fashion. Meanwhile Pirogov bowed slightly and said with his usual pleasantness:

"You will excuse me . . ."

"Get out!" Schiller drawled.

This puzzled Lieutenant Pirogov. Such treatment was completely new to him. The smile that had barely appeared on his face suddenly vanished. With a sense of distressed dignity, he said:

"I find it strange, my dear sir . . . you must have failed to notice . . . I am an officer . . ."

"What is an officer! I am a Swabian German. Mineself" (here Schiller banged his fist on the table) "I can be an officer: a year and a half a Junker,[11] two years a sub-lieutenant, and tomorrow I'm right away an officer. But I don't want to serve. I'll do this to an officer—poof!" Here Schiller held his hand to his mouth and poofed on it.

Lieutenant Pirogov saw that there was nothing left for him but to withdraw. Nevertheless, such treatment, not at all befitting his rank, was disagreeable to him. He stopped several times on the stairs, as if wishing to collect his wits and think how to make Schiller sensible of his insolence. He finally concluded that Schiller could be excused because his head was full of beer; besides, he pictured the pretty blonde and decided to consign it all to oblivion. Next morning, Lieutenant Pirogov showed up very early at the tinsmith's shop. In the front room he was met by the pretty blonde, who asked in a rather stern voice that was very becoming to her little face:

"What can I do for you?"

"Ah, good morning, my little dear! You don't recognize me? Sly thing, such pretty eyes you have!" at which Lieutenant Pirogov was going to chuck her nicely under the chin with his finger.

But the blonde uttered a timorous exclamation and asked with the same sternness:

"What can I do for you?"

"Let me look at you, that's all," Lieutenant Pirogov said with a very pleasant smile, getting closer to her; but, noticing that the timorous blonde wanted to slip out the door, he added, "I'd like to order some spurs, my little dear. Can you make spurs for me? Though to love you, what's needed is not spurs but a bridle. Such pretty hands!"

Lieutenant Pirogov was always very courteous in conversations of this sort.

"I'll call my husband right now," the German lady cried and left, and a few minutes later Pirogov saw Schiller come out with sleepy eyes, barely recovered from yesterday's drinking. Looking at the officer, he recalled as in a vague dream what had happened yesterday. He did not remember how it had been, but felt that he had done something stupid, and therefore he received the officer with a very stern air.

"I can't take less than fifteen roubles for spurs," he said, wishing to get rid of Pirogov, because as an honorable German he was very ashamed to look at anyone who had seen him in an improper position. Schiller liked to drink without any witnesses, with two or three friends, and at such times even locked himself away from his workmen.

"Why so much?" Pirogov asked benignly.

"German workmanship," Schiller uttered coolly, stroking his chin. "A Russian would make them for two roubles."

"Very well, to prove that I like you and want to become acquainted with you, I'll pay the fifteen roubles."

Schiller stood pondering for a moment: being an honest German, he felt a bit ashamed. Wishing to talk him out of the order, he announced that it would be two weeks before he could make them. But Pirogov, without any objection, declared his consent.

The German lapsed into thought and stood pondering how to do his work better, so that it would actually be worth fifteen roubles. At that moment, the blonde came into the workshop and began rummaging around on the table, which was all covered with coffeepots. The lieutenant took advantage of Schiller's thoughtfulness, got close to her, and pressed her arm, which was bare up to the shoulder. Schiller did not like that at all.

"*Mein' Frau!*" he cried.

"*Was wollen Sie doch?*" answered the blonde.

"*Geh'n Sie* to the kitchen!"

The blonde withdrew.

"In two weeks, then?" said Pirogov.

"Yes, in two weeks," Schiller replied ponderingly. "I have a lot of work now."

"Good-bye! I'll be back."

"Good-bye," answered Schiller, locking the door behind him.

Lieutenant Pirogov decided not to abandon his quest, even though the German lady had obviously rebuffed him. He did not understand how he could be resisted, the less so as his courtesy and brilliant rank gave him full right to attention. It must be said, however, that Schiller's wife, for all her comeliness, was very stupid. Though stupidity constitutes a special charm in a pretty wife. I, at least, have known many husbands who are delighted with their wives' stupidity and see in it all the tokens of childlike innocence. Beauty works perfect miracles. All inner shortcomings in a beauty, instead of causing repugnance, become somehow extraordinarily attractive; vice itself breathes comeliness in them; but if it were to disappear, then a woman would have to be twenty times more intelligent than a man in order to inspire, if not love, at least respect. However, Schiller's wife, for all her stupidity, was always faithful to her duty, and therefore Pirogov was hard put to succeed in his bold enterprise; but pleasure is always combined with the overcoming of obstacles, and the blonde was becoming more and more interesting for him day by day. He began inquiring about the spurs quite frequently, so that Schiller finally got tired of it. He bent every effort towards quickly finishing the spurs he had begun; finally the spurs were ready.

"Ah, what excellent workmanship!" Lieutenant Pirogov exclaimed when he saw the spurs. "Lord, how well made! Our general doesn't have such spurs."

A sense of self-satisfaction spread all through Schiller's soul. His eyes acquired a very cheerful look, and he was completely reconciled with Pirogov. "The Russian officer is an intelligent man," he thought to himself.

"So, then, you can also make a sheath, for instance, for a dagger or something else?"

"Oh, very much so," Schiller said with a smile.

"Then make me a sheath for a dagger. I'll bring it. I have a very good Turkish dagger, but I'd like to make a different sheath for it."

Schiller was as if hit by a bomb. His brows suddenly knitted. "There you go!" he thought, denouncing himself inwardly for having called down more work on himself. He considered it dishonest to refuse now; besides, the Russian officer had praised his work. Shaking his head a little, he gave his consent; but the kiss Pirogov brazenly planted right on the lips of the pretty blonde threw him into total perplexity.

I consider it not superfluous to acquaint the reader a little more closely with Schiller. Schiller was a perfect German in the full sense of this whole word. From the age of twenty, that happy time when a Russian lives by hit-or-miss, Schiller had already measured out his entire life, and on no account would he make any exceptions. He had resolved to get up at seven, to have dinner at two, to be precise in all things, and to get drunk every Sunday. He had resolved to put together a capital of fifty thousand in ten years, and this was as sure and irresistible as fate, because a clerk will sooner forget to leave his card with his superior's doorman[12] than a German will decide to go back on his word. On no account would he increase his expenses, and if the price of potatoes went up too much compared to usual, he did not spend a kopeck more but merely decreased the quantity, and though he occasionally went a bit hungry, he would nevertheless get used to it. His accuracy went so far as the decision to kiss his wife not more than twice a day, and to avoid somehow kissing her an extra time, he never put more than one teaspoon of pepper in his soup; on Sundays, however, this rule was not fulfilled so strictly, because Schiller then drank two bottles of beer and one bottle of caraway-seed vodka, which he nevertheless always denounced. He drank not at all like an Englishman, who bolts his door right after dinner and gets potted by himself. On the contrary, being a German, he always drank inspiredly, either with the cobbler Hoffmann or with the cabinet-maker Kuntz, also a German and a big drinker. Such was the character of the noble Schiller, who was finally put into an extremely difficult position. Though he was phlegmatic and a German, Pirogov's behavior still aroused something like jealousy in him. He racked his brain and could not figure out how to get rid of this Russian officer. Meanwhile, Pirogov, as he was smoking his pipe in a circle of his comrades—because Providence has so arranged it that where there are officers there are also pipes—smoking his pipe in a circle of his comrades, hinted significantly and with a pleasant smile at a little intrigue with a pretty German lady with whom, in his words, he was already on quite close terms and whom in reality he had all but lost hope of attracting to himself.

One day, while strolling along Meshchanskaya, he kept glancing at the house adorned by Schiller's shingle with its coffeepots and samovars; to his great joy, he saw the blonde's head leaning out the window and watching the passers-by. He stopped, waved his hand, and said: "*Gut Morgen!*" The blonde greeted him as an acquaintance.

"Say, is your husband at home?"

"Yes," answered the blonde.

"And when is he not at home?"

"He's not at home on Sundays," the stupid blonde answered.

"Not bad," Pirogov thought to himself, "I must take advantage of it."

And next Sunday, out of the blue, he appeared before the blonde. Schiller was indeed not at home. The pretty hostess got frightened; but this time Pirogov behaved quite prudently, treated her very respectfully and, bowing, showed all the beauty of his tightly fitted waist. He joked very pleasantly and deferentially, but the silly German woman replied to everything in monosyllables. Finally, having tried to get at her from all sides and seeing that nothing would amuse her, he offered to dance. The German woman accepted at once, because German women are always eager to dance. Pirogov placed great hopes in this: first, she already enjoyed it; second, it would demonstrate his tournure and adroitness; third, while dancing he could get closer and embrace the pretty German, and thus start it all going—in short, the result would be complete success. He started some sort of gavotte, knowing that German women need gradualness. The pretty German stepped out into the middle of the room and raised her beautiful little foot. This position so delighted Pirogov that he rushed to kiss her. The German woman began to scream, thereby increasing her loveliness still more in Pirogov's eyes; he showered her with kisses. When suddenly the door opened and in came Schiller with Hoffmann and the cabinetmaker Kuntz. These worthy artisans were all drunk as cobblers.

But I will let my readers judge of Schiller's wrath and indignation for themselves.

"Ruffian!" he cried in the greatest indignation. "How dare you kiss my wife? You are a scoundrel, not a Russian officer. Devil take it, Hoffmann my friend, I am a German, not a Russian swine!"

Hoffmann responded in the affirmative.

"Oh, I will not the horns have! Take him by the collar, Hoffmann my friend, I will not," he went on, swinging his arms violently, and his face was close in color to the red flannel of his waistcoat. "I have lived in Petersburg for eight years, I have my mother in Swabia and my uncle in Nuremberg; I am a German, not a horned beef! Off with everything, Hoffmann my friend! Hold his arm and leg, Kuntz my comrat!"

And the Germans seized Pirogov by his arms and legs.

He vainly tried to fight them off; the three artisans were the most stalwart fellows of all the Petersburg Germans, and they behaved so rudely and impolitely with him that I confess I can find no words to describe this sorry event.

I'm sure that Schiller was in a bad fever the next day, that he trembled like a leaf, expecting the police to come every moment, that he would have given God knows what for all of yesterday's events to have been a dream. But what's done cannot be undone. Nothing could compare with Pirogov's wrath and indignation. The very thought of such a terrible insult drove him to fury. He thought Siberia and the lash the very least of punishments for Schiller. He flew home so that, having changed, he could go straight to the general and describe for him in the most vivid colors the violence of the German artisans. He also wanted to petition general headquarters at the same time. And if the punishment of general headquarters was insufficient, he would go straight to the state council, or else to the sovereign himself.

But all this ended somehow strangely: he stopped at a pastry shop on his way, ate two puff pastries, read something from *The Northern Bee,* and left the place already in a less wrathful state. Besides, the rather pleasant, cool evening induced him to take a little stroll on Nevsky Prospect; toward nine o'clock he calmed down and decided it was not nice to trouble the general on a Sunday, and besides he had undoubtedly been summoned somewhere; and therefore he went to a soiree given by one of the heads of the college of auditors, where there was a very pleasant gathering of functionaries and officers. He enjoyed the evening he spent there, and so distinguished himself in the mazurka that not only the ladies but even their partners were delighted.

"Marvelous is the working of our world," I thought as I walked down Nevsky Prospect two days ago, calling to mind these two events. "How strangely, how inconceivably our fate plays with us! Do we ever get what we desire? Do we ever achieve that for which our powers seem purposely to prepare us? Everything happens in a contrary way. To this one fate gave wonderful horses, and he drives around indifferently without ever noticing their beauty— while another, whose heart burns with the horse passion, goes on foot and contents himself with merely clicking his tongue as a trotter is led past him. This one has an excellent cook, but unfortunately so small a mouth that it cannot let pass more than a couple of tidbits; another has a mouth as big as the archway of general headquarters, but, alas! has to be satisfied with some German dinner of potatoes. How strangely our fate plays with us!"

But strangest of all are the events that take place on Nevsky Prospect. Oh, do not believe this Nevsky Prospect! I always wrap myself tighter in my cloak and try not to look at the objects I meet at all. Everything is deception, everything is a dream, everything is not what it seems to be! You think this gentleman who goes about in a finely tailored frock coat is very rich? Not a bit of it: he consists entirely of his frock coat. You imagine that these two fat men who stopped at the church under construction are discussing its architecture? Not at all: they're talking about how strangely two crows are sitting facing each other. You think that this enthusiast waving his arms is telling how his wife threw a little ball out the window at a completely unknown officer? Not at all, he's talking about Lafayette.[13] You think these ladies . . . but least of all believe the ladies. Peer less at the shop windows: the knickknacks displayed in them are beautiful, but they smell of a terrible quantity of banknotes. But God forbid you should peer under the ladies' hats! However a beauty's cloak may flutter behind her, I shall never follow curiously after her. Further away, for God's sake, further away from the street lamp! pass it by more quickly, as quickly as possible. You'll be lucky to get away with it pouring its stinking oil on your foppish frock coat. But, along with the street lamp, everything breathes deceit. It lies all the time, this Nevsky Prospect, but most of all at the time when night heaves its dense mass upon it and sets off the white and pale yellow walls of the houses, when the whole city turns into a rumbling and brilliance, myriads of carriages tumble from the bridges, postillions shout and bounce on their horses, and the devil himself lights the lamps only so as to show everything not as it really looks.

The Diary of a Madman

October 3.

TODAY AN EXTRAORDINARY adventure took place. I got up rather late in the morning, and when Mavra brought me my polished boots, I asked what time it was. On hearing that it had long since struck ten, I quickly hastened to get dressed. I confess, I wouldn't have gone to the office at all, knowing beforehand what a sour face the section chief would make. He has long been saying to me: "Why is it you've got such a hotchpotch in your head, brother? You rush about frantically, you sometimes confuse a case so much the devil himself couldn't sort it out, you start the title in lowercase, forget the date or number." Cursed stork! He must be envious that I sit in the director's study and sharpen pens for His Excellency. In short, I wouldn't have gone to the office if it weren't for the hope of seeing the treasurer and maybe cajoling at least some of my pay out of that Jew in advance. What a creature! For him to hand out any money a month ahead—Lord God, the Last Judgment would come sooner! Even if you beg on your life, even if you're destitute—he won't hand out anything, the hoary devil! Yet at home his own cook slaps him in the face. The whole world knows it. I don't see the profit of working in my department. Absolutely no resources. In the provincial government, in the civil courts and treasuries, it's quite a different matter: there, lo and behold, a man squeezes himself into a corner and scribbles away. His tailcoat is vile, his mug begs to be spat in, but just look what sort of country house he rents! Don't even try giving him a gilded china cup: "That," he says, "is a gift fit for a doctor." He wants to be given a pair of trotters, or a droshky, or a beaver coat worth some three hundred roubles. He looks like such a goody-goody, he talks with such delicacy—"Lend me your little knife to trim my little pen"—and then he skins a petitioner so that the man's left in nothing but his shirt. It's true, our work is noble, it's clean everywhere, as you never see it in the provincial government: the tables are mahogany, and the superiors address each other formally. Yes, I confess, if it weren't for the nobility of the work, I'd long since have quit the department.

I put on my old overcoat and took an umbrella, because it was pouring rain. There was nobody in the streets; only peasant women with their skirts pulled over their heads and Russian merchants under umbrellas and messenger boys caught my eye. Of the gentry I met only a fellow clerk. I saw him at an intersection. As I noticed him, I said to myself at once, "Oh-ho! No, dear heart, you're not going to the office, you're rushing after that thing running ahead of you and ogling her little feet." Our fellow clerk is quite a customer! By God, he won't yield to any officer; if a pretty thing in a bonnet passes by, he's sure to tag after her. While I was thinking that, I saw a carriage drive up to a shop I was walking past. I recognized it at once: it was our director's carriage. "But he has no business in that shop," I thought, "it must be his daughter." I pressed myself to the wall. The lackey opened the doors, and she fluttered out of the carriage like a little bird. As she glanced right and left, as she flashed her eyebrows and eyes . . . Lord God! I'm lost, I'm utterly lost! And why does she have to go out in such rainy weather! Go on, now, tell me women don't have a great passion for all these rags. She didn't recognize me, and I tried to wrap myself up the best I could, because the overcoat I had on was very dirty, and old-fashioned besides. Now everyone wears cloaks with tall collars, and mine is short, overlapping; and the broadcloth isn't waterproof at all. Her lapdog didn't manage to get through the door into the shop and was left in the street. I know this dog. She's called Medji. A minute hadn't passed when I suddenly heard a piping little voice: "Hello, Medji!" Well, I'll be! Who said that? I looked around and saw two ladies walking under an umbrella: one a little old lady, the other a young one; but they had already passed by when I heard beside me: "Shame on you, Medji!" What the devil! I saw Medji and the little dog that was following the ladies sniff each other. "Oh-ho!" I said to myself, "what, am I drunk or something? Only that seldom seems to happen with me." "No, Fidèle, you shouldn't think so," I myself saw Medji say it, "I've been bow-wow! I've been bow-wow-wow! very sick." Ah, you pup! I confess, I was very surprised to hear her speak in human language. But later, when I'd thought it over properly, I at once ceased to be surprised. Actually, there have already been many such examples in the world. They say in England a fish surfaced who spoke a couple of words in such a strange language that scholars have already spent three years trying to define them and still haven't found anything out. I also read in the papers about two cows that came to a grocer's and asked for a pound of tea. But, I confess, I was much more surprised when Medji said, "I wrote to you, Fidèle. It must be that Polkan didn't deliver my letter!" May my salary be withheld! Never yet in my life have I heard of a dog being able to write. Only a gentleman can write correctly. Of course, there are sometimes merchants' clerks and even certain serfs who can write a bit; but their writing is mostly mechanical—no commas, no periods, no style.

This surprised me. I confess, lately I had begun sometimes to hear and see things no one had ever seen or heard before. "I'll just follow that little dog," I said to myself, "and find out what she is and what she thinks."

I opened my umbrella and followed the two ladies. They went down Gorokhovaya, turned onto Meshchanskaya, from there to Stolyarnaya, and finally to the Kokushkin Bridge, where they stopped in front of a big house. "I know that building," I said to myself. "That's Zverkov's building." What a pile! And the sorts that live in it: so many cooks, so many out-of-towners! and our fellow clerks—like pups, one on top of the other. I, too, have a friend there, a very good trumpet player. The ladies went up to the fifth floor. "Very well," I thought, "I won't go up now, but I'll note the place and be sure to make use of it at the first opportunity."

October 4.

Today is Wednesday, and so I was in my superior's study. I came earlier on purpose, sat down to work, and sharpened all the pens. Our director must be a very intelligent man. His whole study is filled with bookcases. I read the titles of some of the books: it's all learning, such learning as our kind can't even come close to: all in French, or in German. And to look at his face: pah, such impor- tance shines in his eyes! I've never yet heard him utter an extra word. Except maybe when I hand him some papers, and he asks, "How is it outside?" "Wet, Your Excellency!" Yes, there's no com- parison with our kind! A real statesman. I notice, though, that he has a special liking for me. If only the daughter also . . . ah, con- found it! . . . Never mind, never mind, silence! I read the little *Bee.*[1] What fools these Frenchmen are! So, what is it they want? By God, I'd take the lot of them and give them a good birching! I also read a very pleasant portrayal of a ball there, described by a Kursk landowner. Kursk landowners are good writers. After that I noticed it had already struck twelve-thirty, and our man had never left his bedroom. But around one-thirty an event took place which no pen can describe. The door opened, I thought it was the direc- tor and jumped up from the chair with my papers; but it was she, she herself! Heavens above, how she was dressed! Her gown was white as a swan, and so magnificent, pah! and her glance—the sun, by God, the sun! She nodded and said, "Papá hasn't been here?" Aie, aie, aie! what a voice! A canary, truly, a canary! "Your Excel- lency," I almost wanted to say, "don't punish me, but if it is your will to punish me, punish me with Your Excellency's own hand." But, devil take it, my tongue somehow refused to move, and I said only, "No, ma'am." She looked at me, at the books, and dropped her handkerchief. I rushed headlong, slipped on the cursed par- quet, almost smashed my nose, nevertheless kept my balance and picked up the handkerchief. Heavens, what a handkerchief! The finest cambric—ambrosia, sheer ambrosia! it simply exuded excellency. She thanked me and just barely smiled, so that her sugary lips scarcely moved, and after that she left. I sat for another hour, when suddenly a lackey came in and said, "Go home, Aksenty Ivanovich, the master has already gone out." I can't stand the lackey circle: there is one always sprawled in the front hall who won't even nod his head. Moreover, one of the knaves decided once to offer me some snuff without getting up. But don't you know, stupid churl, that I am an official, a man of noble birth? However, I took my hat and put my overcoat on by myself—because these gentlemen never help you—and left. At home I lay in bed most of the time. Then I copied out some very nice verses: "I was gone from her an hour, / Yet to me it seemed a year; / Life itself for me turned sour, / And the future dark and drear." Must be Pushkin's writing.[2] In the evening, wrapped in my overcoat, I went to Her Excellency's front gates and waited for a long time to see whether she'd come out for a carriage, to have one more look—but no, she didn't come out.

•

November 6.

Furious with the section chief. When I came to the office, he called me over and started talking to me like this: "Well, pray tell me, what are you up to?" "What am I up to? Why, nothing," I replied. "Well, think a little better! You're over forty—it's time you got smart. What are you dreaming of? Do you think I don't know all your pranks? You're dangling after the director's daughter! Well, take a look at yourself, only think, what are you? You're a zero, nothing more. You haven't got a kopeck to your name. Just look at yourself in the mirror, how can you even think of it!" Devil take him, his face bears a slight resemblance to a druggist's bottle, with a tuft of hair curled into a forelock sticking up, smeared with some pomade, so he thinks he's the only one allowed anything. I see, I see why he's angry with me. He's jealous. Maybe he saw the signs of benevolence preferentially bestowed on me. Well, spit on him! Big deal, a court councillor! hangs a gold watch chain on himself, orders thirty-rouble boots—who the devil cares! Am I some sort of nobody, a tailor's son, or a sergeant's? I'm a nobleman. So, I, too, can earn rank. I'm only forty-two—the age at which service just seriously begins. Wait, friend! we, too, will become a colonel and, God willing, maybe something even higher. We'll get ourselves a reputation even better than yours. What, have you taken it into your head that there are no decent men except you? Just give me a Ruch[3] tailcoat, cut in the latest fashion, and let me have the same kind of necktie as you have—you won't hold a candle to me. No income—that's the trouble.

November 8.

Went to the theater. The Russian fool Filatka[4] was playing. Laughed a lot. There was some other vaudeville with funny verses about lawyers, especially about some collegiate registrar, written quite freely, so that I wondered how it passed the censors, and they said outright that merchants cheat people and their sons are debauchers and try to worm their way into the nobility. Also a very funny couplet about journalists: that they like denouncing everything—and the author asked the public for protection. Authors write very funny plays nowadays. I like going to the theater. As soon as I have a penny in my pocket, I just can't keep myself from going. But there are such pigs among our fellow clerks: they decidedly will not go to the theater, the clods, unless you give them a free ticket. One actress sang very well. I remembered the other . . . ah, confound it! . . . never mind, never mind . . . silence.

November 9.

At eight o'clock I went to the office. The section chief assumed such an air as if he didn't notice my arrival. I, for my part, acted as if there had been nothing between us. Looked through and collated papers. Left at four o'clock. Passed by the director's apartment but didn't see anybody. Lay in bed most of the time after dinner.

November 11.

Today I sat in our director's study and sharpened twenty-three pens for him, and for her, aie, aie! . . . four pens for Her Excellency. He likes very much having more pens. Oh, what a head that must be! Quite silent, but in his head, I think, he ponders everything. I wish I knew what he thinks about most; what's cooking in that head? I'd like to have a closer look at these gentlemen's lives, at all these equivocations and courtly tricks—how they are, what they do in their circle—that's what I'd like to find out! I've meant several times to strike up a conversation with His Excellency, only, devil take it, my tongue wouldn't obey me: I'd just say it was cold or warm outside, and be decidedly unable to say anything else. I'd like to peek into the drawing room, where you sometimes see only an open door into yet another room beyond the drawing room. Ah, such rich furnishings! Such mirrors and china! I'd like to peek in there, into that half, Her Excellency's—that's what I'd like! Into the boudoir, with all those little jars and vials standing there, such flowers that you're afraid to breathe on them; with her dress thrown down there, more like air than a dress. I'd like to peek into her bedroom . . . there, I think, there are wonders; there, I think, there is paradise, such as is not even to be found in heaven. To look at the little stool she puts her little foot on when she gets out of bed, at how a snow-white stocking is being put on that foot . . . aie! aie! aie! never mind, never mind . . . silence.

Today, however, it dawned on me clear as daylight: I recalled the conversation of the two little dogs I'd heard on Nevsky Prospect. "Very well," I thought to myself, "I'll find out everything now. I must get hold of the correspondence those rotten little dogs have exchanged. I'll learn a thing or two from it." I confess, I had even called Medji over once and said, "Listen, Medji, we're alone now; I'll lock the door if you like, so no one can see—tell me everything you know about the young miss, what and how she is? I swear to God I won't tell anybody." But the cunning little dog put her tail between her legs, shrank to half her size, and quietly walked out the door as if she hadn't heard anything. I've long suspected dogs of being much smarter than people; I was even certain they could speak, but there was only some kind of stubbornness in them. They're extraordinary politicians: they notice every human step. No, I'll go to Zverkov's building tomorrow at all costs, question Fidèle, and, if I'm lucky, get hold of all the letters Medji has written to her.

November 12.

At two o'clock in the afternoon I set out with the firm intention of seeing Fidèle and questioning her. I can't stand cabbage, the smell of which comes pouring out of all the small shops on Meshchanskaya; besides that, there was such a whiff of hell coming from under the gates of each house that I held my nose and ran for dear life. And those vile artisans produce so much soot and smoke in their workshops that it's decidedly impossible for a gentleman to walk there. When I got to the sixth floor and rang the bell, a girl came out, not so bad looking, with little freckles. I recognized her. It was the same one who was walking with the old lady. She blushed slightly, and I understood at once: You, my sweet, are looking for a fiancé. "What can I do for you?" she said. "I must have a word with your little dog." The girl was stupid! I knew at once she was stupid! At that moment the dog ran in, barking; I wanted to seize her, but she, vile thing, almost seized me by the nose with her teeth. I saw her basket in the corner, however. Aha, just what I need! I went over to it, rummaged in the straw of the wooden box, and, to my greatest satisfaction, pulled out a small bundle of little papers. Seeing that, the nasty little dog first bit me on the calf and then, when she realized I'd taken the papers, began squealing and fawning, but I said, "No, my sweet, good-bye!" and rushed out. I suppose the girl took me for a madman, because she was extremely frightened. On coming home, I wanted to get to work and sort these letters out at once, because I see poorly by candlelight. But Mavra had decided to wash the floor. These stupid Finnish women are always cleaning at the wrong moment. And so I went out to walk around and think this event over. Now I'll finally learn about all these affairs and intentions, all these springs, and finally get to the bottom of it. These letters will reveal everything to me. Dogs are smart folk, they know all the political relations, and so it's all sure to be there: the picture of the man and all his doings. There'll also be something about her who . . . never mind, silence! Toward evening I came home. Lay in bed most of the time.

Well, now, let's see: the letter looks pretty clear. However, there's still something doggy in the writing. Let's read it:

Dear Fidèle,

I still cannot get used to your common-sounding name. As if they couldn't have given you a better one? Fidèle, Rosy—such banal tone! However, that's all beside the point. I'm very glad we've decided to write to each other.

The letter is written very correctly. Punctuation and even tricky spellings all in order. Not even our section chief can write like that, though he keeps saying he studied at some university. Let's see what comes next:

It seems to me that sharing thoughts, feelings, and impressions with others is one of the foremost blessings in the world.

Hm! the thought is drawn from some work translated from the German. Can't recall the title.

I say it from experience, though I've never run farther in the world than the gates of our house. Whose life flows by in pleasure if not mine? My young mistress, whom Papá calls Sophie, loves me to distraction.

Aie, aie! . . . never mind, never mind. Silence.

Papá also pets me very often. I drink tea and coffee with cream. Ah, *ma chère*, I must tell you that I see no pleasure at all in those big, bare bones our Polkan slobbers over in the kitchen. Only bones from wild game are good, and only before anyone has sucked out the marrow. Mixtures of several gravies are very good, only not with capers or herbs; but I know nothing worse than the habit of giving dogs little balls of bread. Some gentleman sitting at the table, after holding all sorts of trash in his hands, begins to roll bread in those same hands, then calls you over and puts the ball in your teeth. It's somehow impolite to refuse, so you eat it; with disgust, but you eat it . . .

Devil knows what this is! Such nonsense! As if there were no better subjects to write about. Let's look at the next page. For something more sensible.

I'm quite ready and willing to inform you of all that goes on in our house. I've already told you a little something about the main gentleman, whom Sophie calls Papá. He's a very strange man.

Ah! at last! Yes, I knew it: they have political views on all subjects. Let's see about Papá:

. . . a very strange man. He's silent most of the time. Speaks very rarely; but a week ago, he talked to himself constantly: "Will I get it or won't I?" He would take a piece of paper in one hand, close the other empty one, and say: "Will I get it or won't I?" Once he addressed the question to me: "What do you think, Medji? Will I get it or won't I?" I could understand none of it, so I sniffed his boot and went away. Then, *ma chère*, a week later Papá came home very happy. All morning gentlemen in uniforms kept coming to him, congratulating him for something. At the table he was merrier than I'd ever seen him before, told jokes, and after dinner he held me up to his neck and said: "Look, Medji, what's this?" I saw some little ribbon. I sniffed it but found decidedly no aroma; finally I licked it on the sly: it was a bit salty.

Hm! This little dog seems to me to be much too . . . she ought to be whipped! Ah! so he's ambitious. That must be taken into consideration.

Good-bye, *ma chère,* I must run, and so on . . . and so forth . . . I'll finish my letter tomorrow. Well, hello! here I am again . . . Today my mistress Sophie . . .

Ah! so we shall see about Sophie. Eh, confound it! . . . Never mind, never mind . . . let's go on.

. . . my mistress Sophie was in a great bustle. She was going to a ball, and I was glad that in her absence I'd be able to write to you. My Sophie is always greatly delighted to be going to a ball, though she's almost always angry as she's being dressed. I simply don't understand, *ma chère,* the pleasure in going to a ball. Sophie comes home from the ball at six o'clock in the morning, and I can almost always tell by her pale and skinny look that the poor thing was given nothing to eat there. I confess, I could never live like that. If I wasn't given hazel grouse with gravy or roast chicken wings, I . . . I don't know what would become of me. Gruel with gravy is also good. But carrots, turnips, and artichokes will never be good . . .

Extremely uneven style. Shows at once that it wasn't written by a man. Begins properly, but ends with some dogginess. Let's have a look at another letter. A bit long. Hm! and no date.

Ah, my dear, how one senses the approach of spring! My heart throbs as if it keeps waiting for something. There is an eternal humming in my ears, so that I often stand for several minutes with uplifted paw, listening at the door. I'll confide to you that I have many wooers. I often sit in the window and look at them. Ah, if you only knew how ugly some of them are. The coarsest of all mutts, terribly stupid, stupidity written all over his face, goes down the street most imposingly, imagining he's the noblest person, thinking everyone is looking only at him. Not a bit of it. I didn't even pay attention, just as if I hadn't seen him. And what a frightful Great Dane stops outside my window! If he stood on his hind legs—

something the boor is surely incapable of doing—he'd be a whole head taller than my Sophie's Papá, who is also quite tall and fat. This blockhead must be terribly impudent. I growled at him a little, but he couldn't have cared less. He didn't flinch! stuck his tongue out, hung his enormous ears, and stared in the window—what a clod! But don't think, *ma chère,* that my heart is indifferent to all suitors—oh, no . . . If you saw a certain gallant who climbs over the fence from the neighbors' house, by the name of Trésor. Ah, *ma chère,* he has such a cute muzzle!

Pah, devil take it! . . . What rot! . . . How can one fill letters with such silliness? Give me a man! I want to see a man; I demand food—such as nourishes and delights my soul; and instead I get these trifles . . . let's skip a page, maybe it will get better:

. . . Sophie sat at her table sewing something. I was looking out the window, because I enjoy watching passers-by. When suddenly a lackey came in and said: "Teplov!" "Show him in," Sophie cried and rushed to embrace me . . . "Ah, Medji, Medji! If you knew who he is: dark hair, a kammerjunker,[5] and such eyes! dark and glowing like fire"—and Sophie ran to her room. A moment later a young kammerjunker with dark side-whiskers came in, went up to the mirror, smoothed his hair, and glanced around the room. I growled a little and kept my place. Sophie came out soon and bowed gaily to his scraping; and I, as if noticing nothing, just went on looking out the window; however, I cocked my head a little to one side and tried to hear what they were talking about. Ah, *ma chère,* such nonsense they talked about! They talked about a lady who performed one figure instead of another during a dance; also how a certain Bobov looked just like a stork in his jabot and nearly fell down; how a certain Miss Lidin fancies she has blue eyes, whereas they're green—and the like. "Well," thought I to myself, "and if we compare the kammerjunker with Trésor!" Heavens, what a difference! First of all, the kammerjunker has a perfectly smooth, broad face with side-whiskers around it, as if someone had tied it with a black band; while Trésor has a slender little muzzle and a white spot right on his forehead. Between Trésor's waist and the kammerjunker's there's no comparing. The eyes, the gestures, the manners are not at all alike. Oh, what a difference! I don't know, *ma chère,* what she finds in her Teplov. Why does she admire him so? . . .

To me it also seems that there's something wrong here. It can't be that a kammerjunker could enchant her so. Let's see further on:

It seems to me that if she likes that kammerjunker, she'll soon be liking the clerk who sits in Papá's study. Ah, *ma chère,* if you only knew how ugly he is. A perfect turtle in a sack . . .

What clerk might this be? . . .

He has the strangest last name. He always sits and sharpens pens. The hair on his head looks very much like hay. Papá always sends him out instead of a servant.

I think the vile little dog is aiming at me. How is my hair like hay?

Sophie can never help laughing when she looks at him.

You're lying, you cursed dog! What a vile tongue! As if I don't know it's a matter of envy. As if I don't know whose tricks these are. These are the section chief's tricks. The man has sworn undying hatred—and so he injures me, he keeps injuring me at every step. However, let's look at another letter. Maybe the thing will explain itself.

Ma chère Fidèle, you must excuse my not writing for so long. I've been in perfect ecstasy. It's entirely correct what some writer has said, that love is a second life. Besides, there are big changes in our house now. The kammerjunker now comes every day. Sophie loves him to distraction. Papá is very happy. I even heard from our Grigory, who sweeps the floor and almost always talks to himself, that there will be a wedding soon; because Papá absolutely wants to see Sophie married to a general, or a kammerjunker, or an army colonel . . .

Devil take it! I can't read any more . . . It's all either kammerjunker or general. All that's best in the world, all of it goes either to kammerjunkers or generals. You find a poor treasure for yourself, hope to reach out your hand to it—a kammerjunker or a general plucks it away from you. Devil take it! I wish I could become a general myself: not so as to get her hand and the rest of it, no, I want to be a general simply to see how they'll fawn and perform all those various courtly tricks and equivocations, and then to tell them I spit on them both. Devil take it. How annoying! I've torn the stupid dog's letters to shreds.

December 3.

It can't be. Lies! The wedding won't take place! So what if he's a kammerjunker. It's nothing more than a dignity; it's not anything visible that you can take in your hands. He's not going to have a third eye on his forehead because he's a kammerjunker. His nose isn't made of gold, it's the same as mine or anybody else's; he doesn't eat with it, he smells; he doesn't cough, he sneezes. Several times already I've tried to figure out where all these differences come from. What makes me a titular councillor, and why on earth am I a titular councillor? Maybe I'm some sort of count or general and only seem to be a titular councillor? Maybe I myself don't know who I am. There are so many examples in history: some simple fellow, not only not a nobleman, but simply some tradesman or even peasant—and it's suddenly revealed that he's some sort of dignitary, or sometimes even an emperor. If even a muzhik sometimes turns out like that, what, then, may become of a nobleman? Suddenly, for instance, I walk in wearing a general's uniform: an epaulette on my right shoulder, and an epaulette on my left shoulder, a blue ribbon over my shoulder—what then? How is my beauty going to sing? What is Papá himself, our director, going to say? Oh, he's a man of great ambition! He's a Mason, a downright Mason, though he pretends to be this and that, I noticed right away he's a Mason: whenever he shakes a person's hand, he only holds out two fingers. But can't I be promoted this minute to governor general, or intendant, or something else like that? I'd like to know, what makes me a titular councillor? Why precisely a titular councillor?

December 5.

I spent the whole morning today reading the newspapers. There are strange doings in Spain. I couldn't even make them out properly. They write that the throne is vacant and that the officials are in a difficult position about the selection of an heir, which is causing disturbances. This seems terribly strange to me. How can a throne be vacant? They say some doña should ascend the throne.[6] A doña cannot ascend a throne. Simply cannot. There should be a king on a throne. But, they say, there is no king. It cannot be that there was no king. A state cannot be without a king. There is a king, only he's somewhere unknown. Possibly he's right there, but either some sort of family reasons, or apprehensions about neighboring powers, such as France and other countries, have forced him into hiding, or there are other reasons of some sort.

December 8.

I was just about to go to the office, but various reasons and reflections held me back. I couldn't get these Spanish affairs out of my head. How can a doña be made a queen? They won't allow it. And, first of all, England won't allow it. And besides, the political affairs of the whole of Europe: the Austrian emperor, our sovereign . . . I confess, these events so crushed and shook me that I was decidedly unable to busy myself with anything all day long. Mavra observed to me that I was extremely distracted at the table. And, indeed, it seems I absentmindedly threw two plates on the floor, which proceeded to break. After dinner, I strolled around the toboggan slides. Couldn't arrive at anything constructive. Mostly lay in bed and reasoned about the affairs in Spain.

The Year 2000, 43rd of April.

This day—is a day of the greatest solemnity! Spain has a king. He has been found. I am that king. Only this very day did I learn of it. I confess, it came to me suddenly in a flash of lightning. I don't understand how I could have thought and imagined that I was a titular councillor. How could such a wild notion enter my head? It's a good thing no one thought of putting me in an insane asylum. Now everything is laid open before me. Now I see everything as on the palm of my hand. And before, I don't understand, before everything around me was in some sort of fog. And all this happens, I think, because people imagine that the human brain is in the head. Not at all: it is brought by a wind from the direction of the Caspian Sea. First off, I announced to Mavra who I am. When she heard that the king of Spain was standing before her, she clasped her hands and nearly died of fright. The stupid woman had never seen a king of Spain before. However, I endeavored to calm her down and assured her in gracious words of my benevolence and that I was not at all angry that she sometimes polished my boots poorly. They're benighted folk. It's impossible to tell them about lofty matters. She got frightened, because she's convinced that all kings of Spain are like Philip II. But I explained to her that there was no resemblance between me and Philip II, and that I didn't have a single Capuchin[7] . . . I didn't go to the office . . . To hell with it! No, friends, you won't lure me there now; I'm not going to copy your vile papers!

The 86th of Martober. Between day and night.

Today our manager came to tell me to go to the office, since I hadn't been to work for over three weeks. I went to the office as a joke. The section chief thought I'd bow to him and start apologizing, but I looked at him with indifference—neither too wrathfully nor too benevolently—and sat down at my place as if not noticing anyone. I looked at all that office riffraff and thought: "What if you knew who was sitting amongst you . . . Lord God! what a rumpus you'd raise, and the section chief would start bowing as low to me as he now bows to the director." Some papers were placed in front of me so that I could make an abstract of them. But

I didn't even set a finger to them. A few minutes later everything was in turmoil. They said the director was coming. Many clerks ran up front to show themselves before him. But I didn't budge. When he was passing through our section, everybody buttoned up their tailcoats; but I—nothing of the sort! What is a director that I should stand up before him—never! What sort of director is he? He's a doornail, not a director. An ordinary doornail, a simple doornail, nothing more. The kind used in doors. I was most amused when they slipped me a paper to be signed. They thought I'd write "Chief Clerk So-and-So" at the very bottom of the page. Not a chance! In the central place, where the director of the department signs, I dashed off: "Ferdinand VIII." You should have seen what reverent silence ensued; but I merely waved my hand, saying, "No need for any tokens of homage!" and walked out. From there I went straight to the director's apartment. He was not at home. The lackey didn't want to let me in, but after what I said to him, he just dropped his arms. I made my way straight to the boudoir. She was sitting before the mirror, jumped up, and backed away from me. However, I didn't tell her I was the king of Spain. I only said that such happiness awaited her as she could not even imagine, and that despite the machinations of enemies, we would be together. I did not want to say anything more, and walked out. Oh, she's a perfidious being—woman! Only now have I grasped what woman is. Till now no one has found out who she's in love with: I'm the first to discover it. Woman is in love with the devil. Yes, no joking. It's stupid what physicists write, that she's this or that—she loves only the devil. See there, from a box in the first balcony, she's aiming her lorgnette. You think she's looking at that fat one with the star? Not at all, she's looking at the devil standing behind his back. There he is hiding in his tailcoat. There he is beckoning to her with his finger! And she'll marry him. Marry him. And all those high-ranking fathers of theirs, all those who fidget in all directions and worm their way into court and say they're patriots and this and that: income, income is what these patriots want! Mother, father, God—they'll sell them all for money, the ambitious Judases! It's all ambition, and ambition is caused by a little blister under the tongue with a little worm in it the size of a pinhead, and it's all the doing of some barber who lives in Gorokhovaya Street. I don't know what his name is; but it's known for certain that he, together with some midwife, wants to spread Mohammedanism throughout the world, and as a result, they say, in France the majority of people already accepts the faith of Mohammed.

Date none. The day had no date.

Strolled incognito on Nevsky Prospect. His Majesty the emperor drove by. The whole city took their hats off, and I did, too; however, I didn't let on that I was the king of Spain. I considered it unsuitable to reveal myself right there in front of everybody; because, first of all, I have to present myself at court. The only thing holding me up is that I still don't have royal attire. If only I could get some sort of mantle. I was going to order one from a tailor, but they're perfect asses, and, besides, they neglect their work completely; they've thrown themselves into affairs and are mostly busy paving the streets with stones. I decided to make a mantle out of my new uniform, which I had only worn twice. But, to prevent those blackguards from ruining it, I decided to sew it myself, after locking the door so that no one could see. I cut it all up with scissors, because the style has to be completely different.

Don't remember the date. There was no
month, either. Devil knows what there was.

The mantle is all ready and sewn up. Mavra cried out when I put it on. However, I still refrain from presenting myself at court. No deputation from Spain so far. Without deputies it's not proper. There'll be no weight to my dignity. I expect them any moment.

The 1st.

I'm extremely astonished at the slowness of the deputies. What reasons can be holding them up? Can it be France? Yes, that is the most unfavorably disposed power. I went to inquire at the post office whether the Spanish deputies had arrived. But the postmaster is very stupid, he doesn't know anything; no, he says, there are no Spanish deputies here, and if you wish to write letters, we accept them at the set rate. Devil take it! what's a letter! A letter's nonsense. Apothecaries can write letters . . .

Madrid. Thirtieth Februarius.

And so I'm in Spain, and it happened so quickly that I've barely come to my senses. This morning the Spanish deputies came to me, and I got into the carriage together with them. The extraordinary speed seemed strange to me. We drove so quickly that in half an hour we reached the Spanish border. However, there are railroads everywhere in Europe now, and steamships drive very fast. Spain is a strange land: when we entered the first room, I saw a lot of people with shaved heads. I guessed, however, that they must be either grandees or soldiers, since they shave their heads. The behavior of the lord chancellor, who led me by the arm, seemed extremely strange to me; he pushed me into a little room and said, "Sit here, and if you still want to call yourself King Ferdinand, I'll beat the wish out of you." But I, knowing it was nothing but a provocation, replied in the negative—for which the chancellor hit me twice on the back with a stick, so painfully that I nearly cried out, but caught myself, having remembered that this was the knightly custom on entering upon high rank, because in Spain they still preserve knightly customs. Being left alone, I decided to occupy myself with state affairs. I discovered that China and Spain are absolutely one and the same land, and it is only out of ignorance that they are considered separate countries. I advise everyone purposely to write Spain on a piece of paper, and it will come out China. But, nevertheless, I was extremely upset by an event that is going to take place tomorrow. Tomorrow at seven o'clock a strange phenomenon will occur: the earth is going to sit on the moon. This has also been written about by the noted English chemist Wellington. I confess, I felt troubled at heart when I pictured to myself the extraordinary delicacy and fragility of the moon. For the moon is usually made in Hamburg, and made quite poorly. I'm surprised England doesn't pay attention to this. It's made by a lame cooper, and one can see that the fool understands nothing about the moon. He used tarred rope and a quantity of cheap olive oil, and that's why there's a terrible stench all over the earth, so that you have to hold your nose. And that's why the moon itself is such a delicate sphere that people can't live on it, and now only noses live there. And for the same reason, we can't see our own noses, for they're all in the moon. And when I pictured how the earth is a heavy substance and in sitting down may grind our noses into flour, I was overcome with such anxiety that, putting on my stockings and shoes, I hurried to the state council chamber to order the police not to allow the earth to sit on the moon. The shaved grandees, great numbers of whom I found in the state council chamber, were all very intelligent people, and when I said, "Gentlemen, let us save the moon, because the earth wants to sit on it," they all rushed at once to carry out my royal will, and many crawled up the wall in order to get the moon; but just then the lord chancellor came in. Seeing him, they all ran away. I, being the king, was the only one to remain. But, to my surprise, the chancellor hit me with a stick and drove me to my room. Such is the power of popular custom in Spain!

January of the same year,
which came after February.

I still cannot understand what sort of country Spain is. The popular customs and court etiquette are absolutely extraordinary. I do not understand, I do not understand, I decidedly do not understand anything. Today they shaved my head, though I shouted with all my might about my unwillingness to be a monk. But I cannot even remember how I felt when they began dripping cold water on my head. I've never experienced such hell before. I was ready to start raging, so that they were barely able to hold me back. I don't understand the meaning of this strange custom at all. A stupid, senseless custom! The folly of the kings, who still have not abolished it, is incomprehensible to me. Judging by all probabilities, I guess I may have fallen into the hands of the Inquisition, and the one I took for the chancellor may be the grand inquisitor himself. Only I still cannot understand how a king can be made subject to the Inquisition. True, this might come from the French side, especially from Polignac.[8] Oh, he's a sly customer, Polignac! He's sworn to injure me as long as I live. And so he persecutes me, persecutes me; but I know, friend, that you're being led by the Englishman. The Englishman is a great politician. He fusses about everywhere. The whole world knows that when England takes snuff, France sneezes.

The 25th.

Today the grand inquisitor came to my room, but, hearing his footsteps from far off, I hid under a chair. Seeing I wasn't there, he began calling out. First he shouted, "Poprishchin!" but I didn't say a word. Then: "Aksenty Ivanovich! Titular councillor! Nobleman!" I kept silent. "Ferdinand VIII, king of Spain!" I wanted to poke my head out, but then thought, "No, brother, you're not going to hoodwink me! We know you: you'll pour cold water on my head again." Nevertheless, he saw me and chased me out from under the chair with his stick. That cursed stick is extremely painful. However, all this has been rewarded by my present discovery: I've learned that every rooster has his Spain, that it's located under his feathers. The grand inquisitor nevertheless left me in wrath and threatened me with some punishment. But I utterly ignored his impotent anger, knowing that he was acting mechanically, as the Englishman's tool.

The of 34 ʎɹɐnɹqǝℲ th, yrea 349.

No, I no longer have the strength to endure. God! what they're doing to me! They pour cold water on my head! They do not heed, do not see, do not listen to me. What have I done to them? Why do they torment me? What do they want from poor me? What can I give them? I have nothing. It's beyond my strength, I cannot endure all their torments, my head is burning, and everything is whirling before me. Save me! take me! give me a troika of steeds swift as the wind! Take the reins, my driver, ring out, my bells, soar aloft, steeds, and carry me out of this world! Farther, farther, so that there's nothing to be seen, nothing. Here is the sky billowing before me; a little star shines in the distance; a forest races by with dark trees and a crescent moon; blue mist spreads under my feet; a string twangs in the mist; on one side the sea, on the other Italy; and there I see some Russian huts. Is that my house blue in the distance? Is that my mother sitting at the window? Dear mother, save your poor son! shed a tear on his sick head! see how they torment him! press the poor orphan to your breast! there's no place for him in the world! they're driving him out! Dear mother! pity your sick child! . . . And do you know that the Dey of Algiers has a bump just under his nose?

THE NOSE

I

ON THE TWENTY-FIFTH day of March,[1] an extraordinarily strange incident occurred in Petersburg. The barber Ivan Yakovlevich, who lives on Voznesensky Prospect (his family name has been lost, and even on his signboard—which portrays a gentleman with a soaped cheek along with the words "Also Bloodletting"— nothing more appears), the barber Ivan Yakovlevich woke up quite early and sensed the smell of hot bread. Raising himself a little in bed, he saw that his wife, quite a respectable lady, who very much liked her cup of coffee, was taking just-baked loaves from the oven.

"Today, Praskovya Osipovna, I will not have coffee," said Ivan Yakovlevich, "but instead I'd like to have some hot bread with onion."

(That is, Ivan Yakovlevich would have liked the one and the other, but he knew it was utterly impossible to ask for two things at the same time, for Praskovya Osipovna very much disliked such whims.) "Let the fool eat bread; so much the better for me," the wife thought to herself, "there'll be an extra portion of coffee left." And she threw a loaf of bread on the table.

For the sake of propriety, Ivan Yakovlevich put his tailcoat on over his undershirt and, settling at the table, poured out some salt, prepared two onions, took a knife in his hands, and, assuming a significant air, began cutting the bread. Having cut the loaf in two, he looked into the middle and, to his surprise, saw something white. Ivan Yakovlevich poked cautiously with his knife and felt with his finger. "Firm!" he said to himself. "What could it be?"

He stuck in his fingers and pulled out—a nose! . . . Ivan Yakovlevich even dropped his arms; he began rubbing his eyes and feeling it: a nose, precisely a nose! and, what's more, it seemed like a familiar one. Terror showed on Ivan Yakovlevich's face. But this terror was nothing compared to the indignation that came over his wife.

"Where did you cut that nose off, you beast?" she shouted wrathfully. "Crook! Drunkard! I'll denounce you to the police myself! What a bandit! I've heard from three men already that you pull noses so hard when you give a shave that they barely stay attached."

But Ivan Yakovlevich was more dead than alive. He recognized this nose as belonging to none other than the collegiate assessor Kovalev, whom he shaved every Wednesday and Sunday.

"Wait, Praskovya Osipovna! I'll wrap it in a rag and put it in the corner. Let it stay there a while, and later I'll take it out."

"I won't hear of it! That I should leave some cut-off nose lying about my room? . . . You dried-up crust! You only know how to drag your razor over the strop, but soon you won't be able to do your duties at all, you trull, you blackguard! That I should have to answer for you to the police? . . . Ah, you muck-worm, you stupid stump! Out with it! out! take it wherever you like! so that I never hear of it again!"

Ivan Yakovlevich stood totally crushed. He thought and thought and did not know what to think.

"Devil knows how it happened," he said finally, scratching himself behind the ear. "Whether I came home drunk yesterday or not, I can't say for sure. But by all tokens this incident should be unfeasible: for bread is a baking matter, and a nose is something else entirely. I can't figure it out! . . ."

Ivan Yakovlevich fell silent. The thought of the police finding the nose at his place and accusing him drove him to complete distraction. He could already picture the scarlet collar, beautifully embroidered with silver, the sword . . . and he trembled all over. Finally he took his shirt and boots, pulled all this trash on him, and, to the accompaniment of Praskovya Osipovna's weighty admonitions, wrapped the nose in a rag and went out.

He wanted to leave it somewhere, in an iron hitching post under a gateway, or just somehow accidentally drop it and turn down an alley. But unfortunately he kept running into someone he knew, who would begin at once by asking, "Where are you off to?" or "Who are you going to shave so early?"—so that Ivan Yakovlevich could never seize the moment. Another time, he had already dropped it entirely, but a policeman pointed to it from afar with his halberd and said: "Pick that up! You've dropped something there!" And Ivan Yakovlevich had to pick the nose up and put it in his pocket. Despair came over him, especially as there were more and more people in the street as the stores and shops began to open.

He decided to go to St. Isaac's Bridge: might he not somehow manage to throw it into the Neva? . . . But I am slightly remiss for having said nothing yet about Ivan Yakovlevich, a worthy man in many respects.

Ivan Yakovlevich, like every decent Russian artisan, was a terrible drunkard. And though he shaved other people's chins every day, his own was eternally unshaven. Ivan Yakovlevich's tailcoat (Ivan Yakovlevich never went around in a frock coat) was piebald; that is, it was black, but all dappled with brownish-yellow and gray spots; the collar was shiny, and in place of three buttons there hung only threads. Ivan Yakovlevich was a great cynic, and whenever the collegiate assessor Kovalev said to him while being shaved, "Your hands eternally stink, Ivan Yakovlevich"—Ivan Yakovlevich would reply with a question: "And why should they stink?" to which the collegiate assessor would say, "I don't know, brother, but they stink," and for that Ivan Yakovlevich, after a pinch of snuff, would soap him up on the cheeks, and under the nose, and behind the ears, and under the chin—in short, anywhere he liked.

This worthy citizen was already on St. Isaac's Bridge. First he glanced around; then he leaned over the rail, as if looking under the bridge to see if there were lots of fish darting about, and quietly threw down the rag with the nose. He felt as if a three-hundred-pound weight had suddenly fallen from him; Ivan Yakovlevich even grinned. Instead of going to shave the chins of functionaries, he was heading for an institution under a sign that read "Food and Tea" to ask for a glass of punch, when suddenly he saw at the end of the bridge a police officer of noble appearance, with broad side-whiskers, in a three-cornered hat, wearing a sword. He went dead; and meanwhile the policeman was beckoning to him with his finger and saying, "Come here, my good man!"

Ivan Yakovlevich, knowing the rules, took off his peaked cap while still far away and, approaching rapidly, said:

"Good day to your honor!"

"No, no, brother, never mind my honor. Tell me what you were doing standing on the bridge."

"By God, sir, I'm on my way to give a shave and just stopped to see if the river's flowing fast."

"Lies, lies! You won't get off with that. Be so good as to answer!"

"I'm ready to shave you twice a week, sir, or even three times, with no objections," Ivan Yakovlevich answered.

"No, friend, that's trifles. I have three barbers to shave me, and they consider it a great honor. Kindly tell me what you were doing there."

Ivan Yakovlevich blanched . . . But here the incident becomes totally shrouded in mist, and of what happened further decidedly nothing is known.

II

The collegiate assessor Kovalev woke up quite early and went "brr . . ." with his lips—something he always did on waking up, though he himself was unable to explain the reason for it. Kovalev stretched and asked for the little mirror that stood on the table. He wished to look at a pimple that had popped out on his nose the previous evening; but, to his greatest amazement, he saw that instead of a nose he had a perfectly smooth place! Frightened,

Kovalev asked for water and wiped his eyes with a towel: right, no nose! He began feeling with his hand to find out if he might be asleep, but it seemed he was not. The collegiate assessor Kovalev jumped out of bed, shook himself: no nose! . . . He ordered his man to dress him and flew straight to the chief of police.

But meanwhile it is necessary to say something about Kovalev, so that the reader may see what sort of collegiate assessor he was. Collegiate assessors who obtain that title by means of learned diplomas cannot in any way be compared with collegiate assessors who are made in the Caucasus.[2] They are two entirely different sorts. Learned collegiate assessors . . . But Russia is such a wondrous land that, if you say something about one collegiate assessor, all collegiate assessors, from Riga to Kamchatka, will unfailingly take it to their own account. The same goes for all ranks and titles. Kovalev was a Caucasian collegiate assessor. He had held this rank for only two years, and therefore could not forget it for a moment; and to give himself more nobility and weight, he never referred to himself as a collegiate assessor, but always as a major. "Listen, dearie," he used to say on meeting a woman selling shirt fronts in the street, "come to my place; I live on Sadovaya; just ask, 'Where does Major Kovalev live?'—anyone will show you." And if he met some comely little thing, he would give her a secret order on top of that, adding: "Ask for Major Kovalev's apartment, sweetie." For which reason, we shall in future refer to this collegiate assessor as a major.

Major Kovalev had the habit of strolling on Nevsky Prospect every day. The collar of his shirt front was always extremely clean and starched. His side-whiskers were of the sort that can still be seen on provincial and regional surveyors, architects, and regimental doctors, as well as on those fulfilling various police duties, and generally on all men who have plump, ruddy cheeks and play a very good game of Boston: these side-whiskers go right across the middle of the cheek and straight to the nose. Major Kovalev wore many seals, of carnelian, with crests, and the sort that have Wednesday, Thursday, Monday, and so on, carved on them. Major Kovalev had come to Petersburg on business—namely, to seek a post suited to his rank: as vice-governor if he was lucky, or else as an executive in some prominent department. Major Kovalev would not have minded getting married, but only on the chance that the bride happened to come with two hundred thousand in capital. And therefore the reader may now judge for himself what the state of this major was when he saw, instead of a quite accept-able and moderate nose, a most stupid, flat, and smooth place.

As ill luck would have it, not a single coachman appeared in the street, and he had to go on foot, wrapping himself in his cloak and covering his face with a handkerchief as if it were bleeding. "But maybe I just imagined it that way: it's impossible for a nose to van-ish so idiotically," he thought and went into a pastry shop on pur-pose to look at himself in the mirror. Luckily there was no one in the pastry shop; the boys were sweeping the rooms and putting the chairs in place; some of them, sleepy-eyed, brought out hot pastries on trays; yesterday's newspapers, stained with spilt coffee, lay about on tables and chairs. "Well, thank God nobody's here," he said. "Now I can have a look." He timidly approached a mir-ror and looked: "Devil knows, what rubbish!" he said, spitting. "There might at least be something instead of a nose, but there's nothing! . . ."

Biting his lips in vexation, he walked out of the pastry shop and decided, contrary to his custom, not to look at anyone or smile to anyone. Suddenly he stopped as if rooted outside the doors of one house; before his eyes an inexplicable phenomenon occurred: a carriage stopped at the entrance; the door opened; a gentleman in a uniform jumped out, hunching over, and ran up the stairs. What was Kovalev's horror as well as amazement when he recognized him as his own nose! At this extraordinary spectacle, everything seemed to turn upside down in his eyes; he felt barely able to stand; but, trembling all over as if in a fever, he decided that, whatever the cost, he would await his return to the carriage. Two minutes later the nose indeed came out. He was in a gold-embroidered uniform with a big standing collar; he had kidskin trousers on; at his side hung a sword. From his plumed hat it could be concluded that he belonged to the rank of state councillor. By all indications, he was going somewhere on a visit. He looked both ways, shouted, "Here!" to the coachman, got in, and drove off.

Poor Kovalev nearly lost his mind. He did not know what to think of such a strange incident. How was it possible, indeed, that the nose which just yesterday was on his face, unable to drive or walk—should be in a uniform! He ran after the carriage, which luckily had not gone far and was stopped in front of the Kazan Cathedral.

He hastened into the cathedral, made his way through a row of old beggar women with bandaged faces and two openings for the eyes, at whom he had laughed so much before, and went into the church. There were not many people praying in the church: they all stood just by the entrance. Kovalev felt so upset that he had no strength to pray, and his eyes kept searching in all corners for the gentleman. He finally saw him standing to one side. The nose had his face completely hidden in his big standing collar and was praying with an expression of the greatest piety.

"How shall I approach him?" thought Kovalev. "By all tokens, by his uniform, by his hat, one can see he's a state councillor. Devil knows how to go about it!"

He began to cough beside him; but the nose would not abandon his pious attitude for a minute and kept bowing down.

"My dear sir," said Kovalev, inwardly forcing himself to take heart, "my dear sir . . ."

"What can I do for you?" the nose said, turning.

"I find it strange, my dear sir . . . it seems to me . . . you should know your place. And suddenly I find you, and where?—in a church. You must agree . . ."

"Excuse me, I don't understand what you're talking about . . . Explain, please."

"How shall I explain it to him?" thought Kovalev, and, gathering his courage, he began:

"Of course, I . . . anyhow, I'm a major. For me to go around without a nose is improper, you must agree. Some peddler woman selling peeled oranges on Voskresensky Bridge can sit without a nose; but, having prospects in view . . . being acquainted, moreover, with ladies in many houses: Chekhtareva, the wife of a state councillor, and others . . . Judge for yourself . . . I don't know, my dear sir . . ." (Here Major Kovalev shrugged his shoulders.) "Pardon me, but . . . if one looks at it in conformity with the rules of duty and honor . . . you yourself can understand . . ."

"I understand decidedly nothing," replied the nose. "Explain more satisfactorily."

"My dear sir . . ." Kovalev said with dignity, "I don't know how to understand your words . . . The whole thing seems perfectly obvious . . . Or do you want to . . . But you're my own nose!"

The nose looked at the major and scowled slightly.

"You are mistaken, my dear sir. I am by myself. Besides, there can be no close relationship between us. Judging by the buttons on your uniform, you must serve in a different department."

Having said this, the nose turned away and continued praying.

Kovalev was utterly bewildered, not knowing what to do or even what to think. At that moment the pleasant rustle of a lady's dress was heard; an elderly lady all decked out in lace approached, followed by a slim one in a white dress that very prettily outlined her slender waist, wearing a pale yellow hat as light as a pastry. Behind them a tall footman with big side-whiskers and a full dozen collars stopped and opened his snuffbox.

Kovalev stepped closer, made the cambric collar of his shirt front peek out, straightened the seals hanging on his gold watch chain, and, smiling to all sides, rested his attention on the ethereal lady who, bending slightly like a flower in spring, brought her white little hand with its half-transparent fingers to her brow. The smile on Kovalev's face broadened still more when he saw under her hat a rounded chin of a bright whiteness and part of a cheek glowing with the color of the first spring rose. But he suddenly jumped back as if burnt. He remembered that in place of a nose he had absolutely nothing, and tears squeezed themselves from his eyes. He turned with the intention of telling the gentleman in the uniform outright that he was only pretending to be a state councillor, that he was a knave and a scoundrel, and nothing but his own nose . . . But the nose was no longer there; he had already driven off, again probably to visit someone.

This threw Kovalev into despair. He went back and paused for a moment under the colonnade, looking carefully in all directions, in case he might spot the nose. He remembered very well that he was wearing a plumed hat and a gold-embroidered uniform; but he had not noted his overcoat, nor the color of his carriage, nor of his horses, nor even whether he had a footman riding behind and in what sort of livery. Besides, there were so many carriages racing up and down, and at such speed, that it was even difficult to notice anything; and if he had noticed one of them, he would have had no way of stopping it. The day was beautiful and sunny. There were myriads of people on Nevsky; a whole flowery cascade of ladies poured down the sidewalk from the Police to the Anichkin Bridge. There goes an acquaintance of his, a court councillor whom he called Colonel, especially if it occurred in front of strangers. And there is Yarygin, a chief clerk in the Senate, a great friend who always called *remise* when he played eight at Boston. There is another major who got his assessorship in the Caucasus, waving his arm, inviting him to come over . . .

"Ah, devil take it!" said Kovalev. "Hey, cabby, drive straight to the chief of police!"

Kovalev got into the droshky and kept urging the cabby on: "Gallop the whole way!"

"Is the chief of police in?" he cried, entering the front hall.

"No, he's not," the doorman replied, "he just left."

"Worse luck!"

"Yes," the doorman added, "not so long ago, but he left. If you'd have come one little minute sooner, you might have found him at home."

Kovalev, without taking the handkerchief from his face, got into a cab and shouted in a desperate voice:

"Drive!"

"Where to?" said the cabby.

"Straight ahead!"

"How, straight ahead? There's a turn here—right or left?"

This question stopped Kovalev and made him think again. In his situation, he ought first of all to address himself to the Office of Public Order, not because it was related directly to the police, but because its procedures were likely to be much quicker than elsewhere; to seek satisfaction from the authorities in the place where the nose claimed to work would be unreasonable, because it could be seen from the nose's own replies that nothing was sacred for this man, and he could be lying in this case just as he lied when he insisted that he never saw him before. And so Kovalev was about to tell the cabby to drive to the Office of Public Order when it again occurred to him that this knave and cheat, who had already behaved so shamelessly at their first encounter, might again conveniently use the time to slip out of the city somehow, and then all searching would be in vain, or might, God forbid, go on for a whole month. In the end it seemed that heaven itself gave him an idea. He decided to address himself directly to the newspaper office and hasten to take out an advertisement, with a detailed description of all his qualities, so that anyone meeting him could bring him to him or at least inform him of his whereabouts. And so, having decided on it, he told the cabby to drive to the newspaper office, and all the way there he never stopped hitting him on the back with his fist, saying: "Faster, you scoundrel! Faster, you cheat!" "Eh, master!" the coachman replied, shaking his head and whipping up his horse, whose coat was as long as a lapdog's. The droshky finally pulled up, and Kovalev, breathless, ran into a small reception room, where a gray-haired clerk in an old tailcoat and spectacles sat at a table, holding a pen in his teeth and counting the copper money brought to him.

"Who here takes advertisements?" cried Kovalev. "Ah, how do you do!"

"My respects," said the gray-haired clerk, raising his eyes for a moment and lowering them again to the laid-out stacks of coins.

"I wish to place . . ."

"Excuse me. I beg you to wait a bit," said the clerk, setting down a number on a piece of paper with one hand, and with the fingers of the left moving two beads on his abacus.

A lackey with galloons and an appearance indicating that he belonged to an aristocratic household, who was standing by the table with a notice in his hand, deemed it fitting to display his sociability:

"Believe me, sir, the pup isn't worth eighty kopecks, I mean, I wouldn't give eight for it; but the countess loves it, by God, she loves it—and so whoever finds it gets a hundred roubles! To put it proper, between you and me, people's tastes don't correspond at all: if you're a hunter, keep a pointer or a poodle, it'll cost you five hundred, a thousand, but you'll have yourself a fine dog."

The worthy clerk listened to this with a significant air and at the same time made an estimate of the number of letters in the notice. Around them stood a host of old women, shop clerks, and porters holding notices. One announced that a coachman of sober disposition was available for hire; another concerned a little-used carriage brought from Paris in 1814; elsewhere a nineteen-year-old serf girl was released, a good laundress and also fit for other work; a sturdy droshky lacking one spring; a hot young dapple-gray horse, seventeen years old; turnip and radish seeds newly received from London; a country house with all its appurtenances—two horse stalls and a place where an excellent birch or pine grove could be planted; next to that was an appeal to all those desiring to buy old shoes, with an invitation to come to the trading center every day from eight till three. The room into which all this company crowded was small and the air in it was very heavy; but the collegiate assessor Kovalev could not smell it, because he had covered his face with a handkerchief, and because his nose itself was in God knows what parts.

"My dear sir, allow me to ask . . . It's very necessary for me," he finally said with impatience.

"Right away, right away! Two roubles forty-three kopecks! This minute! One rouble sixty-four kopecks!" the gray-haired gentleman was saying as he flung the notices into the old women's and porters' faces. "What can I do for you?" he said at last, turning to Kovalev.

"I ask . . ." said Kovalev, "some swindling or knavery has occurred—I haven't been able to find out. I only ask you to advertise that whoever brings this scoundrel to me will get a sufficient reward."

"What is your name, if I may inquire?"

"No, why the name? I can't tell you. I have many acquaintances: Chekhtareva, wife of a state councillor, Palageya Grigorievna Podtochina, wife of a staff officer . . . God forbid they should suddenly find out! You can simply write: a collegiate assessor, or, better still, one holding the rank of major."

"And the runaway was your household serf?"

"What household serf? That would be no great swindle! The
one that ran away was . . . my nose . . ."

"Hm! what a strange name! And did this Mr. Nosov steal a large
sum of money from you?"

"Nose, I said . . . you've got it wrong! My nose, my own nose,
disappeared on me, I don't know where. The devil's decided to
make fun of me!"

"Disappeared in what fashion? I'm afraid I don't quite understand."

"I really can't say in what fashion; but the main thing is that he's
now driving around town calling himself a state councillor. And
therefore I ask you to announce that whoever catches him should
immediately present him to me within the shortest time. Consider
for yourself, how indeed can I do without such a conspicuous part
of the body? It's not like some little toe that I can put in a boot
and no one will see it's not there. On Thursdays I call on the wife
of the state councillor Chekhtarev; Palageya Grigorievna Podtochina, a staff officer's wife—and she has a very pretty daughter—
they, too, are my very good acquaintances, and consider for
yourself, now, how can I . . . I can't go to them now."

The clerk fell to pondering, as was indicated by his tightly compressed lips.

"No, I can't place such an announcement in the newspaper," he
said finally, after a long silence.

"What? Why not?"

"Because. The newspaper may lose its reputation. If everybody
starts writing that his nose has run away, then . . . People say we
publish a lot of absurdities and false rumors as it is."

"But what's absurd about this matter? It seems to me that it's
nothing of the sort."

"To you it seems so. But there was a similar incident last week.
A clerk came, just as you've come now, brought a notice, it came

to two roubles seventy-three kopecks in costs, and the whole announcement was that a poodle of a black coat had run away. Nothing much there, you'd think? But it turned out to be a lampoon: this poodle was the treasurer of I forget which institution."

"But I'm giving you an announcement not about a poodle, but about my own nose: which means almost about me myself."

"No, I absolutely cannot place such an announcement."

"But my nose really has vanished!"

"If so, it's a medical matter. They say there are people who can attach any nose you like. I observe, however, that you must be a man of merry disposition and fond of joking in company."

"I swear to you as God is holy! Very well, if it's come to that, I'll show you."

"Why trouble yourself!" the clerk went on, taking a pinch of snuff. "However, if it's no trouble," he added with a movement of curiosity, "it might be desirable to have a look."

The collegiate assessor took the handkerchief from his face.

"Extremely strange, indeed!" said the clerk. "The place is perfectly smooth, like a just-made pancake. Yes, of an unbelievable flatness!"

"Well, are you going to argue now? You can see for yourself that you've got to print it. I'll be especially grateful to you; and I'm very glad that this incident has afforded me the pleasure of making your acquaintance . . ."

The major, as may be seen from that, had decided to fawn a bit this time.

"Of course, printing it is no great matter," said the clerk, "only I don't see any profit in it for you. If you really want, you should give it to someone with a skillful pen, who can describe it as a rare work of nature and publish the little article in *The Northern Bee*"[3] (here he took another pinch of snuff), "for the benefit of the young" (here he wiped his nose), "or just for general curiosity."

The collegiate assessor was totally discouraged. He dropped his eyes to the bottom of the newspaper, where theater performances were announced; his face was getting ready to smile, seeing the name of a pretty actress, and his hand went to his pocket to see if he had a blue banknote[4] on him, because staff officers, in Kovalev's opinion, ought to sit in the orchestra—but the thought of the nose ruined everything!

The clerk himself seemed to be moved by Kovalev's difficult situation. Wishing to soften his grief somehow, he deemed it fitting to express his sympathy in a few words:

"I'm truly sorry that such an odd thing has happened to you. Would you care for a pinch? It dispels headaches and melancholy states of mind; it's even good with regard to hemorrhoids."

So saying, the clerk held the snuffbox out to Kovalev, quite deftly flipping back the lid with the portrait of some lady in a hat.

This unintentional act brought Kovalev's patience to an end.

"I do not understand how you find it possible to joke," he said in passion. "Can you not see that I precisely lack what's needed for a pinch of snuff? Devil take your snuff! I cannot stand the sight of it now, not only your vile Berezinsky, but even if you were to offer me rappee itself."

Having said this, he left the newspaper office in deep vexation and went to see the police commissioner, a great lover of sugar. In his house, the entire front room, which was also the dining room, was filled with sugar loaves that merchants brought him out of friendship. Just then the cook was removing the commissioner's regulation boots; his sword and other military armor were already hanging peacefully in the corners, and his three-year-old son was playing with his awesome three-cornered hat; and he himself, after his martial, military life, was preparing to taste the pleasures of peace.

Kovalev entered just as he stretched, grunted, and said: "Ah, now for a nice two-hour nap!" And therefore it could be foreseen that the collegiate assessor's arrival was quite untimely; and I do not know whether he would have been received all that cordially even if he had brought him several pounds of sugar or a length of broadcloth. The commissioner was a great patron of all the arts and manufactures, but preferred state banknotes to them all. "Here's a thing," he used to say, "there's nothing better than this thing: doesn't ask to eat, takes up little space, can always be put in the pocket, drop it and it won't break."

The commissioner received Kovalev rather drily and said that after dinner was no time for carrying out investigations, that nature herself had so arranged it that after eating one should have a little rest (from this the collegiate assessor could see that the police commissioner was not unacquainted with the sayings of the ancient wise men), that a respectable man would not have his nose torn off, and that there were many majors in the world whose underclothes were not even in decent condition, and who dragged themselves around to all sorts of improper places.

That is, a square hit, right between the eyes. It must be noted that Kovalev was an extremely touchy man. He could forgive anything said about himself, but he could never pardon a reference to his rank or title. He even thought that in theatrical plays everything referring to inferior officers could pass, but staff officers should never be attacked. The commissioner's reception so perplexed him that he shook his head and said with dignity, spreading his arms slightly, "I confess, after such offensive remarks on your part, I have nothing to add . . ." and left.

He returned home scarcely feeling his legs under him. It was already dark. Dismal or extremely vile his apartment seemed to him after this whole unsuccessful search. Going into the front room, he saw his lackey Ivan lying on his back on the soiled leather sofa, spitting at the ceiling and hitting the same spot quite successfully. The man's indifference infuriated him; he gave him a whack on the forehead with his hat, adding, "You pig, you're always busy with stupidities!"

Ivan suddenly jumped up from his place and rushed to help him off with his cape.

Going into his bedroom, the major, weary and woeful, threw himself into an armchair and finally, after several sighs, said:

"My God! my God! Why this misfortune? If I lacked an arm or a leg, it would still be better; if I lacked ears, it would be bad, but still more bearable; but lacking a nose, a man is devil knows what: not a bird, not a citizen—just take and chuck him out the window! And if it had been cut off in war or a duel, or if I'd caused it myself—but it vanished for no reason, vanished for nothing, nothing at all! . . . Only, no, it can't be," he added, after reflecting briefly.

"It's incredible that a nose should vanish, simply incredible. I must be dreaming, or just imagining it; maybe, by mistake somehow, instead of water I drank the vodka I use to pat my chin after shaving. That fool Ivan didn't take it away, and I must have downed it."

To make absolutely sure that he was not drunk, the major pinched himself so painfully that he cried out. This pain completely reassured him that he was acting and living in a waking state. He slowly approached the mirror and at first closed his eyes, thinking that the nose might somehow show up where it ought to be; but he jumped back at that same moment, saying:

"What a lampoonish look!"

This was indeed incomprehensible. If it had been a button, a silver spoon, a watch, or something of the sort, that had vanished— but to vanish, and who was it that vanished? and what's more, in his own apartment! . . . Major Kovalev, having put all the circumstances together, supposed it would hardly be unlikely if the blame were placed on none other than Podtochina, the staff officer's wife, who wished him to marry her daughter. He himself enjoyed dallying with her, but kept avoiding a final settlement. And when the mother announced to him directly that she wanted to give him the girl's hand, he quietly eased off with his compliments, saying that he was still young and had to serve some five years more, until he turned exactly forty-two. And therefore the staff officer's wife, probably in revenge, decided to put a spell on him, and to that end hired some sorceress, because it was by no means possible to suppose that the nose had been cut off; no one had come into his room; and the barber Ivan Yakovlevich had shaved him on Wednesday, and the nose had been there for the whole of Wednesday, and even all day Thursday—he remembered that and knew it very well; besides, he would have felt the pain, and the wound undoubtedly could not have healed so quickly and become smooth as a pancake. He made plans in his head: to formally summon the staff officer's wife to court, or to go to her in person and expose her. His reflections were interrupted by the light flickering through all the chinks in the door, signifying that Ivan had already lighted a candle in the front room. Soon Ivan himself appeared, carrying it before him and brightly lighting up the whole bedroom. Kovalev's first impulse was to grab the handkerchief and cover the place where his nose had been just the day before, so that the stupid man would not actually start gaping, seeing such an oddity in his master.

Ivan had just gone back to his closet when an unfamiliar voice came from the front room, saying:

"Does the collegiate assessor Kovalev live here?"

"Come in. Major Kovalev is here," said Kovalev, hastily jumping up and opening the door.

In came a police officer of handsome appearance, with quite plump cheeks and side-whiskers neither light nor dark, the very same one who, at the beginning of this tale, was standing at the end of St. Isaac's Bridge.

"Did Your Honor lose his nose?"

"Right."

"It has now been found."

"What's that you say?" cried Major Kovalev. Joy robbed him of speech. He stared with both eyes at the policeman standing before him, over whose plump lips and cheeks the tremulous candlelight flickered brightly. "How did it happen?"

"By a strange chance: he was intercepted almost on the road. He was getting into a stage coach to go to Riga. And he had a passport long since filled out in the name of some official. The strange thing was that I myself first took him for a gentleman. But fortunately I was wearing my spectacles, and I saw at once that he was a nose. For I'm nearsighted, and if you're standing right in front of me, I'll see only that you have a face, but won't notice any nose or beard. My mother-in-law—that is, my wife's mother—can't see anything either."

Kovalev was beside himself.

"Where is it? Where? I'll run there at once."

"Don't trouble yourself. Knowing you had need of him, I brought him with me. And it's strange that the chief participant in this affair is that crook of a barber on Voznesenskaya Street, who is now sitting in the police station. I've long suspected him of being a drunkard and a thief, and only two days ago he pilfered a card of buttons from a shop. Your nose is exactly as it was."

Here the policeman went to his pocket and took out a nose wrapped in a piece of paper.

"That's it!" cried Kovalev. "That's it all right! Kindly take a cup of tea with me today."

"I'd consider it a great pleasure, but I really can't: I must go to the house of correction . . . The prices of all products have gone up so expensively . . . I've got my mother-in-law—that is, my wife's mother—living with me, and the children—for the oldest in particular we have great hopes: he's a very clever lad, but there's no means at all for his education . . ."

Kovalev understood and, snatching a red banknote from the table, put it into the hand of the officer, who bowed and scraped his way out, and at almost the same moment Kovalev heard his voice in the street, where he delivered an admonition into the mug of a stupid muzhik who had driven his cart right on to the boulevard.

On the policeman's departure, the collegiate assessor remained in some vague state for a few minutes, and only after several minutes acquired the ability to see and feel: such obliviousness came over him on account of the unexpected joy. He carefully took the found nose in his two cupped hands and once again studied it attentively.

"That's it, that's it all right!" Major Kovalev kept repeating. "There's the pimple that popped out on the left side yesterday."

The major almost laughed for joy.

But nothing in this world lasts long, and therefore joy, in the minute that follows the first, is less lively; in the third minute it becomes still weaker, and finally it merges imperceptibly with one's usual state of mind, as a ring in the water, born of a stone's fall, finally merges with the smooth surface. Kovalev began to reflect and realized that the matter was not ended yet: the nose had been found, but it still had to be attached, put in its place.

"And what if it doesn't stick?"

At this question, presented to himself, the major blanched.

With a feeling of inexplicable fear, he rushed to the table and set the mirror before him, so as not to put the nose on somehow askew. His hands were trembling. Carefully and cautiously he applied it to its former place. Oh, horror! The nose did not stick! . . . He held it to his mouth, warmed it a little with his breath, and again brought it to the smooth space between his two cheeks; but in no way would the nose hold on.

"Well, so, stay there, you fool!" he said to it. But the nose was as if made of wood and kept falling to the table with a strange, cork-like sound. The major's face twisted convulsively. "Can it be that it won't grow back on?" he repeated in fear. But no matter how many times he put it in its proper place, his efforts remained unsuccessful.

He called Ivan and sent him for the doctor, who occupied the best apartment on the first floor of the same building. This doctor was an imposing man, possessed of handsome, pitch-black side-whiskers and of a fresh, robust doctress, ate fresh apples in the morning, and kept his mouth extraordinarily clean by rinsing it every morning for nearly three quarters of an hour and polishing his teeth with five different sorts of brushes. The doctor came that same minute. Having asked him how long ago the misfortune had occurred, he raised Major Kovalev's face by the chin and flicked him with his thumb in the very place where the nose had formerly been, which made the major throw his head back so hard that it struck the wall behind. The physician said it was nothing, advised him to move away from the wall a bit, told him to tip his head to the right first, and, having palpated the spot where the nose had been, said, "Hm!" Then he told him to tip his head to the left, said, "Hm!" and in conclusion flicked him again with his thumb, which made Major Kovalev jerk his head back like a horse having its teeth examined. After performing this test, the physician shook his head and said:

"No, impossible. You'd better stay the way you are, because it might come out still worse. Of course, it could be attached; I could perhaps attach it for you now; but I assure you it will be the worse for you."

"Well, that's just fine! How can I stay without a nose?" said Kovalev. "It can't be worse than now. This is simply devil knows what! Where can I show myself with such lampoonery! I have good acquaintances; today alone I have to be at soirees in two houses. I know many people: Chekhtareva, a state councillor's wife, Podtochina, a staff officer's wife . . . though after this act I won't deal with her except through the police. Do me the kindness," Kovalev said in a pleading voice, "isn't there some remedy? Attach it somehow—maybe not perfectly, so long as it holds; I can even prop it up with my hand on dangerous occasions. Besides, I don't dance, so I can't injure it with some careless movement. Regarding my gratitude for your visits, rest assured that everything my means will permit . . ."

"Believe me," the doctor said in a voice neither loud nor soft but extremely affable and magnetic, "I never treat people for profit. That is against my rules and my art. True, I take money for visits, but solely so as not to give offense by refusing. Of course, I could attach your nose; but I assure you on my honor, if you do not believe my word, that it will be much worse. You'd better leave it to the effect of nature herself. Wash it frequently with cold water, and I assure you that you'll be as healthy without a nose as with one. As for the nose, I advise you to put it in a jar of alcohol, or, better still, add two tablespoons of aquafortis and warm vinegar—then you'll get decent money for it. I'll even buy it myself, if you don't put too high a price on it."

"No, no! I won't sell it for anything!" cried the desperate Major Kovalev. "Better let it perish!"

"Excuse me!" said the doctor, bowing out. "I wished to be of use to you . . . Nothing to be done! At least you've seen how I tried."

Having said this, the doctor, with a noble bearing, left the room. Kovalev did not even notice his face but, plunged in profound insensibility, saw only the cuffs of his shirt, clean and white as snow, peeking out from the sleeves of his black tailcoat.

He resolved to write to the staff officer's wife the next day, before filing a complaint, on the chance that she might agree to return to him what she owed without a fight. The content of the letter was as follows:

My dear madam, Alexandra[5] Grigorievna!

I am unable to understand this strange act on your part. Rest assured that in behaving in this fashion you gain nothing and will by no means prevail upon me to marry your daughter. Believe me, I am perfectly well informed concerning the story of my nose, as well as the fact that none other than the two of you are the main participants in it. Its sudden detachment from its place, its flight, its disguising itself first as an official and now finally as its own self, are nothing else but the results of witchcraft, performed either by you or by those who exercise similarly noble occupations. I, for my part, consider it my duty to warn you: if the above-mentioned nose of mine is not back in place this same day, I shall be forced to resort to the shelter and protection of the law.

Nevertheless, with the utmost respect for you, I have the honor of being

> Your humble servant,
>
> *Platon Kovalev*

My dear sir, Platon Kuzmich!

I am extremely astonished by your letter. I confess to you in all frankness, I never expected, the less so with regard to unjust reproaches on your part. I warn you that I have never received the official you mention in my house, either disguised or as his real self. True, Filipp Ivanovich Potanchikov used to visit me. And though he indeed sought my daughter's hand, being himself of good, sober behavior and great learning, I never gave him reasons for any hope. You also mention a nose. If by that you mean that I supposedly led you by the nose and intended to refuse you formally, I am surprised that you speak of it, since I, as you know, was of the completely opposite opinion, and if you were to propose to my daughter in a lawful fashion right now, I would be ready to satisfy you at once, for this has always constituted the object of my liveliest desire, in hopes of which I remain, always ready to be at your service,

> *Alexandra Podtochina*

"No," said Kovalev, after reading the letter. "She's clearly not guilty. She can't be! The way the letter's written, it couldn't have been written by a person guilty of a crime." The collegiate assessor was informed in such matters, because he had been sent on investigations several times while still in the Caucasus. "How, then, how on earth did it happen? The devil alone can sort it all out!" he finally said, dropping his arms.

Meanwhile, rumors of this remarkable incident spread all over the capital, and, as usually happens, not without special additions. Just then everyone's mind was precisely attuned to the extraordinary: only recently the public had been taken up with experiments on the effects of magnetism. What's more, the story about the dancing chairs on Konyushennaya Street was still fresh, and thus it was no wonder people soon began saying that the nose of the collegiate assessor Kovalev went strolling on Nevsky Prospect at exactly three o'clock. Hordes of the curious thronged there every day. Someone said the nose was supposed to be in Junker's shop[6]—and such a crowd and crush formed outside Junker's that the police even had to intervene. One speculator of respectable appearance, with side-whiskers, who sold various kinds of cookies at the entrance to the theater, had some fine, sturdy wooden benches specially made, which he invited the curious to stand on for eighty kopecks per visitor. One worthy colonel left home earlier specifically for that and made his way through the crowd with great difficulty; but to his great indignation, he saw in the shop window, instead of the nose, an ordinary woolen jacket and a lithograph portraying a girl straightening a stocking and a fop with a turned-back waistcoat and a small beard peeping at her from behind a tree—a picture that had been hanging in the same place for over ten years. He walked off saying vexedly, "How is it possible to upset people with such stupid and implausible rumors?"

Then the rumor spread that Major Kovalev's nose went strolling not on Nevsky Prospect but in the Tavrichesky Garden, and had long been going there; that when Khozrev-Mirza[7] lived there, he wondered greatly at this strange sport of nature. Some students from the College of Surgeons went there. One noble, respectable lady, in a special letter, asked the overseer of the garden to show this rare phenomenon to her children and, if possible, with an explanation instructive and edifying for the young.

All these events were an extreme joy for those inevitable frequenters of social gatherings who delight in making the ladies laugh and whose stock was by then completely exhausted. A small portion of respectable and right-minded people was extremely displeased. One gentleman said with indignation that he did not understand how such preposterous inventions could be spread in our enlightened age and that he was astonished that the government paid no attention to it. This gentleman was obviously one of those gentlemen who wish to mix the government into everything, even their daily quarrels with their wives. After that . . . but here again the whole incident is shrouded in mist, and what came later is decidedly unknown.

III

Perfect nonsense goes on in the world. Sometimes there is no plausibility at all: suddenly, as if nothing was wrong, that same nose which had driven about in the rank of state councillor and made such a stir in town was back in place—that is, precisely between the two cheeks of Major Kovalev. This happened on the seventh of April. Waking up and chancing to look in the mirror, he saw: the nose! He grabbed it with his hand—yes, the nose! "Aha!" said Kovalev, and in his joy he nearly burst into a trepak all around the room, but Ivan hindered him by coming in. He ordered a wash at once and, as he was washing, again glanced in the mirror: the nose! Drying himself with a towel, he again glanced in the mirror: the nose!

"Look, Ivan, I think I've got a pimple on my nose," he said, and thought meanwhile, "What a disaster if Ivan says, 'No, sir, not only no pimple, but no nose either!'"

But Ivan said:

"Nothing, sir, no pimple at all—the nose is clean!"

"Good, devil take it!" the major said to himself and snapped his fingers. At that moment the barber Ivan Yakovlevich peeked in the

door, but as timorously as a cat that has just been beaten for stealing lard.

"Tell me first: are your hands clean?" Kovalev cried to him from
afar.

"Yes."

"Lies!"

"By God, they're clean, sir."

"Well, watch yourself now."

Kovalev sat down. Ivan Yakovlevich covered him with a towel
and in an instant, with the aid of a brush, transformed his whole
chin and part of his cheeks into a cream such as is served on merchants' birthdays.

"Look at that!" Ivan Yakovlevich said to himself, glancing at the
nose. Then he tipped the head the other way and looked at it from
the side. "There, now! really, just think of it," he continued and
went on looking at the nose for a long time. At last, lightly, as cautiously as one can imagine, he raised two fingers so as to grasp the
tip of it. Such was Ivan Yakovlevich's system.

"Oh-oh, watch out!" cried Kovalev.

Ivan Yakovlevich dropped his arms, more confused and taken
aback than he had ever been before. Finally he started tickling
carefully under his chin with the razor; and though it was quite
difficult and inconvenient for him to give a shave without holding
on to the smelling part of the body, nevertheless, resting his rough
thumb on the cheek and lower jaw, he finally overcame all obstacles and shaved him.

When everything was ready, Kovalev hastened at once to get
dressed, hired a cab, and drove straight to the pastry shop. Going
in, he cried from afar, "A cup of hot chocolate, boy!" and instantly
went up to the mirror: the nose was there! He gaily turned around
and, with a satirical air, squinting one eye a little, looked at two
military men, one of whom had a nose no bigger than a waistcoat
button. After that, he went to the office of the department where
he had solicited a post as vice-governor or, failing that, as an executive. Passing through the waiting room, he looked in the mirror:
the nose was there! Then he went to see another collegiate assessor, or major, a great mocker, to whom he often said in response to

various needling remarks: "Well, don't I know you, you sharpy!" On the way there, he thought, "If even the major doesn't split from laughing when he sees me, then it's a sure sign that whatever's there is sitting where it should." But from the collegiate assessor— nothing. "Good, good, devil take it!" Kovalev thought to himself. On his way he met Podtochina, the staff officer's wife, with her daughter, greeted them, and was met with joyful exclamations— nothing, then; he was in no way damaged. He talked with them for a very long time and, purposely taking out his snuffbox, spent a very long time in front of them filling his nose from both entrances, murmuring to himself, "There, that's for you, females, hen folk! and even so I won't marry the daughter. Just like that— *par amour,* if you please!" And Major Kovalev strolled on thereafter as if nothing was wrong, on Nevsky Prospect, and in the theaters, and everywhere. And the nose also sat on his face as if nothing was wrong, not even showing a sign that it had ever gone anywhere. And after that Major Kovalev was seen eternally in a good humor, smiling, chasing after decidedly all the pretty ladies, and even stop- ping once in front of a shop in the Merchants' Arcade to buy some ribbon or other, no one knows for what reason, since he was not himself the bearer of any decoration.

Such was the story that occurred in the northern capital of our vast country! Only now, on overall reflection, we can see that there is much of the implausible in it. To say nothing of the strangeness of the supernatural detachment of the nose and its appearance in vari- ous places in the guise of a state councillor—how was it that Kovalev did not realize that he ought not to make an announcement about the nose through the newspaper office? I'm speaking here not in the sense that I think it costly to pay for an announcement: that is nonsense, and I am not to be numbered among the mercenary. But it is indecent, inept, injudicious! And then, too—how did the nose end up in the baked bread and how did Ivan Yakovlevich him- self . . . ? no, that I just do not understand, I decidedly do not under- stand! But what is strangest, what is most incomprehensible of all is how authors can choose such subjects . . . I confess, that is utterly inconceivable, it is simply . . . no, no, I utterly fail to understand. In the first place, there is decidedly no benefit to the fatherland; in the

second place . . . but in the second place there is also no benefit. I
simply do not know what it . . .

And yet, for all that, though it is certainly possible to allow for
one thing, and another, and a third, perhaps even . . . And then,
too, are there not incongruities everywhere? . . . And yet, once
you reflect on it, there really is something to all this. Say what you
like, but such incidents do happen in the world—rarely, but they
do happen.

The Carriage

THE LITTLE TOWN of B. became much gayer when the ———
cavalry regiment was stationed there. Before then, it was awfully
boring. When you happened to drive through it and gaze at the
low cob houses looking out so incredibly sourly, it's impossible to
describe what would come over your heart then—such anguish as
if you'd lost at cards or blurted out something stupid at the wrong
time; in short, no good. The cob has fallen off them on account
of the rain, and the walls, instead of white, have become piebald;
the roofs are in most cases covered with thatch, as is usual in our
southern towns; as for the gardens, they were cut down long ago
on the mayor's orders, to improve appearances. You wouldn't meet
a soul abroad, except maybe a rooster crossing the street, soft as a
pillow owing to the five inches of dust lying on it, which turns to
mud with the slightest rain, and then the streets of the town of
B. fill up with those stout animals the mayor of the place calls
Frenchmen. Poking their serious snouts out of their baths, they set
up such a grunting that the traveler can only urge his horses on
faster. However, it was hard to meet a traveler in the town of B.
Rarely, very rarely, some landowner possessed of eleven peasant
souls, wearing a nankeen frock coat, would rattle down the street
in something halfway between a cart and a britzka, peeking out

from amidst a heap of flour sacks and whipping up a bay mare with
a colt running behind her. The marketplace itself has a rather woeful look: the tailor's house sits quite stupidly, not with the whole
front facing it, but catercorner; across from it some stone building
with two windows has been a-building for fifteen years now; further on, a fashionable plank fence stands all by itself, painted gray
to match the color of the mud, erected as a model for other buildings by the mayor in the time of his youth, when he did not yet
have the habit of napping directly after dinner and taking some
sort of infusion of dried gooseberries before going to bed. In
other places, it's almost all wattle fence; in the middle of the square
stand the smallest shops: in them you could always notice a string
of pretzels, a woman in a red kerchief, a crate of soap, a few
pounds of bitter almonds, shot for small arms, half-cotton cloth,
and two salesclerks playing mumblety-peg by the shop door all the
time. But when the cavalry regiment began to be stationed in the
regional town of B., everything changed. The streets became colorful, animated—in short, acquired a totally different look. The
little, low houses often saw passing by a trim, adroit officer with a
plume on his head, on his way to visit a friend for a chat about
horse breeding, or the excellence of tobacco, or occasionally for a
game of cards, with what might be called the regimental droshky
as the stake, because it managed to pass through everybody's hands
without ever leaving the regiment: today the major was driving
around in it, tomorrow it turned up in the lieutenant's stable, and a
week later, lo and behold, again the major's orderly was greasing it
with lard. The wooden fences between houses were all dotted with
soldiers' caps hanging out in the sun; a gray overcoat was bound to
be sticking up somewhere on a gate; in the lanes you might run
into soldiers with mustaches as stiff as a bootblack's brush. These
mustaches could be seen in all places. If tradeswomen got together
at the market with their dippers, a mustache was sure to be peeking over their shoulders. In the middle of the square, a soldier with
a mustache was sure to be soaping the beard of some village yokel,
who merely grunted, rolling up his eyes. The officers animated
society, which till then had consisted only of the judge, who lived

in the same house as some deacon's widow, and the mayor, a reasonable man, but who slept decidedly all day: from dinner till evening, and from evening till dinner. Society became still more numerous and entertaining when the quarters of the brigadier general were transferred there. Neighboring landowners, whose existence no one had even suspected till then, began coming to the little town more often, to meet the gentlemen officers and on occasion to play a little game of faro, which before had been an extremely vague fancy in their heads, busied with crops, their wives' errands, and hunting hares. It's a great pity I'm unable to remember for what occasion the brigadier general gave a big dinner; enormous preparations went into it: the snick of the chef's knives in the general's kitchen could be heard as far as the town gates. The entire market was completely bought up for this dinner, so that the judge and his deaconess had to eat buckwheat pancakes and cornstarch custard. The small yard of the general's house was entirely filled with droshkies and carriages. The company consisted of men: officers and some neighboring landowners. Among the landowners, the most remarkable was Pythagor Pythagorovich Chertokutsky, one of the chief aristocrats of the B. region, who made the biggest stir at the local elections, coming to them in a jaunty carriage. He had served formerly in one of the cavalry regiments and had numbered among its important and notable officers. At least he was seen at many balls and gatherings, wherever his regiment happened to migrate; the girls of Tambov and Simbirsk provinces might, incidentally, be asked about that. It's quite possible that his favorable repute would have spread to other provinces as well, if he had not retired on a certain occasion, usually known as an unpleasant incident: either he gave someone a slap in his earlier years, or he was given one, I don't remember for sure, only the upshot was that he was asked to retire. However, he by no means lost any of his dignity: wore a high-waisted tailcoat after the fashion of military uniforms, spurs on his boots, and a mustache under his nose, because otherwise the noblemen might have thought he had served in the infantry, which he sometimes scornfully called infantury and sometimes infantary. He visited all the crowded fairs, where the insides of Russia, consisting of nannies, children, daughters, and fat landowners, came for the merrymaking in britzkas, gigs, tarantasses, and such carriages as no one ever saw even in dreams. His nose could smell where a cavalry regiment was stationed, and he always went to meet the gentleman officers. With great adroitness he would leap from his light carriage or droshky before them and make their acquaintance extremely quickly. During the last election, he gave an excellent dinner for the nobility, at which he announced that if he were elected marshal,[1] he would put the nobility on the very best footing. He generally behaved with largesse, as they say in the districts and provinces, married a pretty little thing, with her got a dowry of two hundred souls plus several thousand in capital. The capital went immediately on a sixsome of really fine horses, gilded door latches, a tame monkey for the house, and a Frenchman for a butler. The two hundred souls, together with his own two hundred, were mortgaged with a view to some sort of commercial transactions. In short, he was a real landowner . . . A landowner good and proper. Besides him, there were several other landowners at the general's dinner, but they are not worth talking about. The rest were all army men of the same regiment, including two staff officers: a colonel and a rather fat major. The general was stocky and corpulent himself, though a good commander in the officers' opinion. He spoke in a rather deep, imposing bass. The dinner was extraordinary: sturgeon, beluga, sterlet, bustard, asparagus, quail, partridge, and mushrooms testified that the cook had not sat down to eat since the day before, and that four soldiers, knives in hand, had worked all night helping him with the *fricassées* and *gelées*. The myriads of bottles—tall ones of Lafitte, short-necked ones of Madeira—the beautiful summer day, the windows all thrown wide open, the plates of ice on the table, the gentlemen officers with their bottom button unbuttoned, the owners of trim tailcoats with their shirt fronts all rumpled, the crisscross conversation dominated by the general's voice and drowned in champagne—everything was in harmony with everything else. After dinner they all got up with an agreeable heaviness in their stomachs and, having lit their

long or short chibouks, stepped out on the porch, cups of coffee in
their hands.

The general, the colonel, and even the major had their uniforms
completely unbuttoned, so that their noble silk suspenders showed
slightly, while the gentlemen officers, observing due respect, remained buttoned up except for the bottom three buttons.

"We can have a look at her now," said the general. "Please, my
good fellow," he added, turning to his aide-de-camp, a rather
adroit young man of pleasant appearance, "tell them to bring the
bay mare here! You'll see for yourselves." Here the general drew on
his pipe and let the smoke out. "She still hasn't been well cared
for—cursed little town, not a decent stable in it. The horse, puff,
puff, is quite a decent one!"

"And have you, puff, puff, had her long, Your Excellency?" said
Chertokutsky.

"Puff, puff, puff, well . . . puff, not so long. It's only two years
since I brought her from the stud farm!"

"And was she broken when you got her, or did they break her
here?"

"Puff, puff, pu, pu, pu . . . u . . . u . . . ff, here." Having said
which, the general vanished completely in smoke.

Meanwhile, a soldier sprang out of the stable, the sound of
hooves was heard, another finally appeared in a white coverall, with
an enormous black mustache, leading by the bridle the twitching
and shying horse, which, suddenly raising its head, all but raised the
crouching soldier into the air along with his mustache. "Now, now,
Agrafena Ivanovna!" he said as he led her to the porch.

The mare's name was Agrafena Ivanovna; strong and wild as a
southern beauty, she drummed her hooves on the wooden porch
and suddenly stood still.

The general, lowering his pipe, began looking at Agrafena
Ivanovna with a contented air. The colonel himself stepped down
from the porch and took Agrafena Ivanovna by the muzzle. The
major himself patted Agrafena Ivanovna on the leg. The rest clucked
their tongues.

Chertokutsky got down from the porch and went behind her.

The soldier, standing at attention and holding the bridle, stared straight into the visitor's eyes, as if he wished to jump into them.

"Very, very good," said Chertokutsky, "a shapely horse! How's her gait, Your Excellency, if I may ask?"

"Her gait is good, only . . . devil knows . . . that fool of a vet gave her some sort of pills, and she's been sneezing for two days now."

"Very, very nice. And do you have a corresponding equipage, Your Excellency?"

"Equipage? . . . But this is a saddle horse."

"I know that. But I asked Your Excellency about it so as to learn whether you have corresponding equipages for your other horses."

"Well, as for equipages, I don't have quite enough. I must confess to tell you, I've long wanted to own a modern carriage. I wrote about it to my brother, who is now in Petersburg, but I don't know whether he'll send me one or not."

"It seems to me, Your Excellency," the colonel observed, "that there's no better carriage than a Viennese one."

"You think rightly, puff, puff, puff!"

"I have a surpassing carriage, Your Excellency, real Viennese workmanship."

"Which? The one you came in?"

"Oh, no. This one's just for driving around, for my own use, but that one . . . it's astonishing, light as a feather; and when you get in, it's simply as if—with Your Excellency's permission—as if a nurse were rocking you in a cradle!"

"So it's comfortable?"

"Very, very comfortable; cushions, springs—all just like a picture."

"That's good."

"And so roomy! I mean, Your Excellency, I've never yet seen the like of it. When I was in the service, I used to put ten bottles of rum and twenty pounds of tobacco in the trunk; and besides that I'd take with me some six changes of uniform, linens, and two chibouks, Your Excellency, as long—if you'll permit the expression—as tapeworms, and you could put a whole ox in the pouches."

"That's good."

"I paid four thousand for it, Your Excellency."

"Judging by the price, it must be good. And you bought it yourself?"

"No, Your Excellency, it happened to come to me. It was bought by a friend of mine, a rare person, a childhood friend, you'd get along perfectly with him. Between us there was no yours or mine, it was all the same. I won it from him at cards. Perhaps you'd care to do me the honor, Your Excellency, of coming to dine with me tomorrow and of having a look at the carriage at the same time?"

"I don't know what to say to you. Myself alone, it's somehow . . . Or, if you please, perhaps the gentlemen officers can come along?"

"I humbly invite the gentlemen officers as well. Gentlemen, I would consider myself greatly honored to have the pleasure of seeing you in my house!"

The colonel, the major, and the other officers thanked him with a courteous bow.

"I personally am of the opinion, Your Excellency, that if one buys something, it ought to be good, and if it's bad, there's no point in acquiring it. At my place, when you honor me with your visit tomorrow, I'll show you a thing or two that I've acquired for the management of my estate."

The general looked and let the smoke out of his mouth.

Chertokutsky was extremely pleased to have invited the gentlemen officers; in anticipation, he ordered pâtés and sauces in his head, kept glancing very gaily at the gentlemen officers, who, for their part, also doubled their benevolence toward him, as could be noticed by their eyes and little gestures of a half-bowing sort. Chertokutsky's step grew somehow more casual, his voice more languid: it sounded like a voice heavy with pleasure.

"There, Your Excellency, you will make the acquaintance of the mistress of the house."

"I shall be very pleased," said the general, stroking his mustache.

After which Chertokutsky wanted to go home at once, so as to make all the preparations for receiving his guests at the next day's dinner in good time; he had already picked up his hat, but it happened somehow strangely that he stayed a little longer. Meanwhile the card tables were set up in the room. Soon the whole company broke up into foursomes for whist and settled in different corners of the general's rooms.

Candles were brought. For a long time, Chertokutsky did not know whether to sit down to whist or not. But since the gentlemen officers had begun to invite him, he thought it quite against social rules to decline. He sat down. Imperceptibly, a glass of punch turned up before him, which he, forgetting himself, drank straight off that same minute. Having played two rubbers, Chertokutsky again found a glass of punch under his hand, which he, forgetting himself, again drank off, after first saying, "It's time, gentlemen, really, it's time I went home." But he sat down again for a second game. Meanwhile the conversation took it's own particular turn in different corners of the room. Those playing whist were rather silent; but the nonplayers sitting to the side on sofas conducted their own conversation. In one corner a cavalry staff captain, putting a pillow under his side and a pipe in his mouth, spoke quite freely and fluently of his amorous adventures and held the full attention of the circle around him. One extremely fat landowner with short arms, somewhat resembling two potatoes growing on him, listened with an extraordinarily sweet look and only tried now and then to send his short arm behind his broad back to get out his snuffbox. In another corner, a rather heated argument sprang up about squadron exercises, and Chertokutsky, who by then had twice played a jack instead of a queen, would suddenly interfere in other people's conversation and cry out from his corner: "What year was that?" or "What regiment?"—not noticing that the question was sometimes completely beside the point. Finally, a few minutes before suppertime, the whist came to an end, though it still went on in words and everyone's head seemed filled with whist. Chertokutsky remembered very well that he had won a lot, but he had nothing in his hands, and, getting up from the table, he stood for a long time in the position of a man who finds no handkerchief in his pocket. Meanwhile supper was served. It goes without saying that there was no shortage of wines and that Chertokutsky almost inadvertently had sometimes to fill his glass because there were bottles standing to right and left of him.

A most lengthy conversation went on at the table, yet it was conducted somehow strangely. One landowner who had served back in the campaign of 1812[2] told about a battle such as never took place, and then, for completely unknown reasons, removed the stopper from a decanter and stuck it into a pastry. In short, when they began to leave, it was already three o'clock in the morning, and the coachmen had to gather up some persons in their arms like shopping parcels, and Chertokutsky, for all his aristocratism, bowed so low and swung his head so much as he sat in his carriage that he brought two burrs home with him on his mustache.

In the house all was completely asleep; the coachman had great difficulty finding the valet, who brought his master through the drawing room and handed him over to the chambermaid, following whom Chertokutsky somehow reached his bedroom and lay down next to his young and pretty wife, who was lying there looking lovely in her white-as-snow nightgown. The movement produced by her husband falling into bed woke her up. She stretched herself, raised her eyelashes, and, quickly squinting three times, opened her eyes with a half-angry smile; but seeing that he was decidedly unwilling to show her any tenderness just then, she vexedly turned on her other side and, putting her fresh cheek on her hand, fell asleep soon after he did.

It was already that time which on country estates is not called *early,* when the young mistress woke up beside her snoring husband. Recalling that he had come home past three o'clock last night, she was sorry to rouse him, and having put on her slippers, which her husband had ordered from Petersburg, with a white jacket draping her like flowing water, she went out to her dressing room, washed with water fresh as her own self, and approached the mirror. Glancing at herself a couple of times, she saw that she was not at all bad looking that day. This apparently insignificant circumstance made her sit for precisely two extra hours before the mirror. At last she dressed herself very prettily and went to take some fresh air in the garden. As if by design, the weather was beautiful then, such as only a southern summer day can boast of. The sun, getting toward noon, blazed down with all the force of its rays, but it was cool strolling in the dense shade of the alleys, and the flowers, warmed by the sun, tripled their fragrance. The pretty mistress quite forgot that it was already twelve and her husband was still asleep. There already came to her ears the after-dinner snoring of the two coachmen and one postilion, who slept in the stables beyond the garden. But she went on sitting in the dense alley, from which a view opened onto the high road, and gazing absentmindedly at its unpeopled emptiness, when dust suddenly rising in the distance caught her attention. Looking closer, she soon made out several carriages. At their head drove a light, open two-seater; in it sat the general, his thick epaulettes gleaming in the sun, with the colonel beside him. It was followed by another, a four-seater; in it sat the major, with the general's aide-de-camp and two officers on the facing seats; following that carriage came the regimental droshky known to all the world, owned this time by the corpulent major; after the droshky came a four-place *bon-voyage* in which four officers sat holding a fifth on their lap . . . behind the *bonvoyage* three officers pranced on handsome dapple-bay horses.

"Can they be coming here?" the mistress of the house thought. "Ah, my God! they've actually turned onto the bridge!" She cried out, clasped her hands, and ran across flower beds and flowers straight to her husband's bedroom. He lay in a dead sleep.

"Get up, get up! Get up quickly!" she cried, pulling him by the arm.

"Ah?" said Chertokutsky, stretching without opening his eyes.

"Get up, poopsy! Do you hear? Guests!"

"Guests? What guests?" Having said which, he uttered a little moo, like a calf feeling for its mother's teats with its muzzle. "Mm . . ." he grunted, "give me your little neck, moomsy! I'll kiss you."

"Sweetie, get up quickly, for God's sake. The general and the officers! Ah, my God, you've got a burr on your mustache!"

"The general? Ah, so he's coming already? But why the devil didn't anybody wake me up? And the dinner, what about the dinner—is everything properly prepared?"

"What dinner?"

"Didn't I order it?"

"You? You came home at four o'clock in the morning and never told me anything, no matter how I asked. I didn't wake you up, poopsy, because I felt sorry for you—you hadn't had any sleep . . ." These last words she pronounced in an extremely languid and pleading voice.

Chertokutsky, his eyes popping out, lay in bed for a moment as if thunderstruck. Finally he jumped up in nothing but his shirt, forgetting that it was quite indecent.

"Ah, what a horse I am!" he said, slapping himself on the forehead. "I invited them for dinner. What can we do? Are they far off?"

"I don't know . . . they must be here by now."

"Sweetie . . . hide somewhere! . . . Hey, who's there? Go, my girl—what, fool, are you afraid? The officers will come any minute. Tell them the master isn't here, tell them he won't be home today, that he left in the morning, do you hear? And tell all the servants. Go quickly!"

Having said that, he hastily grabbed his dressing gown and ran to hide in the carriage shed, supposing he would be completely safe there. But, after installing himself in a corner of the shed, he saw that even there he might somehow be visible. "Now, this will be better," flashed in his head, and he instantly folded down the steps of a nearby carriage, jumped in, closed the doors, covered himself with the apron and the rug for greater safety, and became perfectly still, crouched there in his dressing gown.

Meanwhile the carriages drove up to the porch.

The general stepped out and shook himself, followed by the colonel, straightening the plumes on his hat. Then the fat major jumped down from the droshky, holding his saber under his arm. Then the slim lieutenants who had been holding the sub-lieutenant on their laps leaped down from the *bonvoyage*, and finally the horse-prancing officers dismounted.

"The master's not at home," said a lackey, coming out to the porch.

"How, not at home? But, in any case, he'll be home by dinnertime?"

"No, sir, he's gone for the whole day. He may be back around this time tomorrow."

"Well, look at that!" said the general. "How can it be? . . ."

"Some stunt, I must say!" the colonel said, laughing.

"Ah, no, it isn't done," the general went on with displeasure. "Pah . . . the devil . . . If you can't receive, why go inviting?"

"I don't understand how anyone could do it, Your Excellency," said one young officer.

"What?" said the general, who was in the habit of always uttering this interrogative word when speaking with his officers.

"I said, Your Excellency, how can anyone act in such a way?"

"Naturally . . . Well, if something's happened, let people know, at least, or don't invite them."

"So, Your Excellency, there's no help for it, let's go back!" said the colonel.

"Certainly, nothing else to be done. However, we can have a look at the carriage even without him. He surely hasn't taken it with him. Hey, you there, come here, brother!"

"What's your pleasure?"

"You're a stable boy?"

"I am, Your Excellency."

"Show us the new carriage your master acquired recently."

"It's here in the shed, sir."

The general went into the shed together with the officers.

"If you wish, I'll move it out a little, it's a bit dark in here."

"Enough, enough, that's good!"

The general and the officers walked around the carriage, thoroughly examining the wheels and springs.

"Well, nothing special," said the general, "a most ordinary carriage."

"Most ungainly," said the colonel, "absolutely nothing good about it."

"It seems to me, Your Excellency, that it's hardly worth four thousand," said one of the young officers.

"What?"

"I said, Your Excellency, that it seems to me it's not worth four thousand."

"Four thousand, hah! It's not even worth two. There's simply nothing to it. Unless there's something special inside . . . Be so kind, my good fellow, as to undo the cover . . ."

And before the officers' eyes Chertokutsky appeared, sitting in his dressing gown and crouched in an extraordinary fashion.

"Ah, you're here! . . ." said the amazed general.

Having said which, the general at once slammed the doors, covered Chertokutsky with the apron again, and drove off with the other gentlemen officers.

THE PORTRAIT

PART I

NOWHERE DID SO many people stop as in front of the art shop in the Shchukin market. This shop, indeed, presented the most heterogeneous collection of marvels: the pictures were for the most part painted in oils and covered with a dark green varnish, in gaudy, dark-yellow frames. Winter with white trees, a completely red evening like the glow of a fire, a Flemish peasant with a pipe and a dislocated arm, looking more like a turkey with cuffs than a human being—these were their usual subjects. To them should be added a few engraved prints: the portrait of Khozrev-Mirza[1] in a lambskin hat, the portraits of some generals in three-cornered hats, with crooked noses. Moreover, the doors of such a shop are usually hung with sheaves of popular prints on large sheets, which witness to the innate giftedness of the Russian man. On one was the tsarevna Miliktrisa Kirbitievna,[2] on another the city of Jerusalem, whose houses and churches were unceremoniously rolled over with red paint, which invaded part of the ground and two praying Russian peasants in mittens. These works usually have few purchasers, but a heap of viewers. Some bibulous lackey is sure to be there gaping at them, holding covered dishes from the restaurant for his master, who without doubt will sup a none-too-hot soup. In front of them there is sure to be standing a soldier in an overcoat, that cavalier of

340

the flea market, with a couple of penknives to sell, and an Okhta[3] market woman with a box full of shoes. Each admires in his own way: the peasants usually poke their fingers; gentlemen study seriously; lackey boys and boy artisans laugh and tease each other with caricatures; old lackeys in frieze overcoats look on only so as to stand somewhere and gape; and young Russian market women hasten there by instinct, to hear what people are gabbing about and look at what they are looking at.

Just then the young artist Chartkov, passing by, stopped involuntarily in front of the shop. His old overcoat and unstylish clothes showed him to be a man who was selflessly devoted to his work and had no time to concern himself with his attire, which always has some mysterious attraction for the young. He stopped in front of the shop and at first laughed to himself at these ugly pictures. In the end, an involuntary pondering came over him: he began thinking about who might have need of these works. That the Russian populace should stare at *Yeruslan Lazarevich*, at the *big eaters* and *big drinkers*, at *Foma and Yerema*,[4] did not seem surprising to him: the subjects portrayed were easily accessible and understandable for the people; but where were the purchasers for these motley, dirty daubings in oil? Who needed these Flemish peasants, these red and blue landscapes, which displayed some pretense to a slightly higher step of art, while showing all the depths of its humiliation? They seemed not altogether the works of a self-taught child. Otherwise, for all the insensitive caricature of the whole, some sharp impulse would have burst through in them. But here one could only see dull-witted, impotent, decrepit giftlessness arbitrarily placing itself among the arts, when it belonged among the lowest crafts—a giftlessness which was faithful to its calling, however, and introduced its craft into art itself. The same colors, the same manner, the same practiced, habituated hand, belonging rather to a crudely made automaton than to a man! . . . He stood for a long time before these grimy paintings, finally not thinking about them at all, and meanwhile the owner of the shop, a gray little man in a frieze overcoat, with a chin unshaved since Sunday, had long been talking to him, bargaining and setting a price, before even finding out what he liked and wanted.

"For these peasants here and this little landscape, I'm asking twenty-five roubles. What painterliness! It simply hits you in the eye. We just got them from the exchange; the varnish is still wet. Or there's this winter, take this winter! Fifteen roubles! The frame is worth a lot by itself. Look, what a winter!" Here the shop owner gave the canvas a light flick, probably to show how good a winter it was. "Shall I have them tied up together and taken along with you? Where do you live? Hey, lad, fetch me the string!"

"Wait, brother, not so fast," the artist said, coming to his senses and seeing that the nimble shop owner had seriously started tying them up together. He felt a bit ashamed not to take anything after standing in the shop for so long, and he said:

"Wait, now, I'll see if there's anything here for me," and, bending down, he started going through some shabby, dusty old daubings piled on the floor and evidently not held in any respect. There were old family portraits, whose descendants were perhaps not even to be found in this world, pictures of total strangers on torn canvases, frames that had lost their gilding—in short, all sorts of decrepit trash. But the artist began to examine them, thinking secretly, "Maybe something will turn up." More than once he had heard stories of great master paintings occasionally being found among the trash sold by cheap print dealers.

The owner, seeing where he was getting to, abandoned his bustling and, assuming his usual position and proper dignity, placed himself by the door again, calling to passers-by and pointing with one hand to the shop: "Here, my friends, see what pictures! Come in, come in! Fresh from the exchange!" He had already shouted his fill, for the most part fruitlessly, and talked to his heart's content with the rag seller who stood across the street by the door of his own shop, and, remembering at last that he had a customer in his shop, he turned his back to the people and went inside. "Well, my friend, have you chosen something?" But the artist had already been standing motionless for some time before a portrait in a big, once magnificent frame, on which traces of gilding now barely gleamed.

It was an old man with a face the color of bronze, gaunt, high-cheekboned; the features seemed to have been caught at a moment of convulsive movement and bespoke an un–northern force. Fiery noon was stamped on them. He was draped in a loose Asiatic costume. Damaged and dusty though the portrait was, when he managed to clean the dust off the face, he could see the marks of a lofty artist's work. The portrait, it seemed, was unfinished; but the force of the brush was striking. Most extraordinary of all were the eyes: in them the artist seemed to have employed all the force of his brush and all his painstaking effort. They simply stared, stared even out of the portrait itself, as if destroying its harmony by their strange aliveness. When he brought the portrait to the door, the eyes stared still more strongly. They produced almost the same impression among the people. A woman who stopped behind him exclaimed, "It's staring, it's staring!" and backed away. He felt some unpleasant feeling, unaccountable to himself, and put the portrait down.

"So, take the portrait!" said the owner.

"How much?" said the artist.

"Why make it expensive? Give me seventy-five kopecks!"

"No."

"Well, then, what will you give me?"

"Twenty kopecks," said the artist, preparing to leave.

"Eh, what kind of price is that? Twenty kopecks won't even pay for the frame. I see, you think you'll buy it tomorrow? Mister, mister, come back! Tack on ten kopecks at least. Take it, then, take it, give me the twenty kopecks. Really, it's just for openers, since you're my first customer."

At which he made a gesture as if to say, "So be it, and perish the picture!"

Thus Chartkov quite unexpectedly bought the old portrait and at the same time thought: "Why did I buy it? What do I need it for?" But there was nothing to be done. He took a twenty-kopeck piece from his pocket, gave it to the owner, took the portrait under his arm, and dragged it home. On the way, he recalled that the twenty kopecks he had paid out were his last. His thoughts suddenly darkened; vexation and an indifferent emptiness came over him in the same moment. "Devil take it! it's vile in this world!" he said, with the feeling of a Russian for whom things are going badly. And he walked on almost mechanically, with hurried steps, insensible to everything. The red light of the evening sun still lingered over half the sky; the houses turned toward it still glowed faintly with its warm light; and meanwhile the cold, bluish radiance of the moon grew stronger. Light, half-transparent shadows fell tail-like on the ground, cast by houses and the legs of passers-by. The artist was beginning gradually to admire the sky, aglow with some transparent, thin, uncertain light, and almost simultaneously the words "What a light tone!" and "It's irksome, devil take it!" flew out of his mouth. And, straightening the portrait, which kept slipping from under his arm, he quickened his pace.

Weary and all in a sweat, he dragged himself to the Fifteenth Line on Vasilievsky Island.[5] Straining and panting, he climbed the stairs, slopped with swill and adorned with the traces of cats and dogs. His knocking at the door brought no response: his man was not at home. He leaned against the window and set himself to waiting patiently, until he finally heard behind him the steps of the lad in the blue shirt, his companion, his model, his paint grinder and floor sweeper, who dirtied it straight away with his boots. The lad was called Nikita, and he spent all his time outside the gates when his master was not at home. Nikita was a long time trying to get the key into the keyhole, which was completely invisible on account of the darkness. At last the door opened. Chartkov went into his front room, which was insufferably cold, as is always the case with artists, something they, however, do not notice. Not handing Nikita his overcoat, he went in it to his studio, a square room, large but low, with frost-covered windows, set about with all sorts of artistic litter: pieces of plaster arms, stretched canvases, sketches begun and abandoned, lengths of fabric draped over chairs. He was very weary, threw off his overcoat, absentmindedly stood the portrait he had bought between two small canvases, and threw himself down on a narrow couch, of which one could not say that it was covered in leather, because the row of brass tacks formerly attaching it had long since existed on its own, and the leather over it also existed on its own, so that Nikita could shove black stockings, shirts, and all the dirty linen under it. Sitting there, sprawling as much as one could on this narrow couch, he finally asked for a candle.

"We have no candles," said Nikita.

"No?"

"And we had none yesterday either," said Nikita.

The artist remembered that in fact they had not had any candles yesterday, so he calmed down and fell silent. He allowed himself to be undressed and put on his well- and much-worn dressing gown.

"And the landlord also came," said Nikita.

"Well, so he came for money? I know," the artist said, waving his hand.

"He didn't come alone," said Nikita.

"With whom, then?"

"I don't know . . . some policeman."

"Why a policeman?"

"I don't know why. He says the rent isn't paid."

"Well, so what will come of it?"

"I don't know. He said, 'If he doesn't want to pay, he can move out.' They're both coming back tomorrow."

"Let them," Chartkov said with sad indifference. And a dreary state of mind came over him completely.

Young Chartkov was an artist with a talent that promised much: in flashes and moments his brush bespoke power of observation, understanding, a strong impulse to get closer to nature. "Watch out, brother," his professor had told him more than once, "you have talent; it would be a sin to ruin it. But you're impatient. Some one thing entices you, some one thing takes your fancy—and you occupy yourself with it, and the rest can rot, you don't care about it, you don't even want to look at it. Watch out you don't turn into a fashionable painter. Even now your colors are beginning to cry a bit too loudly. Your drawing is imprecise, and sometimes quite weak, the line doesn't show; you go for fashionable lighting, which strikes the eye at once. Watch out or you'll fall right into the English type. Beware. You already feel drawn to the world: every so often I see a showy scarf on your neck, a glossy hat . . . It's enticing, you can start painting fashionable pictures, little portraits for money. But that doesn't develop talent, it ruins it. Be patient.

Ponder over every work, drop showiness—let the others make money. You won't come out the loser."

The professor was partly right. Sometimes, indeed, our artist liked to carouse or play the dandy—in short, to show off his youth here and there. Yet, for all that, he was able to keep himself under control. At times he was able to forget everything and take up his brush, and had to tear himself away again as if from a beautiful, interrupted dream. His taste was developing noticeably. He still did not understand all the depth of Raphael, but was already carried away by the quick, broad stroke of Guido, paused before Titian's portraits, admired the Flemish school.[6] The dark surface obscuring the old paintings had not yet been entirely removed for him; yet he already perceived something in them, though inwardly he did not agree with his professor that the old masters surpassed us beyond reach; it even seemed to him that the nineteenth century was significantly ahead of them in certain things, that the imitation of nature as it was done now had become somehow brighter, livelier, closer; in short, he thought in this case as a young man thinks who already understands something and feels it in his proud inner consciousness. At times he became vexed when he saw how some foreign painter, a Frenchman or a German, sometimes not even a painter by vocation, with nothing but an accustomed hand, a quick brush, and bright colors, would produce a general stir and instantly amass a fortune. This would come to his mind not when, all immersed in his work, he forgot drinking and eating and the whole world, but when he would finally come hard up against necessity, when he had no money to buy brushes and paints, when the importunate landlord came ten times a day to demand the rent. Then his hungry imagination enviously pictured the lot of the rich painter; then a thought glimmered that often passes through a Russian head: to drop everything and go on a spree out of grief and to spite it all. And now he was almost in such a situation.

"Yes! be patient, be patient!" he said with vexation. "But patience finally runs out. Be patient! And on what money will I have dinner tomorrow? No one will lend to me. And if I were to go and sell all my paintings and drawings, I'd get twenty kopecks for the lot. They've been useful, of course, I feel that: it was not in vain that each of them was undertaken, in each of them I learned something. But what's the use? Sketches, attempts—and there will constantly be sketches, attempts, and no end to them. And who will buy them, if they don't know my name? And who needs drawings from the antique, or from life class, or my unfinished *Love of Psyche,* or a perspective of my room, or the portrait of my Nikita, though it's really better than the portraits of some fashionable painter? What is it all, in fact? Why do I suffer and toil over the ABC's like a student, when I could shine no worse than the others and have money as they do?"

Having said that, the artist suddenly shuddered and went pale: gazing at him, peering from behind the canvas on the easel, was someone's convulsively distorted face. Two terrible eyes were fixed directly on him, as if preparing to devour him; on the mouth was written the threatening command to keep silent. Frightened, he wanted to cry out and call Nikita, who had already managed to set up a mighty snoring in the front room; but suddenly he stopped and laughed. The feeling of fear instantly subsided. It was the portrait he had bought, which he had quite forgotten about. Moonlight illuminated the room and, falling on it, endowed it with a strange aliveness. He began studying it and cleaning it. Wetting a sponge, he went over it several times, washed off almost all the dust and dirt that had accumulated and stuck to it, hung it on the wall before him, and marveled still more at the extraordinary work: the whole face almost came to life, and the eyes stared at him so that he finally gave a start and stepped back, saying in an amazed voice, "It stares, it stares at you with human eyes!" A story he had heard long ago from his professor suddenly came to his mind, about a certain portrait by the famous Leonardo da Vinci, which the great master had labored over for several years and still considered unfinished, but which, according to the words of Vasari,[7] everyone nevertheless considered a most perfect and finished work of art. Most finished of all in it were the eyes, at which his contemporaries were amazed; even the tiniest, barely visible veins were not omitted but were rendered on the canvas. But here, in the portrait now before him, there was nevertheless something strange. This was no longer art: it even destroyed the har-

mony of the portrait itself. They were alive, they were human eyes!
It seemed as if they had been cut out of a living man and set there.
Here there was not that lofty pleasure which comes over the soul at
the sight of an artist's work, however terrible its chosen subject;
here there was some morbid, anguished feeling. "What is it?" the
artist asked himself involuntarily. "It's nature all the same, it's living
nature—why, then, this strangely unpleasant feeling? Or else the
slavish, literal imitation of nature is already a trespass and seems like
a loud, discordant cry? Or else, if you take the subject indifferently,
unfeelingly, with no feeling for it, it inevitably stands out only in
its terrible reality, not illumined by the light of some incomprehensible, ever-hidden thought, stands out in that reality which is
revealed only when, wishing to understand a beautiful man, one
arms oneself with an anatomical knife, cuts into his insides, and
sees a repulsive man? Why, then, does simple, lowly nature appear
with one artist in such a light that you have no lowly impression;
on the contrary, it seems as if you enjoy it, and after that everything around you flows and moves more calmly and evenly? And
why, with another artist, does that same nature seem low, dirty,
though he has been just as faithful to nature? But no, some radiance is missing. Just as with a natural landscape: however splendid,
it still lacks something if there's no sun in the sky."

He went up to the portrait again, so as to study those wondrous
eyes, and noticed with horror that they were indeed staring at him.
This was no longer a copy from nature, this was that strange aliveness that would radiate from the face of a dead man rising from the
grave. Either it was the light of the moon bringing delirious reveries with it and clothing everything in other images, opposite to
positive daylight, or there was some other cause, only suddenly, for
some reason, he felt afraid to be alone in the room. He quietly
withdrew from the portrait, turned away and tried not to look
at it, and yet his eyes, of themselves, involuntarily cast sidelong
glances at it. Finally he even became frightened of walking about
the room; it seemed to him that some other would immediately
start walking behind him, and he kept timorously looking back.
He had never been a coward; but his imagination and nerves were
sensitive, and that evening he was unable to explain this involun-

tary fear to himself. He sat in the corner, but there, too, it seemed to him that someone was about to look over his shoulder into his face. Not even the snores of Nikita resounding from the front room could drive away his fear. Finally, timorously, without raising his eyes, he stood up, went behind his screen, and got into bed. Through a chink in the screen he could see his room lit up by moonlight, and directly opposite him he could see the portrait on the wall. The eyes were fixed still more terribly, still more meaningly, on him, and seemed not to want to look at anything but him. Filled with an oppressive feeling, he decided to get up, grabbed a bedsheet, and, going over to the portrait, covered it completely.

Having done so, he went back to bed more calmly, began thinking about the poverty and pitifulness of the artist's lot, about the thorny path that lay before him in this world; and meanwhile his eyes involuntarily looked through the chink in the screen at the sheet-covered portrait. The moonlight intensified the whiteness of the sheet, and it seemed to him that the terrible eyes even began to glow through the cloth. In fear, he fixed his eyes on it more intently, as if wishing to assure himself that it was nonsense. But finally, indeed now . . . he saw, saw clearly: the sheet was no longer there . . . the portrait was all uncovered and staring, past whatever was around it, straight into him, simply staring into his insides . . . His heart went cold. And he saw: the old man stirred and suddenly leaned on the frame with both hands. Finally he propped himself on his hands and, thrusting out both legs, leaped free of the frame . . . Now all that could be seen through the chink in the screen was the empty frame. The noise of footsteps sounded in the room, finally coming closer and closer to the screen. The poor artist's heart began to pound harder. Breathless with fear, he expected the old man to look behind the screen at any moment. And then he did look behind the screen, with the same bronze face, moving his big eyes. Chartkov tried to cry out and found that he had no voice, tried to stir, to make some movement, but his limbs would not move. Open-mouthed and with bated breath, he looked at this terrible phantom, tall, in a loose Asian robe, waiting for what he would do. The old man sat down almost at his feet and then took something from under the folds of his loose garment. It was a sack. The old man untied it and, taking it by the corners, shook it upside down: with a dull sound, heavy packets shaped like long posts fell to the floor, and each was wrapped in blue paper and had "1,000 Gold Roubles" written on it. Thrusting his long, bony hands from the wide sleeves, the old man began to unwrap the packets. Gold gleamed. However great the oppressive feeling and frantic fear of the artist, still all of him gazed at the gold, staring fixedly as it was unwrapped by the bony hands, gleaming, clinking thinly and dully, and then wrapped up again. Here he noticed one packet that had rolled farther away than the rest, just near the leg of his bed, by its head. He seized it almost convulsively and looked fearfully to see whether the old man would notice. But it seemed the old man was very busy. He gathered up all his packets, put them back into the sack, and, without looking at him, went out from behind the screen. Chartkov's heart pounded heavily as he heard the shuffle of the retreating steps in the room. He clutched his packet tighter in his hand, his whole body trembling over it, when suddenly he heard the footsteps approaching the screen again—evidently the old man had remembered that one packet was missing. And now—he looked behind the screen again. Filled with despair, the artist clutched the packet in his hand with all his might, tried as hard as he could to make some movement, cried out—and woke up.

He was bathed in a cold sweat; his heart could not have pounded any harder; his chest was so tight that it was as if the last breath was about to fly out of it. "Could it have been a dream?" he said, clutching his head with both hands; but the terrible aliveness of the apparition was not like a dream. Awake now, he saw the old man going into the frame, even caught a glimpse of the skirts of his loose clothing, and his hand felt clearly that a moment before it had been holding something heavy. Moonlight lit up the room, drawing out of its dark corners now a canvas, now a plaster arm, now some drapery left on the floor, now trousers and a pair of unpolished boots. Only here did he notice that he was not lying in bed but standing right in front of the portrait. How he got there— that he simply could not understand. He was still more amazed that the portrait was all uncovered and there was in fact no sheet over it. In motionless fear he gazed at it and saw living, human eyes peer straight into him. Cold sweat stood out on his brow; he wanted to back away, but felt as if his feet were rooted to the ground. And he saw—this was no longer a dream—the old man's features move, his lips begin to stretch toward him, as if wishing to suck him out . . . With a scream of despair, he jumped back—and woke up.

"Could this, too, have been a dream?" His heart pounding to the point of bursting, he felt around him with his hands. Yes, he was lying on his bed in the same position in which he had fallen asleep. Before him stood the screen; moonlight filled the room. Through the chink in the screen he could see the portrait properly covered with a sheet—as he himself had covered it. And so, this, too, had been a dream! But his clenched hand felt even now as if something had been in it. The pounding of his heart was hard, almost terrible; the heaviness on his chest was unbearable. He looked through the chink and fixed his eyes on the sheet. And now he saw clearly that the sheet was beginning to come away, as if hands were fumbling under it, trying to throw it off. "Lord God, what is this!" he cried out, crossing himself desperately, and woke up.

And this had also been a dream! He jumped from the bed, half demented, frantic, no longer able to explain what was happening to him: the oppression of a nightmare or a household spirit, delirious raving or a living vision. Trying to calm somewhat his mental agitation and the stormy blood that throbbed in tense pulsations through all his veins, he went to the window and opened the vent pane. A chill breath of wind revived him. Moonlight still lay on the roofs and white walls of the houses, though small clouds passed across the sky more often. Everything was still: occasionally there came the distant rattle of a droshky, whose coachman was sleeping somewhere in an out-of-sight alley, lulled by his lazy nag as he waited for a late passenger. He gazed for a long time, thrusting his head out the vent. The sky was already beginning to show signs of approaching dawn; finally he felt the approach of drowsiness, slammed the vent shut, left the window, went to bed, and soon fell sound asleep, like the dead.

He woke up very late and felt himself in the unpleasant condition that comes over a man after fume poisoning; his head ached unpleasantly. The room was bleak; an unpleasant dampness drizzled through the air, penetrating the cracks in his windows, obstructed by paintings or primed canvases. Gloomy, disgruntled, he sat down like a wet rooster on his tattered couch, not knowing himself what to undertake, what to do, and finally recalled the whole of his dream. As he recalled it, the dream presented itself to his imagination so oppressively alive that he even began to wonder whether it had indeed been a dream and a mere delirium, and not something else, not an apparition. Pulling off the sheet, he studied this terrible portrait in the light of day. The eyes were indeed striking in their extraordinary aliveness, yet he found nothing especially terrible in them; only, it was as if some inexplicable, unpleasant feeling remained in one's soul. For all that, he still could not be completely certain that it had been a dream. It seemed to him that amidst the dream there had been some terrible fragment of reality. It seemed that even in the very gaze and expression of the old man something was as if saying that he had visited him that night; his hand felt the heaviness that had only just lain in it, as if someone had snatched it away only a moment before. It seemed to him that if he had only held on to the packet more tightly, it would surely have stayed in his hand after he woke up.

"My God, if I had at least part of that money!" he said, sighing heavily, and in his imagination all the packets he had seen, with the alluring inscription of "1,000 Gold Roubles" began to pour from the sack. The packets came unwrapped, gold gleamed, was wrapped up again, and he sat staring fixedly and mindlessly into the empty air, unable to tear himself away from such a subject—like a child sitting with dessert in front of him, his mouth watering, watching while others eat. Finally there came a knock at the door, which roused him unpleasantly. His landlord entered with the police inspector, whose appearance, as everyone knows, is more unpleasant for little people than the face of a petitioner is for the rich. The owner of the small house where Chartkov lived was such a creature as owners of houses somewhere on the Fifteenth

Line of Vasilievsky Island or on the Petersburg side or in a remote
corner of Kolomna[8] usually are—a creature of which there are
many in Russia and whose character is as difficult to define as the
color of a worn-out frock coat. In his youth, he had been a captain
and a loudmouth, had also been employed in civil affairs, had been
an expert at flogging, an efficient man, a fop, and a fool; but in his
old age, he had merged all these sharp peculiarities in himself into
some indefinite dullness. He was a widower, he was retired, he
no longer played the fop, stopped boasting, stopped bullying, and
only liked drinking tea and babbling all sorts of nonsense over it;
paced the room, straightened a tallow candle end; visited his tenants punctually at the end of every month for the money; went
outside, key in hand, to look at the roof of his house; repeatedly
chased the caretaker out of the nook where he hid and slept; in
short—a retired man who, after all his rakish life and jolting about
in post chaises, is left with nothing but trite habits.

"Kindly look for yourself, Varukh Kuzmich," the landlord said,
addressing the inspector and spreading his arms. "You see, he
doesn't pay the rent. He doesn't pay."

"And what if I have no money? Just wait, I'll pay up."

"I cannot wait, my dear," the landlord said angrily, gesturing
with the key he was holding. "I've had Potogonkin, a lieutenant
colonel, as a tenant for seven years now; Anna Petrovna Bukhmisterova also rents a shed and a stable with two stalls, she has three
household serfs with her—that's the sort of tenants I have. I am
not, to put it to you candidly, in the habit of letting the rent go
unpaid. Kindly pay what you owe and move out."

"Yes, since that's the arrangement, kindly pay," said the police
inspector, shaking his head slightly and putting one finger behind a
button of his uniform.

"But what to pay with—that's the question. Right now I
haven't got a cent."

"In that case, you'll have to satisfy Ivan Ivanovich with your
professional productions," said the inspector. "Perhaps he'll agree
to be paid in pictures."

"No, my dear fellow, no pictures, thank you. It would be fine if they were pictures with some noble content, something that could be hung on the wall, maybe a general with a star, or a portrait of Prince Kutuzov;[9] but no, he's painted a peasant, a peasant in a shirt, the servant who grinds paints for him. What an idea, to paint a portrait of that swine! He'll get it in the neck from me: he pulled all the nails out of the latches on me, the crook! Look here, what subjects: here he's painted his room. It would be fine if he'd taken a neat, tidy room, but no, he's painted it with all this litter and trash just as it's lying about. Look here, how he's mucked up my room, kindly see for yourself. I've had tenants staying on for seven years now—colonels, Bukhmisterova, Anna Petrovna . . . No, I tell you, there's no worse tenant than a painter: they live like real pigs, God spare us."

And the poor painter had to listen patiently to all that. The police inspector was busy meanwhile studying the paintings and sketches, and showed straight away that his soul was more alive than the landlord's and was even no stranger to artistic impressions.

"Heh," he said, jabbing a finger into one canvas on which a naked woman was portrayed, "the subject's a bit . . . playful. And this one, why is it all black under his nose? Did he spill snuff there or what?"

"A shadow," Chartkov answered sternly and without turning his eyes to him.

"Well, it could have been moved somewhere else, under the nose it's too conspicuous," said the inspector. "And whose portrait is that?" he continued, going up to the portrait of the old man. "Much too terrifying. Was he really as terrible as that? Look how he stares! Eh, what a Gromoboy![10] Who was your model?"

"But that's some . . ." said Chartkov, and did not finish. A crack was heard. The inspector must have squeezed the frame of the portrait too hard, owing to the clumsy way his policeman's hands were made; the side boards split inward, one fell to the floor, and along with it a packet wrapped in blue paper fell with a heavy clank. The inscription "1,000 Gold Roubles" struck Chartkov's eyes. He rushed like a madman to pick it up, seized the packet, clutched it convulsively in his hand, which sank from the heavy weight.

"Sounds like the clink of money," said the inspector, hearing something thud on the floor and unable to see it for the quickness of Chartkov's movement as he rushed to pick it up.

"And what business is it of yours what I have?"

"It's this: that you have to pay the landlord for the apartment right now; that you've got money but don't want to pay—that's what."

"Well, I'll pay him today."

"Well, why didn't you want to pay before? Why make the land-lord worry, and bother the police besides?"

"Because I didn't want to touch this money. I'll pay him every-thing by this evening and leave the apartment by tomorrow, because I don't wish to remain with such a landlord."

"Well, Ivan Ivanovich, he's going to pay you," said the inspector, turning to the landlord. "And in the event of your not being prop-erly satisfied by this evening, then I beg your pardon, mister painter."

So saying, he put on his three-cornered hat and went out to the front hall, followed by the landlord, his head bowed, it seemed, in some sort of reflection.

"Thank God they got the hell out of here," said Chartkov when he heard the front door close.

He peeked out to the front hall, sent Nikita for something so as to be left completely alone, locked the door behind him, and, re-turning to his room, began with wildly fluttering heart to unwrap the packet. There were gold roubles in it, every one of them new, hot as fire. Nearly out of his mind, he sat over the heap of gold, still asking himself if he was not dreaming. There was an even thousand of them in the packet, which looked exactly the same as the ones he had seen in his dream. For several minutes he ran his fingers through them, looking at them, and still unable to come to his senses. In his imagination there suddenly arose all the stor-ies about treasures, about boxes with secret compartments, left by forebears to their spendthrift grandchildren in the firm convic-tion of their future ruined condition. He reflected thus: "Mightn't some grandfather have decided even now to leave his grandson a gift, locking it up in the frame of a family portrait?" Full of romantic nonsense, he even began thinking whether there might not be some secret connection with his destiny here: whether the existence of the portrait might not be connected with his own existence, and whether its very acquisition had not been somehow predestined? He began studying the frame of the portrait with curiosity. On one side a groove had been chiseled out, covered so cleverly and inconspicuously with a board that, if the inspector's weighty hand had not broken through it, the roubles might have lain there till the world's end. Studying the portrait, he marveled again at the lofty workmanship, the extraordinary finish of the eyes; they no longer seemed terrible to him, but all the same an unpleasant feeling remained in his soul each time. "No," he said to himself, "whoever's grandfather you were, I'll put you under glass for this and make you a golden frame." Here he placed his hand on the heap of gold that lay before him, and his heart began to pound hard at the touch of it. "What shall I do with it?" he thought, fixing his eyes on it. "Now I'm set up for at least three years, I can shut myself in and work. I have enough for paints now, enough for dinners, for tea, for expenses, for rent; no one will hinder and annoy me anymore; I'll buy myself a good mannequin, order a plaster torso, model some legs, set up a Venus, buy prints of the best pictures. And if I work some three years for myself, unhurriedly, not to sell, I'll beat them all, and maybe become a decent artist."

So he was saying together with the promptings of his reason; but within him another voice sounded more audibly and ringingly. And as he cast another glance at the gold, his twenty-two years and his ardent youth said something different. Now everything he had looked at till then with envious eyes, which he had admired from afar with watering mouth, was in his power. Oh, how his heart leaped in him as soon as he thought of it! To put on a fashionable tailcoat, to break his long fast, to rent a fine apartment, to go at once to the theater, the pastry shop, the . . . all the rest—and, having seized the money, he was already in the street.

First of all he stopped at a tailor's, got outfitted from top to toe, and, like a child, began looking himself over incessantly; bought up lots of scents, pomades; rented, without bargaining, a magnificent apartment on Nevsky Prospect, the first that came along, with mirrors and plate-glass windows; chanced to buy an expensive lorgnette in a shop; also chanced to buy a quantity of various neckties, more than he needed; had his locks curled at a hairdresser's; took a couple of carriage rides through the city without any reason; stuffed himself with sweets in a pastry shop; and went to a French restaurant, of which hitherto he had heard only vague rumors, as of the state of China. There he dined, arms akimbo, casting very proud glances at others, and ceaselessly looking in the mirror and touching his curled locks. There he drank a bottle of champagne, which till then he had also known more from hearsay. The wine went to his head a little, and he left feeling lively, pert, devil-may-care, as the saying goes. He strutted down the sidewalk like a dandy, aiming his lorgnette at everyone. On the bridge, he noticed his former professor and darted nimbly past him as if without noticing him at all, so that the dumbfounded professor stood motionless on the bridge for a long time, his face the picture of a question mark.

All his things, and whatever else there was—easel, canvases, paintings—were transported to the magnificent apartment that same evening. The better objects he placed more conspicuously, the worse he stuck into a corner, and he walked through the magnificent rooms, ceaselessly looking in the mirrors. An irresistible desire was born in him to catch fame by the tail at once and show himself to the world. He could already imagine the cries: "Chartkov, Chartkov! Have you seen Chartkov's picture? What a nimble brush this Chartkov has! What a strong talent this Chartkov has!" He walked about his room in a state of rapture, transported who knows where. The next day, taking a dozen gold roubles, he went to the publisher of a popular newspaper to ask for his magnanimous aid; the journalist received him cordially, called him "most honorable sir" at once, pressed both his hands, questioned him in detail about his name, patronymic, place of residence. And the very next day there appeared in the newspaper, following an advertisement for newly invented tallow candles, an article entitled "On the Extraordinary Talents of Chartkov": "We hasten to delight the educated residents of the capital with a wonderful—in all respects, one may say—acquisition. Everyone agrees that there are many most beautiful physiognomies and most beautiful faces among us, but so far the means have been lacking for transferring them to miracle-working canvas, to be handed on to posterity; now this lack has been filled: an artist has been discovered who combines in himself all that is necessary. Now the beautiful woman may be sure that she will be depicted with all the graciousness of her beauty—ethereal, light, charming, wonderful, like butterflies fluttering over spring flowers. The respectable paterfamilias will see himself with all his family around him. The merchant, the man of war, the citizen, the statesman—each will continue on his path with renewed zeal. Hurry, hurry, come from the fête, from strolling to see a friend or *cousine*, from stopping at a splendid shop, hurry from wherever you are. The artist's magnificent studio (Nevsky Prospect, number such-and-such) is all filled with portraits from his brush, worthy of Van Dycks and Titians. One hardly knows which to be surprised at: their faithfulness and likeness to the originals, or the extraordinary brightness and freshness of the brush. Praised be you, artist! You drew the lucky ticket in the lottery! Viva, Andrei Petrovich!" (The journalist evidently enjoyed taking liberties.) "Glorify yourself and us. We know how to appreciate you. Universal attraction, and money along with it, though some of our fellow journalists rise up against it, will be your reward."

The artist read this announcement with secret pleasure: his face beamed. He was being talked about in print—a new thing for him. He read the lines over several times. The comparison with Van Dyck and Titian pleased him very much. The phrase "Viva, Andrei Petrovich!" also pleased him very much; to be called by his first name and patronymic in print was an honor hitherto completely unknown to him. He began to pace the room rapidly, ruffling his hair, now sitting down on a chair, now jumping up and moving to the couch, constantly picturing himself receiving visitors, men and women, going up to a canvas and making dashing gestures over it with a brush, trying to impart graciousness to the movement of his arm. The next day his bell rang; he rushed to open the door. A lady came in, preceded by a lackey in a livery overcoat with fur lining, and together with the lady came a young eighteen-year-old girl, her daughter.

"Are you M'sieur Chartkov?" asked the lady.

The artist bowed.

"You are written about so much; your portraits, they say, are the height of perfection." Having said this, the lady put a lorgnette to her eye and quickly rushed to examine the walls, on which nothing was hung. "But where are your portraits?"

"Taken down," said the artist, slightly confused. "I've only just moved to this apartment, they're still on the way . . . haven't come yet."

"Have you been to Italy?" said the lady, aiming her lorgnette at him, since she found nothing else to aim it at.

"No, I haven't, but I wanted to . . . however, I've put it off for the time being . . . Here's an armchair, madam, you must be tired . . ."

"No, thank you, I sat in the carriage for a long time. Ah, there, I see your work at last!" said the lady, rushing across the room to the wall and aiming her lorgnette at the sketches, set pieces, perspectives, and portraits standing on the floor. "*C'est charmant! Lise, Lise, venez ici!* A room to Teniers'[11] taste, you see—disorder, disorder, a table with a bust on it, an arm, a palette. There's dust, see how the dust is painted! *C'est charmant!* And there, on that other canvas, a woman washing her face—*quelle jolie figure!* Ah, a peasant! Lise, Lise, a little peasant in a Russian shirt! look—a peasant! So you don't do portraits only?"

"Oh, it's rubbish . . . Just for fun . . . sketches . . ."

"Tell me, what is your opinion regarding present-day portraitists? Isn't it true that there are none like Titian nowadays? None with that strength of color, that . . . a pity I can't express it in Russian" (the lady was a lover of art and had gone running with her lorgnette through all the galleries of Italy). "However, M'sieur Null . . . ah, what a painter! Such an extraordinary brush! I find his faces even more expressive than Titian's. Do you know M'sieur Null?"

"Who is this Null?" asked the artist.

"M'sieur Null. Ah, such talent! He painted her portrait when she was only twelve. You absolutely must come and visit us. Lise, you shall show him your album. You know, we came so that you could start at once on her portrait."

"Why, I'm ready this very minute."

He instantly moved over the easel with a prepared canvas on it, took up the palette, and fixed his eyes on the daughter's pale face. Had he been a connoisseur of human nature, in a single moment he would have read in it the beginnings of a childish passion for balls, the beginnings of boredom and complaints about the length of time before dinner and after dinner, the wish to put on a new dress and run to the fête, the heavy traces of an indifferent application to various arts, imposed by her mother for the sake of loftiness of soul and feelings. But the artist saw in this delicate little face nothing but an almost porcelain transparency of body, so alluring for the brush, an attractive, light languor, a slender white neck, and an aristocratic lightness of figure. And he was preparing beforehand to triumph, to show the lightness and brilliance of his brush, which so far had dealt only with the hard features of crude models, with the stern ancients and copies of some classical masters. He could already picture mentally to himself how this light little face was going to come out.

"You know," said the lady, even with a somewhat touching expression on her face, "I'd like to . . . the dress she's wearing now—I confess, I'd like her not to be wearing a dress we're so used to; I'd like her to be dressed simply and sitting in the shade of greenery, with a view of some fields, with herds in the distance, or a copse . . . so that it won't look as if she were going to some ball or fashionable soiree. Our balls, I confess, are so deadly for the soul, so destructive of what's left of our feelings . . . simplicity, there should be more simplicity."

Alas! it was written on the faces of mother and daughter that they danced themselves away at balls until they nearly turned to wax.

Chartkov got down to work, seated his model, pondered it all somewhat in his head; traced in the air with his brush, mentally establishing the points; squinted his eye a little, stepped back, looked from a distance—and in one hour had begun and finished the rough sketch. Pleased with it, he now got to painting, and the work carried him away. He forgot everything, forgot even that he was in the presence of aristocratic ladies, even began to exhibit some artistic mannerisms, uttering various sounds aloud, humming along every once in a while, as happens with artists who are wholeheartedly immersed in their work. Without any ceremony, just with a movement of his brush, he made his model raise her head, for she had finally become quite fidgety and looked utterly weary.

"Enough, that's enough for the first time," said the lady.

"A little longer," said the artist, forgetting himself.

"No, it's time, Lise, it's three o'clock!" she said, taking out a small watch hanging on a golden chain from her belt and exclaiming, "Ah, how late!"

"Only one little minute," Chartkov said in the simple-hearted and pleading voice of a child.

But the lady did not seem at all disposed to cater to his artistic needs this time, and instead promised a longer sitting the next time.

"That's annoying, though," Chartkov thought to himself. "My hand just got going." And he recalled that no one had interrupted him or stopped him when he was working in his studio on Vasilievsky Island; Nikita used to sit in one spot without stirring—paint him as much as you like; he would even fall asleep in the position he was told. Disgruntled, he put his brush and palette down on a chair and stopped vaguely before the canvas. A compliment uttered by the society lady awakened him from his oblivion. He rushed quickly to the door to see them off; on the stairs he received an invitation to visit, to come the next week for dinner, and with a cheerful look he returned to his room. The aristocratic lady had charmed him completely. Till then he had looked at such beings as something inaccessible, born only to race by in a magnificent carriage with liveried lackeys and a jaunty coachman, casting an indifferent glance at the man plodding along on foot in a wretched cloak. And now suddenly one of these beings had entered his room; he was painting a portrait, he was invited to dinner in an aristocratic house. An extraordinary contentment came over him; he was completely intoxicated and rewarded himself for it with a fine dinner, an evening performance, and again took a carriage ride through the city without any need.

During all those days he was unable even to think about his usual work. He was preparing and waiting only for the moment when the bell would ring. At last the aristocratic lady arrived with her pale daughter. He sat them down, moved the canvas over, with adroitness now and a pretense to worldly manners, and began to paint. The brightness of the sunny day was a great help to him. He saw much in his light model of that which, if caught and transferred to canvas, might endow the portrait with great merit; he saw that he might do something special, if everything was finally executed according to the idea he now had of his model. His heart even began to throb lightly when he sensed that he was about to express something others had never noticed. The work occupied him totally, he was all immersed in his brush, again forgetting about his model's aristocratic origin. With bated breath, he saw the light features and nearly transparent body of a seventeen-year-old girl emerge from under his brush. He picked up every nuance, a slight yellowness, a barely noticeable blue under the eyes, and was even about to catch a small pimple that had broken out on her forehead, when suddenly he heard the mother's voice at his ear. "Ah, why that? There's no need for it," the lady said. "And you've also . . . look, in a few places . . . it seems a bit yellow, and look, here it's just like dark spots." The artist started to explain that it was precisely those spots and the yellowness that had played out so well, and that they made up the pleasing and light tones of the face. To which he received the reply that they did not make up any tones and had not played out in any way, and that it only seemed so to him. "But allow me to touch in a little yellow here, just in this one place," the artist said simple-heartedly. But that precisely he was not allowed to do. It was declared that Lise was merely a bit indisposed that day, and there had never been any yellowness in her face, that it was always strikingly fresh in color. Sadly, he began to wipe out what his brush had brought forth on the canvas. Many barely noticeable features disappeared, and the likeness partly disappeared along with them. Unfeelingly, he began to lend it the general color scheme that is given by rote and turns even faces taken from nature into something coldly ideal, such as is seen in student set pieces. But the lady was pleased that the offensive colors had been quite driven out. She only expressed surprise that the work was taking so long, and added that she had heard he finished a portrait completely in two sittings. The artist found nothing to reply to that. The ladies rose and prepared to leave. He put down his brush, saw them to the door, and after that stood vaguely for a long time on the same spot in front of the portrait. He gazed at it stupidly, and meanwhile those light feminine features raced through his head, those nuances and ethereal tones he had observed and which his brush had mercilessly destroyed. All filled with them, he set the portrait aside and found somewhere in the studio an abandoned head of Psyche, which he had roughly sketched out on canvas once long ago. It was a deftly painted face, but completely ideal, cold, consisting only of general features that had not taken on living flesh. Having nothing to do, he now began going over it, recalling on it all that he had happened to observe in the face of the aristocratic visitor. The features, nuances, and tones he had caught laid themselves down here in that purified form in which they come only when an artist, having looked long enough at the model, withdraws from it and produces a creation equal to it. Psyche began to come to life, and the barely glimpsed idea gradually began to be clothed in visible flesh. The facial type of the young society girl was inadvertently imparted to Psyche, and through that she acquired the distinctive expression which gives a work the right to be called truly original. It seemed he made use of both the parts and the whole of what his model had presented to him, and he became totally caught up in his work. For several days he was occupied with nothing else. And it was at this work that the arrival of his lady acquaintances found him. He had no time to remove the painting from the easel. Both ladies uttered joyful cries of amazement and clasped their hands:

"Lise, Lise! Ah, what a likeness! *Superbe, superbe!* What a good idea to dress her in Greek costume. Ah, such a surprise!"

The artist did not know what to do with the agreeably deceived ladies. Embarrassed and looking down, he said quietly:

"It's Psyche."

"In the guise of Psyche? *C'est charmant!*" the mother said, smiling, and the daughter smiled as well. "Don't you think, Lise, that it's most becoming for you to be portrayed as Psyche? *Quelle idée délicieuse!* But what work! It's Corrège.[12] I confess, I had read and heard about you, but I didn't know you had such talent. No, you absolutely must paint my portrait as well."

The lady evidently also wanted to be presented as some sort of Psyche.

"What am I to do with them?" thought the artist. "If they want it so much themselves, let Psyche pass for whatever they want." And he said aloud:

"Be so good as to sit for a little while, and I'll do a little touching up."

"Ah, no, I'm afraid you might . . . it's such a good likeness now."

But the artist understood that there were apprehensions regarding yellow tints and reassured them by saying that he would only give more brightness and expression to the eyes. For, in all fairness, he felt rather ashamed and wanted to give at least a little more resemblance to the original, lest someone reproach him for decided shamelessness. And, indeed, the features of the young girl did finally begin to show more clearly through the image of Psyche.

"Enough!" said the mother, beginning to fear that the resemblance would finally become too close.

The artist was rewarded with everything: a smile, money, a compliment, a warm pressing of the hand, an open invitation to dinner—in short, he received a thousand flattering rewards. The portrait caused a stir in town. The lady showed it to her lady friends; all were amazed at the art with which the painter had managed to keep the likeness and at the same time endow the model with beauty. This last observation they made, naturally, not without a slight flush of envy on their faces. And the artist was suddenly beset with commissions. It seemed the whole town wanted to be painted by him. The doorbell was constantly ringing. On the one hand, this might have been a good thing, offering him endless practice, diversity, a multitude of faces. But, unfortunately, these were all people who were hard to get along with, hurried people, busy or belonging to society—meaning still busier than any other sort, and therefore impatient in the extreme. From all sides came only the request that it be done well and promptly. The artist saw that it was decidedly impossible to finish his works, that everything had to be replaced by adroitness and quick, facile brushwork. To catch only the whole, only the general expression, without letting the brush go deeper into fine details—in short, to follow nature to the utmost was decidedly impossible. To this it must be added that almost all those being painted had many other claims to various things. The ladies demanded that only their soul and character be portrayed in the main, while the rest sometimes should not even be adhered to, all corners should be rounded, all flaws lightened, or, if possible, avoided altogether. In short, so as to make the face something to admire, if not to fall completely in love with. And as a result of that, when they sat for him, they sometimes acquired such expressions as astonished the artist: one tried to make her face show melancholy, another reverie, a third wanted at all costs to reduce the size of her mouth and compressed it so much that it finally turned into a dot no bigger than a pinhead. And, despite all that, they demanded a good likeness from him and an easy naturalness. Nor were the men any better than the ladies. One demanded to be portrayed with a strong, energetic turn of the head; another with inspired eyes raised aloft; a lieutenant of the guards absolutely insisted that Mars show in his look; a civil dignitary was bent on having more frankness and nobility in his face, and his hand resting on a book on which would be clearly written: "He always stood for truth." At first these demands made the artist break out in a sweat: all this had to be calculated, pondered, and yet he was given very little time. He finally worked the whole business out and no longer had any difficulty. He could grasp ahead of time, from two or three words, how the person wanted to be portrayed. If someone wanted Mars, he put Mars into his face; if someone aimed at Byron, he gave him a Byronic pose and attitude. If a lady wished to be Corinne, Ondine, or Aspasia,[13] he agreed to everything with great willingness and added a dose of good looks on his own, which, as everyone knows, never hurts, and on account of which an artist may even be forgiven the lack of likeness. Soon he himself began to marvel at the wonderful quickness and facility of his brush. And those he painted, it goes without saying, were delighted and proclaimed him a genius.

Chartkov became a fashionable painter in all respects. He began going to dinners, accompanied ladies to galleries and even to fêtes, dressed elegantly, and openly affirmed that an artist must belong to society, that his estate must be upheld, that artists dressed like cobblers, did not know how to behave, did not keep up a high tone, and were totally lacking in cultivation. At home, in his studio, he became accustomed to great neatness and cleanliness, hired two magnificent lackeys, acquired elegant pupils, changed several times a day into various morning suits, had his hair curled, busied himself with improving all the manners by which to receive clients, with the beautifying of his appearance by every means possible, so as to make a pleasing impression on the ladies; in short, it was soon quite impossible to recognize in him that modest artist who had once worked inconspicuously in his hovel on Vasilievsky Island. He now spoke sharply of painters and of art: he maintained that too much merit was granted to painters of the past, that prior to Raphael they had all painted not figures but herrings; that the notion that some sort of holiness could be seen in them existed only in the imagination of the viewers; that even Raphael himself had not always painted well and many of his works were famous only by tradition; that Michelangelo was a braggart, because he only wanted to show off his knowledge of anatomy, that there was no gracefulness in him at all, and that true brilliance, power of the brush and of colors should be looked for only now, in the present age. Here, naturally, things would turn inadvertently to himself.

"No, I do not understand," he would say, "why others strain so much, sitting and toiling over their work. The man who potters for several months over a painting is, in my opinion, a laborer, not an artist. I don't believe there is any talent in him. A genius creates boldly, quickly. Here," he would say, usually turning to his visitors, "this portrait I painted in two days, this little head in one day, this in a few hours, this in a little more than an hour. No, I . . . I confess, I do not recognize as art something assembled line by line. That is craft, not art."

So he spoke to his visitors, and the visitors marveled at the power and facility of his brush, even uttered exclamations on hearing how quickly he worked, and then said to each other: "That's talent, true talent! See how he speaks, how his eyes shine! *Il y a quelque chose d'extraordinaire dans toute sa figure!*"

The artist was flattered to hear such rumors about himself. When printed praise of him appeared in the magazines, he was happy as a child, though this praise had been bought for him with his own money. He carried the printed page around everywhere and, as if inadvertently, showed it to his friends and acquaintances, and this delighted him to the point of the most simple-hearted naïvety. His fame grew, his work and commissions increased. He was already tired of the same portraits and faces, whose poses and attitudes he knew by rote. He painted them now without much enthusiasm, applying himself to sketching only the head anyhow and leaving the rest for his pupils to finish. Before, he had still sought to give some new pose, to impress with force, with effects. Now that, too, became boring to him. His mind was growing weary of thinking up and thinking out. It was more than he could stand, and he had no time: a distracted life and the society in which he tried to play the role of a worldly man—all this took him far from work and thought. His brush was becoming cold and dull, and he imperceptibly locked himself into monotonous, predetermined, long worn-out forms. The monotonous, cold, eternally tidied and, so to speak, buttoned-up faces of the officials, military and civil, did not offer much space for the brush: it began to forget luxurious draperies, strong gestures and passions. To say nothing of group composition, of artistic drama and its lofty design. Before him sat only a uniform, a bodice, a tailcoat, before which an artist feels chilled and all imagination collapses. Even the most ordinary merits were no longer to be seen in his productions, and yet they still went on being famous, though true connoisseurs and artists merely shrugged as they looked at his latest works. And some who had known Chartkov before could not understand how the talent of which signs had shown clearly in him at the very beginning could have disappeared, and vainly tried to understand how the gift could die out in a man just as he reached the full development of his powers.

But the intoxicated artist did not hear this talk. He was already beginning to reach the age of maturity in mind and years, had already begun to gain weight and expand visibly in girth. In newspapers and magazines he was already reading the adjectives "our esteemed Andrei Petrovich," "our honored Andrei Petrovich." He was already being offered respectable posts in the civil service, invited to examinations and committees. He was already beginning, as always happens at a respectable age, to take a firm stand for Raphael and the old masters—not because he was fully convinced of their lofty merit, but so as to shove them in the faces of young artists. He was already beginning, as is the custom of all those entering that age, to reproach the young without exception for immorality and a wrong turn of mind. He was already beginning to believe that everything in the world is done simply, that there is no inspiration from above, and everything must inevitably be subjected to one strict order of accuracy and uniformity. In short, his life had already touched upon the age when everything that breathes of impulse shrinks in a man, when a powerful bow has a fainter effect on his soul and no longer twines piercing music around his heart, when the touch of beauty no longer transforms virginal powers into fire and flame, but all the burnt-out feelings become more accessible to the sound of gold, listen more attentively to its alluring music, and little by little allow it imperceptibly to lull them completely. Fame cannot give pleasure to one who did not merit it but stole it; it produces a constant tremor only in one who is worthy of it. And therefore all his feelings and longings turned toward gold. Gold became his passion, his ideal, fear, delight, purpose. Bundles of banknotes grew in his coffers, and he, like everyone else to whom this terrible gift is granted, began to be a bore, inaccessible to anything but gold, a needless miser, a purposeless hoarder, and was about to turn into one of those strange beings who are so numerous in our unfeeling world, at whom a man filled with life and heart looks with horror, who seem to him like moving stone coffins with dead men instead of hearts in them. Yet one event shook him deeply and awakened all his living constitution.

One day he found a note on his desk in which the Academy of

Art asked him as a worthy member to come and give his opinion of a new work sent from Italy by a Russian artist who was studying there. This artist was one of his former comrades, who from a young age had borne within himself a passion for art, and with the ardent spirit of a laborer had immersed himself in it with his whole soul, had torn himself away from friends, from family, from cherished habits, and rushed to where under beautiful skies a majestic hothouse of the arts was ripening—to that wonderful Rome, at the name of which the ardent heart of an artist beats so deeply and strongly. There, like a hermit, he immersed himself in work and totally undistracted studies. He was not concerned if people commented on his character, his inability to deal with people, his nonobservance of worldly proprieties, the humiliation he inflicted upon the estate of artists by his poor, unfashionable dress. He could not have cared less whether his brethren were angry with him or not. He disregarded everything, he gave everything to art. He tirelessly visited galleries, spent whole hours standing before the works of great masters, grasped and pursued a wondrous brush. He never finished anything without testing himself several times by these great teachers and reading wordless but eloquent advice for himself in their paintings. He did not enter into noisy discussions and disputes; he stood neither for nor against the purists. He granted its due share to everything equally, drawing from everything only what was beautiful in it, and in the end left himself only the divine Raphael as a teacher. So a great poetic artist, having read many different writings filled with much delight and majestic beauty, in the end might leave himself, as his daily reading, only Homer's *Iliad*, having discovered that in it there is everything one wants, and there is nothing that has not already been reflected in its profound and great perfection. And he came away from this schooling with a majestic idea of creation, a powerful beauty of thought, the lofty delight of a heavenly brush.

On entering the hall, Chartkov found a huge crowd of visitors already gathered before the painting. A profound silence, such as rarely occurs amidst a gathering of connoisseurs, now reigned everywhere. He hastened to assume the significant physiognomy of an expert and approached the painting—but, God, what did he see!

Pure, immaculate, beautiful as a bride, the artist's creation stood before him. Modest, divine, innocent, and simple as genius, it soared above everything. It seemed that the heavenly figures, astonished to have so many eyes directed at them, shyly lowered their beautiful eyelashes. With a sense of involuntary amazement, the experts contemplated this new, unprecedented brush. Here everything seemed to have come together: the study of Raphael, reflected in the lofty nobility of the poses; the study of Correggio, breathing from the ultimate perfection of the brushwork. But most imperiously of all there was manifest the power of creation already contained in the soul of the artist himself. Every least object in the picture was pervaded with it; law and inner force were grasped in everything. Everywhere that flowing roundedness of line had been grasped which belongs to nature and is seen only by the eyes of the creative artist, and which comes out angular in an imitator. One could see how the artist had first taken into his soul everything he had drawn from the external world, and from there, from the spring of his soul, had sent it forth in one harmonious, triumphant song. And it became clear even to the uninitiate what a measureless abyss separates a creation from a mere copy of nature. It is almost impossible to express the extraordinary silence that came over everyone whose eyes were fixed on the painting— not a rustle, not a sound; and the painting meanwhile appeared loftier and loftier with every minute; brightly and wonderfully it detached itself from everything, and all transformed finally into one instant—the fruit of a thought that had flown down to the artist from heaven—an instant for which the whole of human life is only a preparation. Involuntary tears were ready to flow down the faces of the visitors who surrounded the picture. It seemed that all tastes and all brazen or wrongheaded deviations of taste merged into some silent hymn to the divine work. Chartkov stood motionless, openmouthed before the picture, and at last, when the visitors and experts gradually began to stir and to discuss the merits of the work, and when at last they turned to him with the request that he tell them what he thought, he came to himself; he was

about to assume an indifferent, habitual air, was about to produce
the banal, habitual judgment of a jaded artist, something like:
"Yes, of course, it's true, one can't deny the artist a certain talent;
there's something there; one can see he wanted to express something; but as for the essence . . ." And to follow it, naturally, with
such praise as no artist would be the better for. He was about to do
that, but the words died on his lips, tears and sobs burst out in a
discordant response, and like a madman he rushed from the hall.

For a moment he stood motionless and insensible in the middle
of his magnificent studio. His whole being, his whole life was
awakened in one instant, as if youth returned to him, as if the
extinguished sparks of talent blazed up again. The blindfold suddenly fell from his eyes. God! to ruin the best years of his youth so
mercilessly; to destroy, to extinguish the spark of fire that had perhaps flickered in his breast, that perhaps would have developed
by now into greatness and beauty, that perhaps would also have
elicited tears of amazement and gratitude! And to ruin all that, to
ruin it without any mercy! It seemed to him as if those urges and
impulses that used to be familiar to him suddenly revived all at
once in his soul. He seized a brush and approached the canvas. The
sweat of effort stood out on his face; he was all one desire, burning
with one thought: he wanted to portray a fallen angel. This idea
corresponded most of all to his state of mind. But, alas! his figures,
poses, groupings, thoughts came out forced and incoherent. His
brush and imagination were confined too much to one measure,
and the powerless impulse to overstep the limits and fetters he had
imposed on himself now tasted of wrongness and error. He had
neglected the long, wearisome ladder of gradual learning and the
first basic laws of future greatness. Vexation pervaded him. He
ordered all his latest works, all the lifeless, fashionable pictures, all
the portraits of hussars, ladies, and state councillors, taken out of
the studio. Locked up in the room by himself, he ordered that no
one be admitted and immersed himself entirely in his work. Like a
patient youth, like an apprentice, he sat over his task. But how
mercilessly ungrateful was everything that came from under his
brush! At every step he was pulled up short by want of knowledge
of the most basic elements; a simple, insignificant mechanism

chilled his whole impulse and stood as an insuperable threshold for his imagination. The brush turned involuntarily to forms learned by rote, the arms got folded in one studied manner, the head dared not make any unusual turn, even the very folds of the clothing smacked of rote learning and refused to obey and be draped over an unfamiliar pose of the body. And he felt it, he felt it and saw it himself!

"But did I ever really have talent?" he said finally. "Am I not mistaken?" And as he said these words, he went up to his old works, which had once been painted so purely, so disinterestedly, there in the poor hovel on solitary Vasilievsky Island, far from people, abundance, and all sorts of fancies. He went up to them now and began to study them all attentively, and along with them all his former poor life began to emerge in his memory. "Yes," he said desperately, "I did have talent. Everywhere, on everything, I can see signs and traces of it . . ."

He stopped and suddenly shook all over: his eyes met with eyes fixed motionlessly on him. It was that extraordinary portrait he had bought in the Shchukin market. All this time it had been covered up, blocked by other paintings, and had left his mind completely. But now, as if by design, when all the fashionable portraits and pictures that had filled the studio were gone, it surfaced together with the old works of his youth. When he remembered all its strange story, remembered that in some sense it, this strange portrait, had been the cause of his transformation, that the hidden treasure he had obtained in such a miraculous way had given birth to all the vain impulses in him which had ruined his talent—rage nearly burst into his soul. That same moment he ordered the hateful portrait taken out. But that did not calm his inner agitation: all his feelings and all his being were shaken to their depths, and he came to know that terrible torment which, by way of a striking exception, sometimes occurs in nature, when a weak talent strains to show itself on too grand a scale and fails; that torment which gives birth to great things in a youth, but, in passing beyond the border of dream, turns into a fruitless yearning; that dreadful torment which makes a man capable of terrible evildoing. A terrible envy possessed him, an envy bordering on rage. The bile rose in him when he saw some work that bore the stamp of talent. He ground his teeth and devoured it with the eyes of a basilisk.[14] A plan was born in his soul, the most infernal a man ever nursed, and with furious force he rushed to carry it out. He began to buy up all the best that art produced. Having bought a painting for a high price, he would take it carefully to his room, fall upon it with the fury of a tiger, tear it, shred it, cut it to pieces, and trample it with his feet, all the while laughing with delight. The inestimable wealth he had acquired provided him with the means of satisfying this infernal desire. He untied all his bags of gold and opened his coffers. No monster of ignorance ever destroyed so many beautiful works as did this fierce avenger. Whenever he appeared at an auction, everyone despaired beforehand of acquiring a work of art. It seemed as if a wrathful heaven had sent this terrible scourge into the world on purpose, wishing to deprive it of all harmony. This terrible passion lent him some frightful coloration: his face was eternally bilious. Denial and blasphemy against the world were expressed in his features. He seemed the incarnation of that terrible demon whom Pushkin had portrayed ideally.[15] His lips uttered nothing but venomous words and eternal despite. Like some sort of harpy, he would appear in the street and even his acquaintances, spotting him from far off, would try to dodge and avoid the encounter, saying it was enough to poison all the rest of the day.

Fortunately for the world and for the arts, such a strained and violent life could not long continue: the scope of its passions was too exaggerated and colossal for its feeble forces. Attacks of rage and madness began to come more often, and finally it all turned into a most terrible illness. A cruel fever combined with galloping consumption came over him with such fierceness that in three days nothing but a shadow of him remained. This was combined with all the signs of hopeless insanity. Sometimes several men could not hold him back. He would begin to imagine the long forgotten, living eyes of the extraordinary portrait, and then his rage was terrible. All the people around his bed seemed to him like terrible portraits. It doubled, quadrupled in his eyes; all the walls seemed hung with portraits, their motionless, living eyes fixed on him. Frightful portraits stared from the ceiling, from the floor; the room expanded and went on endlessly to make space for more of these motionless eyes. The doctor who had assumed the charge of caring for him, having heard something of his strange story, tried his best to find the mysterious relation between the phantoms he imagined and the circumstances of his life, but never succeeded. The sick man neither understood nor felt anything except his own torments, and uttered only terrible screams and incoherent talk. Finally his life broke off in the last, already voiceless strain of suffering. His corpse was frightful. Nothing could be found of his enormous wealth, either; but seeing the slashed remains of lofty works of art whose worth went beyond millions, its terrible use became clear.

PART II

A great many carriages, droshkies, and barouches stood outside the entrance of a house in which an auction was under way of the belongings of one of those wealthy lovers of art who spend their whole life drowsing sweetly, immersed in their zephyrs and cupids, who innocently pass for Maecenases[16] and simple-heartedly spend on it the millions accumulated by their substantial fathers, and often even by their own former labors. Such Maecenases, as we know, exist no longer, and our nineteenth century has long since acquired the dull physiognomy of a banker who delights in his millions only as numbers on paper. The long room was filled with a most motley crowd of visitors, who had come flying like birds of prey to an unburied body. There was a whole fleet of Russian merchants from the Merchants' Arcade,[17] and even from the flea market, in dark blue German frock coats. Their appearance and the expression of their faces was somehow more firm here, more free, and not marked by that cloying subservience so conspicuous in the Russian merchant when he is in his shop with a customer before him. Here they dropped all decorum, even though there were in this same hall a great many of those counts before whom, in some other place, they would be ready with their bowing to sweep away the dust brought in on their own boots. Here they were completely casual, unceremoniously fingered the books and paintings, wishing to see if the wares were good, and boldly upped the bids offered by aristocratic experts. Here there were many of those inevitable auction-goers whose custom it was to attend one every day in place of lunch; aristocratic experts who considered it their duty not to miss a chance of adding to their collections and who found nothing else to do between twelve and one; and, lastly, those noble gentlemen whose clothes and pockets were quite threadbare, who came daily with no mercenary purpose but solely to see how it would end, who would offer more, who less, who would bid up whom, and who would be left with what. A great many paintings were thrown around without any sense at all; they were mixed in with furniture and books bearing the monogram of their former owner, who probably never had the laudable curiosity to look into them. Chinese vases, marble table tops, new and old pieces of furniture with curved lines, gryphons, sphinxes, and lions' paws, gilded and ungilded, chandeliers, Quinquet lamps[18]— it was all lying in heaps, and by no means in the orderly fashion of shops. It all presented some sort of chaos of the arts. Generally, we experience a dreadful feeling at the sight of an auction: it all smacks of something like a funeral procession. The rooms in which they are held are always somehow gloomy; the windows, blocked by furniture and paintings, emit a scant light, silence spreads over the faces, and the funereal voice of the auctioneer, as he taps with his hammer, intones a panikhida[19] over the poor arts so oddly come together there. All this seems to strengthen still more the strange unpleasantness of the impression.

The auction seemed to be at its peak. A whole crowd of decent people, clustered together, vied excitedly with each other over something. The words "Rouble, rouble, rouble," coming from all sides, gave the auctioneer no time to repeat the rising price, which had already grown four times over the initial one. The surrounding crowd was excited over a portrait that could not have failed to stop anyone with at least some understanding of painting. The lofty brush of an artist was clearly manifest in it. The portrait had evidently already been renewed and restored several times, and it represented the swarthy features of some Asian in loose attire, with an extraordinary, strange expression on his face; but most of all, the people around it were struck by the extraordinary aliveness of the eyes. The more they looked at them, the more the eyes seemed to penetrate into each of them. This strangeness, this extraordinary trick of the artist, occupied almost everyone's attention. Many of the competitors had already given up, because the bids rose incredibly. There remained only two well-known aristocrats, lovers of painting, who simply refused to give up such an acquisition. They were excited and would probably have raised the bid impossibly, if one of the onlookers there had not suddenly said:

"Allow me to interrupt your dispute for a time. I have perhaps more right to this portrait than anyone else."

These words instantly drew everyone's attention to him. He was a trim man of about thirty-five with long black hair. His pleasant face, filled with some carefree brightness, spoke for a soul foreign to all wearisome worldly shocks; in his clothing there was no pretense to fashion: everything in him spoke of the artist. This was, in fact, the painter B., known personally to many of those present.

"Strange as my words may seem to you," he went on, seeing the general attention directed at him, "if you are resolved to listen to a brief story, you will perhaps see that I had the right to speak them. Everything assures me that this portrait is the very one I am looking for."

A quite natural curiosity lit up on the faces of almost all of them, and the auctioneer himself stopped, openmouthed, with the upraised hammer in his hand, preparing to listen. At the beginning of the story, many kept involuntarily turning their eyes to the portrait, but soon they all fixed their eyes on the narrator alone, as his story became ever more engrossing.

"You know that part of the city which is called Kolomna." So he began. "There everything is unlike the other parts of Petersburg; there it is neither capital nor province; you seem to feel, as you enter the streets of Kolomna, that all youthful desires and impulses are abandoning you. The future does not visit there, everything there is silence and retirement; everything has settled out of the movement of the capital. Retired clerks move there to live, and widows, and people of small income who, after some acquaintance with the Senate,[20] condemned themselves to this place for almost their whole lives; pensioned-off cooks who spend all day jostling in the marketplaces, babbling nonsense with some peasant in a small-goods shop, and every day take five kopecks' worth of coffee and four of sugar; and, finally, that whole class of people who may be called by one word: ashen—people whose clothing, faces, hair, eyes have a sort of dull, ashen appearance, like a day on which there is neither storm nor sun in the sky, but simply nothing in particular: a drizzling mist robs all objects of their sharpness. Retired theater ushers, retired titular councillors, retired disciples of Mars with a blind eye and a swollen lip, can be included here. These people are utterly passionless: they walk about without looking at anything, they are silent without thinking about anything. They have few chattels in their rooms, sometimes simply a bottle of pure Russian vodka, which they sip monotonously all day, without any strong rush to the head aroused by a heavy intake such as a young German artisan likes to treat himself to on Sundays—that daredevil of Meshchanskaya Street, who takes sole possession of the pavements once it's past midnight.

"Life in Kolomna is terribly solitary: there is rarely a carriage, except maybe the kind actors go around in, which with its rumbling, jingling, and clanking is all that disturbs the universal silence. There everybody goes on foot; a cabby with no passengers quite often plods along, bringing hay to his bearded little nag. You can find lodgings for five roubles a month, even with morning coffee. Widows living on pensions are the aristocrats of the place—they behave themselves well, sweep their room frequently, discuss the high price of beef and cabbage with their lady friends; there's often a young daughter with them, a silent, speechless, sometimes comely being, a vile little dog, and a wall clock with a sadly ticking pendulum. Then come actors, whose earnings do not allow them to move out of Kolomna—free folk who, like all artists, live for pleasure. Sitting in their dressing gowns, they repair a pistol, glue up various useful household objects from cardboard, play checkers or cards with a visiting friend, spend the morning that way, and do almost the same thing in the evening, with the addition of an

occasional glass of punch. After these aces and the aristocracy of
Kolomna come the extraordinarily puny and piddling. It's as difficult to name them as it is to count the multitude of insects that
generate in stale vinegar. There are old women who pray, old
women who drink, old women who both pray and drink, old
women who get along by incomprehensible means, like ants—
they drag old rags and linens from the Kalinkin Bridge to the flea
market and sell them there for fifteen kopecks; in short, often the
most wretched sediment of mankind, whose condition no philan-
thropic political economist could find the means to improve.

"I mention them in order to show you how often these people
have the need to seek one-time, sudden, temporary assistance, to
resort to borrowing; and then there settle among them a special
sort of moneylenders, who provide them with small sums on a
pledge and at high interest. These small moneylenders are often-
times more unfeeling than any of the big ones, because they
emerge in the midst of poverty and the most manifest beggarly
rags, something not seen by the wealthy moneylender, who deals
only with those who come to him in carriages. And therefore
human feeling dies all too early in their souls. Among these
moneylenders there was one . . . but it will do no harm to inform
you that the event I've begun to tell you about took place in the
last century—namely, during the reign of the late empress Catherine II. You can understand yourselves that the very appearance and
inner life of Kolomna must have changed significantly. And so,
among the moneylenders there was one—an extraordinary being
in all respects—who had long since settled in that part of the city.
He went about in loose Asian attire; the dark color of his face
pointed to his southern origin, but precisely what his nationality
was—Indian, Greek, Persian—no one could say for certain. Tall,
almost extraordinary stature, a swarthy, lean, burnt face, its color
somehow inconceivably terrible, large eyes of an extraordinary
fire, and thick, beetling brows, distinguished him greatly and
sharply from all the ashen inhabitants of the capital. His dwelling
itself was unlike all the other little wooden houses. It was a stone
building, like those once built in great numbers by Genoese merchants—with irregular, unequal-sized windows, iron shutters, and

iron bars. This moneylender differed from other moneylenders in that he was able to supply any sum to anyone, from a destitute old woman to an extravagant courtier. The most brilliant carriages often turned up in front of his house, in the windows of which the heads of magnificent society ladies often appeared. The rumor spread, as usual, that his iron coffers were filled with an inestimable fortune in money, jewelry, diamonds, and various pledges, but that nonetheless he was not mercenary in the same way other money-lenders were. He gave money out willingly, fixing seemingly advantageous terms of payment; but through certain strange math-ematical calculations, he somehow made the interest increase enormously. So, at least, rumor said. But strangest of all, and what could not fail to strike many, was the strange fate that befell all those who took money from him: they all ended their lives in some unfortunate way. Whether this was simply people's opinion, absurd superstitious talk, or a deliberately spread rumor, remained unknown. But within a short period of time several vivid and spectacular examples occurred before everyone's eyes.

"Among the aristocracy of the time, a young man from one of the best families soon drew everyone's eyes, who distinguished himself in the government service while still young—an ardent admirer of everything genuine and lofty, a zealot of everything produced by human art and intellect, a promising Maecenas. He soon deserved to be distinguished by the empress herself, who entrusted him with an important post that agreed perfectly with his own expectations, a post in which he could do much for learn-ing and for the good in general. The young courtier surrounded himself with painters, poets, scholars. He wanted to give work to all, to encourage all. He undertook at his own expense a great many useful publications, commissioned a great many things, announced encouraging awards, spent heaps of money on it, and in the end was ruined. Yet, full of magnanimous impulse, he did not want to abandon his cause, sought to borrow everywhere, and turned at last to the famous moneylender. Having taken a con-siderable loan from him, in a short period of time the man changed completely: he became an enemy, a persecutor of devel-oping minds and talents. In all writings he began to see the bad side, he twisted the meaning of every phrase. As luck would have it, the French Revolution occurred just then. This suddenly served him as a tool for every possible nastiness. He began to see some sort of revolutionary trend in everything, he imagined allusions everywhere. He became suspicious to such a degree that he finally began to suspect his own self, started writing terrible, unjust denunciations, made innumerable people miserable. It goes without saying that such behavior could not fail in the end to reach the throne. The magnanimous empress was horrified and, filled with that nobility of soul which is the adornment of crowned heads, spoke words which, though they could not have been conveyed to us exactly, yet imprinted their deep meaning in the hearts of many. The empress observed that it is not under monarchy that the lofty, noble impulses of the soul are suppressed, it is not there that works of intellect, poetry, and art are scorned and persecuted; that, on the contrary, only monarchs patronize them; that the Shakespeares and Molières flourished under their magnanimous rule, while Dante could not find himself a corner in his republican fatherland; that true geniuses emerge in times of the splendor and power of sovereigns and states, and not at times of outrageous political phenomena and republican terrors, which up to now have never presented the world with a single poet; that poets and artists ought to be held in distinction, for they bring only peace and a beautiful quiet to the soul, not agitation and murmuring; that scholars, poets, and all those who produce art are pearls and diamonds in the imperial crown: by them the epoch of a great sovereign is adorned and acquires still greater splendor. In short, the empress, at the moment of speaking these words, was divinely beautiful. I remember that old people couldn't speak of it without tears. Everyone became concerned with the affair. To the credit of our national pride, it must be noted that there always dwells in the Russian heart a beautiful impulse to take the side of the oppressed. The courtier who had betrayed his trust was duly punished and dismissed from his post. But in the faces of his compatriots he read a much greater punishment. This was a decided and universal scorn. It is impossible to describe how the vain soul suffered; pride, disappointed ambition, ruined hopes all joined together, and in fits of terrible madness and rage his life broke off.

"Another spectacular example also occurred before everyone's eyes. Among the beauties of whom there was no lack in our northern capital, one decidedly held primacy over the rest. She was some miraculous blend of our northern beauty with Mediterranean beauty, a diamond that rarely occurs in the world. My father used to confess that he had never in his life seen anything like her. It seemed that everything came together in her: wealth, intelligence, and inner charm. She had a crowd of wooers, and the most remarkable of them was Prince R., the noblest, the best of all young men, beautiful both in looks and in his chivalrous, magnanimous impulses—the lofty ideal of novels and women, a Grandison[21] in all respects. Prince R. was passionately and madly in love with her; and he was reciprocated with the same burning love. But her family thought the match unequal. The prince's hereditary estates had long ceased to belong to him, his family was in disgrace, and the poor state of his affairs was known to everyone. Suddenly the prince leaves the capital for a time, supposedly in order to straighten out his affairs, and a short while later he reappears surrounded with unbelievable magnificence and splendor. Brilliant balls and banquets make him known at court. The beauty's father turns favorable, and in town a most interesting wedding takes place. Whence came such a change and the bridegroom's unheard-of wealth—that certainly no one could explain; but people murmured on the side that he had entered into certain conditions with the incomprehensible moneylender and taken a loan from him. Be that as it may, the wedding occupied the whole town. Both bride and groom were objects of general envy. Everybody knew of their ardent, constant love, the long languishing suffered on both sides, the high merits of both. Fiery women described beforehand the paradisal bliss that the young spouses were going to enjoy. But it all turned out otherwise. Within a year, a terrible change took place in the husband. His character, hitherto noble and beautiful, was poisoned by the venom of suspicious jealousy, intolerance, and inexhaustible caprices. He became a tyrant and tormentor of his wife and—something no one could have foreseen—resorted to the most inhuman acts, even to beating. Within a year, no one could recognize the woman who so recently had shone and attracted crowds of obedient admirers. At last, unable to endure her hard lot any longer, she made the first mention of divorce. Her husband flew into a fury at the very thought of it. On a first violent impulse, he burst into her room with a knife in his hand and undoubtedly would have stabbed her then and there had he not been seized and held back. In a fit of frenzy and despair, he turned the knife against himself—and in the most terrible sufferings ended his life.

"Besides these two examples, which happened before the eyes of the whole of society, a great many were told of which had occurred in the lower classes, almost all of them having a terrible end. Here an honest, sober man became a drunkard; there a merchant's salesclerk stole from his employer; there a cabby, after several years of honest work, put a knife into a client over a penny. It was impossible that these occurrences, sometimes told with additions, should fail to bring some sort of involuntary terror to the humble inhabitants of Kolomna. No one doubted the presence of unclean powers in this man. It was said that he offered hair-raising terms, such as no unfortunate man ever dared repeat to anyone afterwards; that his money had a burning quality, that it became red-hot by itself and bore some strange signs . . . in short, there was a great deal of every sort of absurd talk. And the remarkable thing was that this whole Kolomna populace, this whole world of poor old women, minor officials, minor artists, and, in short, all the small fry we've just named, agreed to suffer and endure the last extremity rather than turn to the dreadful moneylender; old women were even found dead of starvation, preferring the death of their bodies to the destruction of their souls. Those who met him in the street felt an involuntary fear. A passer-by would cautiously back away and glance behind him for a long time afterwards, watching his immensely tall figure disappear in the distance. His appearance alone held so much of the extraordinary that it would have made anyone ascribe a supernatural existence to him. The strong features, more deeply chiseled than ever happens in a man; the hot, bronze complexion; the immense thickness of the eyebrows, the unbearably frightening eyes, even the loose folds of his Asian clothing—all seemed to say that the passions of others all paled before the passion that moved in his body. My father, each time he met him, would stand motionless, and each time could not help saying: 'The devil, the very devil!' But I must hasten to acquaint you with my father, who, incidentally, is the real subject of this story.

"My father was a man remarkable in many respects. He was an artist such as few are, one of those wonders that Russia alone brings forth from her inexhaustible womb, a self-taught artist who found rules and laws in his own soul, without teachers or school, driven only by his thirst for perfection, and following, for reasons perhaps unknown to himself, no path but that which his own soul indicated—one of those natural-born wonders whom contemporaries often abuse with the offensive word 'ignoramus' and whom the castigations of others and their own failures do not cool down but only lend new zeal and strength, so that in their souls they go far beyond the works that earned them the title of 'ignoramus.' With lofty inner instinct, he sensed the presence of a thought in every object; he grasped the true meaning of the term 'historical painting' on his own; grasped why a simple head, a simple portrait by Raphael, Leonardo da Vinci, Titian, Correggio, could be called a historical painting, and why a huge picture on a historical subject remained a *tableau de genre,* despite all the artist's claim to historical painting. Both inner sense and personal conviction turned his brush to Christian subjects, the highest and last step of the sublime. He had none of the ambition or irritability so inseparable from the character of many artists. He was of firm character, an honest, direct, even crude man, covered on the outside with a somewhat tough bark, not without a certain pride in his soul, who spoke of people at once sharply and condescendingly. 'Why look at them?' he used to say. 'I don't work for them. I won't take my works to their drawing rooms, they'll be put in a church. Whoever understands me will be grateful—if not, they'll pray to God anyway. There's no point in blaming a man of society for not understanding painting: he understands cards instead, he can appreciate good wine, horses—why should a gentleman know more than that? Otherwise he'll take up one thing or another, turn smart, and then there'll be no getting rid of him! To each his own; let everybody tend to his affairs. As I see it, he's a better man who says outright that he doesn't understand than one who plays the hypocrite, saying he knows something when he doesn't and simply mucking everything up.' He worked for little money—that is, just for what he needed to support his family and give him the chance to work. Besides that, he never refused to help others or give a helping hand to a poor artist. He had the simple, pious faith of his ancestors, and that may be why the lofty expression which brilliant talents were never able to achieve appeared of itself on the faces he portrayed. In the end, through the constancy of his labors and his steadfastness on the path he had marked out for himself, he began to gain respect even on the part of those who had abused him as an ignoramus and a homemade talent. He was constantly given commissions by the Church and was never without work. One of his works occupied him greatly. I no longer remember what the subject was, I know only that he had to include the spirit of darkness in the picture. He thought for a long time about what image to give him; he wanted to realize in his face all that burdens and oppresses man. As he reflected thus, the image of the mysterious moneylender sometimes passed through his head, and he would think involuntarily, 'There's the one I should paint the devil after.' Consider his astonishment, then, when one day, as he was working in his studio, he heard a knock at the door and immediately afterwards the terrible moneylender came in. He could not help feeling some inner tremor, which passed involuntarily through his whole body.

"'You are an artist?' he said to my father, without any ceremony.

"'An artist,' my father said in perplexity, waiting for what would follow.

"'Very well. Paint my portrait. I may die soon. I have no children, but I do not want to die altogether, I want to live on. Can you paint my portrait as if it were perfectly alive?'

"My father thought, 'What could be better? He's inviting himself to be the devil in my painting.' He gave his word. They

arranged the time and the price, and the next day my father seized
his palette and brushes and went to him. The high courtyard, the
dogs, the iron doors and bars, the arched windows, the coffers
covered with strange carpets, and, finally, the extraordinary host
himself, who sat motionless before him—all this made a strange
impression on him. The windows, as if by design, were blocked up
and encumbered below, so that light came only from above. 'Devil
take it, how well his face is lighted now!' he said to himself, and he
began to paint greedily, as if fearing that the fortunate lighting
might somehow disappear. 'What force!' he repeated to himself. 'If
I depict him even half the way he is now, he'll kill all my saints and
angels; they'll pale beside him. What diabolical force! He'll simply
leap out of my canvas if I'm the least bit faithful to nature. What
extraordinary features!' he constantly repeated, his zeal increasing,
and he could already see certain features beginning to come over
on canvas. But the closer he came to them, the more he felt some
heavy, anxious feeling, incomprehensible to himself. However,
despite that, he resolved to pursue every inconspicuous trait and
expression with literal precision. First of all he set to work on the
eyes. There was so much power in those eyes that it seemed impossible even to think of conveying them exactly as they were in
nature. However, he determined at all costs to search out the least
detail and nuance in them, to grasp their mystery . . . But as soon
as he began to penetrate and delve into them with his brush, there
arose such a strange revulsion in his soul, such inexplicable distress,
that he had to lay his brush aside for a time and then begin again.
In the end he could no longer endure it, he felt that these eyes had
pierced his soul and produced an inconceivable anxiety in it. The
next day, and the third, it became still stronger. He felt frightened.
He threw down his brush and declared flatly that he was no longer
able to paint him. You should have seen the change these words
produced in the strange moneylender. He fell at his feet and
beseeched him to finish the portrait, saying that his fate and his
existence in the world depended on it, that he had already touched
his living features with his brush, and that if he conveyed them
faithfully, his life by some supernatural force would be retained in
the portrait, that through it he would not die entirely, and that he

had to be present in the world. My father felt horrified by these words: they seemed so strange and frightening to him that he threw down both brushes and palette and rushed headlong from the room.

"The thought of it troubled him all day and all night, and in the morning he received the portrait from the moneylender, brought by some woman, the only being in his service, who announced straight away that her master did not want the portrait, would pay nothing for it, and was sending it back. In the evening of the same day, he learned that the moneylender had died and was to be buried by the rites of his own religion. All this seemed inexplicably strange to him. And after that a perceptible change occurred in his character: he felt himself in an uneasy state of anxiety, the cause of which he could not understand, and soon he did something no one would have expected of him. For some time, the works of one of his pupils had begun to attract the attention of a small circle of experts and amateurs. My father had always seen talent in him and was particularly well-disposed toward him for that. Suddenly he became jealous of him. General concern and talk about the young man became unbearable to him. Finally, to crown his vexation, he found out that his pupil had been invited to do the pictures for a rich, newly constructed church. This made him explode. 'No, I won't let that greenhorn triumph!' he said. 'It's too early, brother, for you to be shoving old men into the ditch! I'm still strong, thank God. We'll see who shoves whom.' And this straightforward, honorable man turned to intrigue and scheming, something he had previously always scorned; he succeeded, finally, in having a competition for the pictures announced, and other painters could also enter their works in it. After that he shut himself in his room and ardently took up his brush. It seemed he wanted to put his whole strength, his whole self into it. And, indeed, it turned out to be one of his best works. No one doubted that he would take first place. The paintings were exhibited, and beside it all the others were as night to day. Then suddenly one of the members present, a clergyman if I'm not mistaken, made an observation that struck everyone. 'There is, indeed, much talent in the artist's picture,' he said, 'but there is no holiness in the faces;

there is, on the contrary, something demonic in the eyes, as if the painter's hand was guided by an unclean feeling.' Everyone looked and could not but be convinced of the truth of these words. My father rushed up to his picture, as if to verify this offensive observation, and saw with horror that he had given almost all the figures the moneylender's eyes. Their gaze was so demonically destructive that he involuntarily shuddered. The picture was rejected, and he had to hear, to his indescribable vexation, the first place awarded to his pupil. It is impossible to describe the rage in which he returned home. He almost gave my mother a beating, chased the children away, broke all his brushes and his easel, snatched the portrait of the moneylender from the wall, asked for a knife, and ordered a fire made in the fireplace, intending to cut it to pieces and burn it. At that point he was found by a friend who came into the room, himself also a painter, a happy fellow, always pleased with himself, not carried away by any far-reaching desires, who worked happily at whatever came along and was even happier to get down to dining and carousing.

"'What are you doing? What are you going to burn?' he said, and went up to the portrait. 'Good heavens, it's one of your best works. It's that moneylender who died recently; but it's a most perfect thing. You simply got him, not between the eyes but right in them. No eyes have ever stared the way you've made them stare.'

"'And now I'll see how they stare in the fire,' said my father, making a move to hurl it into the fireplace.

"'Stop, for God's sake!' said the friend, holding him back. 'Better give it to me, if you find it such an eyesore.'

"My father resisted at first, but finally consented, and the happy fellow, extremely pleased with his acquisition, took the portrait home.

"After he left, my father suddenly felt himself more at ease. Just as if, along with the portrait, a burden had fallen from his soul. He was amazed himself at his wicked feeling, his envy, and the obvious change in his character. Having considered his behavior, he was saddened at heart and said, not without inner grief:

"'No, it is God punishing me. My painting deserved to suffer disgrace. It was intended to destroy my brother. The demonic feel-

ing of envy guided my brush, and demonic feeling was bound to
be reflected in it.'

"He immediately went to look for his former pupil, embraced
him warmly, asked his forgiveness, and tried his best to smooth
over his guilt before him. His work again went on as serenely as
before; but pensiveness now showed more often on his face. He
prayed more, was more often taciturn, and did not speak so sharply
about people; the external roughness of his character somehow
softened. Soon one circumstance shook him still more. He had not
seen the friend who had begged the portrait from him for a long
time. He was just about to go and see him when the man suddenly
walked into his room unexpectedly. After a few words and questions on both sides, he said:

"'Well, brother, you weren't wrong to want to burn the portrait. Devil take it, there's something strange in it . . . I don't
believe in witches, but like it or not, there's some unclean power
sitting in it . . .'

"'Meaning what?' said my father.

"'Meaning that once I hung it in my room, I felt such anguish
as if I wanted to put a knife in somebody. Never in my whole life
have I known what insomnia is, and now I had not only insomnia
but such dreams . . . I myself can't tell whether they were dreams
or something else—as if some evil spirit was strangling me—and
the accursed old man kept appearing in them. In short, I can't tell
you what a state I was in. Nothing like it has ever happened to me.
I wandered about like a lunatic all those days. I kept feeling some
kind of fear, expecting something unpleasant. I felt I couldn't say a
cheerful and sincere word to anybody: just as if some sort of spy
was sitting next to me. And it was only when I gave the portrait to
my nephew, who asked for it himself, that I suddenly felt as if a
weight had fallen from my shoulders: I suddenly felt cheerful, as
you see me now. Well, brother, you cooked up quite a devil!'

"My father listened to the story all the while with undivided
attention, and finally said:

"'And the portrait is now with your nephew?'

"'My nephew, hah! He couldn't stand it,' the cheerful fellow
said. 'The moneylender's very soul must have transmigrated into it:

he jumps out of the frame, walks around the room; and what my nephew tells, the mind simply can't grasp. I'd have taken him for a madman if I hadn't experienced some of it myself. He, too, sold it to some art collector, but that one couldn't bear it either and also unloaded it on somebody.'

"This story made a strong impression on my father. He fell to pondering seriously, lapsed into hypochondria, and in the end became fully convinced that his brush had served as a tool of the devil, that part of the moneylender's life had indeed passed somehow into the portrait and was now troubling people, inspiring them with demonic impulses, seducing the artist from his path, generating terrible torments of envy, and so on and so forth. Three misfortunes which befell him after that, three sudden deaths— his wife's, his daughter's, and his young son's—he considered as heaven's punishment of him, and he was absolutely resolved to leave this world. As soon as I turned nine, he enrolled me in the Academy of Art and, after paying off his creditors, withdrew to an isolated monastery, where he was soon tonsured a monk. There he amazed all the brothers by his strictness of life and unremitting observance of all monastery rules. The superior of the monastery, learning of his skill with the brush, requested that he paint the central icon in the church. But the humble brother said flatly that he was unworthy to take up his brush, that it had been defiled, that he would have to purify his soul with labors and great sacrifices before he would be worthy of setting about such a task. They did not wish to force him. He increased the strictness of monastery life for himself as far as possible. Finally even that became insufficient and not strict enough for him. With the blessing of his superior, he withdrew to the wilderness in order to be completely alone. There he built himself a hut out of branches, ate nothing but raw roots, dragged stones on his back from one place to another, stood in one place from dawn till sunset with his arms raised to heaven, ceaselessly reciting prayers. In short, he seemed to seek out all possible degrees of endurance and that inconceivable self-denial of which examples may be found only in the lives of the saints. Thus for a long time, over the course of several years, he exhausted his body, strengthening it at the same time with the vivifying power of prayer. Finally one day he came to the monastery and said firmly to the superior, 'Now I am ready. God willing, I will accomplish my work.' The subject he chose was the Nativity of Jesus. For a whole year he sat over it without leaving his cell, barely sustaining himself with strict fare, praying ceaselessly. At the end of a year, the picture was ready. It was indeed a miracle of the brush. You should know that neither the brothers nor the superior had much knowledge of painting, but everyone was struck by the extraordinary holiness of the figures; the feeling of divine humility and meekness in the face of the most pure Mother leaning over the Child, the profound intelligence in the eyes of the divine Child, as if they already perceived something in the distance, the solemn silence of the kings, struck by the divine wonder and prostrate at his feet, and, finally, the holy, inexpressible silence enveloping the whole picture—all this was expressed with such harmonious force and power of beauty that it produced a magical impression. The brothers all fell on their knees before the new icon, and the superior, moved to tenderness, said, 'No, it is not possible for a man, with the aid of human art only, to produce such a picture. A higher, holy power guided your brush, and the blessing of heaven rests on your work.'

"Just then I finished my studies at the Academy, was given a gold medal and along with it the joyous hope of going to Italy—the best of dreams for a twenty-year-old painter. It only remained for me to bid farewell to my father, from whom I had parted twelve years earlier. I confess, even his very image had long since vanished from my memory. I had heard something about the strict holiness of his life and imagined beforehand meeting a hermit with a hard appearance, alien to everything in the world except his cell and his prayer, wasted away, dried up with eternal watching and fasting. What was my astonishment when there stood before me a beautiful, almost divine elder! No traces of exhaustion were to be seen on his face; it shone with the brightness of heavenly joy. A beard white as snow and fine, almost ethereal hair of the same silvery color flowed picturesquely down his breast and the folds of his black cassock, falling to the very rope tied around his poor monastic garb; but the most amazing thing for me was to hear from his lips such words and thoughts about art as, I confess, I shall long bear in my soul, and I wish sincerely that every brother of mine could do likewise.

"'I have been waiting for you, my son,' he said when I approached to receive his blessing. 'The path which your life will henceforth follow lies before you. This path is pure, do not deviate from it. You have talent, and talent is God's most precious gift—do not ruin it. Seek, study everything you see, submit everything to your brush, but learn to find the inner thought in everything, and try most of all to comprehend the lofty mystery of creation. Blessed is the chosen one who possesses it. No subject in nature is low for him. In the lowly the artist-creator is as great as he is in the great; for him the contemptible is no longer contemptible, for the beautiful soul of the creator shines invisibly through it, and the contemptible is given lofty expression, for it has passed through the purgatory of his soul. For man, art contains a hint of the divine, heavenly paradise, and this alone makes it higher than all else. As solemn peace is higher than all worldly trouble; as creation is higher than destruction; as an angel in the pure innocence of his bright soul is higher than all the innumerable powers and proud passions of Satan—so is a lofty artistic creation higher than anything that exists in the world. Give all in sacrifice to it and love it with all your passion. Not passion that breathes of earthly lust, but quiet, heavenly passion, without which man is powerless to rise above the earth and is unable to give the wondrous sounds of peace. For artistic creation comes down to earth to pacify and reconcile all people. It cannot instill murmuring in the soul, but in the sound of prayer strives eternally toward God. But there are moments, dark moments . . .'

"He paused, and I noticed that his bright countenance suddenly darkened, as if some momentary cloud passed over it.

"'There was one event in my life,' he said. 'To this day I cannot understand what that strange image was whose portrait I painted. It was exactly like some diabolical phenomenon. I know the world rejects the existence of the devil, and therefore I will not speak of him. I will say only that I painted it with loathing, that I felt no love for my work at the time. I wanted forcefully to subject myself and to be faithful to nature, soullessly, having stifled everything. It was not a work of art, and therefore the feelings that overcome people as they look at it are stormy, troubling feelings—not the feelings of an artist, for an artist breathes peace even in the midst of trouble. I have been told that this portrait keeps changing hands and spreading its tormenting impressions, producing feelings of envy in an artist, a dark hatred for his brother, a spiteful yearning to persecute and oppress. May the Most High preserve you from such passions! Nothing is more terrible than they. Better to endure all the bitterness of possible persecution than cause even a shadow of persecution for someone else. Save the purity of your soul. He who has talent in him must be purer in soul than anyone else. Another will be forgiven much, but to him it will not be forgiven. A man who leaves the house in bright, festive clothes needs only one drop of mud splashed from under a wheel, and people all surround him, point their fingers at him, and talk about his slovenliness, while the same people ignore many spots on other passers-by who are wearing everyday clothes. For on everyday clothes the spots do not show.'

"He blessed me and embraced me. Never in my life had I been so sublimely moved. With veneration rather than filial feeling, I leaned on his breast and kissed his flowing silver hair. A tear glistened in his eye.

"'My son, fulfill one request for me,' he said at the very moment of parting. 'Perhaps you will chance to see somewhere the portrait of which I have spoken. You will recognize it at once by its extraordinary eyes and their unnatural expression. Destroy it at all costs . . .'

"You may judge for yourselves, how could I not promise to fulfill it faithfully? For all of fifteen years, I have never chanced to come across anything the least bit like the description given by my father, but now, suddenly, at this auction . . ."

Here, before finishing what he was saying, the painter turned his eyes to the wall in order to look at the portrait again. The whole crowd of his listeners instantly made the same movement, seeking the extraordinary portrait with their eyes. But to their great astonishment, it was no longer on the wall. A vague stir and murmuring went through the crowd, and after that the word "Stolen!" was clearly heard. Someone had managed to take it, seeing that the listeners' attention had been carried away by the story. And for a long time all those present remained perplexed, not knowing whether they had indeed seen those extraordinary eyes or it had merely been a dream, imagined just for an instant, by their eyes weary from the long examination of old paintings.

THE OVERCOAT

IN THE DEPARTMENT of . . . but it would be better not to say in which department. There is nothing more irascible than all these departments, regiments, offices—in short, all this officialdom. Nowadays every private individual considers the whole of society insulted in his person. They say a petition came quite recently from some police chief, I don't remember of what town, in which he states clearly that the government's decrees are perishing and his own sacred name is decidedly being taken in vain. And as proof he attached to his petition a most enormous tome of some novelistic work in which a police chief appears on every tenth page, in some places even in a totally drunken state. And so, to avoid any unpleasantness, it would be better to call the department in question *a certain department*. And so, *in a certain department there served a certain clerk*; a not very remarkable clerk, one might say—short, somewhat pockmarked, somewhat red-haired, even with a somewhat nearsighted look, slightly bald in front, with wrinkles on both cheeks and a complexion that is known as hemorrhoidal . . . No help for it! the Petersburg climate is to blame. As for his rank (for with us rank must be announced first of all), he was what is called an eternal titular councillor, at whom, as is known, all sorts of writers have abundantly sneered and jeered, having the praiseworthy custom of exerting themselves against those who can't bite. The clerk's last name was Bashmachkin. From the name itself one can already see that it once came from *bashmak,* or "shoe"; but when, at what time, and in what way it came from *bashmak*—none of that is known. His father, his grandfather, even his brother-in-law, and absolutely all the Bashmachkins, went around in boots, merely having them resoled three times a year. His name was Akaky Akakievich. The reader will perhaps find that somewhat strange and farfetched, but he can be assured that it was not fetched at all, but that such circumstances occurred of themselves as made it quite impossible to give him any other name, and here is precisely how it came about.

Akaky Akakievich was born, if memory serves me, during the night of the twenty-third of March. His late mother, a clerk's widow and a very good woman, decided, as was fitting, to have the baby baptized. The mother was still lying in bed opposite the door, and to her right stood the godfather, a most excellent man, Ivan Ivanovich Yeroshkin, who served as a chief clerk in the Senate,[1] and the godmother, the wife of a police officer, a woman of rare virtue, Arina Semyonovna Belobriushkova. The new mother was offered a choice of any of three names, whichever she wished to choose: Mokky, Sossy, or to name the baby after the martyr Khozdazat. "No," thought the late woman, "what sort of names are those?" To please her, they opened the calendar[2] to another place; again three names came out: Trifily, Dula, and Varakhasy. "What a punishment," the old woman said. "Such names, really, I've never heard the like. If only it were Varadat or Varukh, not Trifily and Varakhasy." They turned another page: out came Pavsikakhy and Vakhtisy. "Well, I see now," the old woman said, "it's evidently his fate. If so, better let him be named after his father. His father was Akaky, so let the son also be Akaky." Thus it was that Akaky Akakievich came about. As the child was being baptized, he cried and made such a face as if he anticipated that he would be a titular councillor. And so, that is how it all came about. We have told it so that the reader could see for himself that it happened entirely from necessity and that to give him any other name was quite impossible.

When and at what time he entered the department and who appointed him, no one could recall. However many directors and other superiors came and went, he was always to be seen in one and the same place, in the same position, in the same capacity, as the same copying clerk, so that after a while they became convinced that he must simply have been born into the world ready-made, in a uniform, and with a balding head. In the department he was shown no respect at all. The caretakers not only did not rise from their places when he passed, but did not even look at him, as if a mere fly had flown through the reception room. His superiors treated him somehow with cold despotism. Some chief clerk's assistant simply shoved papers under his nose without even saying "Copy them," or "Here's a nice, interesting little case," or something pleasant, as is customary in well-bred offices. And he took them, looking only at the papers, without regarding the one who put them there or whether he had the right to do so. He took them and immediately settled down to copying them. The young clerks poked fun at him and cracked jokes, to the extent that office wit allowed; told right in front of him various stories they had made up about him, about his landlady, a seventy-year-old crone, saying that she beat him, asking when their wedding was to be, dumping torn-up paper over his head and calling it snow. But not one word of response came from Akaky Akakievich, as if no one was there; it did not even affect the work he did: amidst all this pestering, he made not a single error in his copy. Only when the joke was really unbearable, when they jostled his arm, interfering with what he was doing, would he say, "Let me be. Why do you offend me?" And there was something strange in the words and in the voice in which they were uttered. Something sounded in it so conducive to pity that one recently appointed young man who, following the example of the others, had first allowed himself to make fun of him, suddenly stopped as if transfixed, and from then on everything seemed changed before him and acquired a different look. Some unnatural power pushed him away from his comrades, whose acquaintance he had made thinking them decent, well-mannered men. And long afterwards, in moments of the greatest merriment, there would rise before him the figure of the little clerk with the balding brow, uttering his penetrating words: "Let me be. Why do you offend me?"—and in these penetrating words rang other words: "I am your brother." And the poor young man would bury his face in his hands, and many a time in his life he shuddered to see how much inhumanity there is in man, how much savage coarseness is concealed in refined, cultivated manners, and God! even in a man the world regards as noble and honorable . . .

It would hardly be possible to find a man who lived so much in his work. It is not enough to say he served zealously—no, he served with love. There, in that copying, he saw some varied and pleasant world of his own. Delight showed in his face; certain letters were his favorites, and when he came to one of them, he was beside himself: he chuckled and winked and helped out with his lips, so that it seemed one could read on his face every letter his pen traced. If his zeal had been rewarded correspondingly, he might, to his own amazement, have gone as far as state councillor; yet his reward, as his witty comrades put it, was a feather in his hat and hemorrhoids where he sat. However, it was impossible to say he went entirely unnoticed. One director, being a kindly man and wishing to reward him for long service, ordered that he be given something more important than the usual copying—namely, he was told to change an already existing document into a letter to another institution; the matter consisted merely in changing the heading and changing some verbs from first to third person. This was such a task for him that he got all in a sweat, rubbed his forehead, and finally said, "No, better let me copy something." After that he was left copying forever. Outside this copying nothing seemed to exist for him. He gave no thought to his clothes at all: his uniform was not green but of some mealy orange. The collar he wore was narrow, low, so that though his neck was not long, it looked extraordinarily long protruding from this collar, as with those head-wagging plaster kittens that foreign peddlers carry about by the dozen on their heads. And there was always something stuck to his uniform: a wisp of straw or a bit of thread; moreover, he had a special knack, as he walked in the street, of getting under a window at the precise moment when some sort of trash was being thrown out of it, and, as a result, he was eternally carrying around melon or watermelon rinds and other such rubbish on his hat. Not once in his life did he ever pay attention to what was going on or happening every day in the street, which, as is known, his young fellow clerk always looks at, his pert gaze so keen that he even notices when someone on the other side of the street has the footstrap of his trousers come undone—which always provokes a sly smile on his face.

But Akaky Akakievich, even if he looked at something, saw in everything his own neat lines, written in an even hand, and only when a horse's muzzle, coming out of nowhere, placed itself on his shoulder and blew real wind from its nostrils onto his cheek— only then would he notice that he was not in the middle of a line, but rather in the middle of the street. Coming home, he would sit down straight away at the table, hastily slurp up his cabbage soup and eat a piece of beef with onions, without ever noticing their taste, and he would eat it all with flies and whatever else God sent him at the time. Noticing that his stomach was full, he would get up from the table, take out a bottle of ink, and copy documents he had brought home. If there chanced to be none, he made copies especially for his own pleasure, particularly if the document was distinguished not by the beauty of its style but by its being addressed to some new or important person.

Even in those hours when the gray Petersburg sky fades completely and all clerical folk have eaten their fill and finished dinner, each as he could, according to his salary and his personal fancy— when all have rested after the departmental scratching of pens, the rushing about seeing to their own and other people's needful occupations, and all that irrepressible man heaps voluntarily on himself even more than is necessary—when clerks hasten to give the remaining time to pleasure: the more ambitious rushing to the theater; another going out to devote it to gazing at silly hats; another to a party, to spend it paying compliments to some pretty girl, the star of a small clerical circle; still another, and this happens most often, simply going to his own kind, to some fourth or third floor, two small rooms with a front hall and a kitchen, with some claim to fashion, a lamp or other object that cost great sacrifices, the giving up of dinners, outings—in short, even at that time when all clerks disperse to their friends' small apartments to play cutthroat whist, sipping tea from glasses, with one-kopeck rusks, puffing smoke through long chibouks, repeating while the cards are being dealt some gossip blown over from high society, something a Russian man can never give up under any circumstances, or even, when there is nothing to talk about, retelling the eternal joke about the commandant who was brought word that the horse of Falconet's monument[3] had had its tail docked—in short, even when everything strives for diversion—Akaky Akakievich did not give himself up to any diversion. No one could say he had ever been seen at any party. When he had written his fill, he would go to bed, smiling beforehand at the thought of the next day: What would God send him to copy tomorrow? So flowed the peaceful life of this man who, with a salary of four hundred, was able to content himself with his lot, and so it might have flowed on into extreme old age, had it not been for the various calamities strewn along the path of life, not only of titular, but even of privy, actual, court, and other councillors, even of those who neither give counsel nor take any themselves.

There exists in Petersburg a powerful enemy of all who earn a salary of four hundred roubles or thereabouts. This enemy is none other than our northern frost, though, incidentally, people say it is very healthful. Toward nine o'clock in the morning, precisely the hour when the streets are covered with people going to their offices, it starts dealing such strong and sharp flicks to all noses indiscriminately that the poor clerks decidedly do not know where to put them. At that time, when even those who occupy high positions have an ache in their foreheads from the cold and tears come to their eyes, poor titular councillors are sometimes defenseless. The whole of salvation consists in running as quickly as possible, in your skimpy overcoat, across five or six streets and then standing in the porter's lodge, stamping your feet good and hard, thereby thawing out all your job-performing gifts and abilities, which had become frozen on the way. Akaky Akakievich had for a certain time begun to feel that he was somehow getting it especially in the back and shoulder, though he tried to run across his allotted space as quickly as possible. He thought finally that the sin might perhaps lie with his overcoat. Examining it well at home, he discovered that in two or three places—namely, on the back and shoulders—it had become just like burlap; the broadcloth was so worn out that it was threadbare, and the lining had fallen to pieces. It should be known that Akaky Akakievich's overcoat also served as an object of mockery for the clerks; they even deprived it of the noble name of overcoat and called it a housecoat. Indeed, it was somehow strangely constituted: its collar diminished more and more each year, for it went to mend other parts. The mending did not testify to any skill in the tailor, and the results were in fact crude and unsightly. Seeing what the situation was, Akaky Akakievich decided that the overcoat had to be taken to Petrovich the tailor, who lived somewhere on a fourth floor, up a back entrance, and who, in spite of his blind eye and the pockmarks all over his face, performed the mending of clerkly and all other trousers and tailcoats quite successfully—to be sure, when he was sober and not entertaining any other projects in his head. Of this tailor, of course, not much should be said, but since there exists a rule that the character of every person in a story be well delineated, there's no help for it, let us have Petrovich here as well. In the beginning he was simply called Grigory and was some squire's serf; he began to be called Petrovich when he was freed and started drinking rather heavily on feast days—first on great feasts, and then on all church feasts indiscriminately, wherever a little cross appeared on the calendar. In this respect he was true to the customs of his forebears and, in arguing with his wife, used to call her a worldly woman and a German.[4] Now that we've mentioned the wife, we ought to say a couple of words about her as well; but, unfortunately, not much is known about her, except that Petrovich had a wife, and that she even wore a bonnet, not a kerchief; but it seems she could not boast of her beauty; at least, when meeting her, only guardsmen looked under her bonnet, winking their mustaches and emitting some special noise.

Climbing the stairway leading to Petrovich, which, to do it justice, was all dressed with water and swill, and redolent throughout of that spiritous smell that makes the eyes smart and is inevitably present in all back stairways of Petersburg houses—climbing the stairway, Akaky Akakievich was thinking about how much Petrovich would ask, and mentally decided not to pay more than two roubles. The door was open, because the mistress of the house, while cooking fish, had filled the kitchen with so much smoke that even the cockroaches themselves could no longer be seen. Akaky Akakievich passed through the kitchen, unnoticed even by the mistress herself, and finally went into the room, where he saw Petrovich sitting on a wide, unpainted wooden table, his legs tucked under him like a Turkish pasha's. His feet, after the custom of tailors sitting over their work, were bare. The eye was struck first of all by his big toe, very familiar to Akaky Akakievich, with a somehow disfigured nail, thick and strong as tortoise shell. From Petrovich's neck hung a skein of silk and thread, and on his knees lay some rag. He had already spent three minutes trying to put a thread through the eye of a needle and missing, and therefore he was very angry with the darkness and even with the thread itself, grumbling under his breath, "Won't go through, the barbarian! Get the better of me, you rascal!" Akaky Akakievich was upset that he had come precisely at a moment when Petrovich was angry: he liked dealing with Petrovich when the latter was already a bit under the influence, or, as his wife used to put it, "got himself tight on rotgut, the one-eyed devil." In that condition, Petrovich usually gave in and agreed very willingly, and even bowed and thanked him each time. Later, it's true, his wife would come, lamenting that her husband had been drunk and had asked too little; but a ten-kopeck piece would be added, and the deal was in the hat. Now, however, Petrovich seemed to be in a sober state, and therefore tough, intractable, and liable to demand devil knows what price. Akaky Akakievich grasped that fact and was, as they say, about to backtrack, but the thing was already under way. Petrovich squinted at him very intently with his only eye, and Akaky Akakievich involuntarily said:

"Good day, Petrovich!"

"Good day to you, sir," said Petrovich, and cocked his eye at Akaky Akakievich's hands, trying to see what sort of booty he was bringing.

"I've come to you, Petrovich, sort of . . ."

It should be known that Akaky Akakievich expressed himself mostly with prepositions, adverbs, and finally such particles as have decidedly no meaning. If the matter was very difficult, he even had the habit of not finishing the phrase at all, so that very often he would begin his speech with the words "That, really, is altogether sort of . . ." after which would come nothing, and he himself would forget it, thinking everything had been said.

"What's this?" said Petrovich, at the same time giving his uniform a thorough inspection with his only eye, beginning with the collar, then the sleeves, back, skirts, and buttonholes—all of which was quite familiar to him, since it was his own handiwork. Such is the custom among tailors: it's the first thing they do when they meet someone.

"And I've come, Petrovich, sort of . . . this overcoat, the broadcloth . . . you see, in all other places it's quite strong, it got a bit dusty and so it seems as if it's old, but it's new, only in one place it's a bit sort of . . . on the back, and here on one shoulder it's a bit worn, and on this shoulder a little bit—you see, that's all. Not much work . . ."

Petrovich took the housecoat, laid it out on the table first, examined it for a long time, shook his head, and reached his hand out to the windowsill to get his round snuffbox with the portrait of some general on it—which one is not known, because the place where the face was had been poked through by a finger and then pasted over with a rectangular piece of paper. Having taken a pinch, Petrovich stretched the housecoat on his hands and examined it against the light and again shook his head. Then he turned it inside out and shook his head once more, once more opened the lid with the general pasted over with paper, and, having filled his nose with snuff, closed the box, put it away, and finally said:

"No, impossible to fix it—bad wardrobe."

At these words, Akaky Akakievich's heart missed a beat.

"Why impossible, Petrovich?" he said, almost in a child's pleading voice. "It's only a bit worn on the shoulders—surely you have some little scraps . . ."

"Little scraps might be found, we might find some little scraps," said Petrovich, "but it's impossible to sew them on—the stuff's quite rotten, touch it with a needle and it falls apart."

"Falls apart, and you patch it over."

"But there's nothing to put a patch on, nothing for it to hold to, it's too worn out. They pass it off as broadcloth, but the wind blows and it flies to pieces."

"Well, you can make it hold. Otherwise, really, it's sort of . . . !"

"No," Petrovich said resolutely, "it's impossible to do anything. The stuff's no good. You'd better make yourself foot cloths out of it when the winter cold comes, because socks don't keep you warm. It's Germans invented them so as to earn more money for themselves." (Petrovich liked needling the Germans on occasion.) "And it appears you'll have to have a new overcoat made."

At the word "new" all went dim in Akaky Akakievich's eyes, and everything in the room became tangled before him. The only thing he saw clearly was the general with paper pasted over his face who was on the lid of Petrovich's snuffbox.

"How's that—new?" he said, still as if in sleep. "I have no money for that."

"Yes, new," Petrovich said with barbaric calm.

"Well, if it must be a new one, what would it, sort of . . ."

"You mean, how much would it cost?"

"Yes."

"Three times fifty and then some would have to go into it," Petrovich said and pressed his lips together meaningfully. He very much liked strong effects, liked somehow to confound one completely all of a sudden and then glance sideways at the face the confounded one pulls at such words.

"A hundred and fifty roubles for an overcoat?" poor Akaky Akakievich cried out—cried out, perhaps, for the first time in all his born days, for he was always distinguished by the softness of his voice.

"Yes, sir," said Petrovich, "depending also on the overcoat. If we put a marten on the collar, plus a hood with silk lining, it may come to two hundred."

"Please, Petrovich," Akaky Akakievich said in a pleading voice, not hearing and not trying to hear all Petrovich's words and effects, "fix it somehow, so that it can serve a while longer at least."

"Ah, no, that'll be work gone for naught and money wasted," said Petrovich, and after these words Akaky Akakievich left, totally annihilated.

And Petrovich, on his departure, stood for a long time, his lips pressed together meaningfully, without going back to work, feeling pleased that he had not lowered himself or betrayed the art of tailoring.

When he went outside, Akaky Akakievich was as if in a dream. "So it's that, that's what it is," he said to himself. "I really didn't think it would come out sort of . . ." and then, after some silence, he added, "So that's how it is! that's what finally comes out! and I really never would have supposed it would be so." Following that, a long silence again ensued, after which he said, "So that's it! Such an, indeed, altogether unexpected, sort of . . . it's altogether . . . such a circumstance!" Having said this, instead of going home, he went in the entirely opposite direction, without suspecting it himself. On the way, a chimney sweep brushed against him with his whole dirty flank, blackening his whole shoulder; a full hat-load of lime poured down on him from the top of a house under construction. He did not notice any of it, and only later, when he ran into an on-duty policeman who, having set aside his halberd, was shaking snuff from his snuff bottle onto his callused fist, only then did he recover his senses slightly, and that only because the policeman said, "What're you doing, barging into my mug! Don't you have enough sidewalk?" This made him look around and turn back home. Only here did he begin to collect his thoughts, see his situation clearly for what it was, and start talking to himself, not in snatches now but sensibly and frankly, as with a reasonable friend with whom one could discuss the most heartfelt and intimate things. "Ah, no," said Akaky Akakievich, "it's impossible to talk with Petrovich now: now he's sort of . . . his wife must somehow have given him a beating. I'll do better to come to him on Sunday morning: he'll be cockeyed and sleepy after Saturday night, and he'll need the hair of the dog, and his wife won't give him any money, and just then I'll sort of . . . ten kopecks in his hand, he'll be more tractable then, and then the overcoat sort of . . ." So Akaky Akakievich reasoned with himself, encouraged himself, and waited for the next Sunday, when, seeing from afar Petrovich's wife leave the house for somewhere, he went straight to him. Petrovich was indeed badly cockeyed after Saturday, could hardly hold his head up, and was quite sleepy; but for all that, as soon as he learned what it was about, it was as if the devil gave him a nudge. "Impossible," he said, "be so good as to order a new one." Here Akaky Akakievich gave him a ten-kopeck piece. "Thank you, sir, I'll fortify myself a bit for your health," said Petrovich, "but concerning the overcoat, please don't trouble yourself—it's no good for anything good. I'll make you a new overcoat, I'll do it up famously, that I will."

Akaky Akakievich tried to mention mending again, but Petrovich did not listen to the end and said, "I'll make you a new one without fail, please count on me for that, I'll do my best. It may even be in today's fashion, the collar fastened by little silver clasps with appliqué."

Here Akaky Akakievich saw that he could not get around a new overcoat, and his spirits wilted completely. How, indeed, with what, with what money to make it? Of course, he could count partly on his future holiday bonus, but that money had been placed and distributed long ago. He needed to get new trousers, to pay an old debt to the shoemaker for putting new vamps on his old boot tops, and he had to order three shirts from the seamstress and a couple of pairs of that item of underwear which it is indecent to mention in print—in short, absolutely all the money was to be spent; and even if the director was so gracious as to allot him a forty-five- or fifty-rouble bonus, instead of forty, all the same only a trifle would be left, which in the overcoat capital would be like a drop in the ocean. Though he knew, of course, that Petrovich had a trick of suddenly asking devil knows how incongruously high a price, so that his own wife sometimes could not keep herself from exclaiming, "Have you lost your mind, fool that you are! One day he takes a job for nothing, and now the evil one gets him to ask more than he's worth himself." Though he knew, of course, that Petrovich would agree to do it for eighty roubles—even so, where to get the eighty roubles? Now, it might be possible to find half; half could be produced; maybe even a little more; but where to get the other half? . . . But first the reader should learn where the one half would come from. Akaky Akakievich was in the habit of setting aside a half kopeck for every rouble he spent, putting it into a little box with a lock and key and a small hole cut in the lid for dropping money through. At the end of every half year he inspected the accumulated sum of copper and exchanged it for small silver. Thus he continued for a long time, and in this way, over the course of several years, he turned out to have saved a total of more than forty roubles. And so, one half was in hand; but where to get the other half? Where to get the other forty roubles? Akaky Akakievich thought and thought and decided that he would have to cut down his usual expenses, at least for a year; to abolish the drinking of tea in the evening, to burn no candles in the evening, and if there was a need to do something, to go to the landlady's room and work by her candle; to make the lightest and most careful steps possible when walking in the street, over cobbles and pavements, almost on tiptoe, thereby avoiding the rapid wearing out of soles; to send his linen to the laundry as seldom as possible, and to prevent soiling it by taking it off each time on coming home, remaining in a half-cotton dressing gown, a very old one, spared even by time itself. Truth to tell, it was a bit difficult for him at first to get used to such limitations, but later it somehow became a habit and went better; he even accustomed himself to going entirely without food in the evenings; but instead he was nourished spiritually, bearing in his thoughts the eternal idea of the future overcoat. From then on it was as if his very existence became somehow fuller, as if he were married, as if some other person were there with him, as if he were not alone but some pleasant life's companion had agreed to walk down the path of life with him—and this companion was none other than that same overcoat with its cotton-wool quilting, with its sturdy lining that knew no wear. He became somehow livelier, even firmer of character, like a man who has defined and set a goal for himself. Doubt, indecision—in short, all hesitant and uncertain features—disappeared of themselves from his face and actions. Fire occasionally showed in his eyes, the most bold and valiant thoughts even flashed in his head: Might he not indeed put a marten on the collar? These reflections led him nearly to distraction. Once, as he was copying a paper, he even nearly made a mistake, so that he cried "Oh!" almost aloud and crossed himself. In the course of each month, he stopped at least once to see Petrovich, to talk about the overcoat, where it was best to buy broadcloth, and of what color, and at what price, and he would return home somewhat preoccupied yet always pleased, thinking that the time would finally come when all this would be bought and the overcoat would be made. Things went even more quickly than he expected. Contrary to all expectations, the director allotted Akaky Akakievich not forty or forty-five but a whole sixty roubles; whether he sensed that Akaky Akakievich needed an overcoat, or it happened that way of itself, in any case he acquired on account of it an extra twenty roubles. This circumstance speeded the course of things. Another two or three months of going a bit hungry—and Akaky Akakievich had, indeed, about eighty roubles. His heart, generally quite calm, began to throb. The very next day he went shopping with Petrovich. They bought very good broadcloth—and no wonder, because they had begun thinking about it six months before and had hardly ever let a month go by without stopping at a shop and inquiring about prices; and Petrovich himself said that better broadcloth did not exist. For the lining they chose chintz, but of such good, sturdy quality that, according to Petrovich, it was even better than silk and looked more attractive and glossy. They did not buy a marten, because it was indeed expensive; but instead they chose a cat, the best they could find in the shop, a cat which from afar could always be taken for a marten. Petrovich fussed with the overcoat for a whole two weeks, because there was a lot of quilting to do; otherwise it would have been ready sooner. For his work,

Petrovich took twelve roubles—it simply couldn't have been less: decidedly everything was sewn with silk, in small double seams, and afterwards Petrovich went along each seam with his own teeth, imprinting it with various designs. It was . . . it's hard to say precisely which day, but it was probably the most festive day in Akaky Akakievich's life, when Petrovich finally brought the overcoat. He brought it in the morning, just before it was time to go to the office. At no other time could the overcoat have come so appropriately, because very bitter frosts were already setting in and, it seemed, were threatening to get still worse. Petrovich came with the overcoat as befits a good tailor. His face acquired a more important expression than Akaky Akakievich had ever seen before. It seemed he felt in full measure that he had done no small thing and had suddenly revealed in himself the abyss that separates tailors who only put in linings and do repairs from those who sew new things. He took the overcoat out of the handkerchief in which he had brought it; the handkerchief was fresh from the laundry, and he proceeded to fold it and put it in his pocket for further use. Having taken out the overcoat, he looked very proud and, holding it in both hands, threw it deftly around Akaky Akakievich's shoulders; then he pulled it down and straightened the back with his hands; then he draped it over Akaky Akakievich unbuttoned. Akaky Akakievich, being a man of a certain age, wanted to try the sleeves; Petrovich helped him on with the sleeves—it turned out that with the sleeves it was also good. In short, it appeared that the overcoat was just right and fitted perfectly. Petrovich did not miss the chance of saying that it was only because he lived without a shingle, on a small street, and, besides, had known Akaky Akakievich for a long time, that he was asking so little; that on Nevsky Prospect he would pay seventy-five roubles for the work alone. Akaky Akakievich did not want to discuss it with Petrovich, and besides was afraid of all those mighty sums with which Petrovich liked to blow smoke. He paid him, thanked him, and left for the office at once in the new overcoat. Petrovich followed him out and, standing in the street, went on for a long time looking at the overcoat in the distance, then went purposely to the side, so as to

make a detour down a crooked lane, run back out to the street
ahead of him, and thus look at his overcoat from the other direction—that is, straight in the face. Meanwhile, Akaky Akakievich
walked on in the most festive disposition of all his feelings. At each
instant of every minute he felt that there was a new overcoat on his
shoulders, and several times he even smiled from inner satisfaction.
In fact, there were two profits: one that it was warm, the other that
it was good. He did not notice the road at all and suddenly found
himself at the office; in the porter's lodge he took the overcoat off,
looked it all over, and entrusted it to the porter's special care. In
some unknown way everyone in the department suddenly learned
that Akaky Akakievich had a new overcoat and that the housecoat
no longer existed. Everyone immediately ran out to the porter's
lodge to look at Akaky Akakievich's new overcoat. They began
to congratulate him, to cheer him, so that at first he only smiled,
but then even became embarrassed. And when everyone accosted
him and began saying that they should drink to the new overcoat,
and that he should at least throw a party for them all, Akaky
Akakievich was completely at a loss, did not know what to do,
how to reply, or how to excuse himself from it. After several
minutes, blushing all over, he began assuring them quite simple-
heartedly that it was not a new overcoat at all, that it was just
so, that it was an old overcoat. Finally one of the clerks, even some
sort of assistant to the chief clerk, probably in order to show
that he was by no means a proud man and even kept company
with subordinates, said, "So be it, I'll throw a party instead of
Akaky Akakievich and invite everyone tonight for tea: today also
happens to be my name day." Naturally, the clerks straight away
congratulated the chief clerk's assistant and willingly accepted the
invitation. Akaky Akakievich tried to begin excusing himself, but
everyone started to say that it was impolite, that it was simply a
shame and a disgrace, and it was quite impossible for him not to
accept. Afterwards, however, he was pleased when he remembered
that he would thus even have occasion to take a stroll that evening
in his new overcoat. For Akaky Akakievich the whole of that day
was like the greatest festive holiday. He came home in the happiest

state of mind, took off his overcoat and hung it carefully on the wall, having once more admired the broadcloth and the lining, and then he purposely took out for comparison his former house-coat, completely fallen to pieces. He looked at it and even laughed himself: so far was the difference! And for a long time afterwards, over dinner, he kept smiling whenever he happened to think of the condition of his housecoat. He dined cheerfully and wrote nothing after dinner, no documents, but just played a bit of the Sybarite in his bed until it turned dark. Then, without tarrying, he got dressed, put on his overcoat, and left.

Precisely where the clerk who had invited him lived, we unfortunately cannot say: our memory is beginning to fail us badly, and whatever there is in Petersburg, all those houses and streets, has so mixed and merged together in our head that it is very hard to get anything out of it in a decent fashion. Be that as it may, it is at least certain that the clerk lived in a better part of town—meaning not very near to Akaky Akakievich. Akaky Akakievich had first to pass through some deserted, sparsely lit streets, but as he approached the clerk's home, the streets became livelier, more populous, and better lit. Pedestrians flashed by more frequently, ladies began to appear, beautifully dressed, some of the men wore beaver collars, there were fewer cabbies with their wooden-grill sleds studded with gilded nails—on the contrary, coachmen kept passing in raspberry-colored velvet hats, with lacquered sleds and bearskin rugs, or carriages with decorated boxes flew down the street, their wheels shrieking over the snow. Akaky Akakievich looked at it all as at something new. It was several years since he had gone out in the evening. He stopped curiously before a lighted shop window to look at a picture that portrayed some beautiful woman taking off her shoe and thus baring her whole leg, not a bad leg at all; and behind her back, from another room, some man stuck his head out, with side-whiskers and a handsome imperial under his lip. Akaky Akakievich shook his head and chuckled, and then went on his way. Why did he chuckle? Was it because he had encountered something totally unfamiliar, of which everyone nevertheless still preserves some sort of intuition; or had he thought, like many other clerks, as follows: "Well, these Frenchmen! what can you say,

if they want something sort of . . . it's really sort of . . ." But maybe
he didn't think even that—it's really impossible to get inside a
man's soul and learn all he thinks.

At last he reached the house where the chief clerk's assistant
lived. The chief clerk's assistant lived in grand style: the stairway
was lighted, the apartment was on the second floor. Entering the
front hall, Akaky Akakievich saw whole rows of galoshes on
the floor. Among them, in the middle of the room, a samovar
stood hissing and letting out clouds of steam. On the walls hung
overcoats and cloaks, some among them even with beaver collars
or velvet lapels. Behind the walls, noise and talk could be heard,
which suddenly became clear and loud as the door opened and a
lackey came out with a tray laden with empty glasses, a pitcher
of cream, and a basket of rusks. It was evident that the clerks had
gathered long ago and had already finished their first glass of tea.
Akaky Akakievich, having hung up his overcoat himself, went into
the room, and before him simultaneously flashed candles, clerks,
pipes, and card tables, while his hearing was struck vaguely by a
rush of conversation arising on all sides and the noise of chairs
being moved. He stopped quite awkwardly in the middle of the
room, looking about and trying to think what to do. But he was
already noticed, greeted with cries, and everyone went at once to
the front hall and again examined his overcoat. Akaky Akakievich
was somewhat embarrassed, yet being a pure-hearted man, he
could not help rejoicing to see how everyone praised his overcoat.
After that, naturally, everyone dropped both him and his overcoat
and turned, as usual, to the tables set up for whist. All of this—
the noise, the talk, the crowd of people—all of it was somehow
strange to Akaky Akakievich. He simply did not know what to do,
where to put his hands and feet, or his whole self; he finally sat
down with the players, looked at the cards, looked into the face of
one or another, and in a short while began to yawn, feeling himself
bored, the more so as it was long past the time when he customarily went to bed. He tried to take leave of the host, but the host
would not let him go, saying that they absolutely had to drink a
glass of champagne to the new coat. An hour later a supper was
served which consisted of mixed salad, cold veal, pâté, sweet pas-

try, and champagne. Akaky Akakievich was forced to drink two
glasses, after which he felt that the room had become merrier, yet
he was unable to forget that it was already midnight and long since
time to go home. So that the host should not somehow decide to
detain him, he quietly left the room, went to the front hall to find
his overcoat, which he saw, not without regret, lying on the floor,
shook it, cleaned every feather off it, put it over his shoulders,
went downstairs and outside. Outside it was still light. Some small-
goods shops, those permanent clubs for servants and various others, were open; those that were closed still showed a stream of light
the whole length of the door chink, indicating that they were not
yet devoid of company and that the housemaids and servants were
probably finishing their talks and discussions, while their masters
were thrown into utter perplexity as to their whereabouts. Akaky
Akakievich walked along in a merry state of mind, and even suddenly ran, for some unknown reason, after some lady who passed
by like lightning, every part of whose body was filled with extraordinary movement. However, he stopped straight away and again
walked very slowly, as before, marveling to himself at this spright-
liness of unknown origin. Soon there stretched before him those
deserted streets which even in the daytime are none too cheerful,
much less in the evening. Now they had become still more desolate and solitary: street lamps flashed less often—evidently the supply of oil was smaller; there were wooden houses, fences; not a
soul anywhere; only snow glittered in the streets, and sleepy low
hovels with closed shutters blackened mournfully. He approached
a place where the street was intersected by an endless square that
looked like a terrible desert, with houses barely visible on the
other side.

Far away, God knows where, a light flashed in some sentry box
that seemed to be standing at the edge of the world. Here Akaky
Akakievich's merriment somehow diminished considerably. He
entered the square not without some inadvertent fear, as if his
heart had a foreboding of something bad. He looked behind him
and to the sides: just like a sea all around him. "No, better not to
look," he thought and walked with closed eyes, and when he
opened them to see how far the end of the square was, he sud-

denly saw before him, almost in front of his nose, some mustached people, precisely what sort he could not even make out. His eyes grew dim, his heart pounded in his chest. "That overcoat's mine!" one of them said in a thundering voice, seizing him by the collar. Akaky Akakievich was about to shout "Help!" when the other one put a fist the size of a clerk's head right to his mouth and said, "Just try shouting!" Akaky Akakievich felt only that his overcoat was taken off him, he was given a kick with a knee and fell face down in the snow, and then felt no more. After a few minutes, he came to his senses and got to his feet, but no one was there. He felt it was cold in the field and the overcoat was gone; he began to shout, but his voice seemed never to reach the ends of the square. In desperation, shouting constantly, he started running across the square, straight to the sentry box, beside which stood an on-duty policeman, leaning on his halberd, watching with apparent curiosity, desirous of knowing why the devil a man was running toward him from far away and shouting. Akaky Akakievich, running up to him, began shouting in a breathless voice that he had been asleep, not on watch, and had not seen how a man was being robbed. The policeman replied that he had seen nothing; that he had seen him being stopped by two men in the middle of the square but had thought they were his friends; and that, instead of denouncing him for no reason, he should go to the inspector tomorrow and the inspector would find out who took the overcoat. Akaky Akakievich came running home in complete disorder: the hair that still grew in small quantities on his temples and the back of his head was completely disheveled; his side, chest, and trousers were covered with snow. The old woman, his landlady, hearing a terrible knocking at the door, hastily jumped out of bed and ran with one shoe on to open it, holding her nightgown to her breast out of modesty; but when she opened the door she stepped back, seeing what state Akaky Akakievich was in. When he told her what was the matter, she clasped her hands and said he must go straight to the superintendent, that the inspector would cheat him, make promises and then lead him by the nose; and that it was best to go to the superintendent, that he was a man of her acquaintance, because Anna, the Finnish woman who used to work for her as a cook, had now got herself hired at the superintendent's as a nanny, and that she often saw him herself as he drove past their house, and that he also came to church every Sunday, prayed, and at the same time looked cheerfully at everyone, and therefore was by all tokens a good man. Having listened to this decision, Akaky Akakievich plodded sadly to his room, and how he spent the night we will leave to the judgment of those capable of entering at least somewhat into another man's predicament.

Early in the morning he went to the superintendent but was told that he was asleep; he came at ten and again was told: asleep; he came at eleven o'clock and was told that the superintendent was not at home; at lunchtime the scriveners in the front room refused to let him in and insisted on knowing what his business was, what necessity had brought him there, and what had happened. So that finally, for once in his life, Akaky Akakievich decided to show some character and said flatly that he had to see the superintendent himself, in person, that they dared not refuse to admit him, that he had come from his department on official business, and that he would make a complaint about them and they would see. The scriveners did not dare to say anything against that, and one of them sent to call the superintendent. The superintendent took the story about the theft of the overcoat somehow extremely strangely. Instead of paying attention to the main point of the case, he began to question Akaky Akakievich—why was he coming home so late, and had he not stopped and spent some time in some indecent house?—so that Akaky Akakievich was completely embarrassed and left him not knowing whether the case of his overcoat would take its proper course or not. He did not go to the office all that day (the only time in his life). The next day he arrived all pale and in his old housecoat, which now looked still more lamentable. Though some of the clerks did not miss their chance to laugh at Akaky Akakievich even then, still the story of the theft of the overcoat moved many. They decided straight away to take up a collection for him, but they collected a mere trifle, because the clerks had already spent a lot, having subscribed to a portrait of the director and to some book, at the suggestion of the section chief, who was a friend of the author—and so, the sum turned out to be quite trifling. One of them, moved by compassion, decided at least to help Akaky Akakievich with good advice, telling him not to go to the police because, though it might happen that a policeman, wishing to gain the approval of his superior, would somehow find the overcoat, still the overcoat would remain with the police unless he could present legal proofs that it belonged to him; and the best thing would be to address a certain *important person,* so that the *important person,* by writing and referring to the proper quarters, could get things done more successfully. No help for it, Akaky Akakievich decided to go to the *important person.* What precisely the post of the *important person* was, and in what it consisted, remains unknown. It should be realized that this *certain important person* had become an important person only recently, and till then had been an unimportant person. However, his position even now was not considered important in comparison with other, still more important ones. But there will always be found a circle of people for whom something unimportant in the eyes of others is already important. He tried, however, to increase his importance by many other means—namely, he introduced the custom of lower clerks meeting him on the stairs when he came to the office; of no one daring to come to him directly, but everything going in the strictest order: a collegiate registrar should report to a provincial secretary, a provincial secretary to a titular or whatever else, and in this fashion the case should reach him. Thus everything in holy Russia is infected with imitation, and each one mimics and apes his superior. It is even said that some titular councillor, when he was made chief of some separate little chancellery, at once partitioned off a special room for himself, called it his "office room," and by the door placed some sort of ushers with red collars and galloons, who held the door handle and opened it for each visitor, though the "office room" could barely contain an ordinary writing desk. The ways and habits of the *important person* were imposing and majestic, but of no great complexity. The chief principle of his system was strictness. "Strictness, strictness, and—strictness," he used to say, and with the last word usually looked very importantly into the face of the person he was addressing. Though, incidentally, there was no reason for any of it, because the dozen or so clerks who constituted the entire administrative machinery of the office were properly filled with fear even without that; seeing him from far off, they set their work aside and waited, standing at attention, until their superior passed through the room. His usual conversation with subordinates rang with strictness and consisted almost entirely of three phrases: "How dare you? Do you know with whom you are speaking? Do you realize who is standing before you?" However, he was a kind man at heart, good to his comrades, obliging, but the rank of general had completely bewildered him. On receiving the rank of general, he had somehow become confused, thrown off, and did not know how to behave at all. When he happened to be with his equals, he was as a man ought to be, a very decent man, in many respects even not a stupid man; but as soon as he happened to be in the company of men at least one rank beneath him, he was simply as bad as could be: he kept silent, and his position was pitiable, especially since he himself felt that he could be spending his time incomparably better. In his eyes there could sometimes be seen a strong desire to join in some interesting conversation and circle, but he was stopped by the thought: Would it not be excessive on his part, would it not be familiar, would he not be descending beneath his importance? On account of such reasoning, he remained eternally in the same silent state, only uttering some monosyllabic sounds from time to time, and in this way he acquired the title of a most boring person. It was to this *important person* that our Akaky Akakievich came, and came at a most unfavorable moment, very inopportune for himself, though very opportune for the important person.

The important person was in his office and was talking away very, very merrily with a recently arrived old acquaintance and childhood friend, whom he had not seen for several years. Just then it was announced to him that a certain Bashmachkin was there. "Who's that?" he asked curtly. "Some clerk," came the reply. "Ah! he can wait, now isn't a good time," said the important man. Here it should be said that the important man was stretching it a bit: the time was good, he had long since discussed everything with his friend and their conversation had long since been interspersed with lengthy silences, while they patted each other lightly on the thigh, saying: "So there, Ivan Abramovich!" "So it is, Stepan Varlamovich!" But, for all that, he nevertheless told the clerk to wait, in order to show his friend, a man who had not been in the service and had been living for a long time on his country estate, what lengths of time clerks spent waiting in his anteroom. At last, having talked, or, rather, been silent his fill, and having smoked a cigar in an easy chair with a reclining back, at last he suddenly recollected, as it were, and said to his secretary, who stood in the doorway with papers for a report, "Ah, yes, it seems there's a clerk standing there. Tell him he may come in." Seeing Akaky Akakievich's humble look and his old uniform, he turned to him suddenly and said, "What can I do for you?" in a voice abrupt and firm, which he had purposely studied beforehand in his room, alone and in front of a mirror, a week prior to receiving his present post and the rank of general. Akaky Akakievich, who had been feeling the appropriate timidity for a good while already, became somewhat flustered and explained as well as he could, so far as the freedom of his tongue permitted, adding the words "sort of" even more often than at other times, that the overcoat was perfectly new and he had been robbed in a brutal fashion, and that he was addressing him so that through his intercession, as it were, he could sort of write to the gentleman police superintendent or someone else and find the overcoat. For some reason, the general took this to be familiar treatment.

"What, my dear sir?" he continued curtly. "Do you not know the order? What are you doing here? Do you not know how cases are conducted? You ought to have filed a petition about it in the chancellery; it would pass to the chief clerk, to the section chief, then be conveyed to my secretary, and my secretary would deliver it to me . . ."

"But, Your Excellency," said Akaky Akakievich, trying to collect the handful of presence of mind he had and feeling at the same time that he was sweating terribly, "I made so bold as to trouble you, Your Excellency, because secretaries are, sort of . . . unreliable folk . . ."

"What, what, what?" said the important person. "Where did you pick up such a spirit? Where did you pick up such ideas? What is this rebelliousness spreading among the young against their chiefs and higher-ups!"

The important person seemed not to notice that Akaky Akakievich was already pushing fifty. And so, even if he might be called a young man, it was only relatively—that is, in relation to someone who was seventy years old.

"Do you know to whom you are saying this? Do you realize who is standing before you? Do you realize that? Do you realize, I ask you?"

Here he stamped his foot, raising his voice to such a forceful note that even someone other than Akaky Akakievich would have been frightened by it. Akaky Akakievich was simply stricken, he swayed, shook all over, and was quite unable to stand: if the caretakers had not come running at once to support him, he would have dropped to the floor. He was carried out almost motionless. And the important person, pleased that the effect had even surpassed his expectations, and thoroughly delighted by the thought that his word could even make a man faint, gave his friend a sidelong glance to find out how he had taken it all, and saw, not without satisfaction, that his friend was in a most uncertain state and was even, for his own part, beginning to feel frightened himself.

How he went down the stairs, how he got outside, nothing of that could Akaky Akakievich remember. He could not feel his legs or arms. Never in his life had he been given such a bad roasting by a general, and not his own general at that. He walked, his mouth gaping, through the blizzard that whistled down the streets, blowing him off the sidewalk; the wind, as always in Petersburg, blasted him from all four sides out of every alley. He instantly caught a quinsy, and he reached home unable to utter a word; he was all swollen and took to his bed. So strong at times is the effect of a proper roasting! The next day he was found to be in a high fever. Owing to the generous assistance of the Petersburg climate, the illness developed more quickly than might have been expected, and when the doctor came, after feeling his pulse, he found nothing else to do but prescribe a poultice, only so as not to leave the sick man without the beneficent aid of medical science; but he nevertheless declared straight off that within a day and a half it would inevitably be kaput for him. After which he turned to the landlady and said, "And you, dearie, don't waste any time, order him a pine coffin at once, because an oak one will be too expensive for him." Whether Akaky Akakievich heard these fatal words spoken, and, if he heard them, whether they made a tremendous effect on him, whether he regretted his wretched life—none of this is known, because he was in fever and delirium the whole time. Visions, one stranger than another, kept coming to him: first he saw Petrovich and ordered him to make an overcoat with some sort of snares for thieves, whom he kept imagining under the bed, and he even called the landlady every other minute to get one thief out from under his blanket; then he asked why his old housecoat was hanging before him, since he had a new overcoat; then he imagined that he was standing before the general, listening to the proper roasting, and kept murmuring, "I'm sorry, Your Excellency!"— then, finally, he even blasphemed, uttering the most dreadful words, so that his old landlady even crossed herself, never having heard anything like it from him, the more so as these words immediately followed the words "Your Excellency." After that he talked complete gibberish, so that it was impossible to understand anything; one could only see that his disorderly words and thoughts turned around one and the same overcoat. At last poor Akaky Akakievich gave up the ghost. Neither his room nor his belongings were sealed, because, first, there were no heirs, and, second, there was very little inheritance left—namely, a bunch of goose quills, a stack of white official paper, three pairs of socks, two or three buttons torn off of trousers, and the housecoat already familiar to the reader. To whom all this went, God knows: that, I confess, did not even interest the narrator of this story. Akaky Akakievich was taken away and buried. And Petersburg was left without Akaky Akakievich, as if he had never been there. Vanished and gone was the being, protected by no one, dear to no one, interesting to no one, who had not even attracted the attention of a naturalist— who does not fail to stick a pin through a common fly and examine it under a microscope; a being who humbly endured office mockery and went to his grave for no particular reason, but for whom, all the same, though at the very end of his life, there had flashed a bright visitor in the form of an overcoat, animating for an instant his poor life, and upon whom disaster then fell as unbearably as it falls upon the kings and rulers of this world . . . Several days after his death, a caretaker was sent to his apartment from the office with an order for him to appear immediately—the chief demanded it. But the caretaker had to return with nothing, reporting that the clerk could come no more, and to the question "Why?" expressed himself with the words: "It's just that he's already dead, buried three days ago . . ." Thus they learned at the office about the death of Akaky Akakievich, and by the next day a new clerk was sitting in his place, a much taller one, who wrote his letters not in a straight hand but much more obliquely and slantwise.

But who could imagine that this was not yet all for Akaky Akakievich, that he was fated to live noisily for a few days after his death, as if in reward for his entirely unnoticed life? Yet so it happened, and our poor story unexpectedly acquires a fantastic ending. The rumor suddenly spread through Petersburg that around the Kalinkin Bridge and far further a dead man had begun to appear at night in the form of a clerk searching for some stolen overcoat and, under the pretext of this stolen overcoat, pulling from all shoulders, regardless of rank or title, various overcoats: with cat, with beaver, with cotton quilting, raccoon, fox, bearskin coats—in short, every sort of pelt and hide people have thought up for covering their own. One of the clerks from the office saw the dead man with his own eyes and recognized him at once as Akaky Akakievich; this instilled such fear in him, however, that he ran away as fast as his legs would carry him and thus could not take a good look, but only saw from far off how the man shook his finger at him. From all sides came ceaseless complaints that the backs and shoulders—oh, not only of titular, but even of privy councillors themselves, were completely subject to chills on account of this nocturnal tearing off of overcoats. An order was issued for the police to catch the dead man at all costs, dead or alive, and punish him in the harshest manner, as an example to others, and in this they nearly succeeded. Namely, a neighborhood policeman on duty had already quite seized the dead man by the collar in Kiriushkin Lane, catching him red-handed in an attempt to pull a frieze overcoat off some retired musician who had whistled on a flute in his day. Having seized him by the collar, he shouted and summoned his two colleagues, whom he charged with holding him while he went to his boot just for a moment to pull out his snuffbox, so as to give temporary refreshment to his nose, frostbitten six times in his life. But the snuff must have been of a kind that even a dead man couldn't stand. The policeman had no sooner closed his right nostril with his finger, while drawing in half a handful with the left, than the dead man sneezed so hard that he completely bespattered the eyes of all three of them. While they tried to rub them with their fists, the dead man vanished without a trace, so that they did not even know whether or not they had indeed laid hands on him. After that, on-duty policemen got so afraid of dead men that they grew wary of seizing living ones and only shouted from far off: "Hey, you, on your way!" and the dead clerk began to appear even beyond the Kalinkin Bridge, instilling no little fear in all timorous people.

We, however, have completely abandoned the *certain important person,* who in fact all but caused the fantastic turn taken by this, incidentally perfectly true, story. First of all, justice demands that we say of this *certain important person* that, soon after the departure of the poor, roasted-to-ashes Akaky Akakievich, he felt something akin to regret. He was no stranger to compassion: his heart was open to many good impulses, though his rank often prevented their manifestation. As soon as his out-of-town friend left his office, he even fell to thinking about poor Akaky Akakievich. And after that, almost every day he pictured to himself the pale Akaky Akakievich, unable to endure his superior's roasting. He was so troubled by the thought of him that a week later he even decided to send a clerk to him, to find out about him and whether he might indeed somehow help him; and when he was informed that Akaky Akakievich had died unexpectedly of a fever, he was even struck, felt remorse of conscience, and was in low spirits the whole day. Wishing to divert himself somehow and forget the unpleasant impression, he went for the evening to one of his friends, where he found a sizable company, and, best of all, everyone there was of nearly the same rank, so that he felt no constraint whatsoever. This had a surprising effect on his state of mind. He grew expansive, became pleasant in conversation, amiable—in short, he spent the evening very pleasantly. At supper he drank two glasses of champagne—an agent known to have a good effect with regard to gaiety. The champagne disposed him toward various extravagances; to wit: he decided not to go home yet, but to stop and see a lady of his acquaintance, Karolina Ivanovna, a lady of German origin, it seems, toward whom he felt perfectly friendly relations. It should be said that the important person was a man no longer young, a good husband, a respectable father of a family. Two sons, one of whom already served in the chancellery, and a comely sixteen-year-old daughter with a slightly upturned but pretty little nose, came every day to kiss his hand, saying, "*Bonjour,* papa." His wife, still a fresh woman and not at all bad looking, first gave him her hand to kiss and then, turning it over, kissed his hand. Yet the important person, perfectly satisfied, incidentally, with domestic family tendernesses, found it suitable to have a lady for friendly relations in another part of the city. This lady friend was no whit better or younger than his wife; but there exist such riddles in the world, and it is not our business to judge of them. And so, the important person went downstairs, got into his sleigh, and said to the driver, "To Karolina Ivanovna's," and, himself wrapped quite luxuriantly in a warm overcoat, remained in that pleasant state than which no better could be invented for a Russian man, when you are not thinking of anything and yet thoughts come into your head by themselves, each more pleasant than the last, without even causing you the trouble of chasing after and finding them. Filled with satisfaction, he kept recalling all the gay moments of that evening, all his words that had made the small circle laugh; he even repeated many of them in a half whisper and found them as funny as before, and therefore it was no wonder that he himself chuckled heartily. Occasionally, however, a gusty wind interfered with him, suddenly bursting from God knows where and for no apparent reason, cutting at his face, throwing lumps of snow into it, hoisting the collar of his coat like a sail, or suddenly, with supernatural force, throwing it over his head, thereby causing him the eternal trouble of extricating himself from it. Suddenly the important person felt someone seize him quite firmly by the collar. Turning around, he noticed a short man in an old, worn-out uniform, in whom, not without horror, he recognized Akaky Akakievich. The clerk's face was pale as snow and looked exactly like a dead man's. But the important person's horror exceeded all bounds when he saw the dead man's mouth twist and, with the horrible breath of the tomb, utter the following words: "Ah! here you are at last! At last I've sort of got you by the collar! It's your overcoat I need! You didn't solicit about mine, and roasted me besides—now give me yours!" The poor *important person* nearly died. However full of character he was in the chancellery and generally before subordinates, and though at a mere glance at his manly appearance and figure everyone said, "Oh, what character!"—here, like a great many of those who are powerful in appearance, he felt such fear that he even became apprehensive, not without reason, of some morbid fit. He quickly threw the overcoat off his shoulders and shouted to the driver in a voice not his own, "Home at top speed!" The driver, hearing a voice that was usually employed at decisive moments and even accompanied by something much more effective, drew his head between his shoulders just in case, swung his knout, and shot off like an arrow. In a little over six minutes the important person was already at the door of his house. Pale, frightened, and minus his overcoat, he came to his own place instead of Karolina Ivanovna's, plodded to his room somehow or other, and spent the night in great disorder, so that the next morning over tea his daughter told him directly, "You're very pale today, papa." But papa was silent—not a word to anyone about what had happened to him, or where he had been, or where he had wanted to go.

This incident made a strong impression on him. He even began to say "How dare you, do you realize who is before you?" far less often to his subordinates; and if he did say it, it was not without first listening to what the matter was. But still more remarkable was that thereafter the appearances of the dead clerk ceased altogether: evidently the general's overcoat fitted him perfectly; at least there was no more talk about anyone having his overcoat torn off. However, many active and concerned people refused to calm down and kept saying that the dead clerk still appeared in the more remote parts of the city. And, indeed, one policeman in Kolomna saw with his own eyes a phantom appear from behind a house; but, being somewhat weak by nature, so that once an ordinary adult pig rushing out of someone's private house had knocked him down, to the great amusement of the coachmen standing around, for which jeering he extorted a half kopeck from each of them to buy snuff—so, being weak, he did not dare to stop it, but just followed it in the darkness, until the phantom suddenly turned around, stopped, and asked, "What do you want?" and shook such a fist at him as is not to be found even among the living. The policeman said, "Nothing," and at once turned to go back. The phantom, however, was much taller now, had an enormous mustache, and, apparently making its way toward the Obukhov Bridge, vanished completely into the darkness of the night.

NOTES

UKRAINIAN TALES

St. John's Eve

1. The Russian and Ukrainian stove was a large, elaborate structure used for heating and cooking, which one could also sit or sleep on and even get into in order to wash.

2. The names of three half-legendary heroes from Ukrainian history: Ivan Podkova was a Cossack leader who seized the Moldavian throne in 1578 and was later executed by the Polish king; Karp Poltora Kozhukha was hetman of the Ukraine from 1638 to 1642; Sagaidachny (Pyotr Konashevich), also a Ukrainian hetman, led Cossack campaigns against the Turks and Tartars in 1616–21.

3. A Ukrainian saying, meaning to lie at confession, as Gogol himself explains in a note to the story.

4. The Poles and Lithuanians, whose territories bordered the Ukraine, were traditional enemies of the Cossacks, though they sometimes made alliances with each other against common enemies. The narrator refers to them in somewhat familiar, disrespectful terms. "Crimeans" here refers to the Crimean Tartars, a Muslim people inhabiting the Crimean peninsula, descendants of the Mongols.

5. *Kutya* (pronounced koot-YAH) is a special dish made from rice (or barley or wheat) and raisins, sweetened with honey, offered to people after a church service in commemoration of the dead and sometimes also on Christmas Eve.

6. Father Afanasy represents an exaggeration of the view of Roman Catholics (such as Poles and Lithuanians) taken by the Ukrainians, who belong to the Eastern Orthodox Church.

7. The Zaporozhye (meaning "beyond the rapids" on the Dnieper River) was a territory in the southeastern Ukraine where the Cossacks lived and pre-

served some measure of independence from the Russian state during the sixteenth to eighteenth centuries.

8. The Cossacks customarily shaved their heads but grew a topknot on the top of the head, priding themselves on its length.

9. That is, the feast in honor of the nativity of Saint John the Baptist, celebrated on June 24; in folklore the night before the feast is a time of magic and mystification.

10. "Yaga" is the second half of the name Baba-yaga, the wicked witch of Russian folktales, here used generically.

11. A Ukrainian folk dance and the music for it.

12. Probably a slighting reference to the Jews, who often kept taverns in the Ukraine.

The Night Before Christmas

1. See note 5 to "St. John's Eve."

2. See note 1 to "St. John's Eve."

3. The period of fast preceding the feast of Sts. Peter and Paul on June 29.

4. A *panikhida* is an Orthodox prayer service in memory of the dead.

5. A Zaporozhets was a Cossack from the Zaporozhye (see note 7 to "St. John's Eve").

6. The only food permitted on the last day of the Advent fast (i.e., Christmas Eve).

7. The Setch was the sociopolitical and military organization of the Ukrainian Cossacks in the Zaporozhye—a form of republic headed by a chief. The freedoms of the Setch were gradually curtailed in the eighteenth century, and in 1775 it was finally abolished.

8. The term *hetman* (from the German *Hauptmann*) originally referred to the commander in chief of the Polish army. The Cossacks used it as the title of their own elected chief. It is comically misapplied here.

9. Grigory Alexandrovich, Prince Potemkin (1739-91), field marshal and statesman, in 1774 became the favorite of the empress Catherine II (1729-96) and thereafter guided Russian state policy.

10. The Italian *carabinieri* were members of an army corps also used as a police force—a degrading function in the opinion of the Cossacks.

11. On "Crimeans" see note 4 to "St. John's Eve." The allusion is to the Russian conquest of the Crimea from the Turks in 1771.

12. The empress is addressing the dramatist Denis Fonvizin (1745-92), whose plays *The Brigadier* and *The Minor* are classics of the Russian theater and the best Russian prose comedies before Gogol's own *Inspector General*.

13. Jean de La Fontaine (1621-95), the great French poet and fabulist.

14. The iconostasis is an icon-bearing partition with three doors that spans the width of an Orthodox church, separating the sanctuary from the body of the church.

The Terrible Vengeance

1. See note 5 to "The Night Before Christmas."

2. *Księdzy* is the plural of *ksiądz*, Polish for priest; adopted by Russian, the word acquired pejorative connotations as referring to Roman Catholic priests (see note 6 to "St. John's Eve"). Rebaptizing implied that the priests did not consider the Orthodox Ukrainians to be Christians.

3. The Zaporozhtsy under the leadership of Sagaidachny (see note 2 to "St. John's Eve") campaigned against the Crimean Tartar khanate, remnant of the Golden Horde of the Mongols, and fought them on the shore of the Sivash (the "Salt Lake") in 1620.

4. See note 1 to "St. John's Eve."

5. The Uniates are adherents of the so-called Union of Brest (*Unia* in Latin), declared at the church council at Brest in 1595, by which western Russian churches were placed under the jurisdiction of the pope of Rome, with the understanding that, while accepting the dogmas of Roman Catholicism, they would retain the rites of the Eastern Orthodox Church. The *Unia* aroused great dissension at the time, and has been a cause of struggle in the Ukraine and elsewhere to this day.

6. The Pospolitstvo was the combined nobility of Poland and Lithuania, united under one scepter in 1569.

7. See note 8 to "The Night Before Christmas."

8. The enemy of Christ whose appearance in the "last days" is prophesied in Revelation (11:7), and of whom Saint John writes in his first epistle: ". . . and as you have heard that antichrist is coming, so now many antichrists have come . . ." (1 John 2:18).

9. See note 4 to "The Night Before Christmas." It is a popular belief that the soul does not leave this world until forty days after death.

10. See note 2 to "St. John's Eve" and note 3 above.

11. See footnote (author's note) on p. 15.

12. The Liman (an inlet of the Black Sea near Odessa) and the Crimea are in the very south of the Ukraine, as far as possible from Kiev; Galicia, extending to the northern slopes of the Carpathians, is now divided between the western Ukraine and eastern Poland; geographically, it is to the right, not the left, looking south from Kiev.

13. See note 10 above. Bogdan Khmelnitsky (1593-1657), hetman of the Ukrainian Cossacks, rose up against the Poles in 1648.

14. That is, Stefan Batory, a Hungarian prince who was king of Poland from 1575 to 1586.

Ivan Fyodorovich Shponka and His Aunt

1. *Pirozhki* (plural of *pirozhok*) are small pastries with sweet or savory fillings.

2. A tax farmer was a private person authorized by the government to collect various taxes in exchange for a fixed fee.

3. Latin for "knows," meaning that the student has learned the lesson.

4. A concentrate produced by allowing wine to freeze and then removing the frozen portion.

5. See note 1 to "St. John's Eve."

6. Adult male serfs were known in Russia as "souls." Censuses for tax purposes were taken at intervals of as much as fifteen years, between which the number of souls on an estate might of course increase (or decrease).

7. The feast of Saint Philip falls on November 14 and marks the beginning of the Advent fast.

8. A book entitled *The Journey of Trifon Korobeinikov,* an account written by the Moscow clerk Trifon Korobeinikov of his journey to Mount Athos with a mission sent by the tsar Ivan IV ("the Terrible"). First published in the eighteenth century, it went through forty editions, testifying to its immense popularity. Korobeinikov also wrote *Description of the Route from Moscow to Constantinople* after a second journey in 1594.

Old World Landowners

1. Mythological symbol of conjugal love, Philemon and Baucis were a Phrygian couple who welcomed Zeus and Hermes, traveling in disguise, when their compatriots refused them hospitality. In return, they were spared the flood that the divinities sent the Phrygians as a punishment. Their thatched cottage became a temple in which they ministered, and they asked that one of them not die without the other. In old age they were changed into trees.

2. Ukrainian (Little Russian) names frequently end in *o,* which would be Russified by the addition of a *v.*

3. Peter III (1728–62) became emperor of Russia in 1762 and was assassinated at the instigation of his wife, the empress Catherine II, who thereafter ruled alone.

4. Louise de La Baume Le Blanc, Duchess of La Vallière (1644–1710), was a favorite of Louis XIV. She ended her life as a Carmelite nun.

5. A volunteer defense force in the Ukraine during the war with Napoleon in 1812.

6. See note 1 to "Ivan Fyodorovich Shponka and His Aunt."

7. A dish made from grain (wheat, buckwheat, oats, rye, millet) boiled with water or milk.

8. See note 1 to "St. John's Eve."

9. The armies of Catherine II fought successfully against the Turks in the latter part of the eighteenth century.

10. It was customary in Russia to lay a dead person out on a table until the coffin was prepared.

11. See note 5 to "St. John's Eve."

12. The final hymn of the Orthodox funeral service.

13. "Small open," a French card-playing term.

14. Patties of cottage cheese mixed with flour and eggs and fried.

Viy

1. Russian seminary education was open to the lower classes and was often subsidized by state scholarships; seminarians were thus not necessarily preparing for the priesthood.

2. Herodias, wife of Herod the tetrarch and mother of Salome, ordered the beheading of John the Baptist (Matthew 14:1-11); Potiphar, an officer of the Egyptian pharaoh, bought Joseph as a slave and made him overseer of his house; his wife falsely accused Joseph of trying to lie with her (Genesis 39).

3. See note 7 to "Old World Landowners."

4. See note 8 to "St. John's Eve."

5. Earlier of the two summer fasts (see note 3 to "The Night Before Christmas").

6. "Master" in Latin.

7. Thus in the original. The French *bon mot* means a clever or witty saying.

8. See note 14 to "The Night Before Christmas."

9. See note 4 to "The Night Before Christmas."

The Story of How Ivan Ivanovich Quarreled with Ivan Nikiforovich

1. A word of Hungarian origin meaning a frock coat, caftan, or jacket lined with fur.

2. A Tartar word referring, in different regions, to different sorts of jackets—here, probably a simple caftan trimmed with leather on the hem, cuffs, and front.

3. Moscow printers and publishers of the early nineteenth century.

4. In Russian, the godfather and godmother of the same person call each other *kum* and *kuma,* as do all others thus related through the same baptism.

5. A *zertsalo* was a small three-faced glass pyramid bearing an eagle and certain edicts of the emperor Peter the Great (1682-1725) that stood on the desk in every government office.

6. A special dorsal section of flesh running the entire length of a salmon or sturgeon, removed in one piece and either salted or smoked; considered a great delicacy in Russia.

7. The fourth-century saints Basil the Great, Gregory the Theologian, and John Chrysostom, sometimes venerated together by the Orthodox Church.

8. St. Philip's Day marks the beginning of the six-week Advent fast (see note 7 to "Ivan Fyodorovich Shponka and His Aunt").

9. In chapter I his last name is Pupopuz, meaning something like "bellybutton." Golopuz means "bare belly."

10. See note 14 to "Old World Landowners."

PETERSBURG TALES

Nevsky Prospect

1. The Neva River divides into three main branches as it flows into the Gulf of Finland, marking out the three main areas of the city of St. Petersburg: on the left bank of the Neva is the city center; between the Neva and the Little Neva is Vasilievsky Island; and between the Little Neva and the Nevka is the Petersburg side. The Vyborg side, Peski ("the Sands") and the Moscow gate, neighborhoods well within the limits of present-day Petersburg, were once quite remote from each other.

2. Ganymede, the son of King Tros, after whom the city of Troy was named, was the most beautiful of young men and was therefore chosen by the gods to be Zeus's cupbearer.

3. An extremely tall, needle-shaped spire topped by a figure of a ship on the Admiralty building, one of the landmarks of Petersburg.

4. The reference is to the image of the Madonna in the fresco *The Adoration of the Magi,* in the chapel of Santa Maria dei Bianchi in Città della Pieve, painted by the Italian master Pietro Vannucci, called Il Perugino (1446–1523).

5. The star figured on the decoration of a number of Russian military and civil orders.

6. The cemetery in Okhta, a suburb of Petersburg on a small tributary of the Neva.

7. An amusingly ironic assortment of names: F. V. Bulgarin (1789-1859) and N. I. Grech (1787-1867), journalists and minor writers of much influence in their time, were editors of the reactionary and semiofficial magazine *The Northern Bee,* and at least one of them (Bulgarin) was also a police informer. They were archenemies of Russia's greatest poet, Alexander Pushkin (1799-1837), who enjoyed mocking them in epigrams. A. A. Orlov (1791-1840) was the author of primitive, moralistic novels for a popular audience, derided by Bulgarin and Grech, though, as Pushkin pointed out in an article, Bulgarin's novels differed little from Orlov's.

8. The reference is to vaudevilles about simple folk popular in the 1830s, featuring a character named Filatka.

9. *Dmitri Donskoy* is a historical tragedy by the mediocre poet Nestor Kukolnik (1809-68), a great success in its day. *Woe from Wit,* a comedy in verse by Alexander Griboedov (1795-1829), stands as the first real masterpiece of the Russian theater.

10. Friedrich Schiller (1759-1805), poet, playwright, historian, and literary theorist, is one of the greatest figures of German literature. The fantastic tales of E.T.A. Hoffmann (1776-1822) are known the world over.

11. In Russian, the German word *Junker,* meaning "young lord," refers to a

lower officer's rank open only to the nobility (and thus, of course, not to the tinsmith Schiller).

12. A junior clerk was expected to call at his superior's home to wish him good health on his name day and feast days, and to leave his card as evidence of having done so.

13. Marie-Joseph, Marquis de Lafayette (1757-1834), French general and statesman, took the side of the Colonies in the American war of independence, and was active as a liberal royalist in the French revolutions of 1789 and 1830.

The Diary of a Madman

1. See note 7 to "Nevsky Prospect."

2. The lines are in fact by the minor poet and playwright N. P. Nikolev (1758-1815).

3. Ruch was a prominent Moscow tailor of the time.

4. See note 8 to "Nevsky Prospect."

5. The German title *Kammerjunker* ("gentleman of the bedchamber") was adopted by the Russian imperial court.

6. The reference is to the problem of royal succession in Spain following the death of Ferdinand VII in 1833. His three-year-old daughter, Isabella II, was put on the throne and ruled for thirty-five years, despite the efforts of the king's brother, Don Carlos, to depose her.

7. Under the stern and very Catholic Philip II (1527-98), the Inquisition reached its height in Spain. The Capuchins were Franciscan friars of the new rule established in 1528.

8. Jules-Armand, Prince de Polignac (1780-1847), French politican, was minister of foreign affairs under Charles X (1757-1836).

The Nose

1. In the first version of the story, the date was April 25th. The date Gogol finally chose, March 25th, is that of the feast of the Annunciation, one of the major feasts in the Christian calendar. This fact has seemed to support commentators seeking a specifically religious and even apocalyptical significance in "The Nose."

2. Bribery and other administrative abuses evidently worked more quickly in the Caucasus than in the capital or the Russian provinces.

3. See note 7 to "Nevsky Prospect."

4. The denominations of Russian paper currency were distinguished by color: a blue banknote had a value of five roubles, a red of ten roubles.

5. Gogol's slip, perpetuated in all Russian editions; her name is, of course, Palageya.

6. A fashionable shop in Petersburg, located on the corner of Nevsky Prospect and Bolshaya Morskaya Street.

7. Grand admiral and later grand vizier of the Ottoman empire under the

sultan Mahmud II (1785-1839), Khozrev-Mirza came to Petersburg in August 1829 at the head of a special embassy, following the murder in Teheran of the Russian ambassador, the poet Alexander Griboedov (see note 9 to "Nevsky Prospect"). During his stay, he lived in the Tavrichesky Palace.

The Carriage

1. Marshal of the nobility was the highest elective office in a province before the reforms of the 1860s. Governors and administrators were appointed by the tsar.

2. That is, in the war against Napoleon.

The Portrait

1. See note 7 to "The Nose."

2. A character from the popular story "Bova Korolevich," often portrayed in Russian folk prints, or *lubok,* during the eighteenth and nineteenth centuries.

3. That is, from the outskirts of the city (see note 6 to "Nevsky Prospect").

4. Yeruslan Lazarevich is a Russian version of the Rustem of Persian tales; he and the other folk figures listed here were also popular images in *lubok*.

5. The streets on Vasilievsky Island (see note 1 to "Nevsky Prospect"), called "lines," were laid out in a grid and numbered.

6. Raphael Sanzio (1483-1520), who worked in Perugia, Florence, and Rome, was commonly considered the greatest of all painters by Russians of Gogol's time; Guido Reni (1575-1642) was known for the elegance of his brushwork, the correctness of his drawing, and the brilliance of his colors; Titian (1477-1576) was perhaps the greatest of the Venetian masters. For Russians, the Flemish school was represented by Peter Paul Rubens (1577-1640) and Antoine (or Sir Anthony) van Dyck (1599-1641), who collaborated with Rubens for some time and later became court painter for Charles I of England.

7. Giorgio Vasari (1511-74), painter and architect, a pupil of Michelangelo, is best known for his *Lives* of the Italian artists of the Renaissance. The portrait in question is Leonardo's *Mona Lisa*.

8. See note 1 to "Nevsky Prospect." Kolomna was a suburb to the west of Petersburg.

9. Mikhail Illarionovich Golenishchev-Kutuzov, prince of Smolensk (1745-1813), Russian field marshal, led campaigns in Poland, Turkey, and the Crimea, was defeated by Napoleon at Austerlitz, and successfully commanded the Russian army during Napoleon's disastrous Russian expedition of 1812.

10. A hero of the narrative poem *Twelve Sleeping Maidens,* by V. A. Zhukovsky (1783-1852), Gromoboy sold his soul to the devil.

11. Either David Teniers the Elder (1582-1649), or his son, David Teniers the Younger (1610-90), Flemish painters known for their realistic scenes of popular life, interiors, and so on.

12. The lady uses the French form of the name of the Italian painter Antonio

Allegri da Correggio (1494-1534), known for his audacious use of aerial perspective and the sensuality of his mythological scenes.

13. The typical Byronic pose is a full profile with an open-collared shirt. Corinne is the heroine of a novel of the same name by the French writer Mme. de Staël (1766-1817); Ondine is the heroine of a poem of the same name by V. A. Zhukovsky, based on the tale by the German Romantic writer Friedrich de La Motte-Fouqué (1777-1843); Aspasia (fifth century B.C.), an Athenian courtesan famous for her beauty and intelligence, belonged to Socrates' circle and was the lover of the general and statesman Pericles.

14. The basilisk is a legendary monster, hatched by a toad from a cock's egg, whose look is said to kill.

15. The reference is to the poem "The Demon" (1824), by Alexander Pushkin (see note 7 to "Nevsky Prospect").

16. The words "immersed in their zephyrs and cupids" are paraphrased from a line about a ruined landowner and lover of ballet in Griboedov's *Woe from Wit* (see note 9 to "Nevsky Prospect"); the name of Gaius Maecenas (c. 70-8 B.C.), Roman statesman and important patron of literature, has become proverbial.

17. A shopping place that still exists in Petersburg.

18. A special design of oil lamp with a double draft and a reservoir higher than the wick, named for its French inventor.

19. See note 4 to "The Night Before Christmas."

20. The Senate in Petersburg acted as a civil court as well as a legislative body.

21. The noble and virtuous hero of *The History of Sir Charles Grandison* (1753-54), by Samuel Richardson (1689-1761).

The Overcoat

1. See note 20 to "The Portrait."

2. That is, the church calendar, which lists saints' days and feast days, among other things; a child would be named for the saint (or one of the saints) on whose day it was born.

3. The famous equestrian statue of Peter the Great on the Senate square in Petersburg, by French sculptor Étienne-Maurice Falconet (1716-91).

4. That is, one whose neglect of Orthodox feast days made her comparable to an unbeliever and even a sober Lutheran.

ABOUT THE
TRANSLATORS

RICHARD PEVEAR has published translations of Alain, Yves Bonnefoy, Alberto Savinio, Pavel Florensky, and Henri Volohonsky, as well as two books of poetry. He has received fellowships or grants for translation from the National Endowment for the Arts, the Ingram Merrill Foundation, the Guggenheim Foundation, the National Endowment for the Humanities, and the French Ministry of Culture.

LARISSA VOLOKHONSKY was born in Leningrad. She has translated works by the prominent Orthodox theologians Alexander Schmemann and John Meyendorff into Russian. Together, Pevear and Volokhonsky have translated *Dead Souls* by Nikolai Gogol and *The Brothers Karamazov, Crime and Punishment, Notes from Underground,* and *Demons* by Fyodor Dostoevsky. They were awarded the PEN Book-of-the-Month Club Translation Prize for their version of *The Brothers Karamazov,* and, more recently, *Demons* was one of three nominees for the same prize. They are married and live in France.